MW01581778

UNDISCOVERED COUNTRY

VOLUME TWO

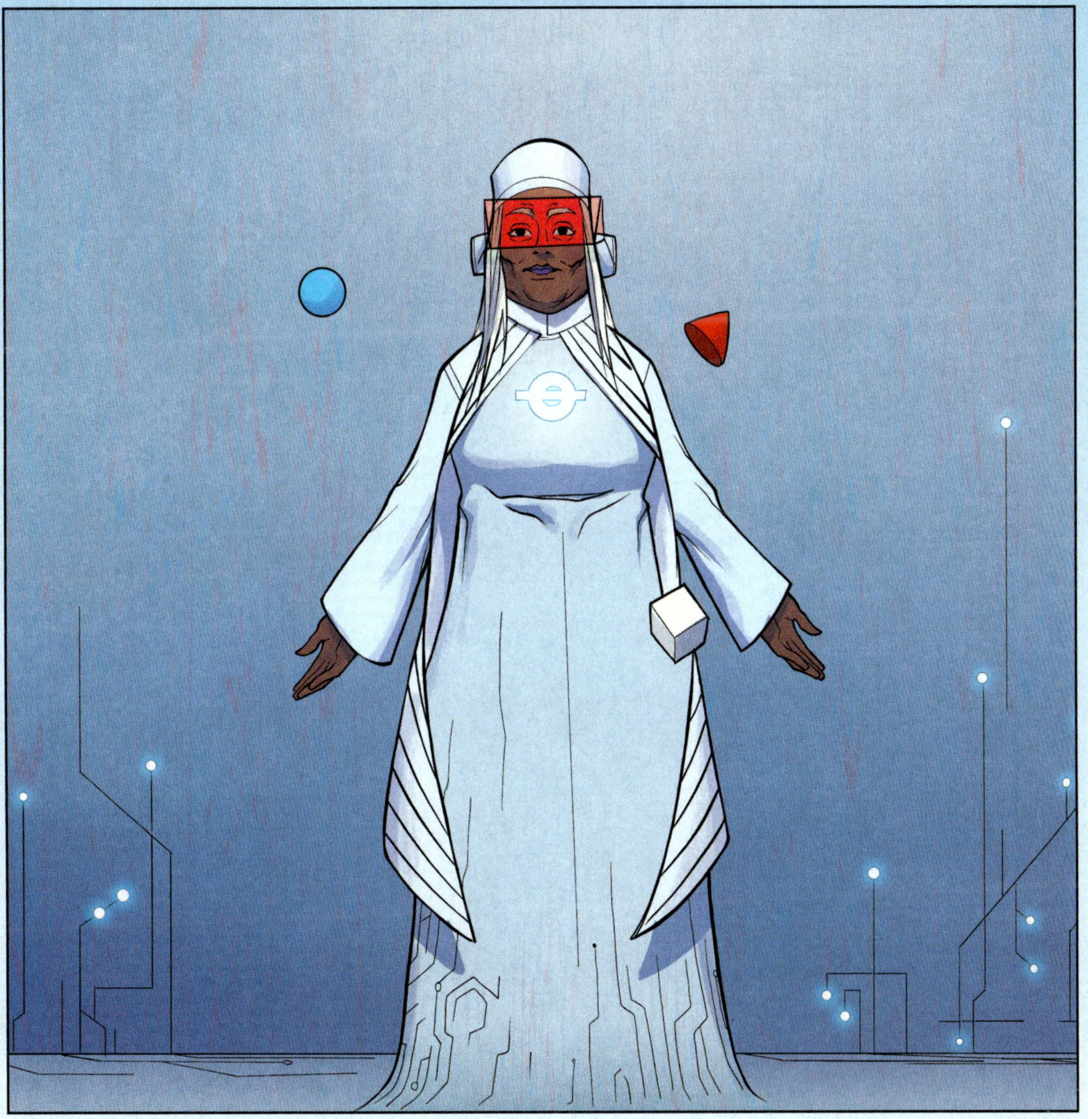

UNITY

UNDISCOVERED COUNTRY

VOLUME TWO

UNITY

Production & design by **RYAN BREWER**
Cover design by **DREW GILL**
Logo design by **MAURO CORRADINI**

IMAGE COMICS, INC. • Todd McFarlane: President • Jim Valentino: Vice President • Marc Silvestri: Chief Executive Officer • Erik Larsen: Chief Financial Officer • Robert Kirkman: Chief Operating Officer • Eric Stephenson: Publisher / Chief Creative Officer • Nicole Lapalme: Controller • Leanna Caunter: Accounting Analyst • Sue Korpela: Accounting & HR Manager • Marla Eizik: Talent Liaison • Jeff Boison: Director of Sales & Publishing Planning • Dirk Wood: Director of International Sales & Licensing • Alex Cox: Director of Direct Market Sales • Chloe Ramos: Book Market & Library Sales Manager • Emilio Bautista: Digital Sales Coordinator • Jon Schlaffman: Specialty Sales Coordinator • Kat Salazar: Director of PR & Marketing • Drew Fitzgerald: Marketing Content Associate • Heather Doornink: Production Director • Drew Gill: Art Director • Hilary DiLoreto: Print Manager • Tricia Ramos: Traffic Manager • Melissa Gifford: Content Manager • Erika Schnatz: Senior Production Artist • Ryan Brewer: Production Artist • Deanna Phelps: Production Artist • IMAGECOMICS.COM

UNDISCOVERED COUNTRY, VOL. 2. First printing. March 2021. Published by Image Comics, Inc. Office of publication: PO BOX 14457, Portland, OR 97293. Copyright © 2021 Last Mile Productions, LLC. All rights reserved. Contains material originally published in single magazine form as UNDISCOVERED COUNTRY #7-12. "Undiscovered Country," its logos, and the likenesses of all characters herein are trademarks of Last Mile Productions, LLC, unless otherwise noted. "Image" and the Image Comics logos are registered trademarks of Image Comics, Inc. No part of this publication may be reproduced or transmitted, in any form or by any means (except for short excerpts for journalistic or review purposes), without the express written permission of Last Mile Productions, LLC, or Image Comics, Inc. All names, characters, events, and locales in this publication are entirely fictional. Any resemblance to actual persons (living or dead), events, or places, without satirical intent, is coincidental. Printed in the USA. For international rights, contact: foreignlicensing@imagecomics.com. ISBN: 978-1-5343-1840-3.

Written by
SCOTT SNYDER & CHARLES SOULE

Layouts by
GIUSEPPE CAMUNCOLI

Finishes by
LEONARDO MARCELLO GRASSI

Colored by
MATT WILSON

Lettered by
CRANK!

Edited by
WILL DENNIS

Assistant edited by
TYLER JENNES

CHAPTER SEVEN

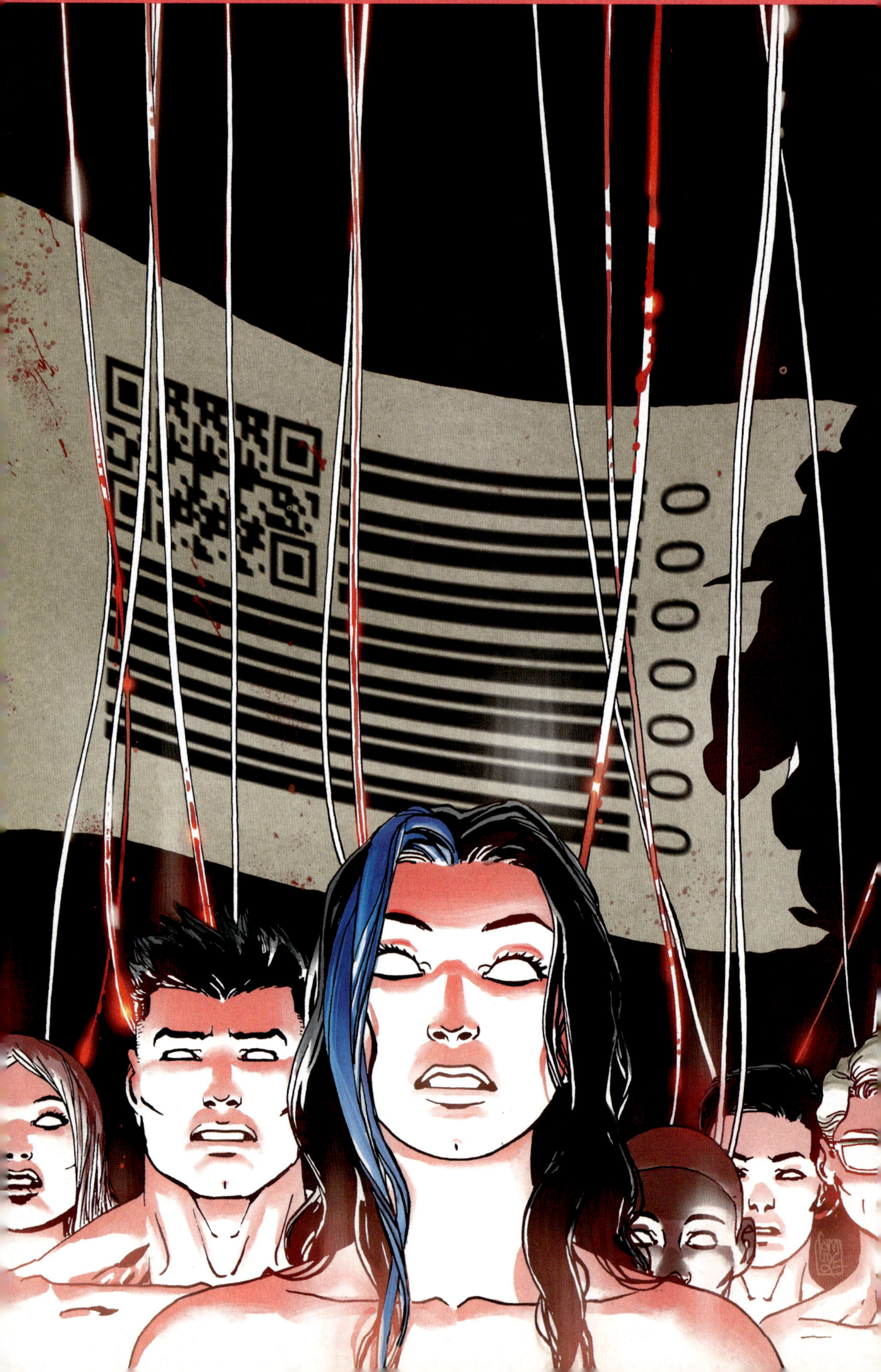

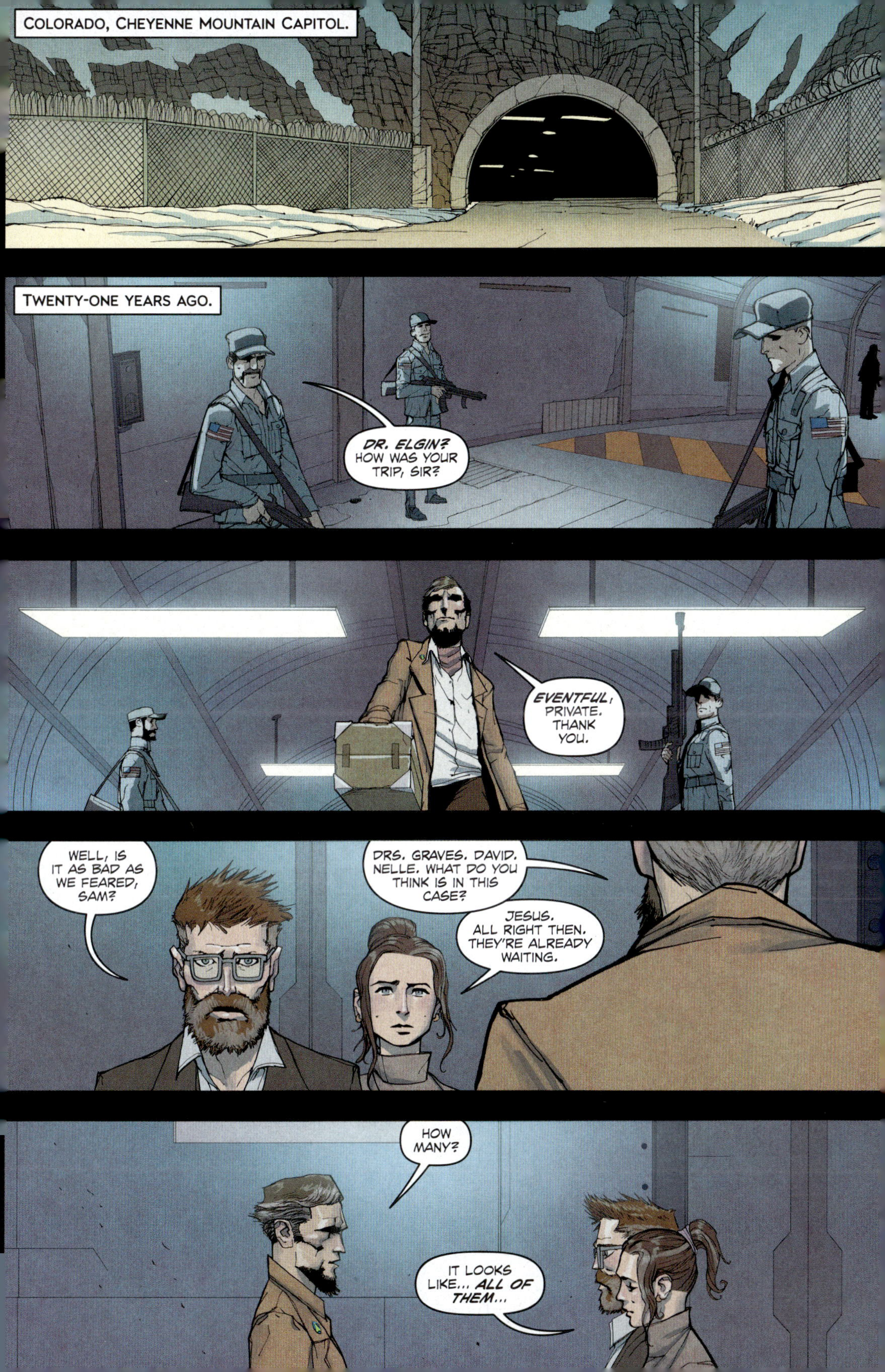
COLORADO, CHEYENNE MOUNTAIN CAPITOL.
TWENTY-ONE YEARS AGO.
DR. ELGIN? HOW WAS YOUR TRIP, SIR?
EVENTFUL, PRIVATE. THANK YOU.
WELL, IS IT AS BAD AS WE FEARED, SAM?
DRS. GRAVES. DAVID. NELLE. WHAT DO YOU THINK IS IN THIS CASE?
JESUS. ALL RIGHT THEN. THEY'RE ALREADY WAITING.
HOW MANY?
IT LOOKS LIKE... ALL OF THEM...

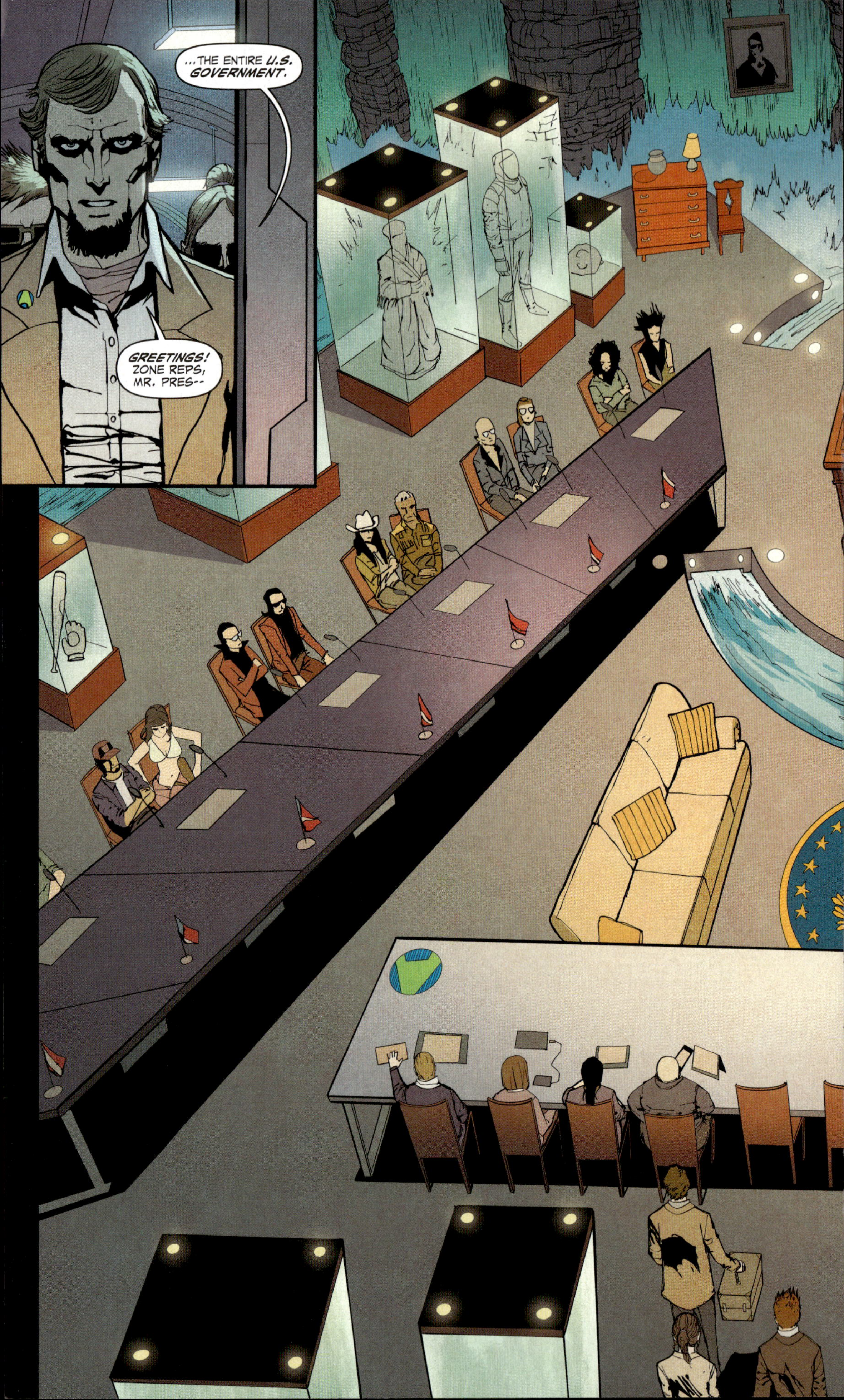
...THE ENTIRE U.S. GOVERNMENT.
GREETINGS! ZONE REPS, MR. PRES--

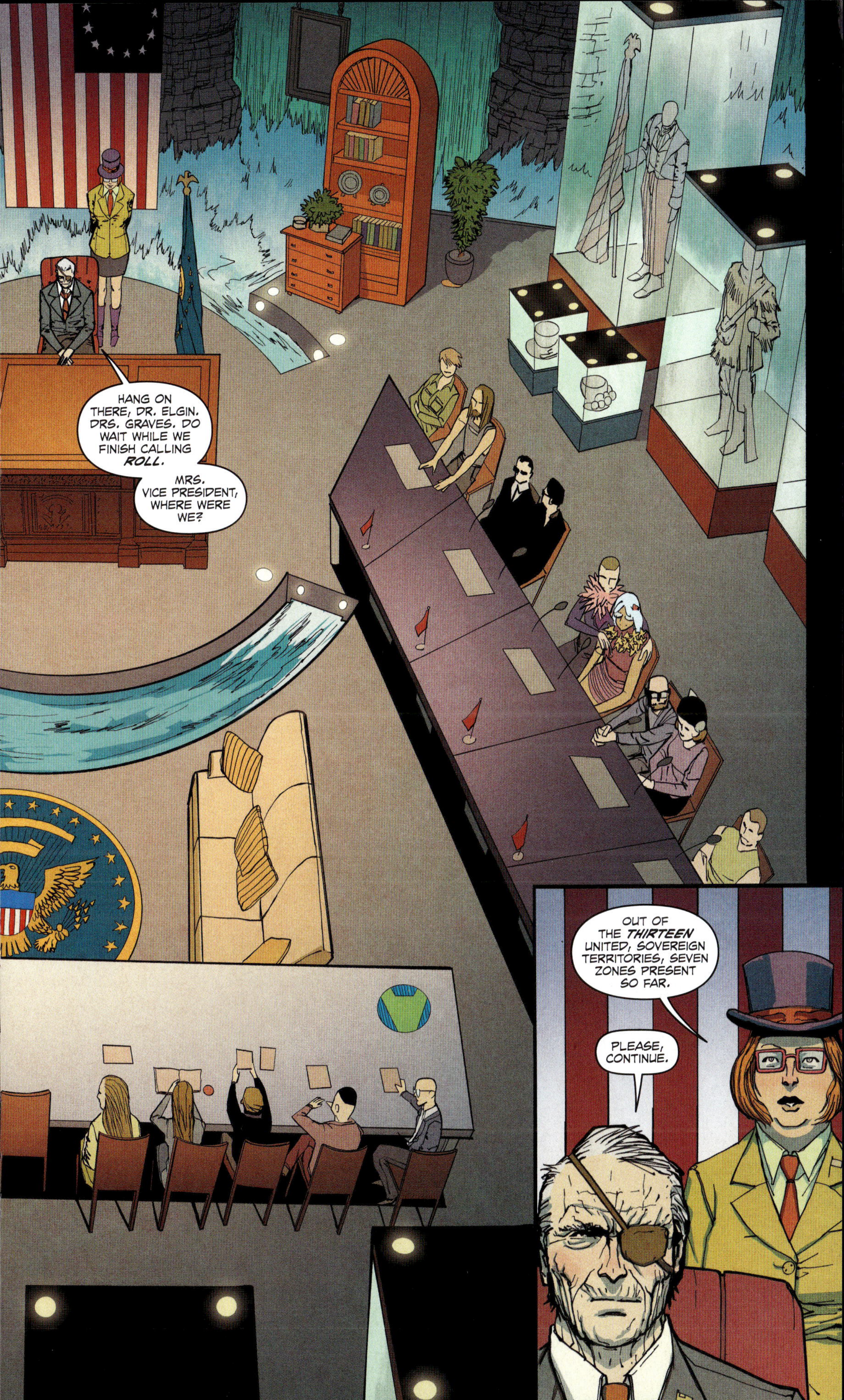
HANG ON THERE, DR. ELGIN. DRS. GRAVES. DO WAIT WHILE WE FINISH CALLING ROLL.
MRS. VICE PRESIDENT, WHERE WERE WE?
OUT OF THE THIRTEEN UNITED, SOVEREIGN TERRITORIES, SEVEN ZONES PRESENT SO FAR.
PLEASE, CONTINUE.

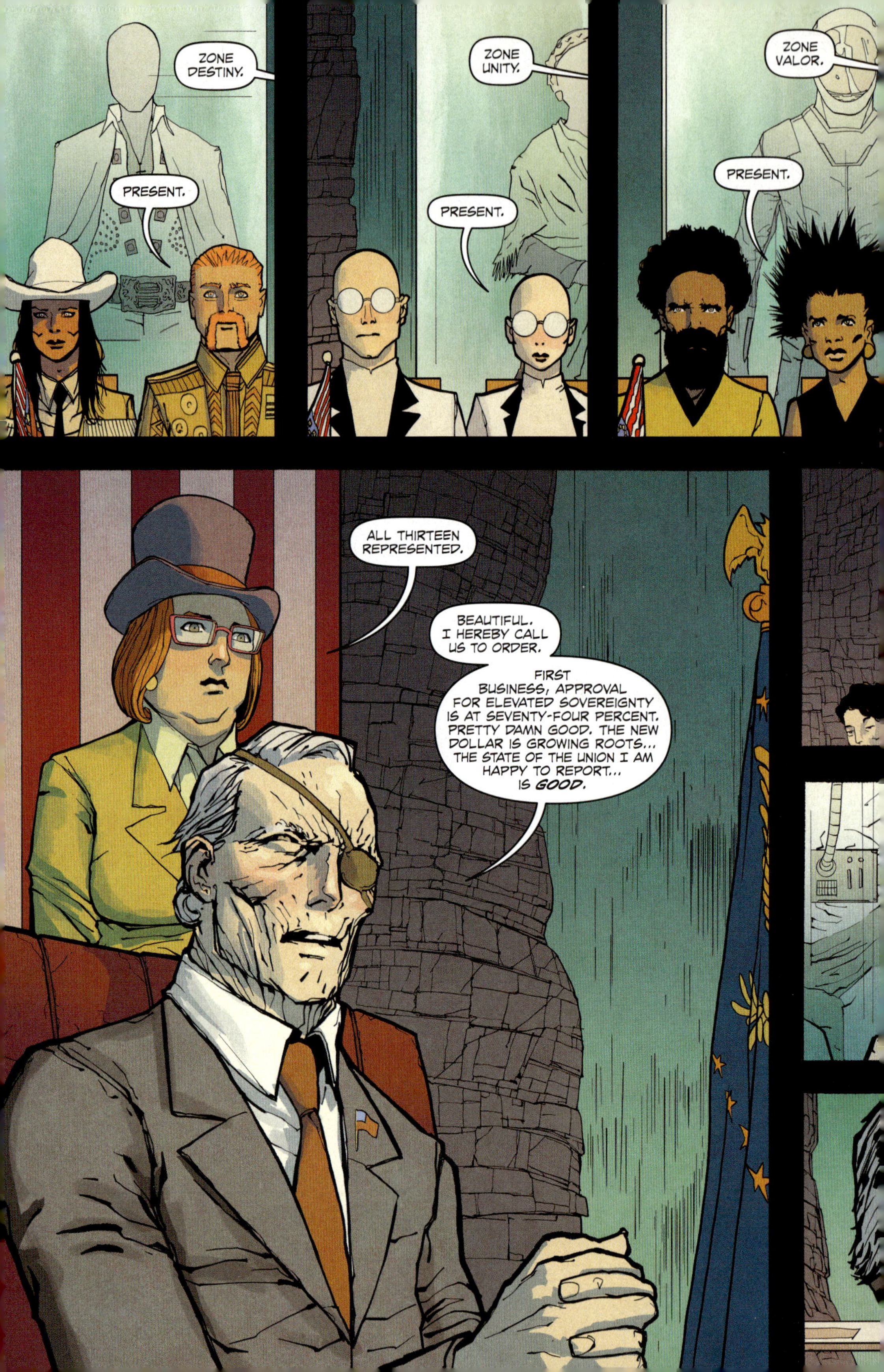
ZONE DESTINY.
PRESENT.
ZONE UNITY.
PRESENT.
ZONE VALOR.
PRESENT.
ALL THIRTEEN REPRESENTED.
BEAUTIFUL. I HEREBY CALL US TO ORDER.
FIRST BUSINESS, APPROVAL FOR ELEVATED SOVEREIGNTY IS AT SEVENTY-FOUR PERCENT. PRETTY DAMN GOOD. THE NEW DOLLAR IS GROWING ROOTS... THE STATE OF THE UNION I AM HAPPY TO REPORT... IS *GOOD*.

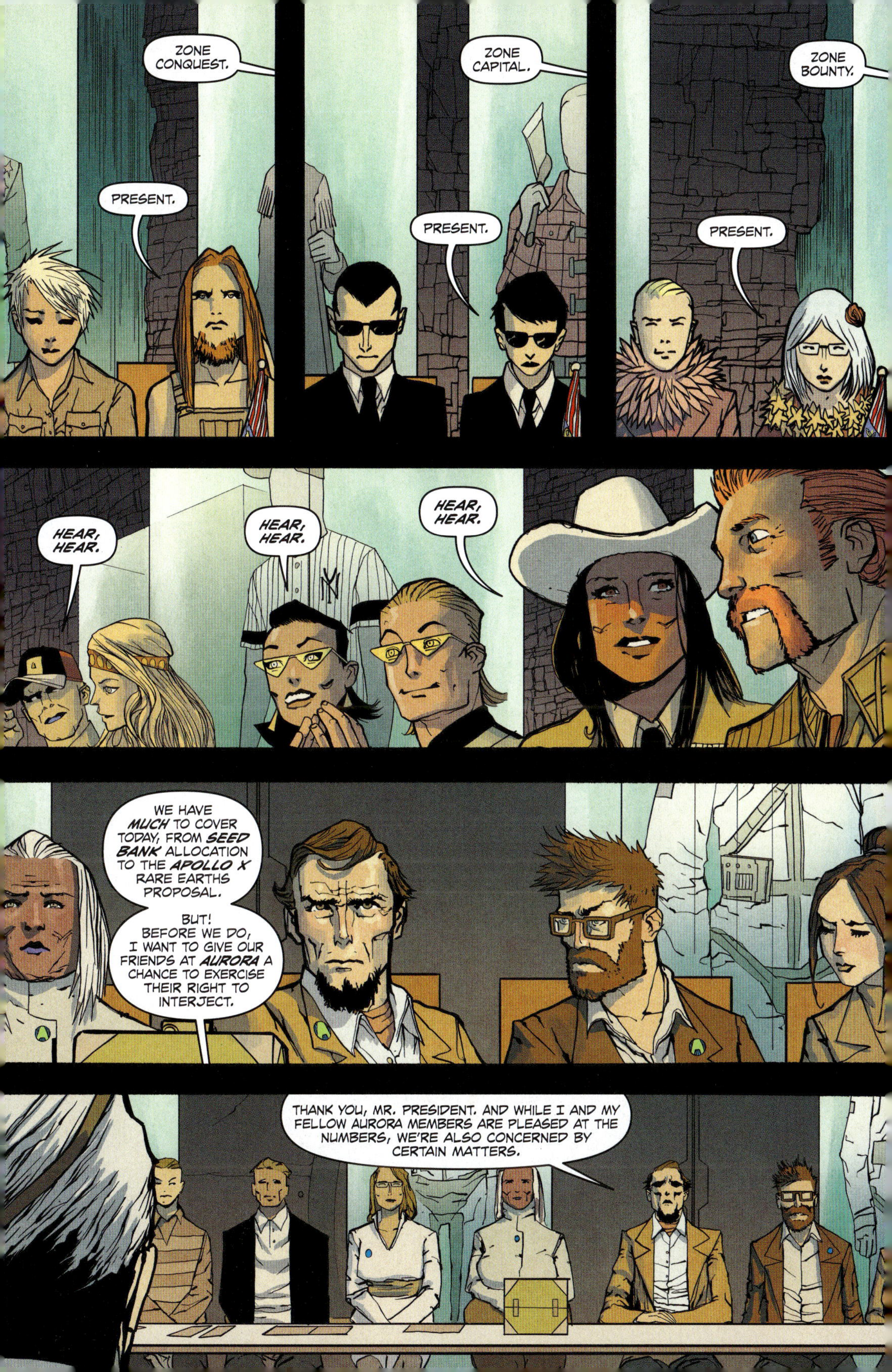
ZONE CONQUEST.
PRESENT.
ZONE CAPITAL.
PRESENT.
ZONE BOUNTY.
PRESENT.
HEAR, HEAR.
HEAR, HEAR.
HEAR, HEAR.
WE HAVE MUCH TO COVER TODAY, FROM SEED BANK ALLOCATION TO THE APOLLO X RARE EARTHS PROPOSAL.
BUT! BEFORE WE DO, I WANT TO GIVE OUR FRIENDS AT AURORA A CHANCE TO EXERCISE THEIR RIGHT TO INTERJECT.
THANK YOU, MR. PRESIDENT. AND WHILE I AND MY FELLOW AURORA MEMBERS ARE PLEASED AT THE NUMBERS, WE'RE ALSO CONCERNED BY CERTAIN MATTERS.

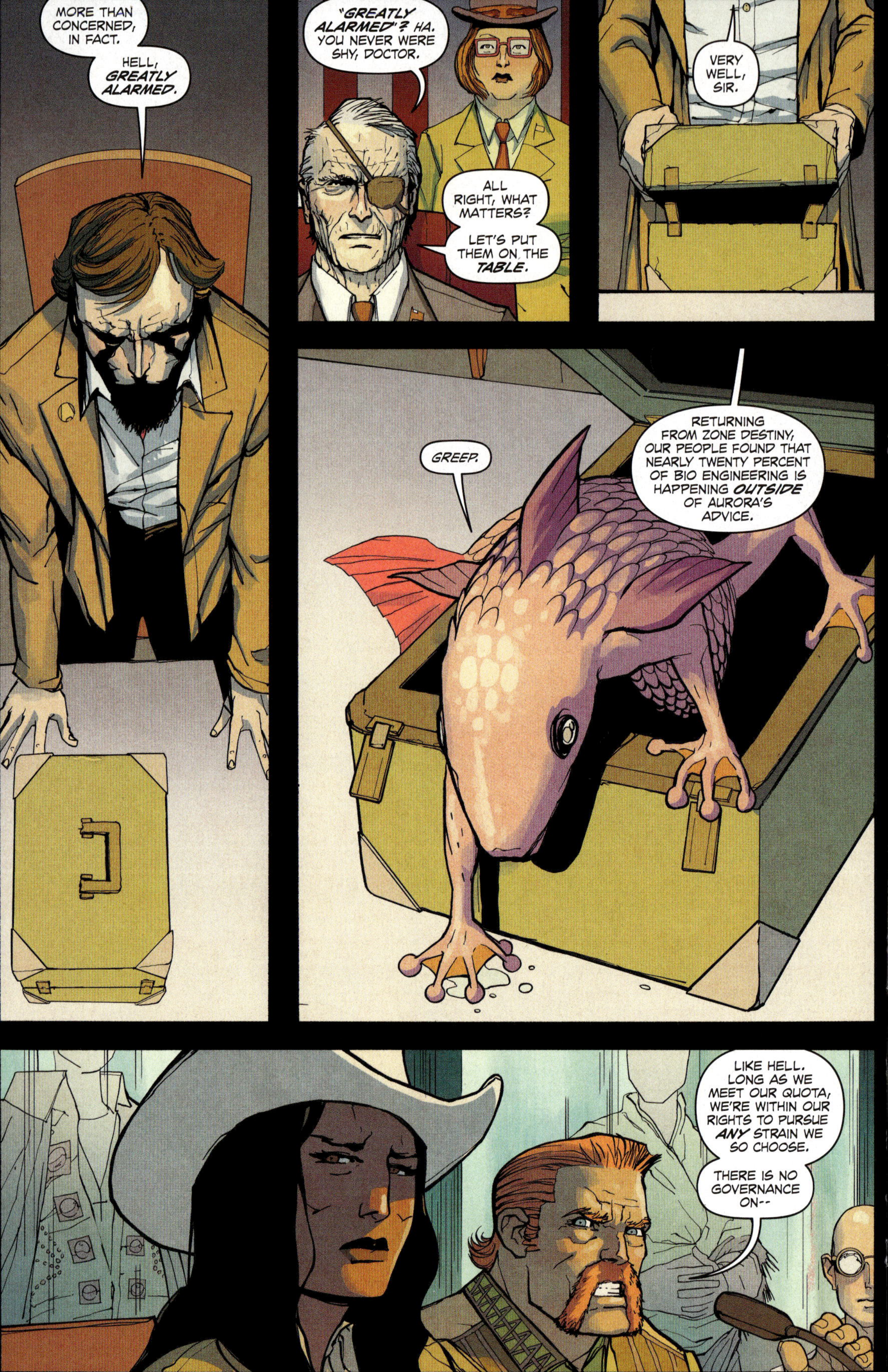
MORE THAN CONCERNED, IN FACT.
HELL, GREATLY ALARMED.
"GREATLY ALARMED"? HA. YOU NEVER WERE SHY, DOCTOR.
ALL RIGHT, WHAT MATTERS?
LET'S PUT THEM ON THE TABLE.
VERY WELL, SIR.
GREEP.
RETURNING FROM ZONE DESTINY, OUR PEOPLE FOUND THAT NEARLY TWENTY PERCENT OF BIO ENGINEERING IS HAPPENING OUTSIDE OF AURORA'S ADVICE.
LIKE HELL. LONG AS WE MEET OUR QUOTA, WE'RE WITHIN OUR RIGHTS TO PURSUE ANY STRAIN WE SO CHOOSE.
THERE IS NO GOVERNANCE ON--

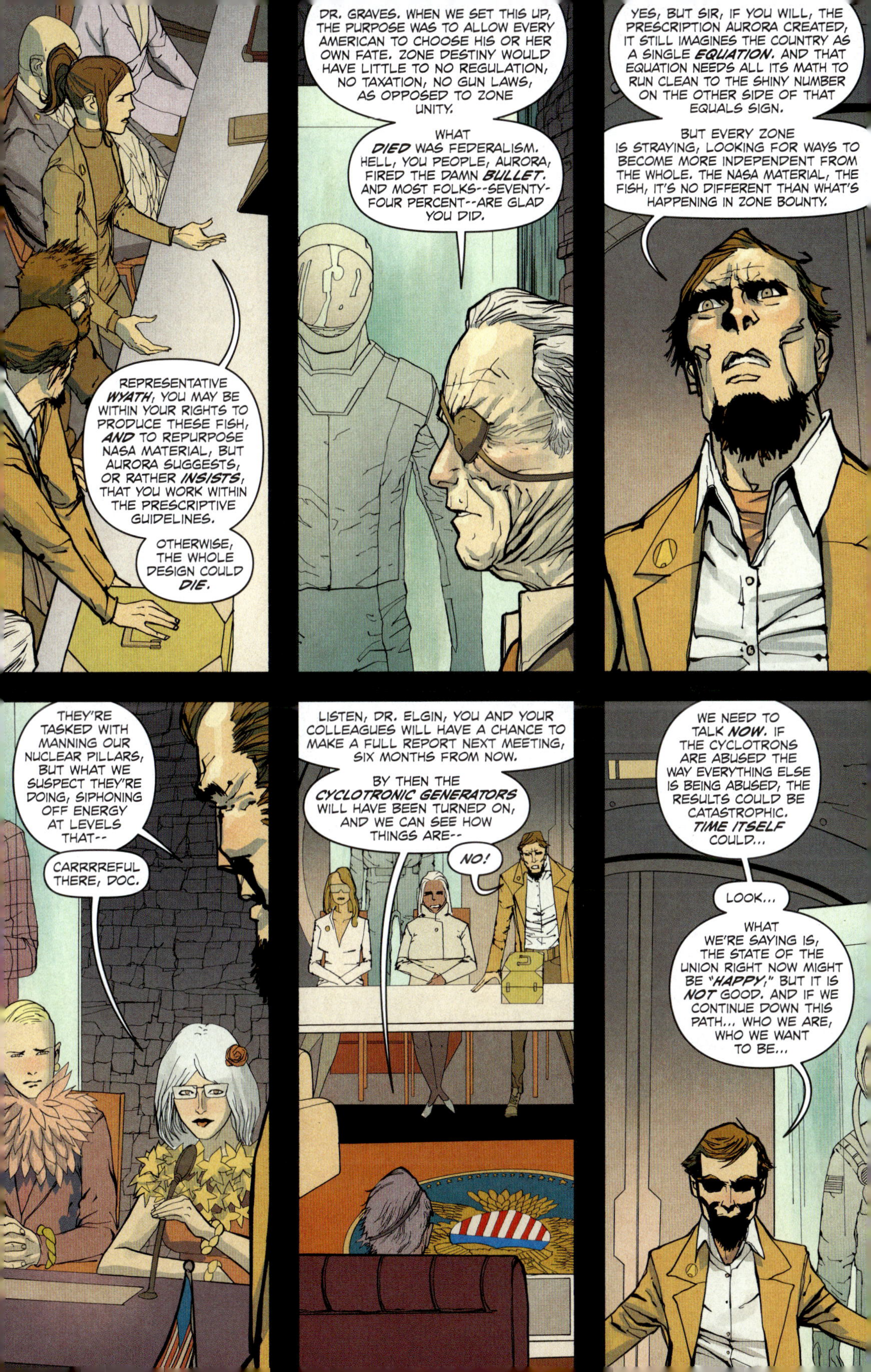
REPRESENTATIVE WYATH, YOU MAY BE WITHIN YOUR RIGHTS TO PRODUCE THESE FISH, AND TO REPURPOSE NASA MATERIAL, BUT AURORA SUGGESTS, OR RATHER INSISTS, THAT YOU WORK WITHIN THE PRESCRIPTIVE GUIDELINES.
OTHERWISE, THE WHOLE DESIGN COULD DIE.
DR. GRAVES. WHEN WE SET THIS UP, THE PURPOSE WAS TO ALLOW EVERY AMERICAN TO CHOOSE HIS OR HER OWN FATE. ZONE DESTINY WOULD HAVE LITTLE TO NO REGULATION, NO TAXATION, NO GUN LAWS, AS OPPOSED TO ZONE UNITY.
WHAT DIED WAS FEDERALISM. HELL, YOU PEOPLE, AURORA, FIRED THE DAMN BULLET. AND MOST FOLKS--SEVENTY-FOUR PERCENT--ARE GLAD YOU DID.
YES, BUT SIR, IF YOU WILL, THE PRESCRIPTION AURORA CREATED, IT STILL IMAGINES THE COUNTRY AS A SINGLE EQUATION. AND THAT EQUATION NEEDS ALL ITS MATH TO RUN CLEAN TO THE SHINY NUMBER ON THE OTHER SIDE OF THAT EQUALS SIGN.
BUT EVERY ZONE IS STRAYING, LOOKING FOR WAYS TO BECOME MORE INDEPENDENT FROM THE WHOLE. THE NASA MATERIAL, THE FISH, IT'S NO DIFFERENT THAN WHAT'S HAPPENING IN ZONE BOUNTY.
THEY'RE TASKED WITH MANNING OUR NUCLEAR PILLARS, BUT WHAT WE SUSPECT THEY'RE DOING, SIPHONING OFF ENERGY AT LEVELS THAT--
CARRRREFUL THERE, DOC.
LISTEN, DR. ELGIN, YOU AND YOUR COLLEAGUES WILL HAVE A CHANCE TO MAKE A FULL REPORT NEXT MEETING, SIX MONTHS FROM NOW.
BY THEN THE CYCLOTRONIC GENERATORS WILL HAVE BEEN TURNED ON, AND WE CAN SEE HOW THINGS ARE--
NO!
WE NEED TO TALK NOW. IF THE CYCLOTRONS ARE ABUSED THE WAY EVERYTHING ELSE IS BEING ABUSED, THE RESULTS COULD BE CATASTROPHIC. TIME ITSELF COULD...
LOOK...
WHAT WE'RE SAYING IS, THE STATE OF THE UNION RIGHT NOW MIGHT BE "HAPPY," BUT IT IS NOT GOOD. AND IF WE CONTINUE DOWN THIS PATH... WHO WE ARE, WHO WE WANT TO BE...

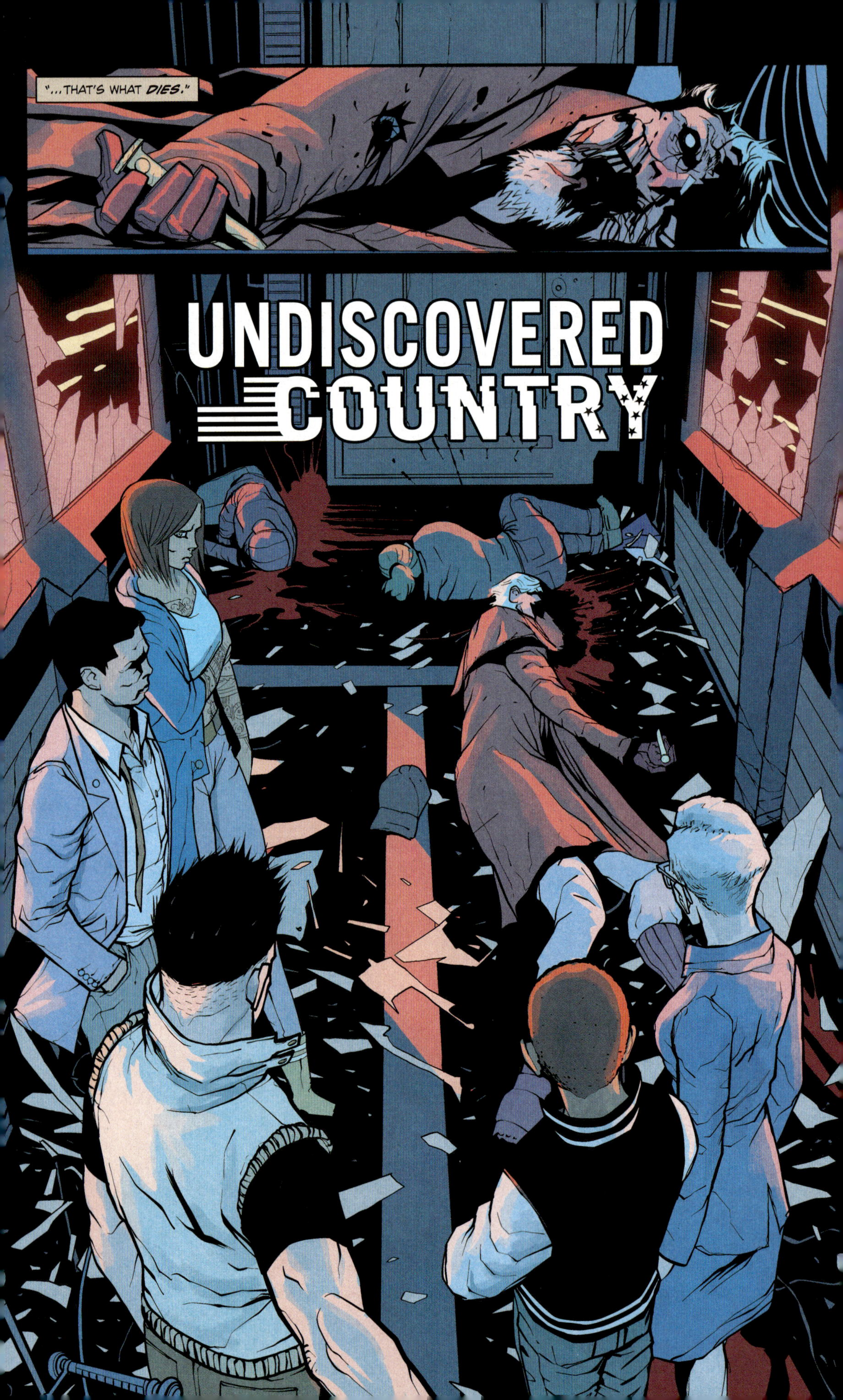
"...THAT'S WHAT DIES."
UNDISCOVERED COUNTRY

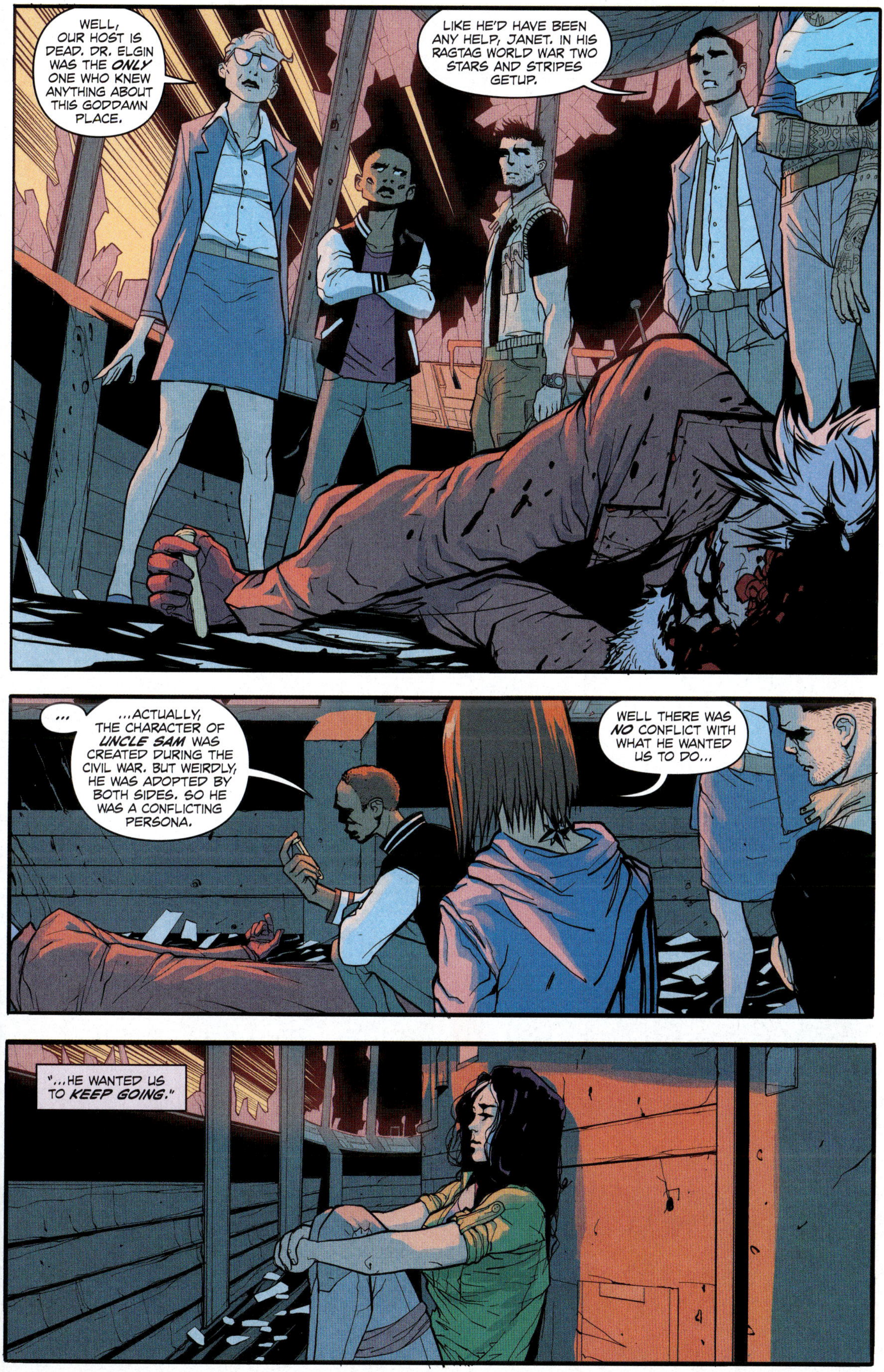
WELL, OUR HOST IS DEAD. DR. ELGIN WAS THE ONLY ONE WHO KNEW ANYTHING ABOUT THIS GODDAMN PLACE.
LIKE HE'D HAVE BEEN ANY HELP, JANET. IN HIS RAGTAG WORLD WAR TWO STARS AND STRIPES GETUP.
...
...ACTUALLY, THE CHARACTER OF UNCLE SAM WAS CREATED DURING THE CIVIL WAR. BUT WEIRDLY, HE WAS ADOPTED BY BOTH SIDES. SO HE WAS A CONFLICTING PERSONA.
WELL THERE WAS NO CONFLICT WITH WHAT HE WANTED US TO DO...
"...HE WANTED US TO KEEP GOING."

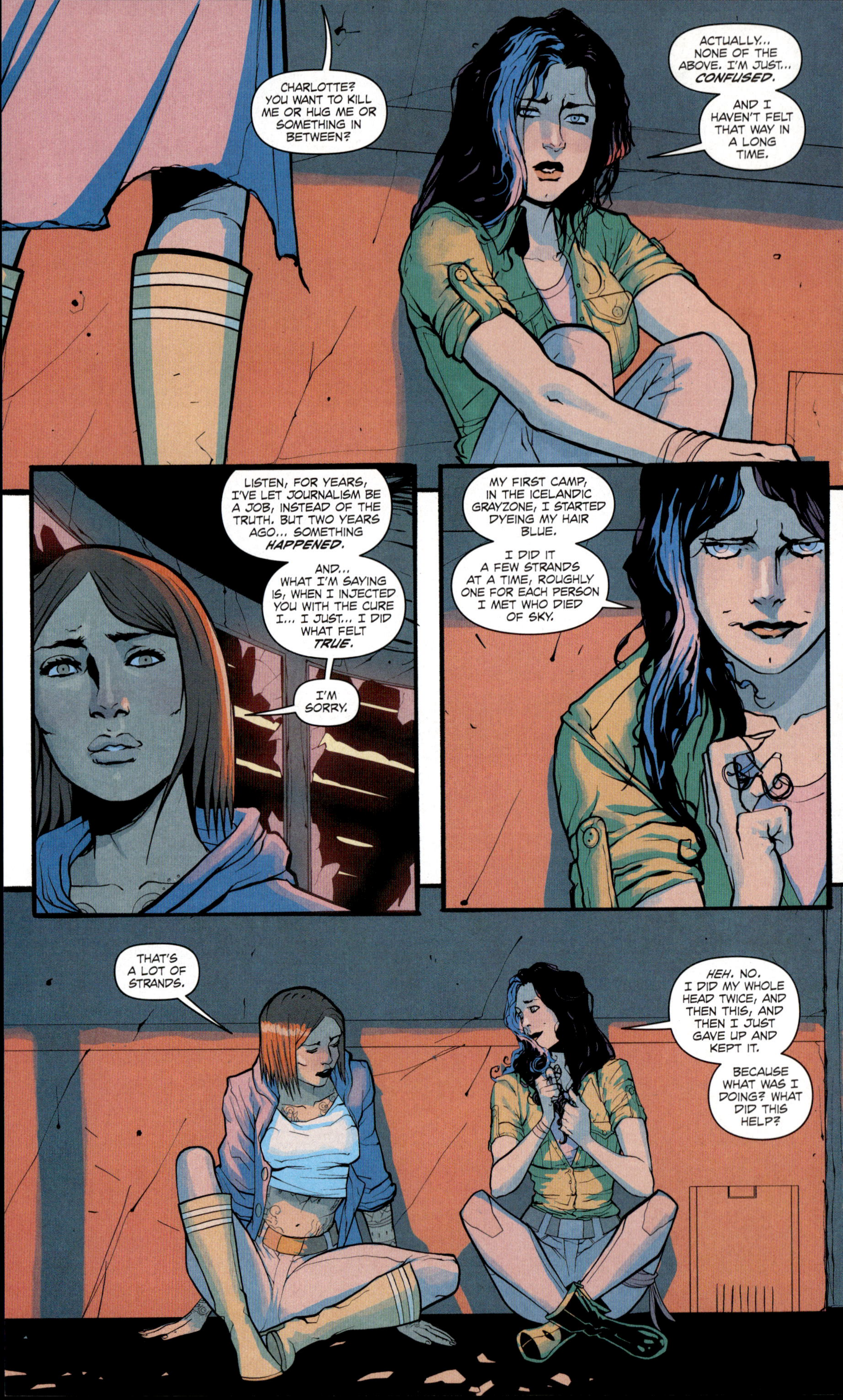
CHARLOTTE? YOU WANT TO KILL ME OR HUG ME OR SOMETHING IN BETWEEN?
ACTUALLY... NONE OF THE ABOVE. I'M JUST... CONFUSED.
AND I HAVEN'T FELT THAT WAY IN A LONG TIME.
LISTEN, FOR YEARS, I'VE LET JOURNALISM BE A JOB, INSTEAD OF THE TRUTH. BUT TWO YEARS AGO... SOMETHING HAPPENED.
AND... WHAT I'M SAYING IS, WHEN I INJECTED YOU WITH THE CURE I... I JUST... I DID WHAT FELT TRUE.
I'M SORRY.
MY FIRST CAMP, IN THE ICELANDIC GRAYZONE, I STARTED DYEING MY HAIR BLUE.
I DID IT A FEW STRANDS AT A TIME, ROUGHLY ONE FOR EACH PERSON I MET WHO DIED OF SKY.
THAT'S A LOT OF STRANDS.
HEH. NO. I DID MY WHOLE HEAD TWICE, AND THEN THIS, AND THEN I JUST GAVE UP AND KEPT IT.
BECAUSE WHAT WAS I DOING? WHAT DID THIS HELP?

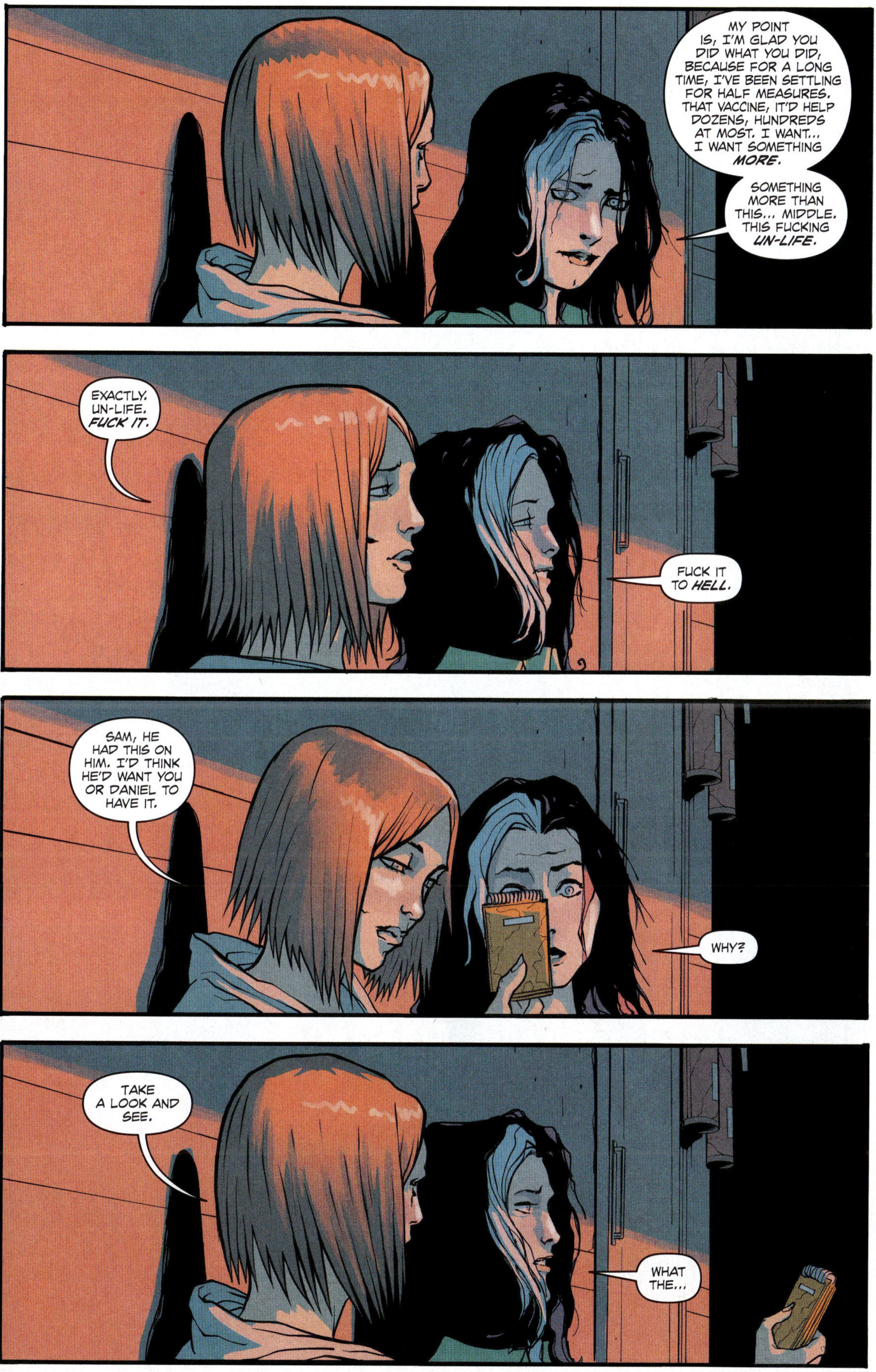
MY POINT IS, I'M GLAD YOU DID WHAT YOU DID, BECAUSE FOR A LONG TIME, I'VE BEEN SETTLING FOR HALF MEASURES. THAT VACCINE, IT'D HELP DOZENS, HUNDREDS AT MOST. I WANT... I WANT SOMETHING MORE.
SOMETHING MORE THAN THIS... MIDDLE. THIS FUCKING UN-LIFE.
EXACTLY. UN-LIFE. FUCK IT.
FUCK IT TO HELL.
SAM, HE HAD THIS ON HIM. I'D THINK HE'D WANT YOU OR DANIEL TO HAVE IT.
WHY?
TAKE A LOOK AND SEE.
WHAT THE...

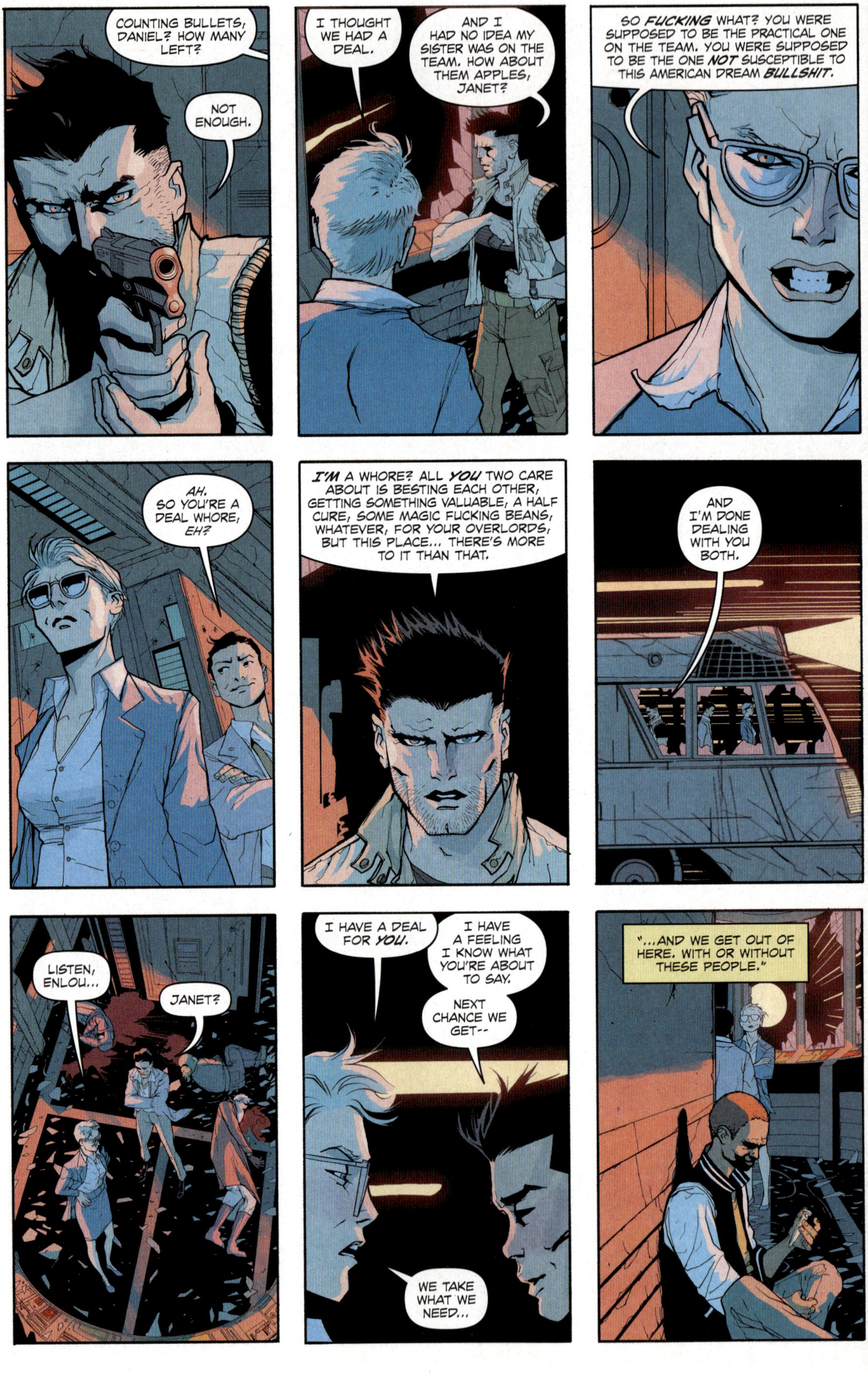
COUNTING BULLETS, DANIEL? HOW MANY LEFT?
NOT ENOUGH.
I THOUGHT WE HAD A DEAL.
AND I HAD NO IDEA MY SISTER WAS ON THE TEAM. HOW ABOUT THEM APPLES, JANET?
SO FUCKING WHAT? YOU WERE SUPPOSED TO BE THE PRACTICAL ONE ON THE TEAM. YOU WERE SUPPOSED TO BE THE ONE NOT SUSCEPTIBLE TO THIS AMERICAN DREAM BULLSHIT.
AH. SO YOU'RE A DEAL WHORE, EH?
I'M A WHORE? ALL YOU TWO CARE ABOUT IS BESTING EACH OTHER, GETTING SOMETHING VALUABLE, A HALF CURE, SOME MAGIC FUCKING BEANS, WHATEVER, FOR YOUR OVERLORDS, BUT THIS PLACE... THERE'S MORE TO IT THAN THAT.
AND I'M DONE DEALING WITH YOU BOTH.
LISTEN, ENLOU...
JANET?
I HAVE A DEAL FOR YOU.
I HAVE A FEELING I KNOW WHAT YOU'RE ABOUT TO SAY.
NEXT CHANCE WE GET--
WE TAKE WHAT WE NEED...
"...AND WE GET OUT OF HERE. WITH OR WITHOUT THESE PEOPLE."

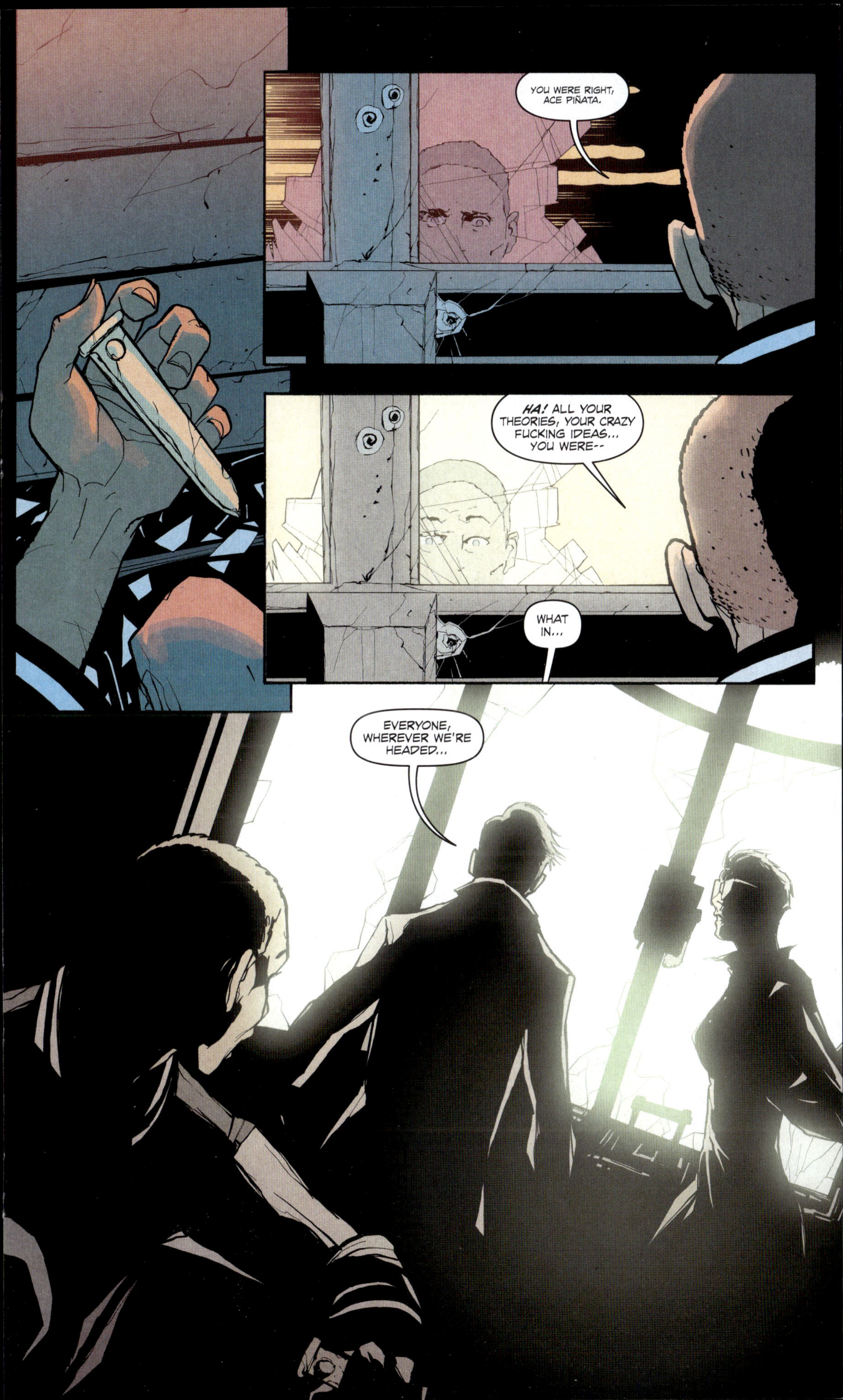
YOU WERE RIGHT, ACE PIÑATA.
HA! ALL YOUR THEORIES, YOUR CRAZY FUCKING IDEAS... YOU WERE--
WHAT IN...
EVERYONE, WHEREVER WE'RE HEADED...

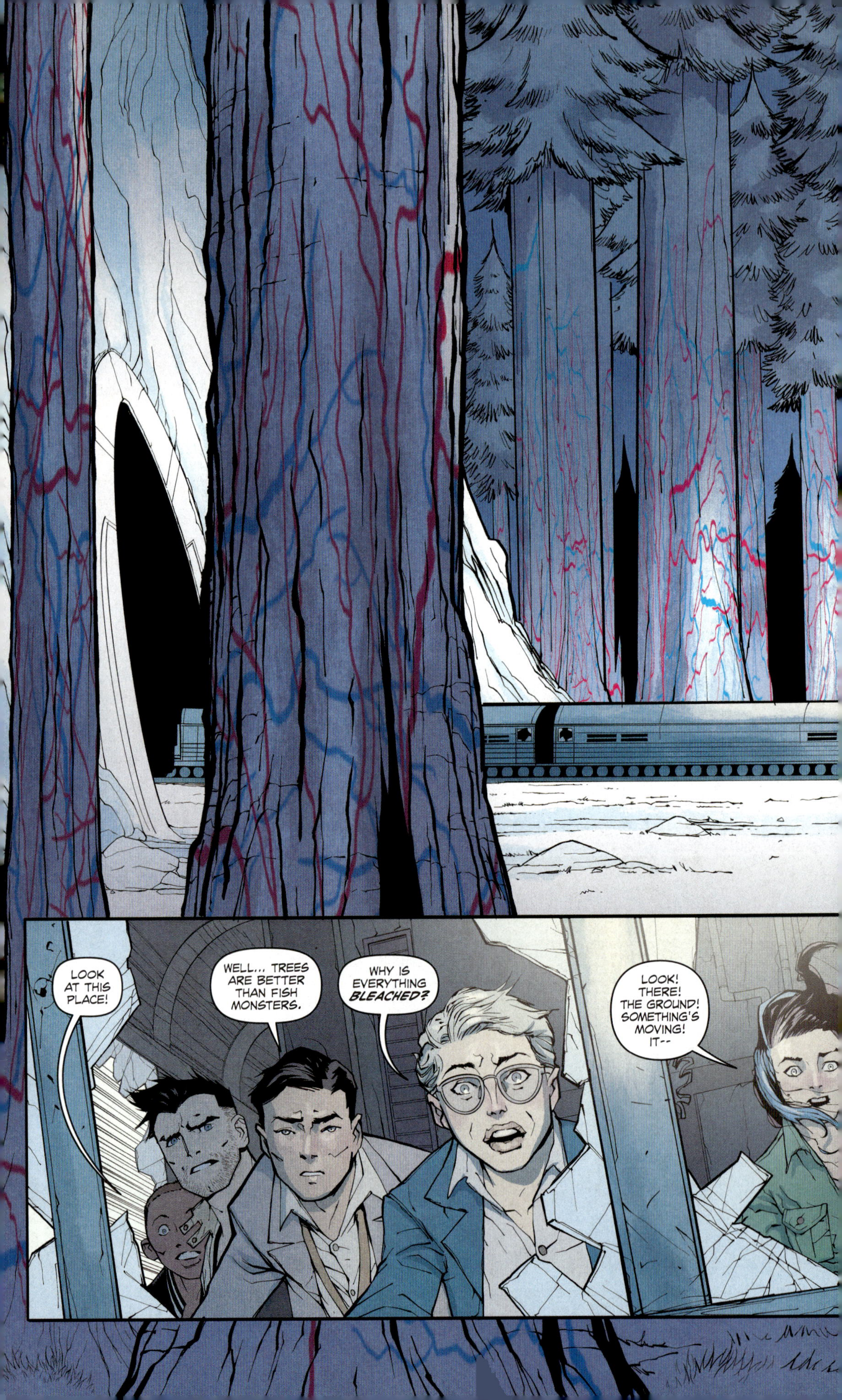
LOOK AT THIS PLACE!
WELL... TREES ARE BETTER THAN FISH MONSTERS.
WHY IS EVERYTHING *BLEACHED?*
LOOK! THERE! THE GROUND! SOMETHING'S MOVING! IT--

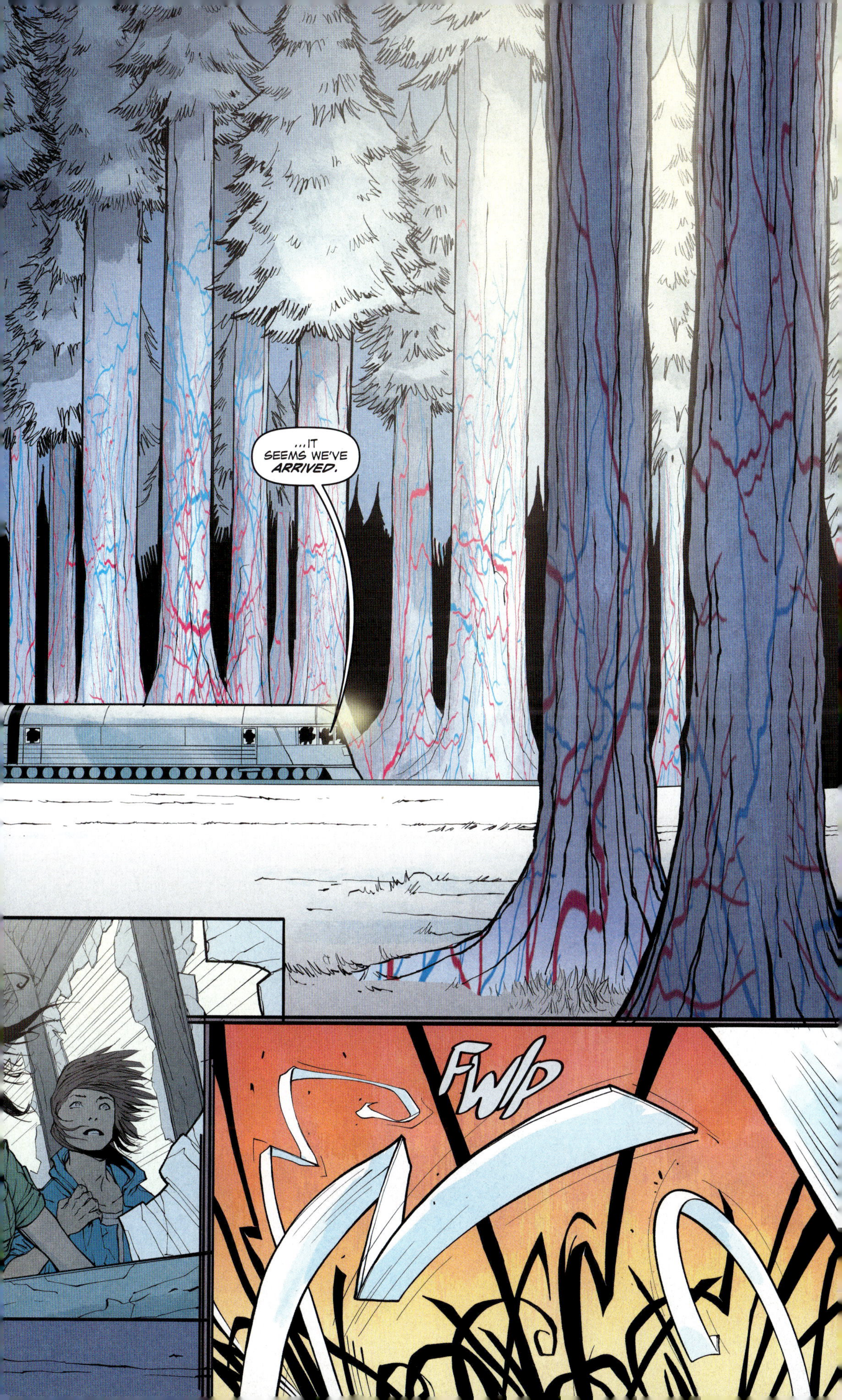
...IT SEEMS WE'VE *ARRIVED*.
FWIP

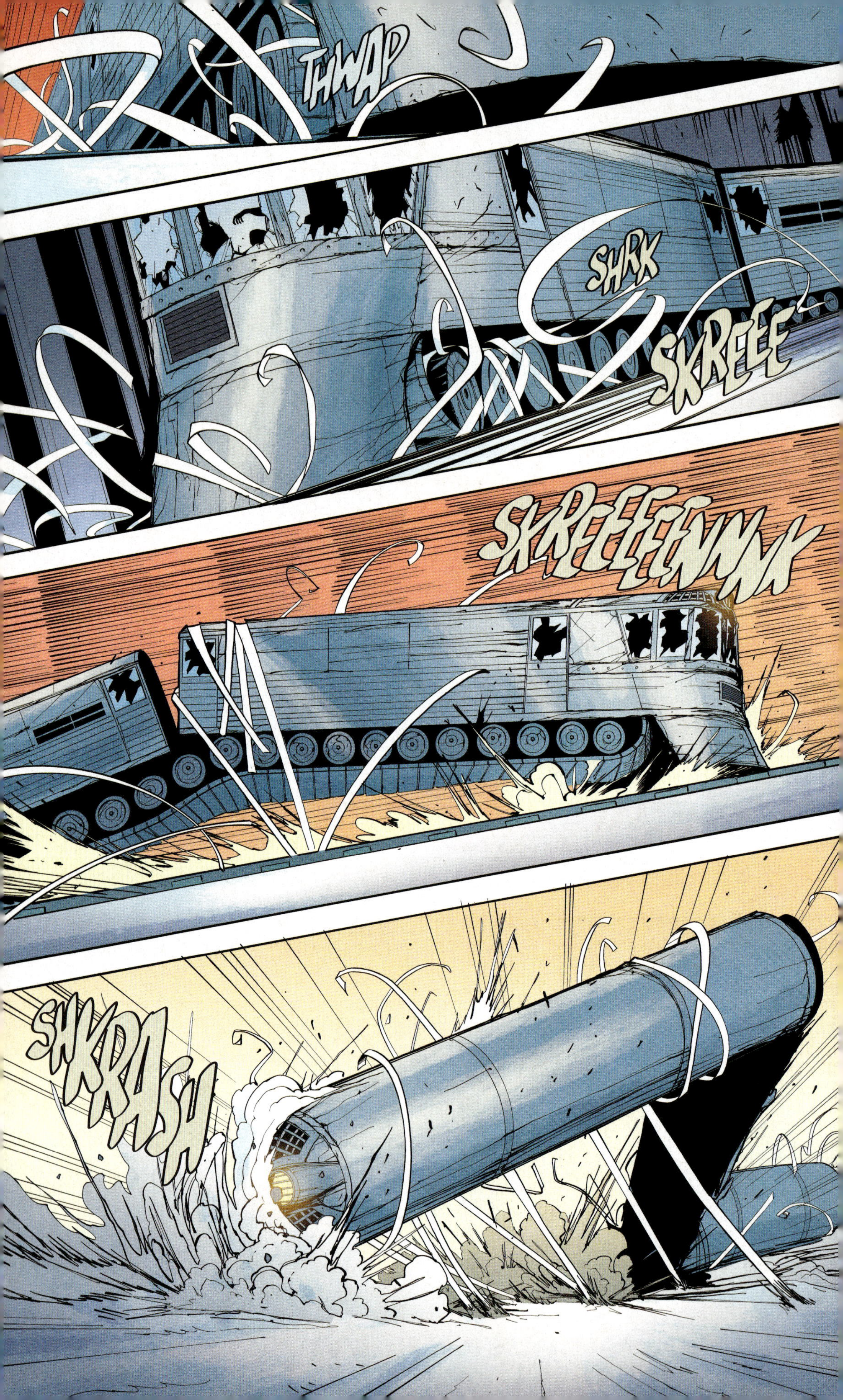
THWAP
SHRK
SKREEE
SKREEEEENNNK
SHKRASH

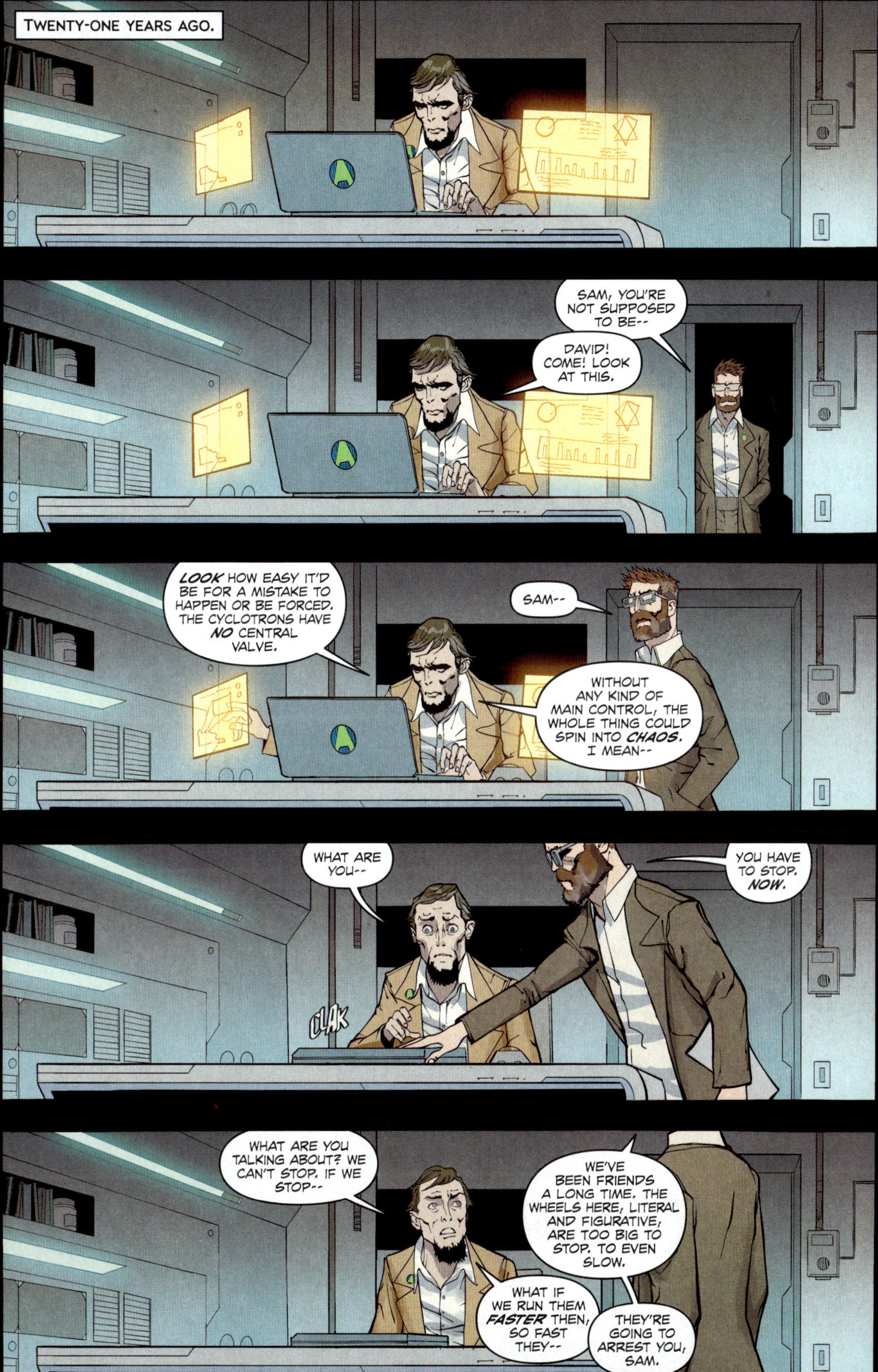
TWENTY-ONE YEARS AGO.
SAM, YOU'RE NOT SUPPOSED TO BE--
DAVID! COME! LOOK AT THIS.
LOOK HOW EASY IT'D BE FOR A MISTAKE TO HAPPEN OR BE FORCED. THE CYCLOTRONS HAVE NO CENTRAL VALVE.
SAM--
WITHOUT ANY KIND OF MAIN CONTROL, THE WHOLE THING COULD SPIN INTO CHAOS. I MEAN--
WHAT ARE YOU--
YOU HAVE TO STOP. NOW.
CLAK
WHAT ARE YOU TALKING ABOUT? WE CAN'T STOP. IF WE STOP--
WE'VE BEEN FRIENDS A LONG TIME. THE WHEELS HERE, LITERAL AND FIGURATIVE, ARE TOO BIG TO STOP. TO EVEN SLOW.
WHAT IF WE RUN THEM FASTER THEN, SO FAST THEY--
THEY'RE GOING TO ARREST YOU, SAM.

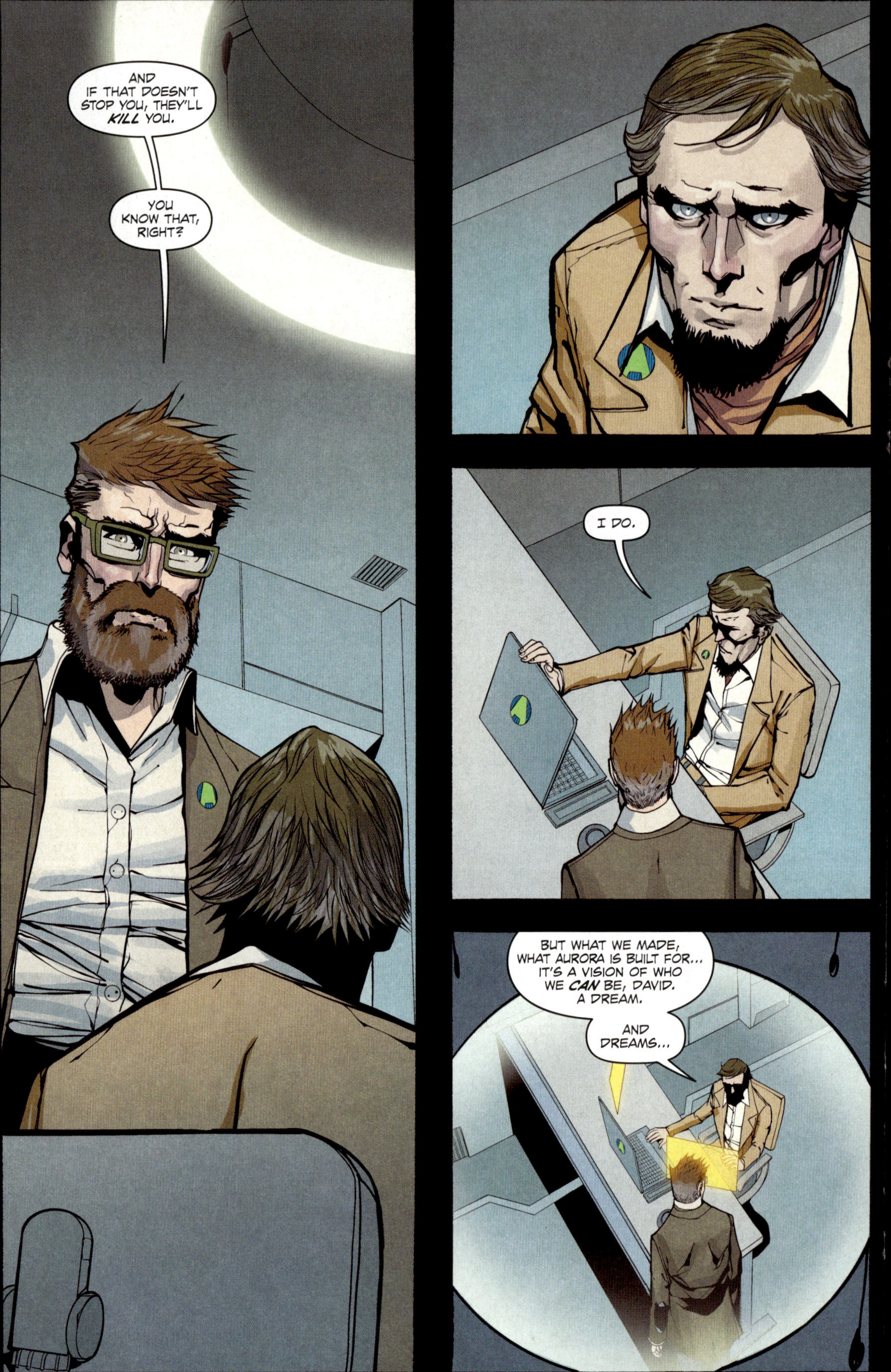
AND IF THAT DOESN'T STOP YOU, THEY'LL *KILL* YOU.
YOU KNOW THAT, RIGHT?
I DO.
BUT WHAT WE MADE, WHAT AURORA IS BUILT FOR... IT'S A VISION OF WHO WE *CAN* BE, DAVID. A DREAM.
AND DREAMS...

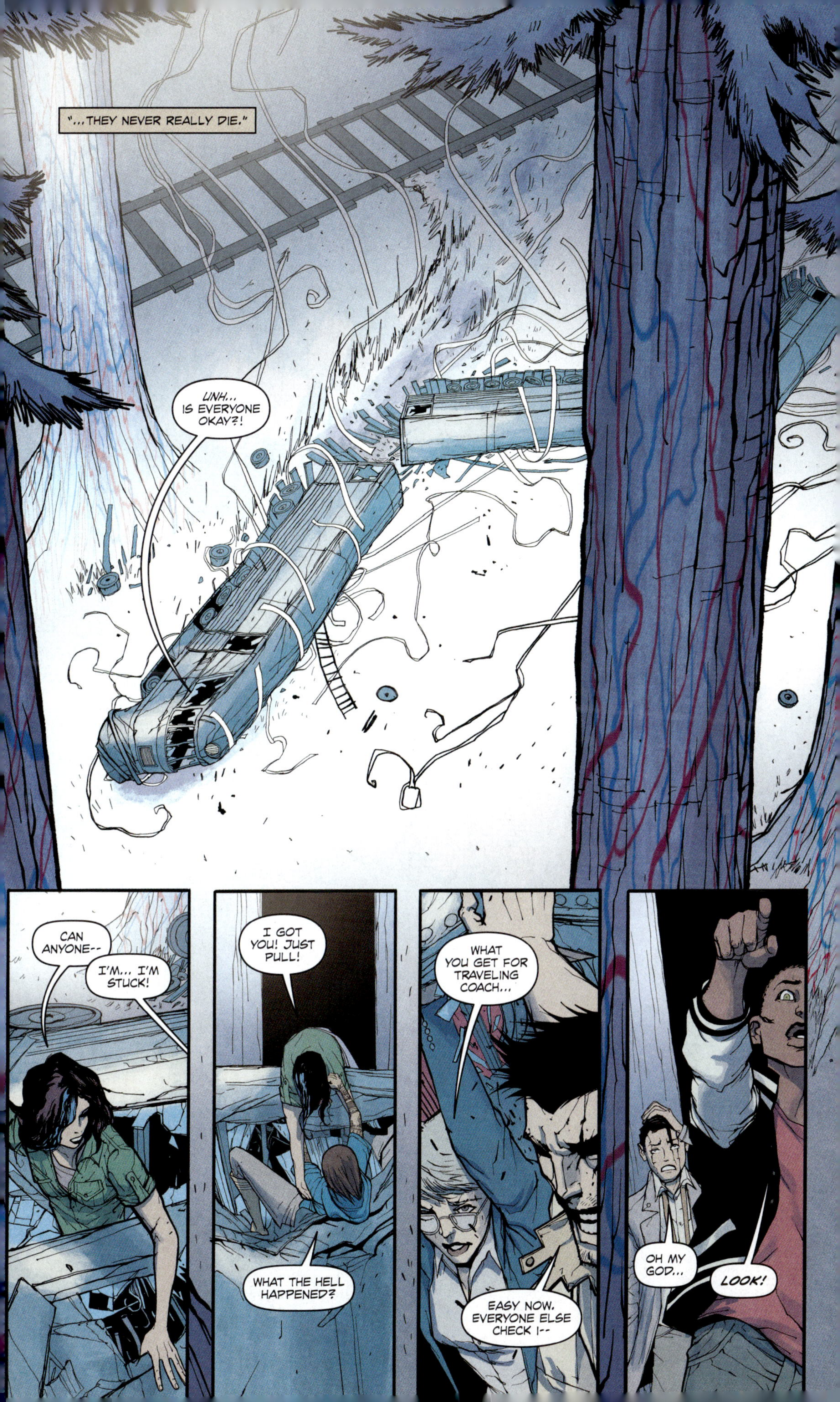
"...THEY NEVER REALLY DIE."
UNH... IS EVERYONE OKAY?!
CAN ANYONE--
I'M... I'M STUCK!
I GOT YOU! JUST PULL!
WHAT THE HELL HAPPENED?
WHAT YOU GET FOR TRAVELING COACH...
EASY NOW. EVERYONE ELSE CHECK I--
OH MY GOD...
LOOK!

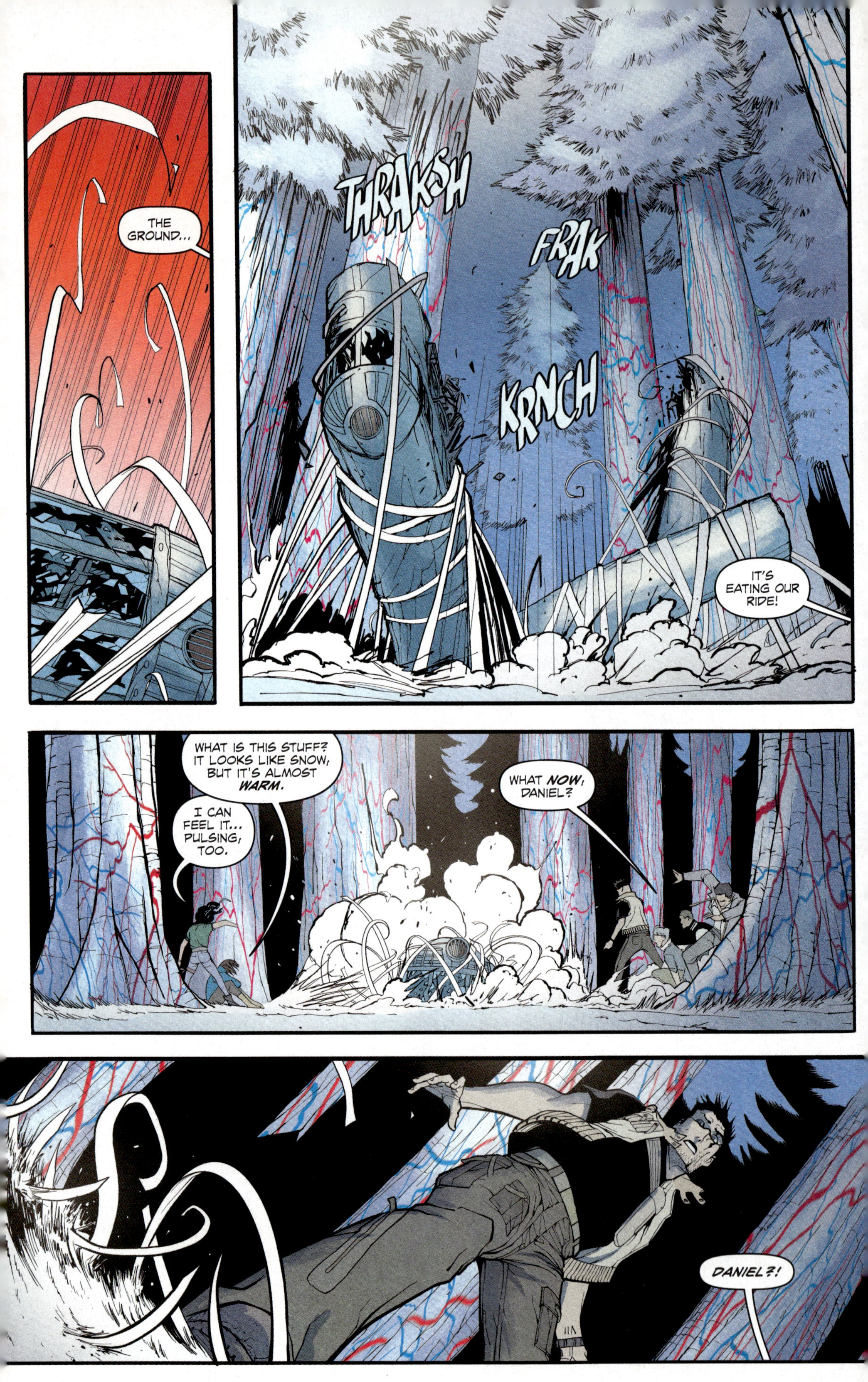
THE GROUND...
THRAKSH
FRAK
KRNCH
IT'S EATING OUR RIDE!
WHAT IS THIS STUFF? IT LOOKS LIKE SNOW, BUT IT'S ALMOST WARM.
I CAN FEEL IT... PULSING, TOO.
WHAT NOW, DANIEL?
DANIEL?!

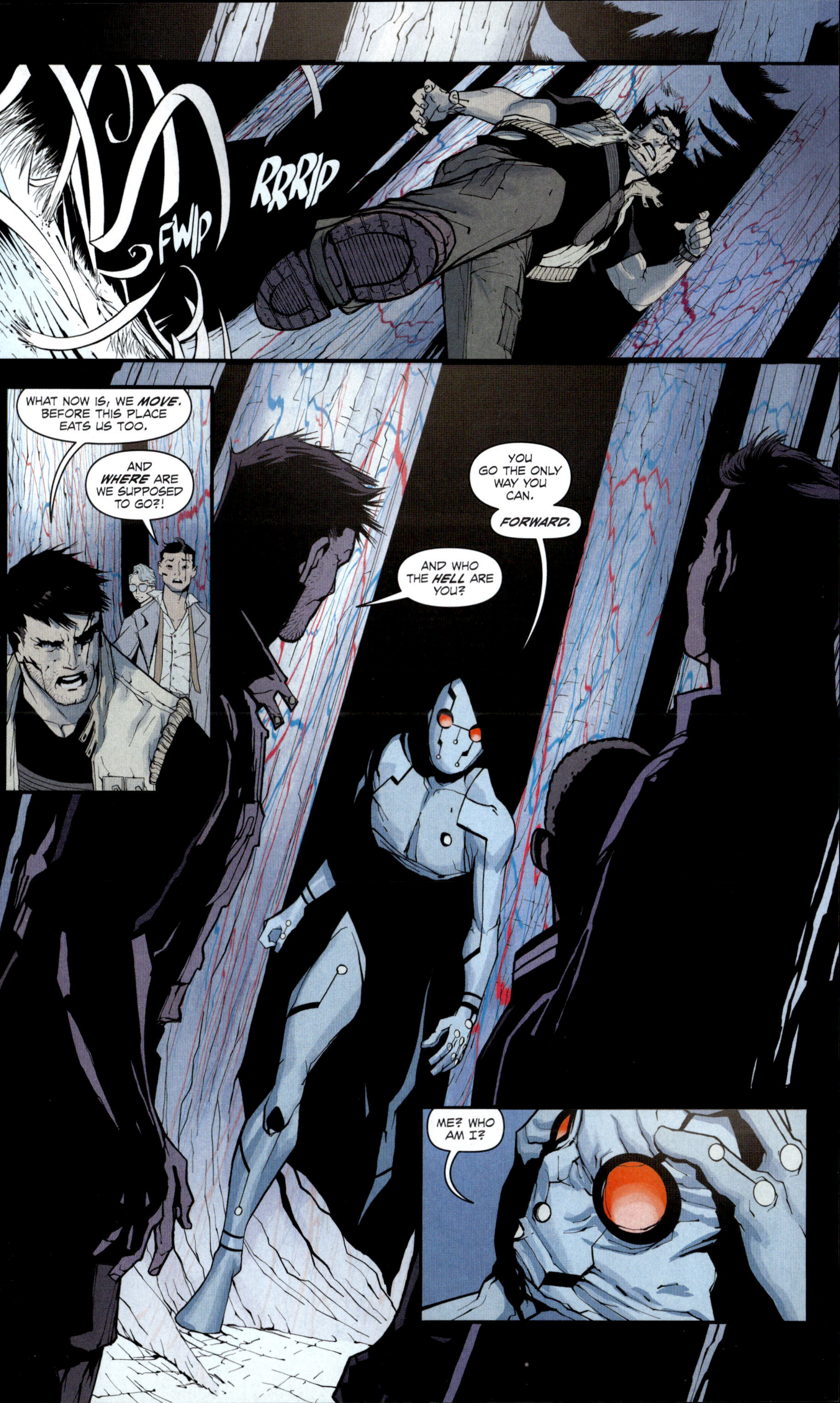
FWIP
RRRIP
WHAT NOW IS, WE MOVE. BEFORE THIS PLACE EATS US TOO.
AND WHERE ARE WE SUPPOSED TO GO?!
YOU GO THE ONLY WAY YOU CAN.
FORWARD.
AND WHO THE HELL ARE YOU?
ME? WHO AM I?

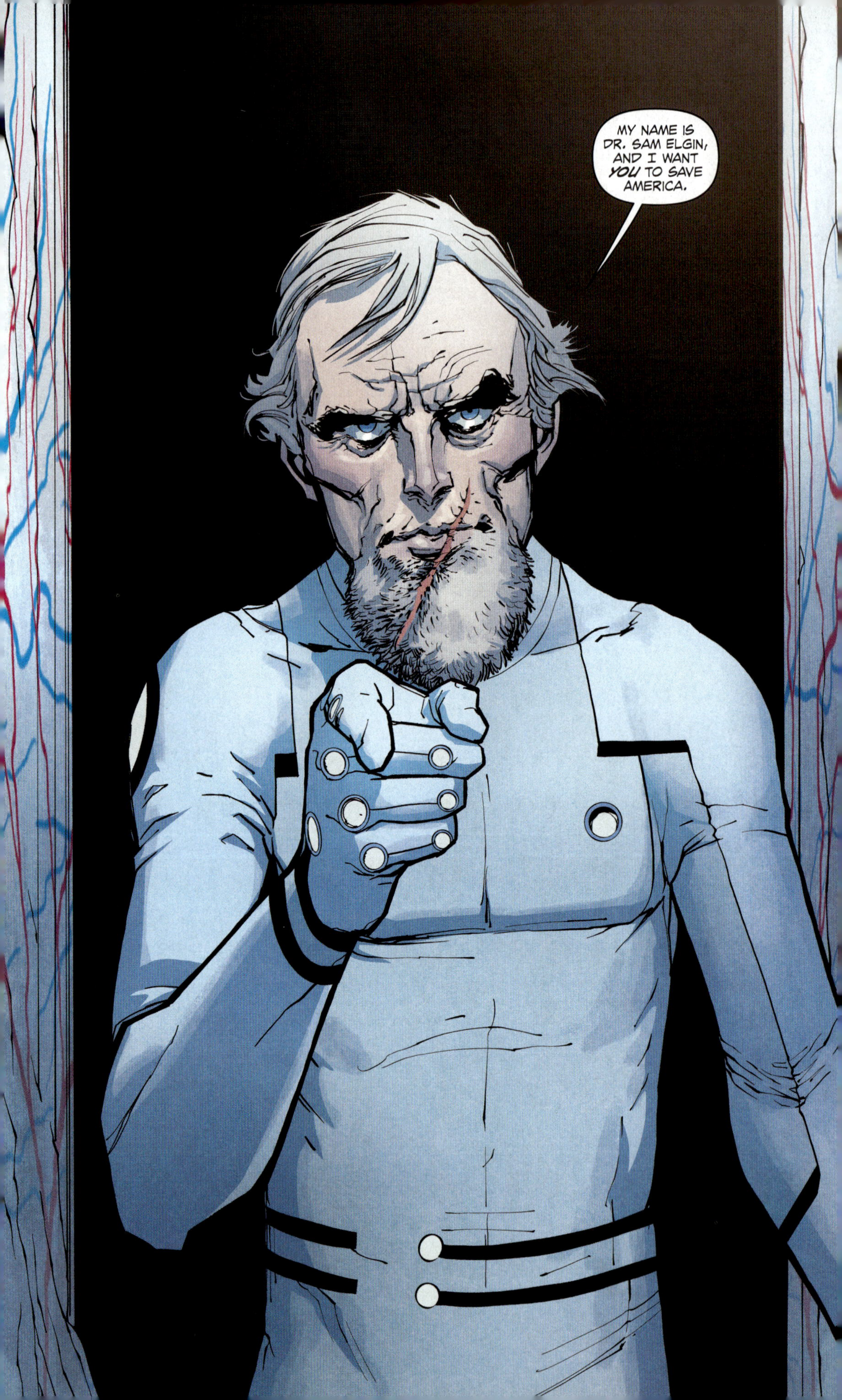
MY NAME IS DR. SAM ELGIN, AND I WANT *YOU* TO SAVE AMERICA.

The Lafayette Group

"The closure of the American border, while impressive, is not yet perfect, and we are still receiving limited intelligence from inside the country. We do not know how long this will last, and we fully expect that the United States government will close these leaks soon--or will find and eradicate our agents. They are not backing down from the scenario described by their President just under two weeks ago. The US has locked itself away, and it does not seem likely to open up again at any point in the near future. That is strange enough, and we do not yet fully understand the implications. But stranger still...

...the vast majority of the American population had no idea it was going to happen."

--Report filed by Dr. Warren Antone,
July 27, 2029.

FROM THE ARCHIVES OF THE LAFAYETTE GROUP.
FOR OFFICIAL USE ONLY.

CHAPTER EIGHT

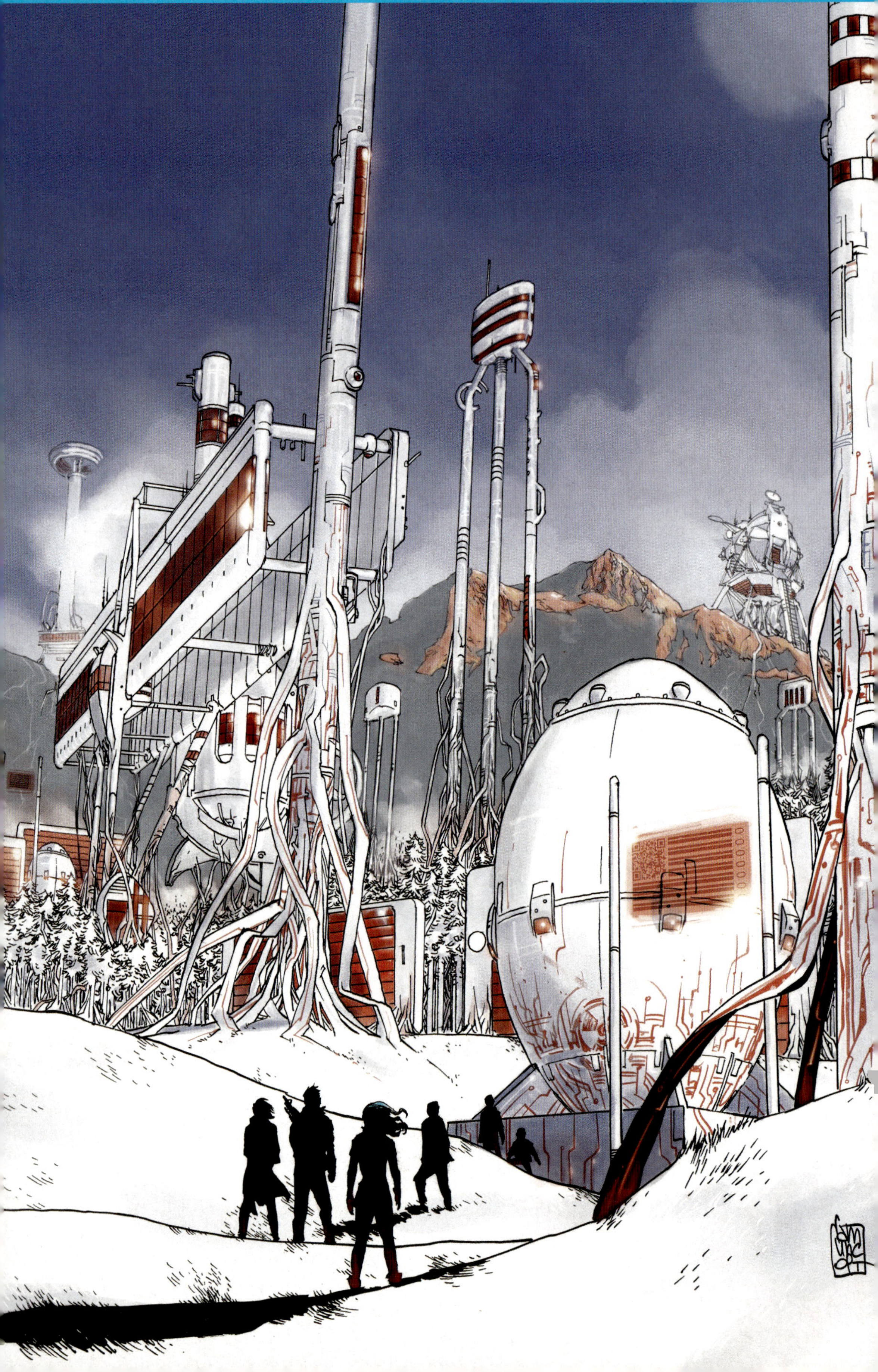

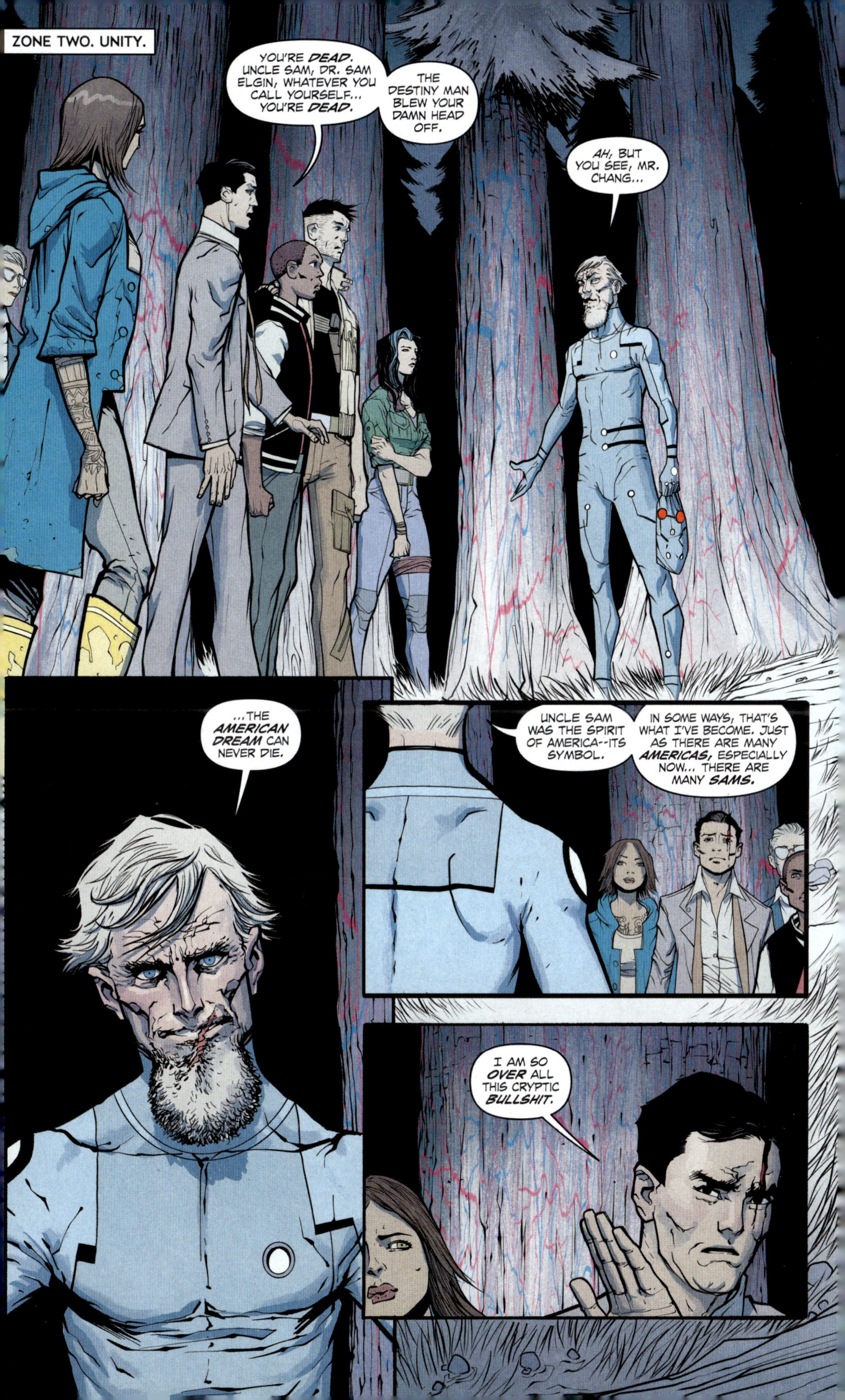
ZONE TWO. UNITY.
YOU'RE DEAD. UNCLE SAM, DR. SAM ELGIN, WHATEVER YOU CALL YOURSELF... YOU'RE DEAD.
THE DESTINY MAN BLEW YOUR DAMN HEAD OFF.
AH, BUT YOU SEE, MR. CHANG...
...THE AMERICAN DREAM CAN NEVER DIE.
UNCLE SAM WAS THE SPIRIT OF AMERICA--ITS SYMBOL.
IN SOME WAYS, THAT'S WHAT I'VE BECOME. JUST AS THERE ARE MANY AMERICAS, ESPECIALLY NOW... THERE ARE MANY SAMS.
I AM SO OVER ALL THIS CRYPTIC BULLSHIT.

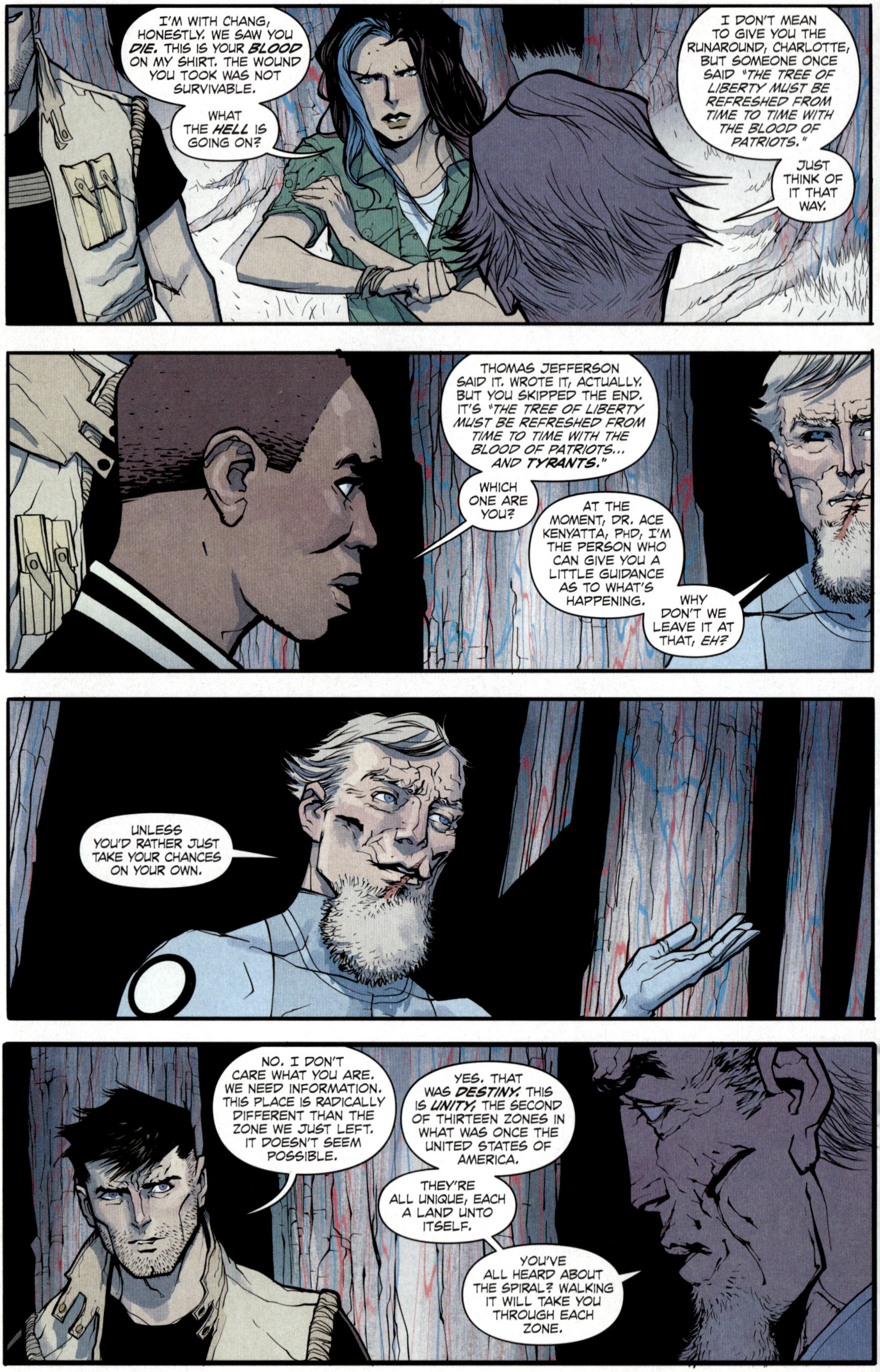
I'M WITH CHANG, HONESTLY. WE SAW YOU DIE. THIS IS YOUR BLOOD ON MY SHIRT. THE WOUND YOU TOOK WAS NOT SURVIVABLE.
WHAT THE HELL IS GOING ON?
I DON'T MEAN TO GIVE YOU THE RUNAROUND, CHARLOTTE, BUT SOMEONE ONCE SAID "THE TREE OF LIBERTY MUST BE REFRESHED FROM TIME TO TIME WITH THE BLOOD OF PATRIOTS."
JUST THINK OF IT THAT WAY.
THOMAS JEFFERSON SAID IT. WROTE IT, ACTUALLY. BUT YOU SKIPPED THE END. IT'S "THE TREE OF LIBERTY MUST BE REFRESHED FROM TIME TO TIME WITH THE BLOOD OF PATRIOTS... AND TYRANTS."
WHICH ONE ARE YOU?
AT THE MOMENT, DR. ACE KENYATTA, PHD, I'M THE PERSON WHO CAN GIVE YOU A LITTLE GUIDANCE AS TO WHAT'S HAPPENING.
WHY DON'T WE LEAVE IT AT THAT, EH?
UNLESS YOU'D RATHER JUST TAKE YOUR CHANCES ON YOUR OWN.
NO. I DON'T CARE WHAT YOU ARE. WE NEED INFORMATION. THIS PLACE IS RADICALLY DIFFERENT THAN THE ZONE WE JUST LEFT. IT DOESN'T SEEM POSSIBLE.
YES. THAT WAS DESTINY. THIS IS UNITY, THE SECOND OF THIRTEEN ZONES IN WHAT WAS ONCE THE UNITED STATES OF AMERICA.
THEY'RE ALL UNIQUE, EACH A LAND UNTO ITSELF.
YOU'VE ALL HEARD ABOUT THE SPIRAL? WALKING IT WILL TAKE YOU THROUGH EACH ZONE.

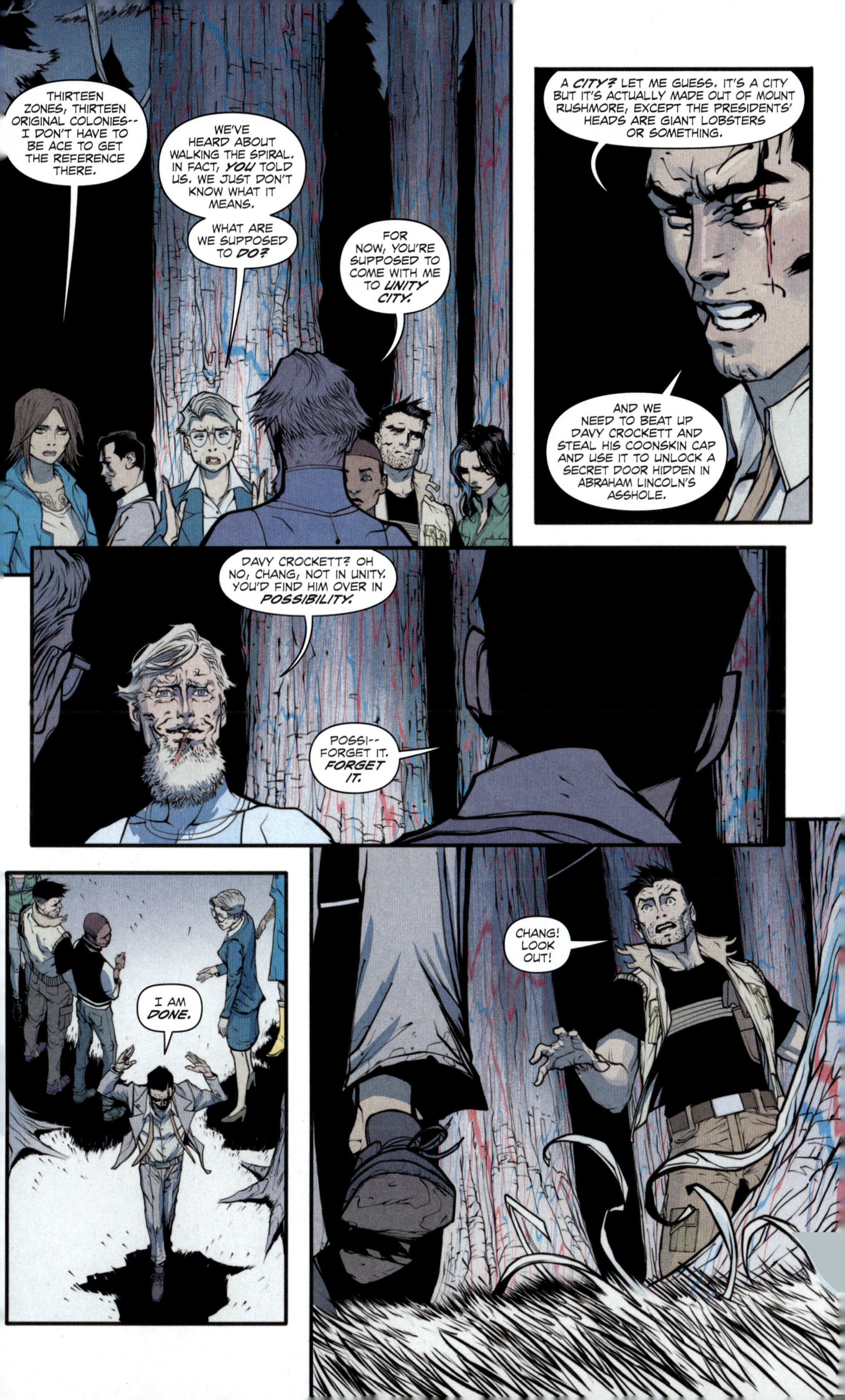
THIRTEEN ZONES, THIRTEEN ORIGINAL COLONIES-- I DON'T HAVE TO BE ACE TO GET THE REFERENCE THERE.
WE'VE HEARD ABOUT WALKING THE SPIRAL. IN FACT, YOU TOLD US. WE JUST DON'T KNOW WHAT IT MEANS.
WHAT ARE WE SUPPOSED TO DO?
FOR NOW, YOU'RE SUPPOSED TO COME WITH ME TO UNITY CITY.
A CITY? LET ME GUESS. IT'S A CITY BUT IT'S ACTUALLY MADE OUT OF MOUNT RUSHMORE, EXCEPT THE PRESIDENTS' HEADS ARE GIANT LOBSTERS OR SOMETHING.
AND WE NEED TO BEAT UP DAVY CROCKETT AND STEAL HIS COONSKIN CAP AND USE IT TO UNLOCK A SECRET DOOR HIDDEN IN ABRAHAM LINCOLN'S ASSHOLE.
DAVY CROCKETT? OH NO, CHANG, NOT IN UNITY. YOU'D FIND HIM OVER IN POSSIBILITY.
POSSI-- FORGET IT. FORGET IT.
I AM DONE.
CHANG! LOOK OUT!

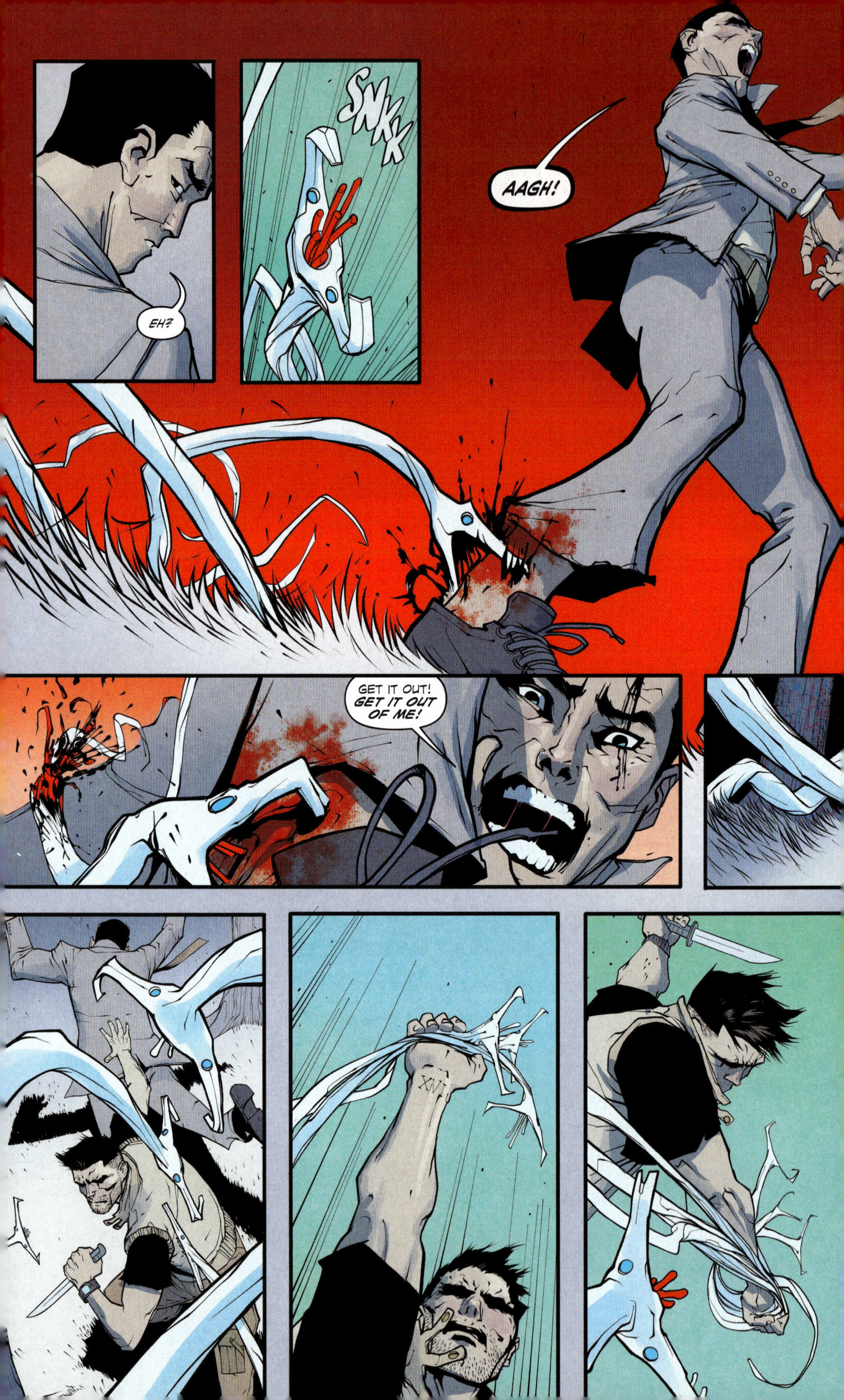
EH?
SNKK
AAGH!
GET IT OUT!
GET IT OUT
OF ME!

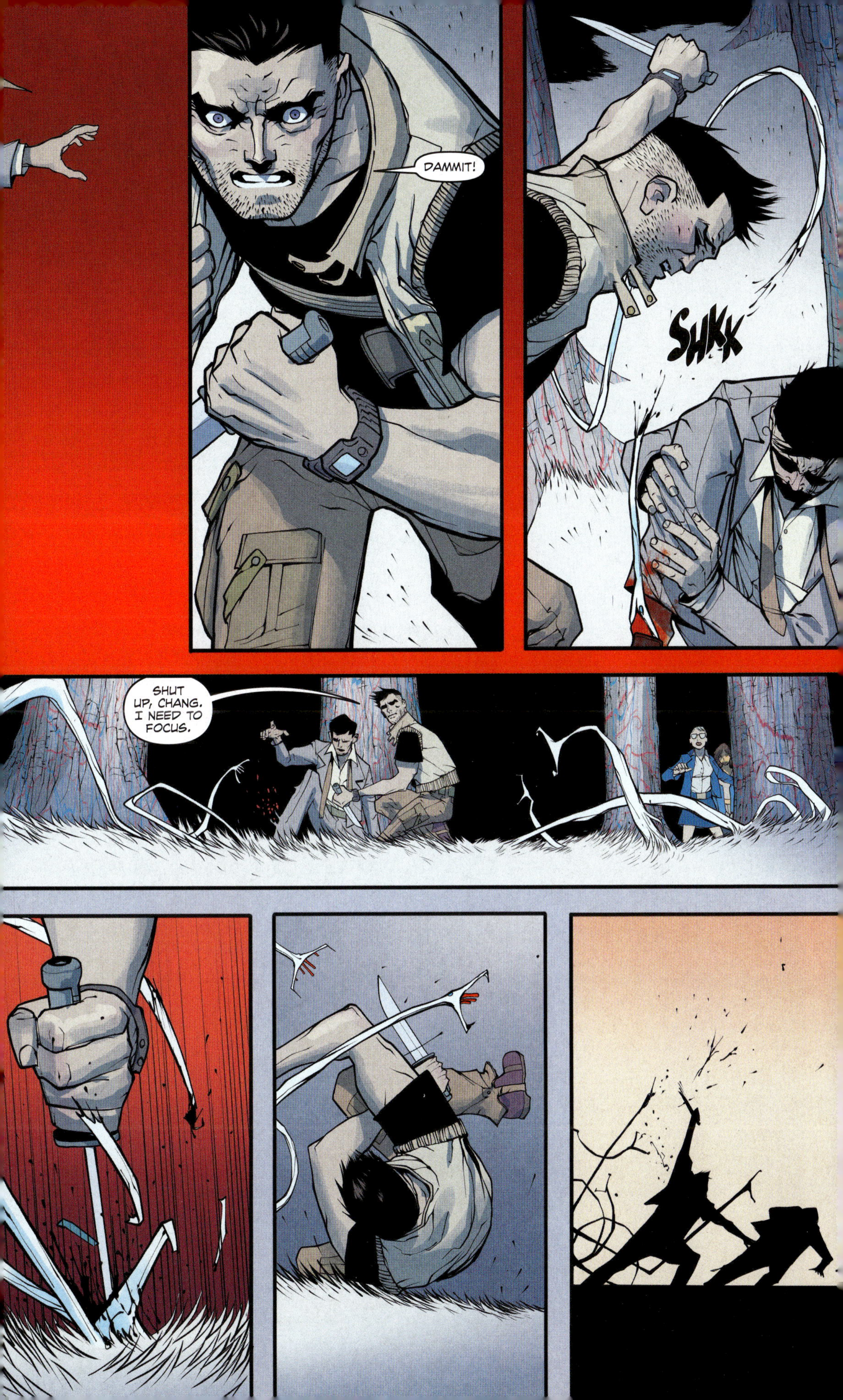
DAMMIT!
SHKK
SHUT UP, CHANG. I NEED TO FOCUS.

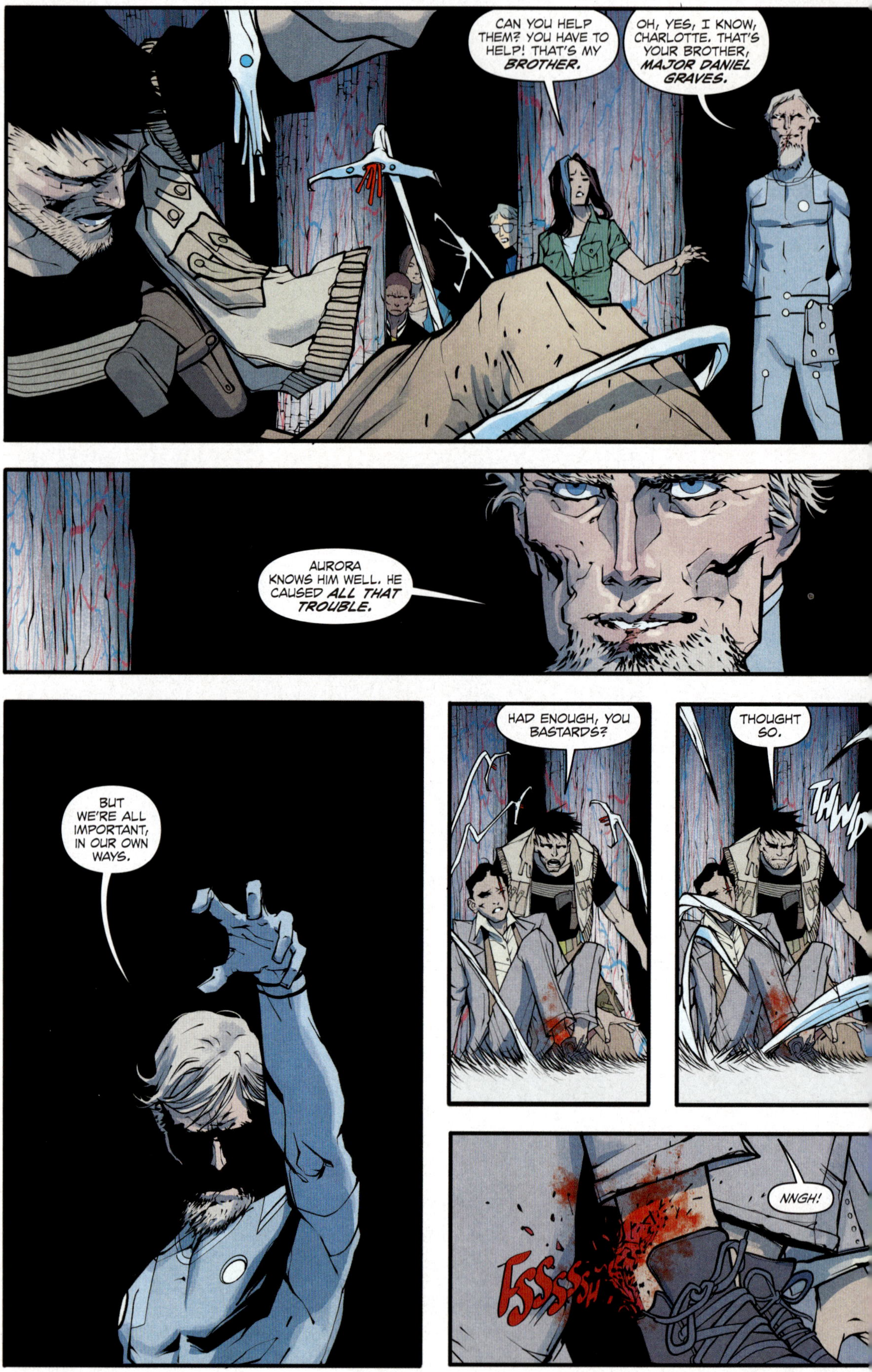
CAN YOU HELP THEM? YOU HAVE TO HELP! THAT'S MY BROTHER.
OH, YES, I KNOW, CHARLOTTE. THAT'S YOUR BROTHER, MAJOR DANIEL GRAVES.
AURORA KNOWS HIM WELL. HE CAUSED ALL THAT TROUBLE.
BUT WE'RE ALL IMPORTANT, IN OUR OWN WAYS.
HAD ENOUGH, YOU BASTARDS?
THOUGHT SO.
THWIP
NNGH!
FSSSSSH

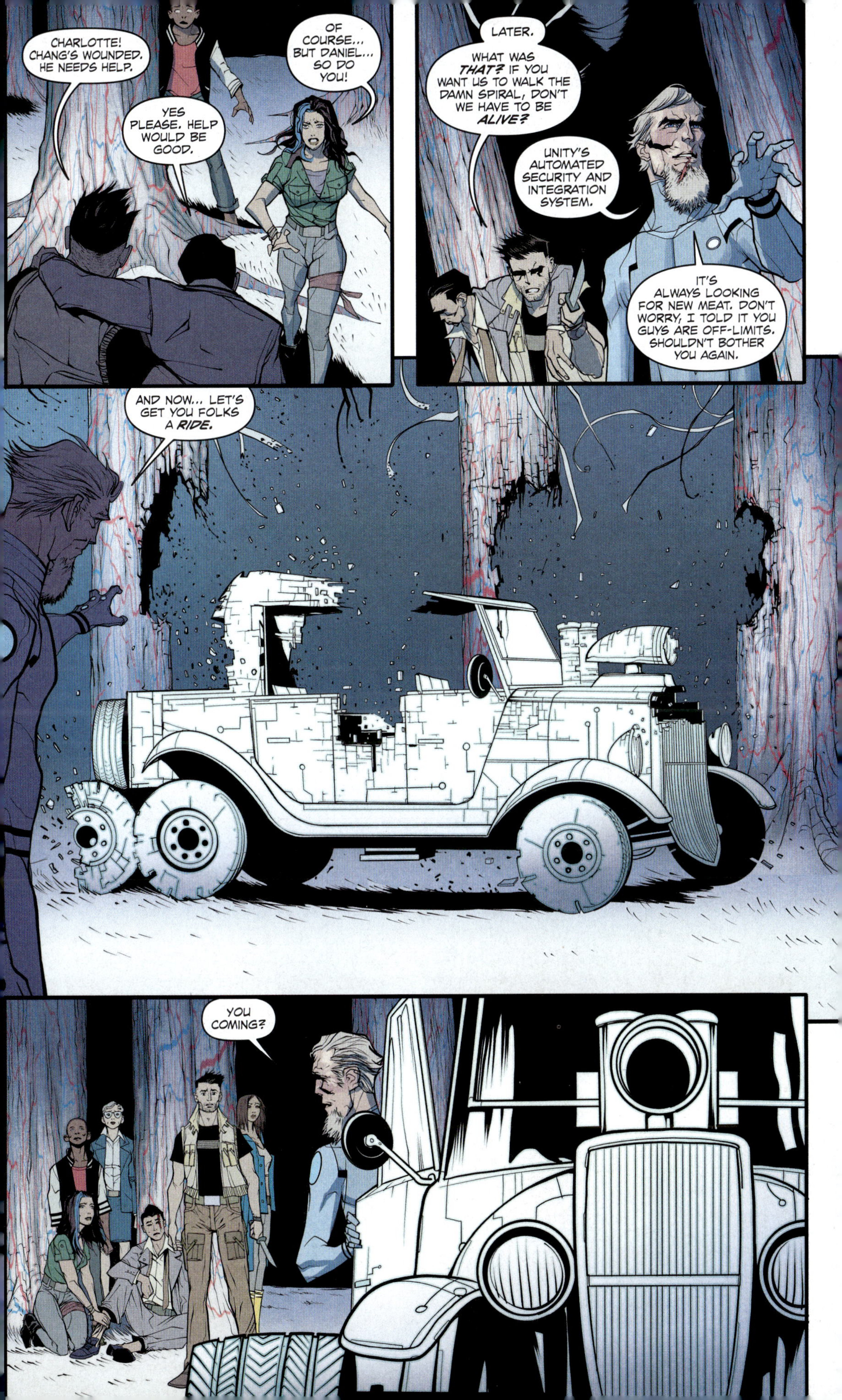

CHARLOTTE! CHANG'S WOUNDED. HE NEEDS HELP.
YES PLEASE. HELP WOULD BE GOOD.
OF COURSE... BUT DANIEL... SO DO YOU!
LATER.
WHAT WAS *THAT?* IF YOU WANT US TO WALK THE DAMN SPIRAL, DON'T WE HAVE TO BE *ALIVE?*
UNITY'S AUTOMATED SECURITY AND INTEGRATION SYSTEM.
IT'S ALWAYS LOOKING FOR NEW MEAT. DON'T WORRY; I TOLD IT YOU GUYS ARE OFF-LIMITS. SHOULDN'T BOTHER YOU AGAIN.
AND NOW... LET'S GET YOU FOLKS A *RIDE.*
YOU COMING?

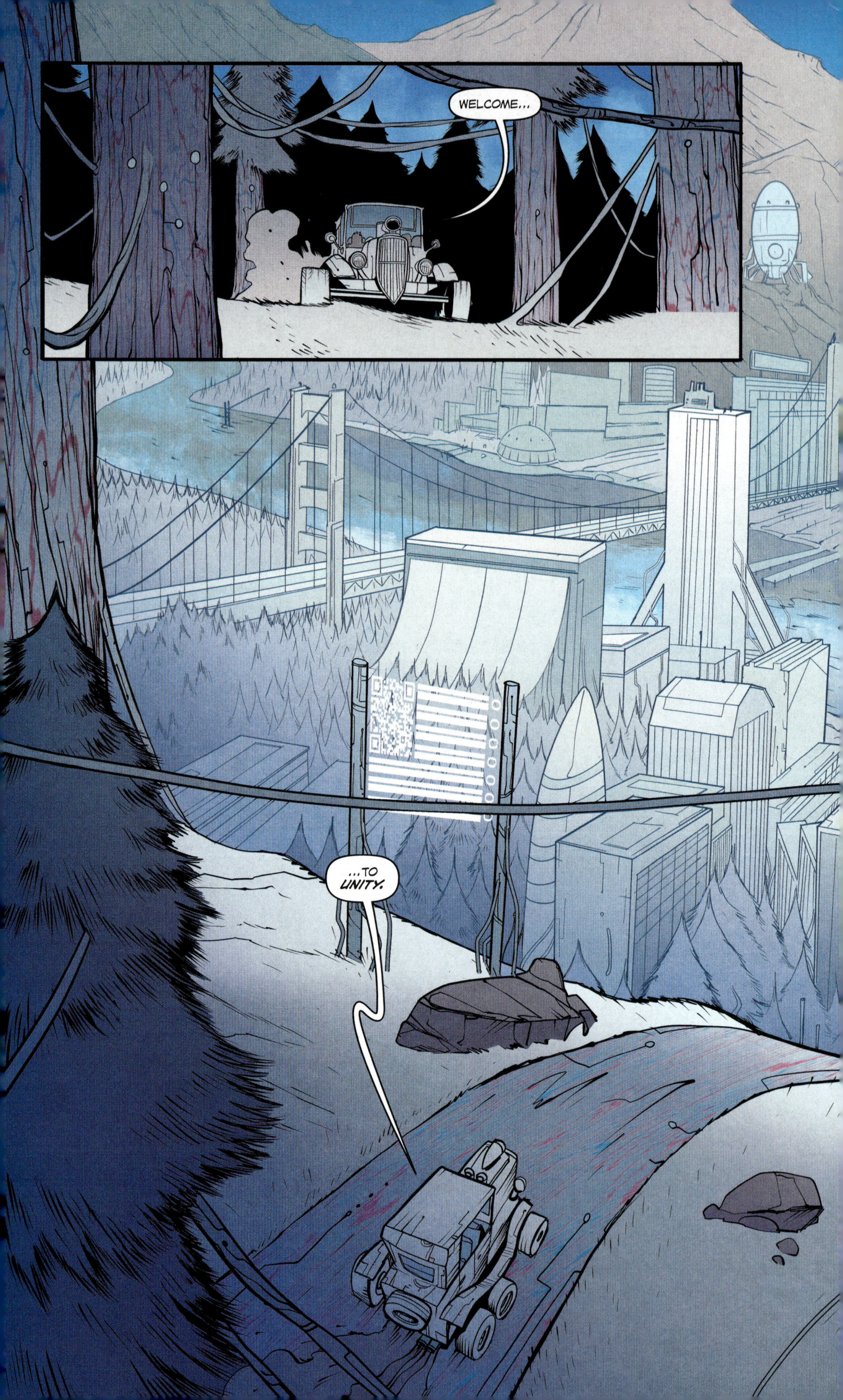
WELCOME...
...TO UNITY.

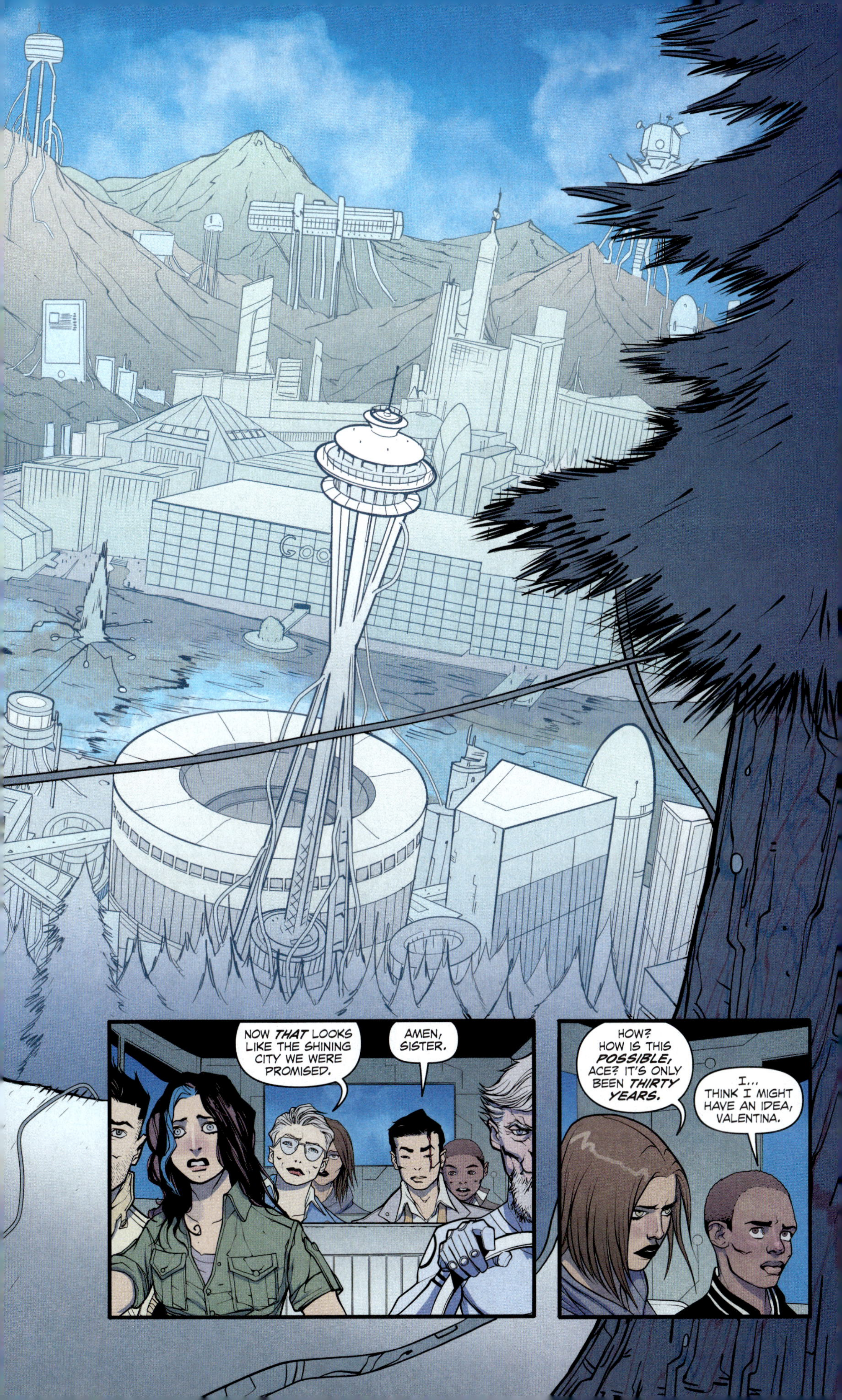
Goo
NOW *THAT* LOOKS LIKE THE SHINING CITY WE WERE PROMISED.
AMEN, SISTER.
HOW? HOW IS THIS *POSSIBLE,* ACE? IT'S ONLY BEEN *THIRTY YEARS.*
I... THINK I MIGHT HAVE AN IDEA, VALENTINA.

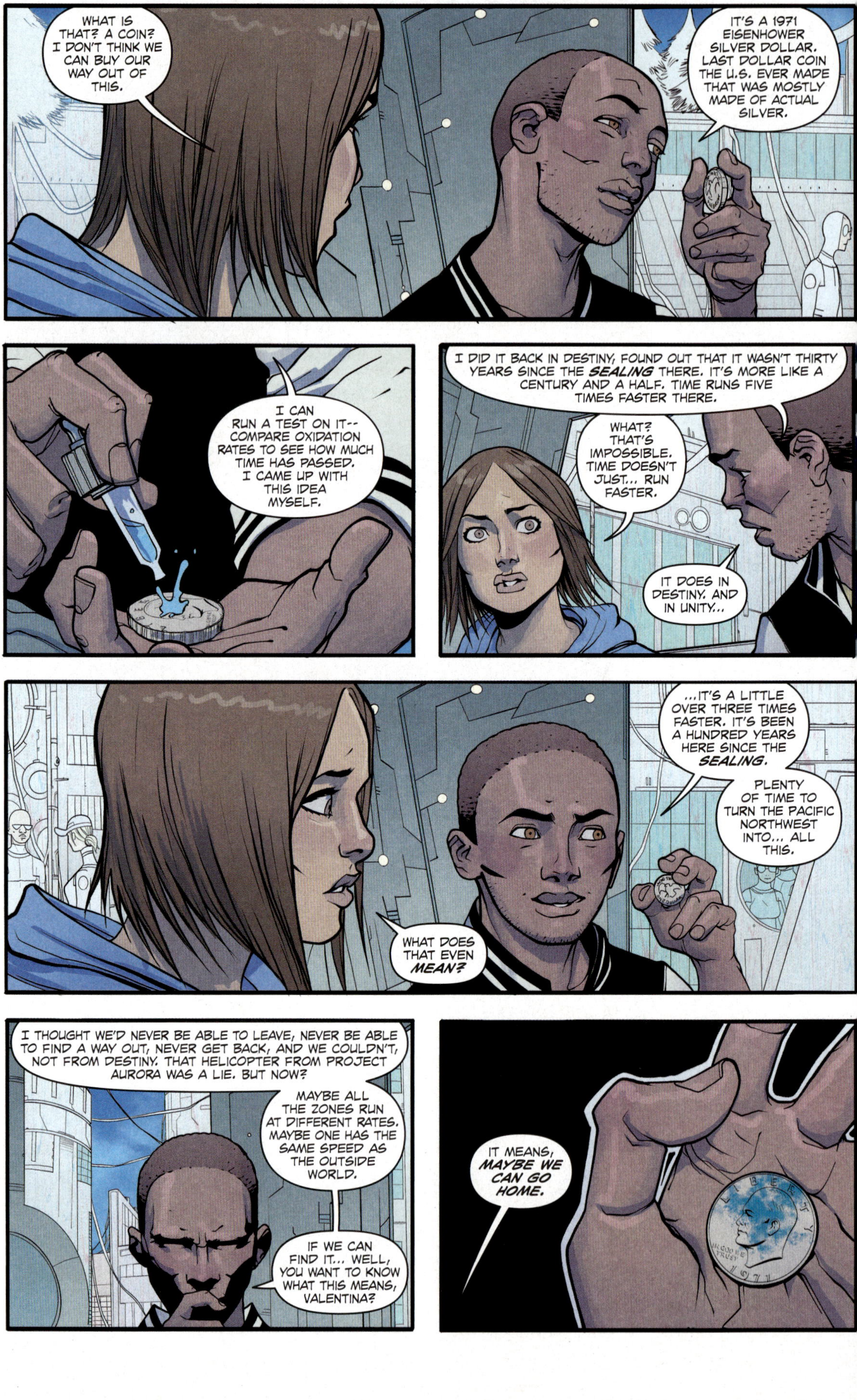
WHAT IS THAT? A COIN? I DON'T THINK WE CAN BUY OUR WAY OUT OF THIS.
IT'S A 1971 EISENHOWER SILVER DOLLAR. LAST DOLLAR COIN THE U.S. EVER MADE THAT WAS MOSTLY MADE OF ACTUAL SILVER.
I CAN RUN A TEST ON IT-- COMPARE OXIDATION RATES TO SEE HOW MUCH TIME HAS PASSED. I CAME UP WITH THIS IDEA MYSELF.
I DID IT BACK IN DESTINY, FOUND OUT THAT IT WASN'T THIRTY YEARS SINCE THE SEALING THERE. IT'S MORE LIKE A CENTURY AND A HALF. TIME RUNS FIVE TIMES FASTER THERE.
WHAT? THAT'S IMPOSSIBLE. TIME DOESN'T JUST... RUN FASTER.
IT DOES IN DESTINY. AND IN UNITY...
...IT'S A LITTLE OVER THREE TIMES FASTER. IT'S BEEN A HUNDRED YEARS HERE SINCE THE SEALING.
PLENTY OF TIME TO TURN THE PACIFIC NORTHWEST INTO... ALL THIS.
WHAT DOES THAT EVEN MEAN?
I THOUGHT WE'D NEVER BE ABLE TO LEAVE, NEVER BE ABLE TO FIND A WAY OUT, NEVER GET BACK, AND WE COULDN'T, NOT FROM DESTINY. THAT HELICOPTER FROM PROJECT AURORA WAS A LIE. BUT NOW?
MAYBE ALL THE ZONES RUN AT DIFFERENT RATES. MAYBE ONE HAS THE SAME SPEED AS THE OUTSIDE WORLD.
IF WE CAN FIND IT... WELL, YOU WANT TO KNOW WHAT THIS MEANS, VALENTINA?
IT MEANS, MAYBE WE CAN GO HOME.

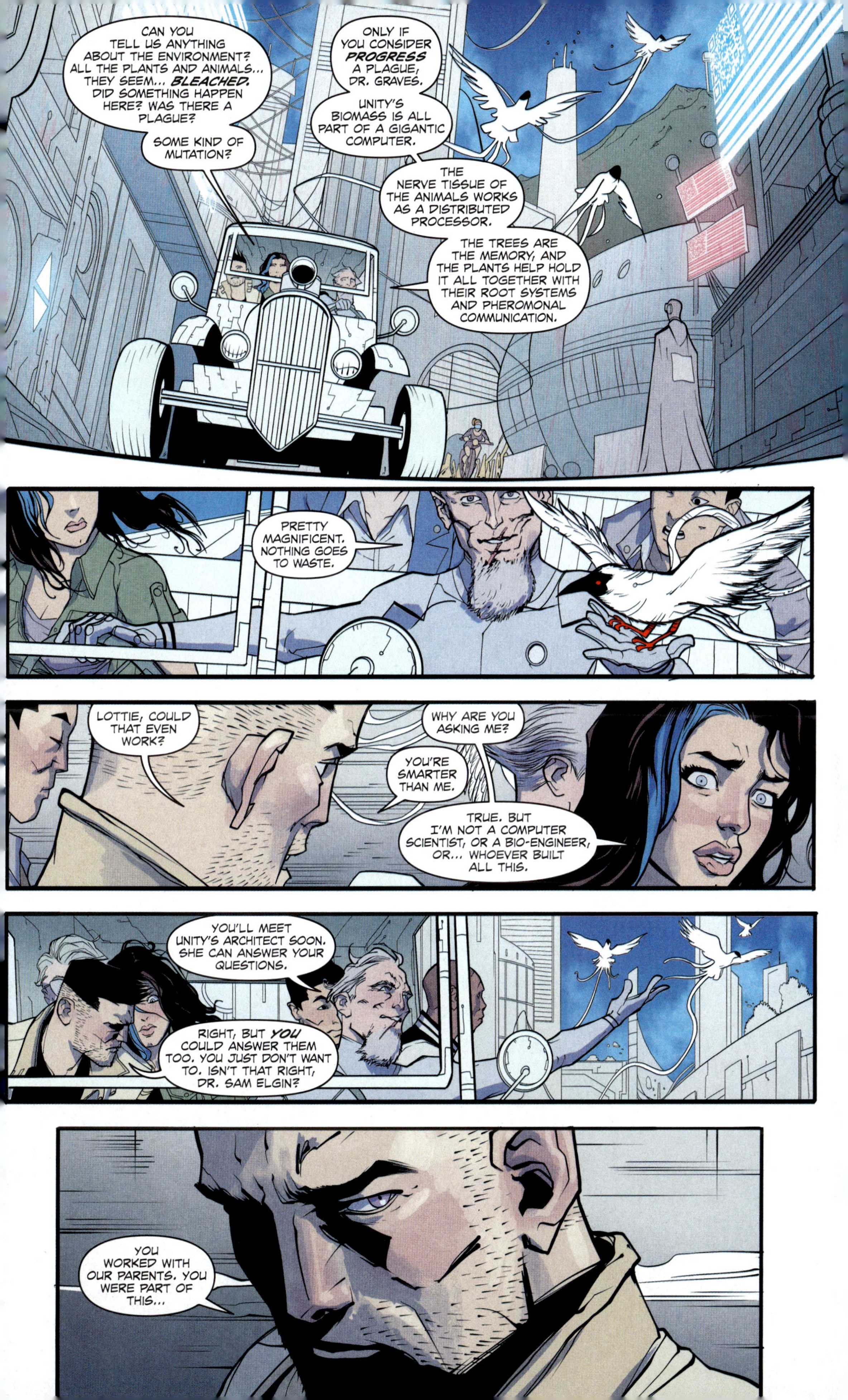
CAN YOU TELL US ANYTHING ABOUT THE ENVIRONMENT? ALL THE PLANTS AND ANIMALS... THEY SEEM... *BLEACHED.* DID SOMETHING HAPPEN HERE? WAS THERE A PLAGUE?
SOME KIND OF MUTATION?
ONLY IF YOU CONSIDER *PROGRESS* A PLAGUE, DR. GRAVES.
UNITY'S BIOMASS IS ALL PART OF A GIGANTIC COMPUTER.
THE NERVE TISSUE OF THE ANIMALS WORKS AS A DISTRIBUTED PROCESSOR.
THE TREES ARE THE MEMORY, AND THE PLANTS HELP HOLD IT ALL TOGETHER WITH THEIR ROOT SYSTEMS AND PHEROMONAL COMMUNICATION.
PRETTY MAGNIFICENT. NOTHING GOES TO WASTE.
LOTTIE, COULD THAT EVEN WORK?
WHY ARE YOU ASKING ME?
YOU'RE SMARTER THAN ME.
TRUE. BUT I'M NOT A COMPUTER SCIENTIST, OR A BIO-ENGINEER, OR... WHOEVER BUILT ALL THIS.
YOU'LL MEET UNITY'S ARCHITECT SOON. SHE CAN ANSWER YOUR QUESTIONS.
RIGHT, BUT *YOU* COULD ANSWER THEM TOO. YOU JUST DON'T WANT TO. ISN'T THAT RIGHT, DR. SAM ELGIN?
YOU WORKED WITH OUR PARENTS. YOU WERE PART OF THIS...

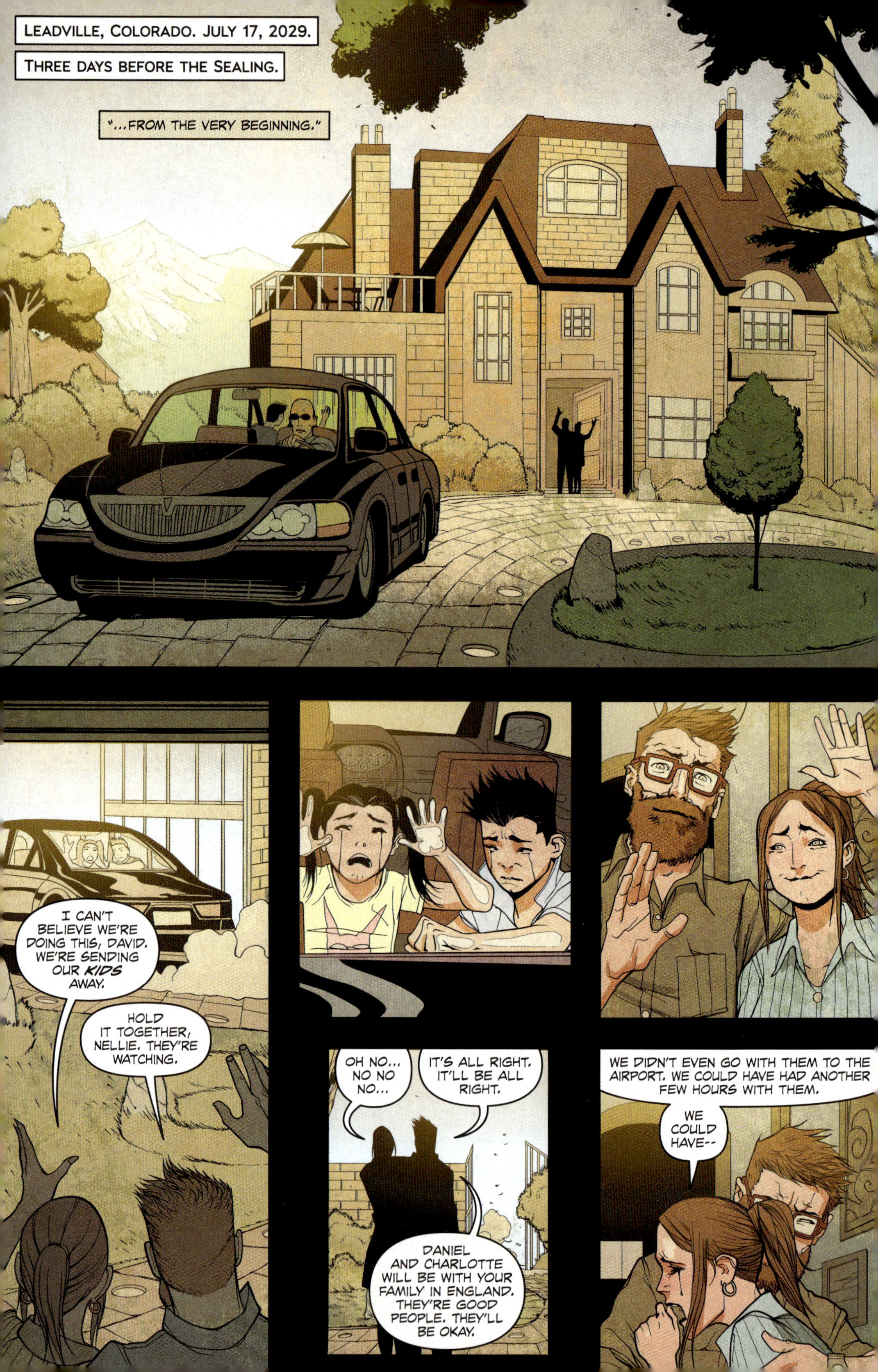
LEADVILLE, COLORADO. JULY 17, 2029.
THREE DAYS BEFORE THE SEALING.
"...FROM THE VERY BEGINNING."
I CAN'T BELIEVE WE'RE DOING THIS, DAVID. WE'RE SENDING OUR KIDS AWAY.
HOLD IT TOGETHER, NELLIE. THEY'RE WATCHING.
OH NO... NO NO NO...
IT'S ALL RIGHT. IT'LL BE ALL RIGHT.
DANIEL AND CHARLOTTE WILL BE WITH YOUR FAMILY IN ENGLAND. THEY'RE GOOD PEOPLE. THEY'LL BE OKAY.
WE DIDN'T EVEN GO WITH THEM TO THE AIRPORT. WE COULD HAVE HAD ANOTHER FEW HOURS WITH THEM.
WE COULD HAVE--

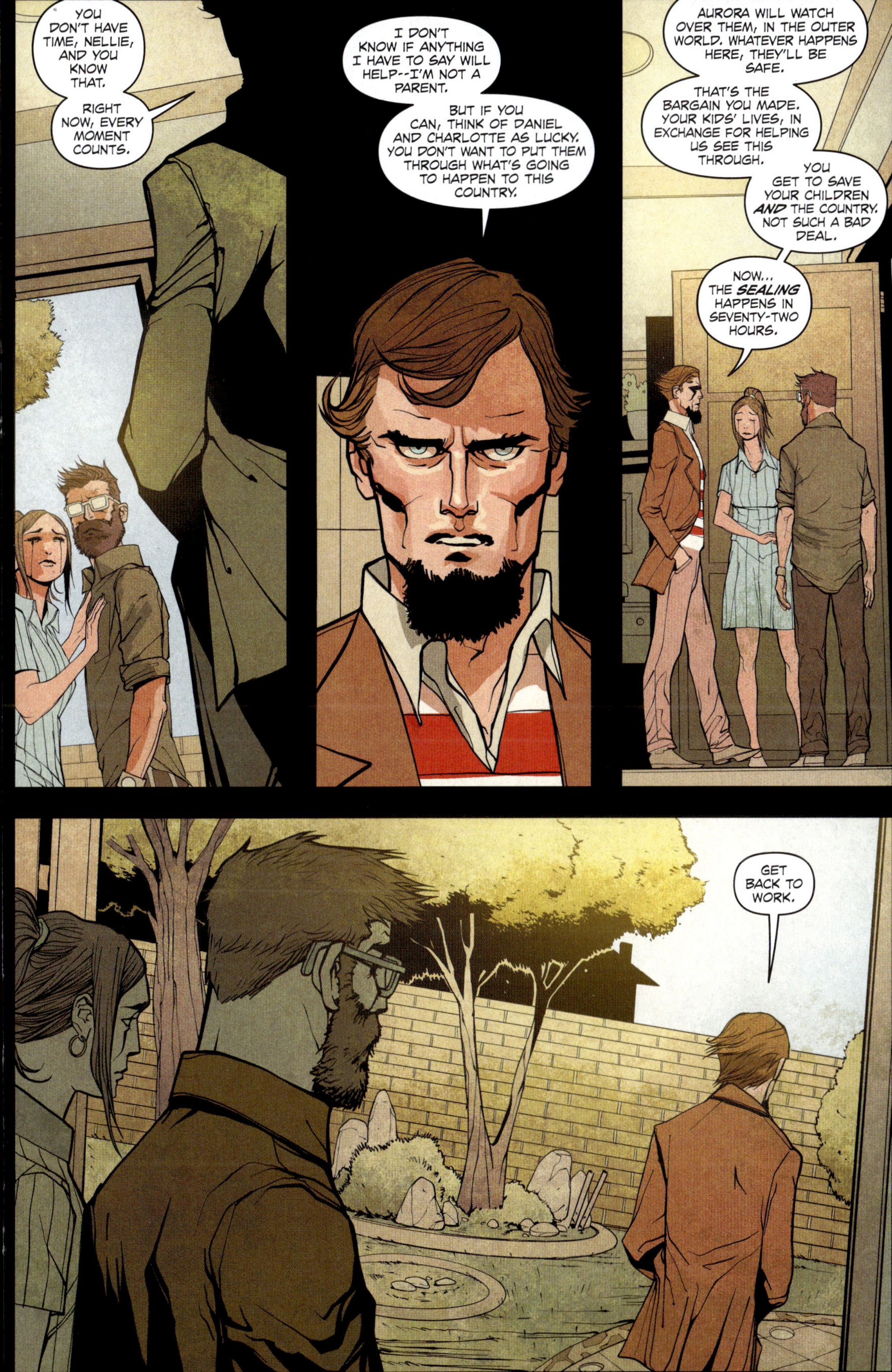
YOU DON'T HAVE TIME, NELLIE, AND YOU KNOW THAT.
RIGHT NOW, EVERY MOMENT COUNTS.
I DON'T KNOW IF ANYTHING I HAVE TO SAY WILL HELP--I'M NOT A PARENT.
BUT IF YOU CAN, THINK OF DANIEL AND CHARLOTTE AS LUCKY. YOU DON'T WANT TO PUT THEM THROUGH WHAT'S GOING TO HAPPEN TO THIS COUNTRY.
AURORA WILL WATCH OVER THEM, IN THE OUTER WORLD. WHATEVER HAPPENS HERE, THEY'LL BE SAFE.
THAT'S THE BARGAIN YOU MADE. YOUR KIDS' LIVES, IN EXCHANGE FOR HELPING US SEE THIS THROUGH.
YOU GET TO SAVE YOUR CHILDREN ***AND*** THE COUNTRY. NOT SUCH A BAD DEAL.
NOW... THE ***SEALING*** HAPPENS IN SEVENTY-TWO HOURS.
GET BACK TO WORK.

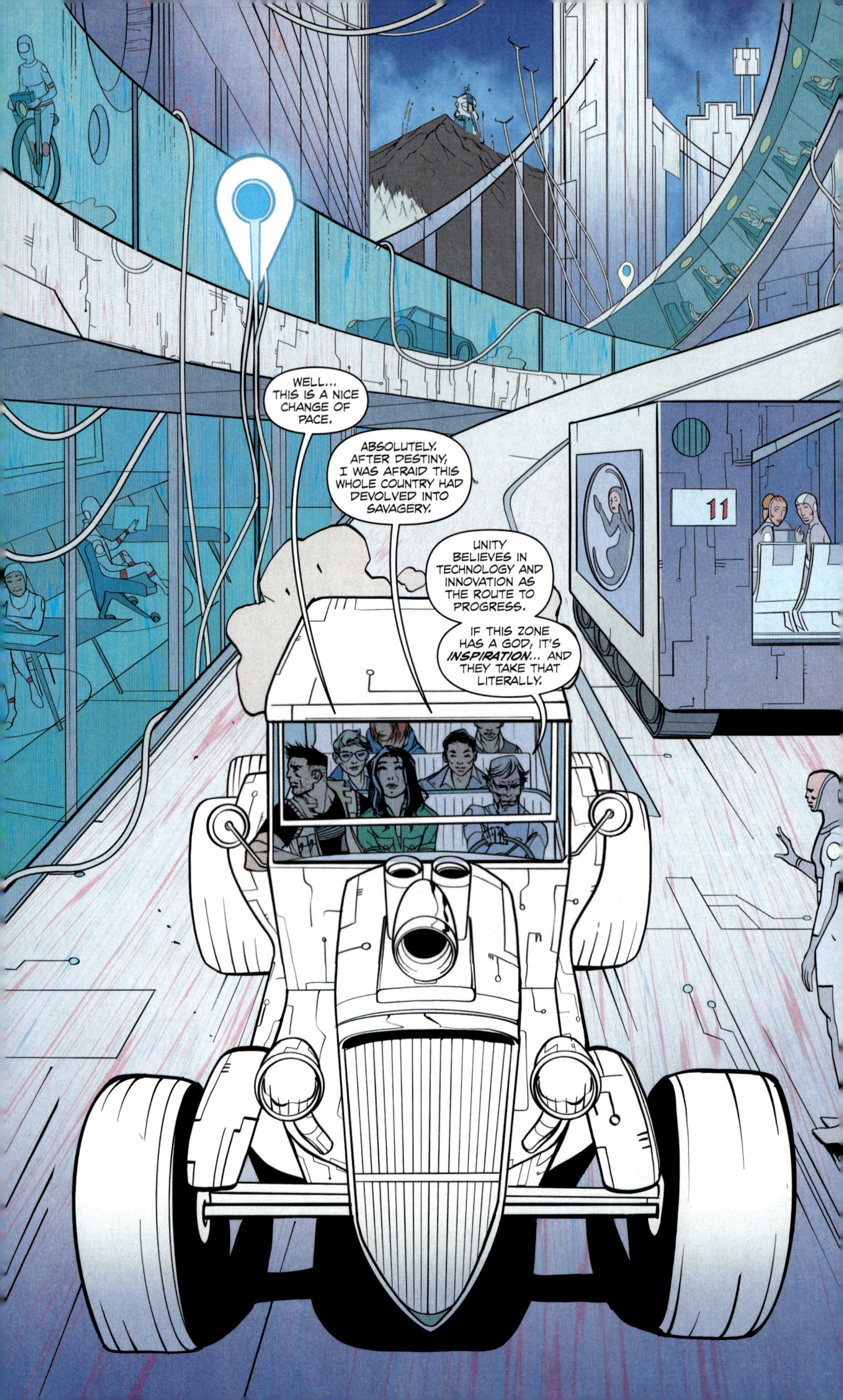
WELL... THIS IS A NICE CHANGE OF PACE.
ABSOLUTELY. AFTER DESTINY, I WAS AFRAID THIS WHOLE COUNTRY HAD DEVOLVED INTO SAVAGERY.
UNITY BELIEVES IN TECHNOLOGY AND INNOVATION AS THE ROUTE TO PROGRESS.
IF THIS ZONE HAS A GOD, IT'S *INSPIRATION*... AND THEY TAKE THAT LITERALLY.
11

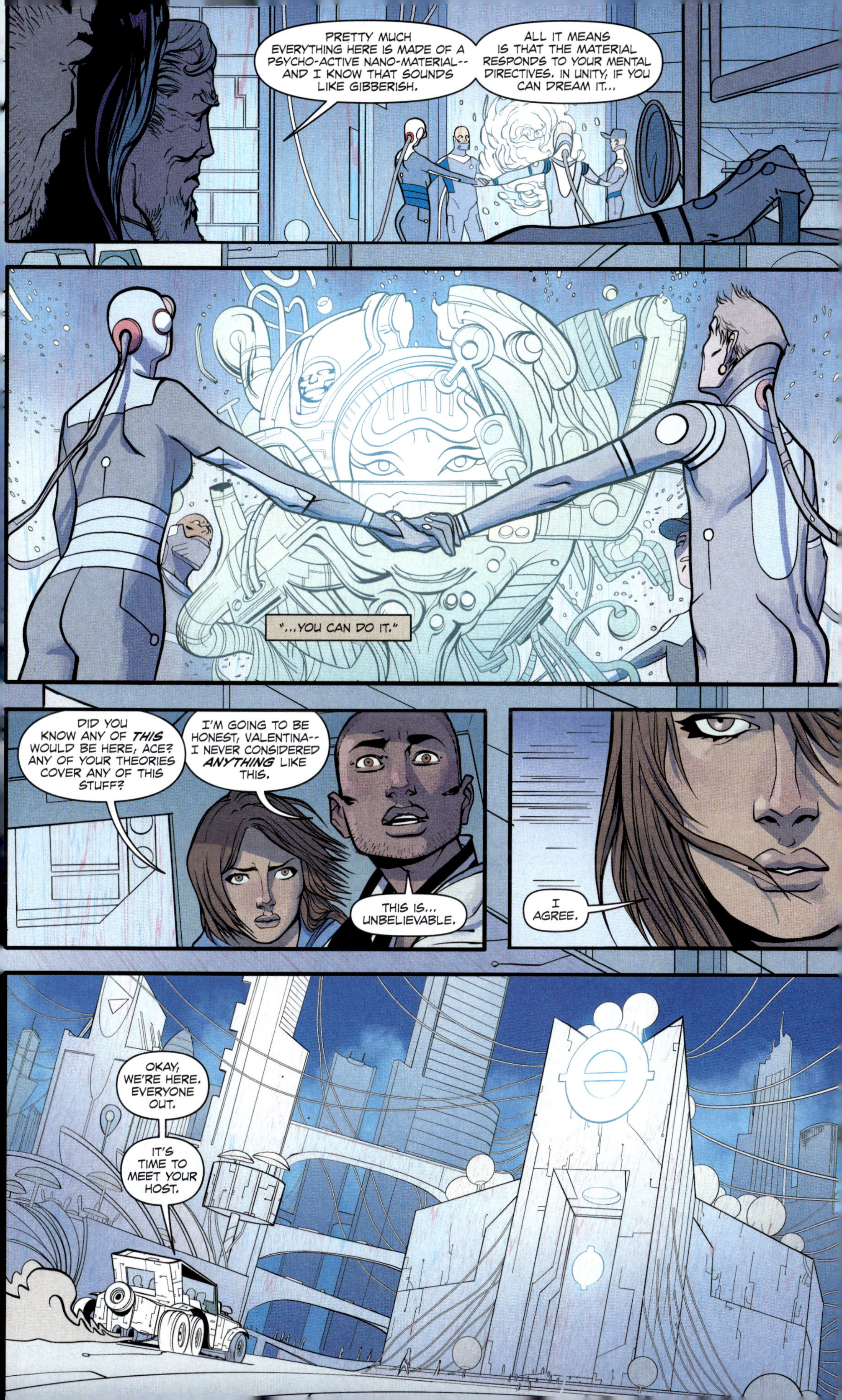
PRETTY MUCH EVERYTHING HERE IS MADE OF A PSYCHO-ACTIVE NANO-MATERIAL-- AND I KNOW THAT SOUNDS LIKE GIBBERISH.
ALL IT MEANS IS THAT THE MATERIAL RESPONDS TO YOUR MENTAL DIRECTIVES. IN UNITY, IF YOU CAN DREAM IT...
"...YOU CAN DO IT."
DID YOU KNOW ANY OF *THIS* WOULD BE HERE, ACE? ANY OF YOUR THEORIES COVER ANY OF THIS STUFF?
I'M GOING TO BE HONEST, VALENTINA-- I NEVER CONSIDERED *ANYTHING* LIKE THIS.
THIS IS... UNBELIEVABLE.
I AGREE.
OKAY, WE'RE HERE. EVERYONE OUT.
IT'S TIME TO MEET YOUR HOST.

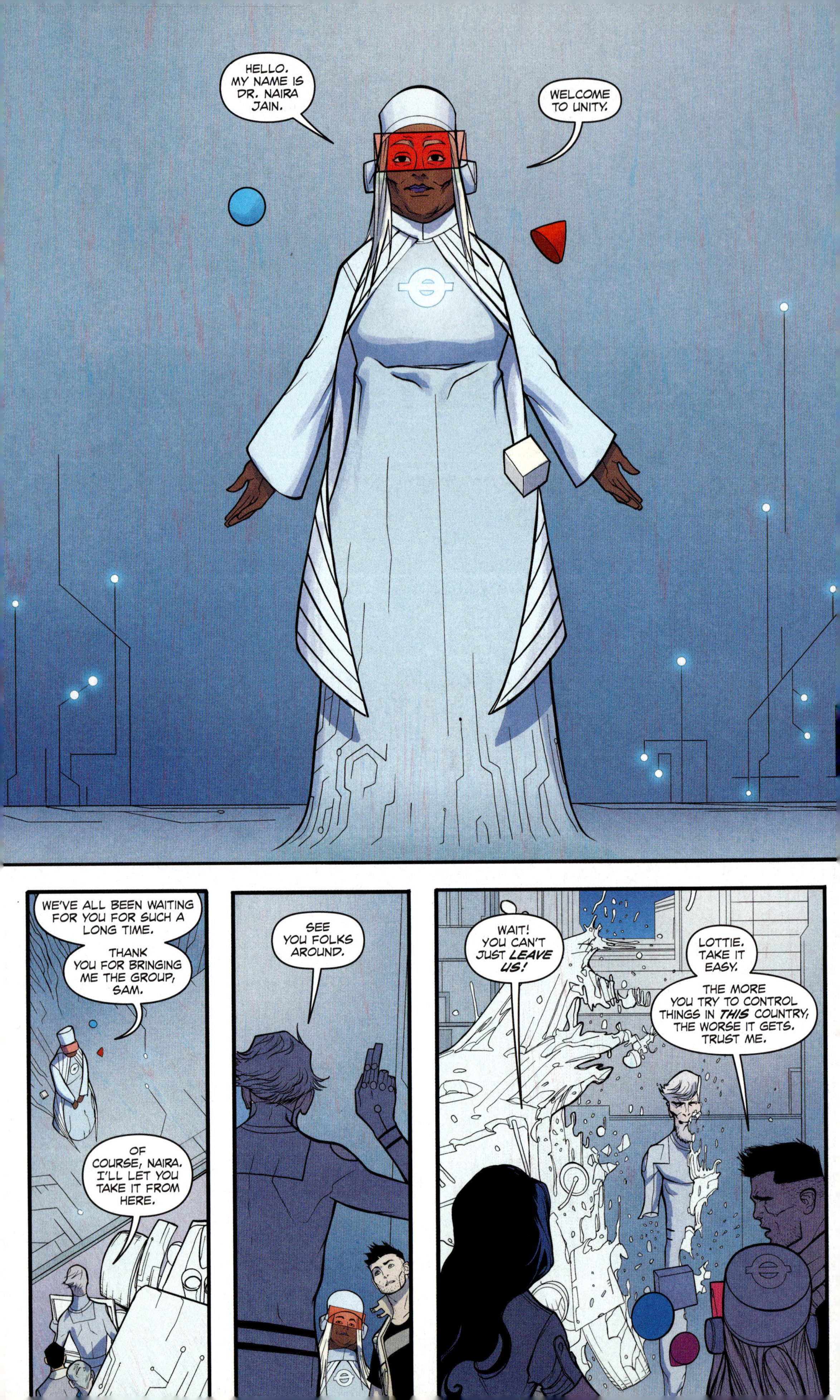
HELLO. MY NAME IS DR. NAIRA JAIN.
WELCOME TO UNITY.
WE'VE ALL BEEN WAITING FOR YOU FOR SUCH A LONG TIME.
THANK YOU FOR BRINGING ME THE GROUP, SAM.
OF COURSE, NAIRA. I'LL LET YOU TAKE IT FROM HERE.
SEE YOU FOLKS AROUND.
WAIT! YOU CAN'T JUST *LEAVE US!*
LOTTIE. TAKE IT EASY.
THE MORE YOU TRY TO CONTROL THINGS IN *THIS* COUNTRY, THE WORSE IT GETS. TRUST ME.

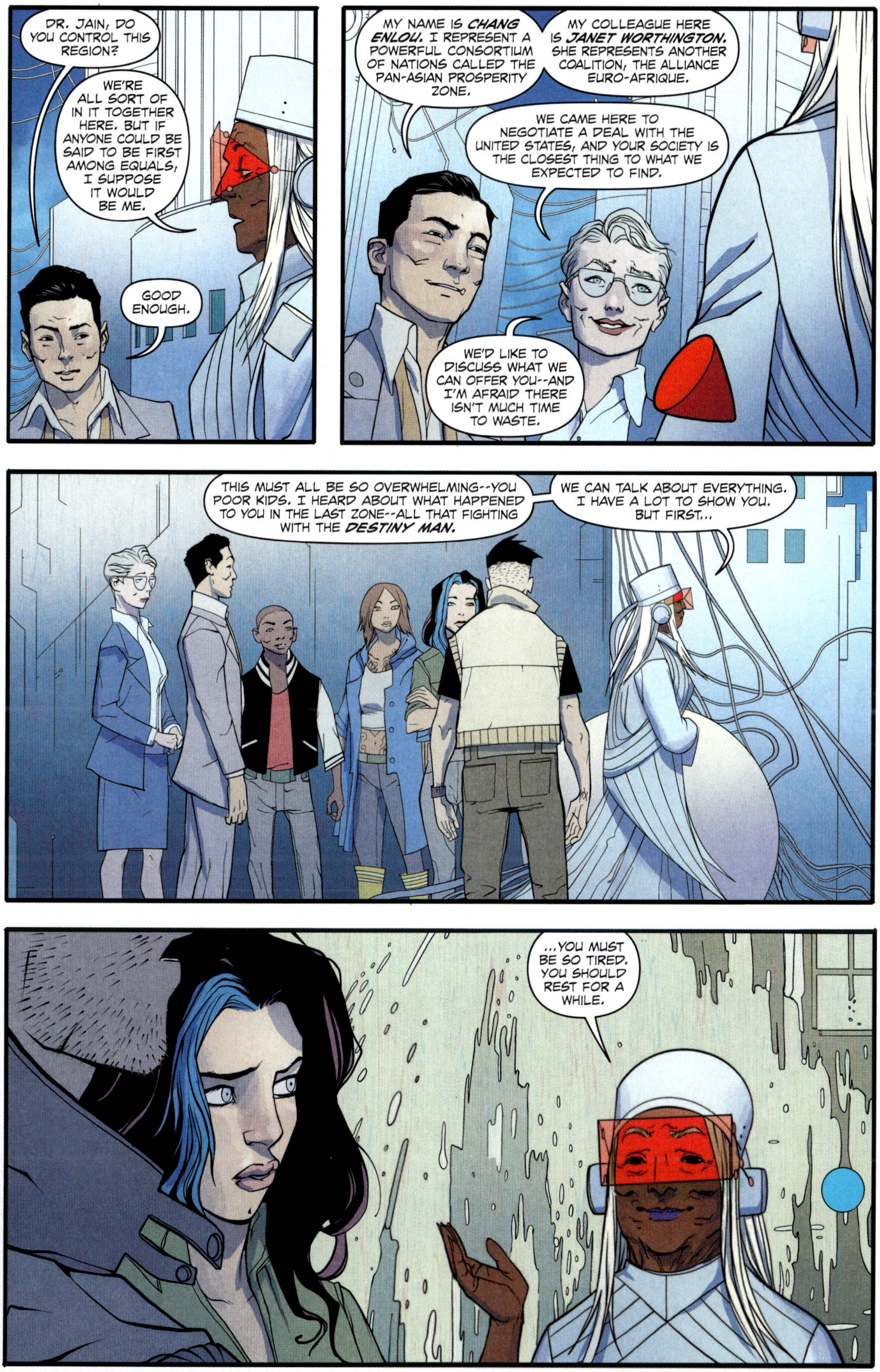
DR. JAIN, DO YOU CONTROL THIS REGION?
WE'RE ALL SORT OF IN IT TOGETHER HERE. BUT IF ANYONE COULD BE SAID TO BE FIRST AMONG EQUALS, I SUPPOSE IT WOULD BE ME.
GOOD ENOUGH.
MY NAME IS CHANG ENLOU. I REPRESENT A POWERFUL CONSORTIUM OF NATIONS CALLED THE PAN-ASIAN PROSPERITY ZONE.
MY COLLEAGUE HERE IS JANET WORTHINGTON. SHE REPRESENTS ANOTHER COALITION, THE ALLIANCE EURO-AFRIQUE.
WE CAME HERE TO NEGOTIATE A DEAL WITH THE UNITED STATES, AND YOUR SOCIETY IS THE CLOSEST THING TO WHAT WE EXPECTED TO FIND.
WE'D LIKE TO DISCUSS WHAT WE CAN OFFER YOU--AND I'M AFRAID THERE ISN'T MUCH TIME TO WASTE.
THIS MUST ALL BE SO OVERWHELMING--YOU POOR KIDS. I HEARD ABOUT WHAT HAPPENED TO YOU IN THE LAST ZONE--ALL THAT FIGHTING WITH THE DESTINY MAN.
WE CAN TALK ABOUT EVERYTHING. I HAVE A LOT TO SHOW YOU. BUT FIRST...
...YOU MUST BE SO TIRED. YOU SHOULD REST FOR A WHILE.

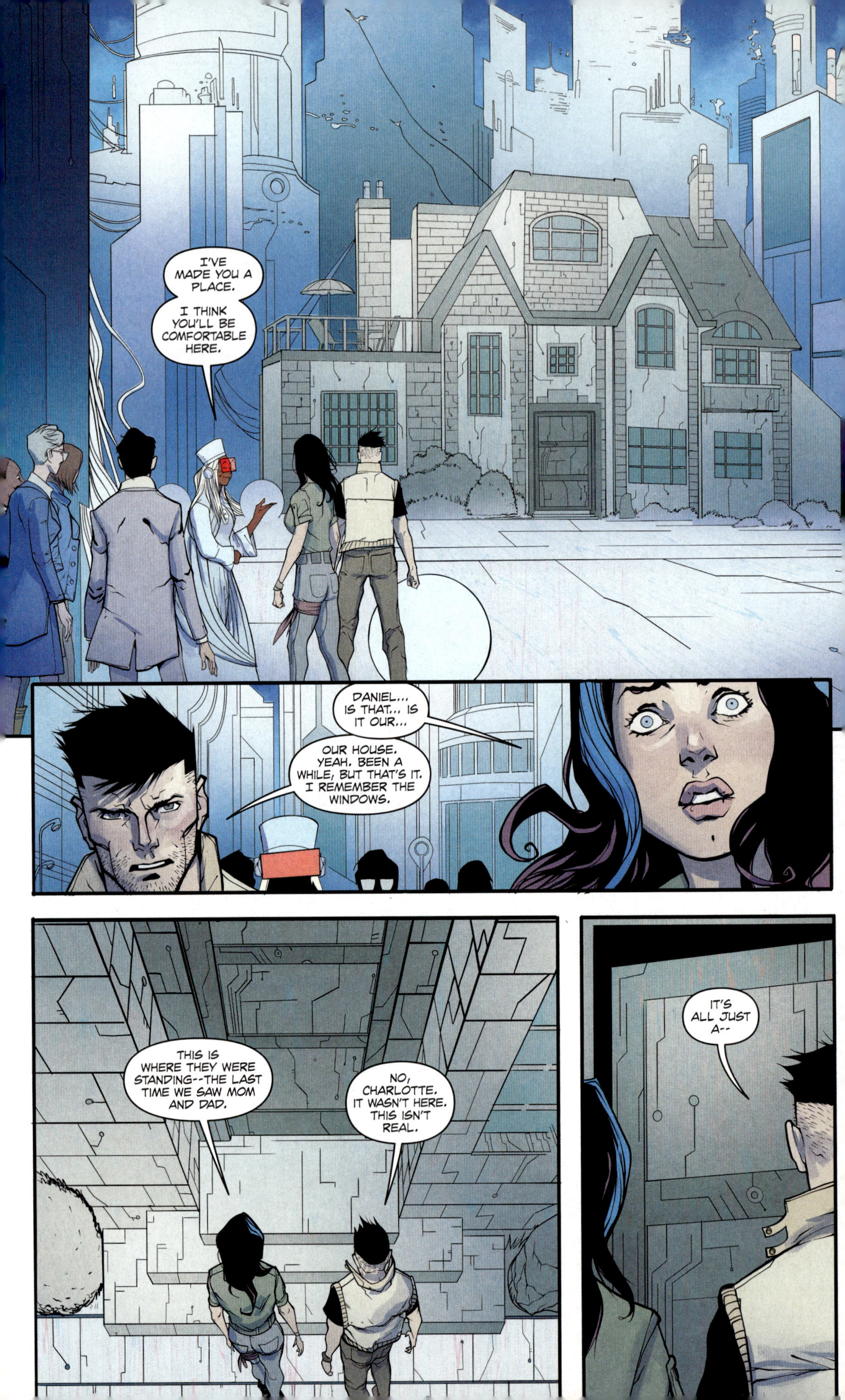
I'VE MADE YOU A PLACE.
I THINK YOU'LL BE COMFORTABLE HERE.
DANIEL... IS THAT... IS IT OUR...
OUR HOUSE. YEAH. BEEN A WHILE, BUT THAT'S IT. I REMEMBER THE WINDOWS.
THIS IS WHERE THEY WERE STANDING--THE LAST TIME WE SAW MOM AND DAD.
NO, CHARLOTTE. IT WASN'T HERE. THIS ISN'T REAL.
IT'S ALL JUST A--

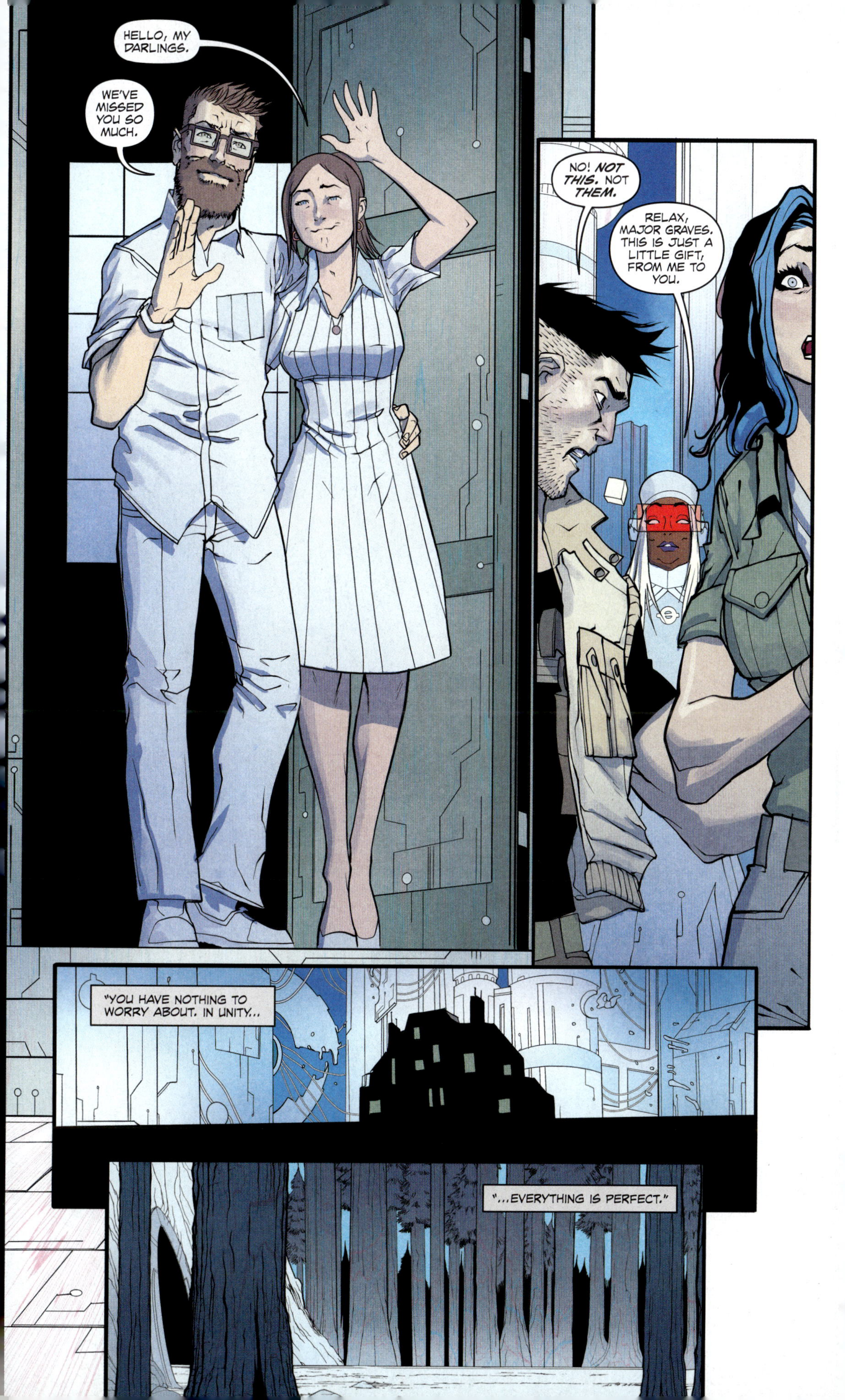
HELLO, MY DARLINGS.
WE'VE MISSED YOU SO MUCH.
NO! NOT THIS. NOT THEM.
RELAX, MAJOR GRAVES. THIS IS JUST A LITTLE GIFT, FROM ME TO YOU.
"YOU HAVE NOTHING TO WORRY ABOUT. IN UNITY...
"...EVERYTHING IS PERFECT."

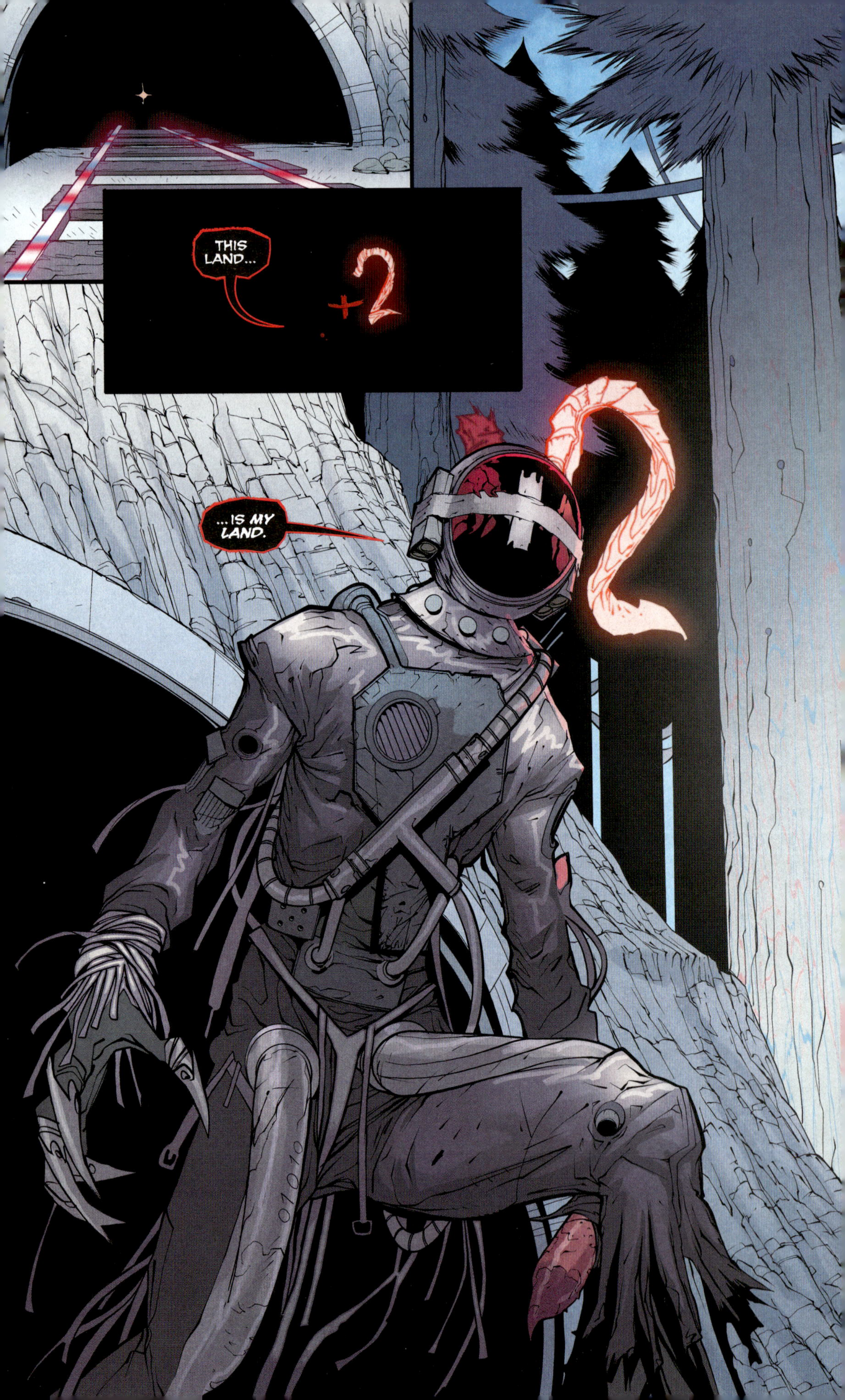
THIS LAND...
...IS MY LAND.

DRONET

"USA USA USA ALL THE WAY! It's your man Piñata here, with a question for you all. If you're America, with all your power and all your people and all your ambition... and let's not kid ourselves, the US always wanted things... If you're a nation like that, do you seal yourself off from the world because you want to just calm everything down, chill out, relax and retire, like some old man going to the nursing home?

Doesn't sound like America to me.

America was like that old high school football star, past his glory days (I apologize for the metaphor if you don't get it... swap in soccer for football, I guess), now just getting by in his life, desperate to go back to that time when he ruled the world.

I think that's what the Sealing is. America's trying to get a bit of that glory back. They're working on something in there. They want something... and that something is... everything.

USA USA USA ALL THE WAY."

—**Posted by Ace Piñata on the 'America Unsealed' Dronet, July 4, 2056.**

CHAPTER NINE

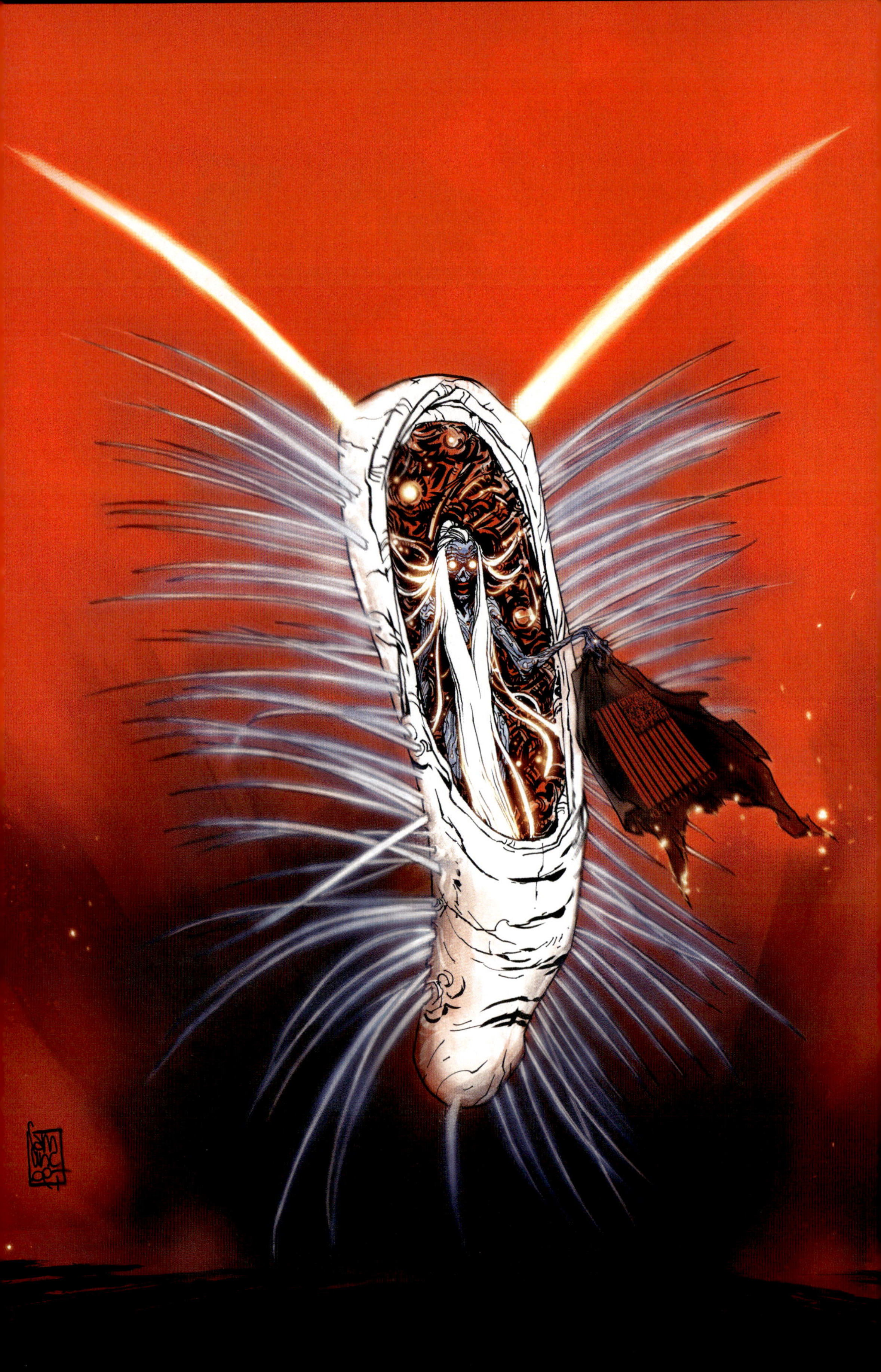

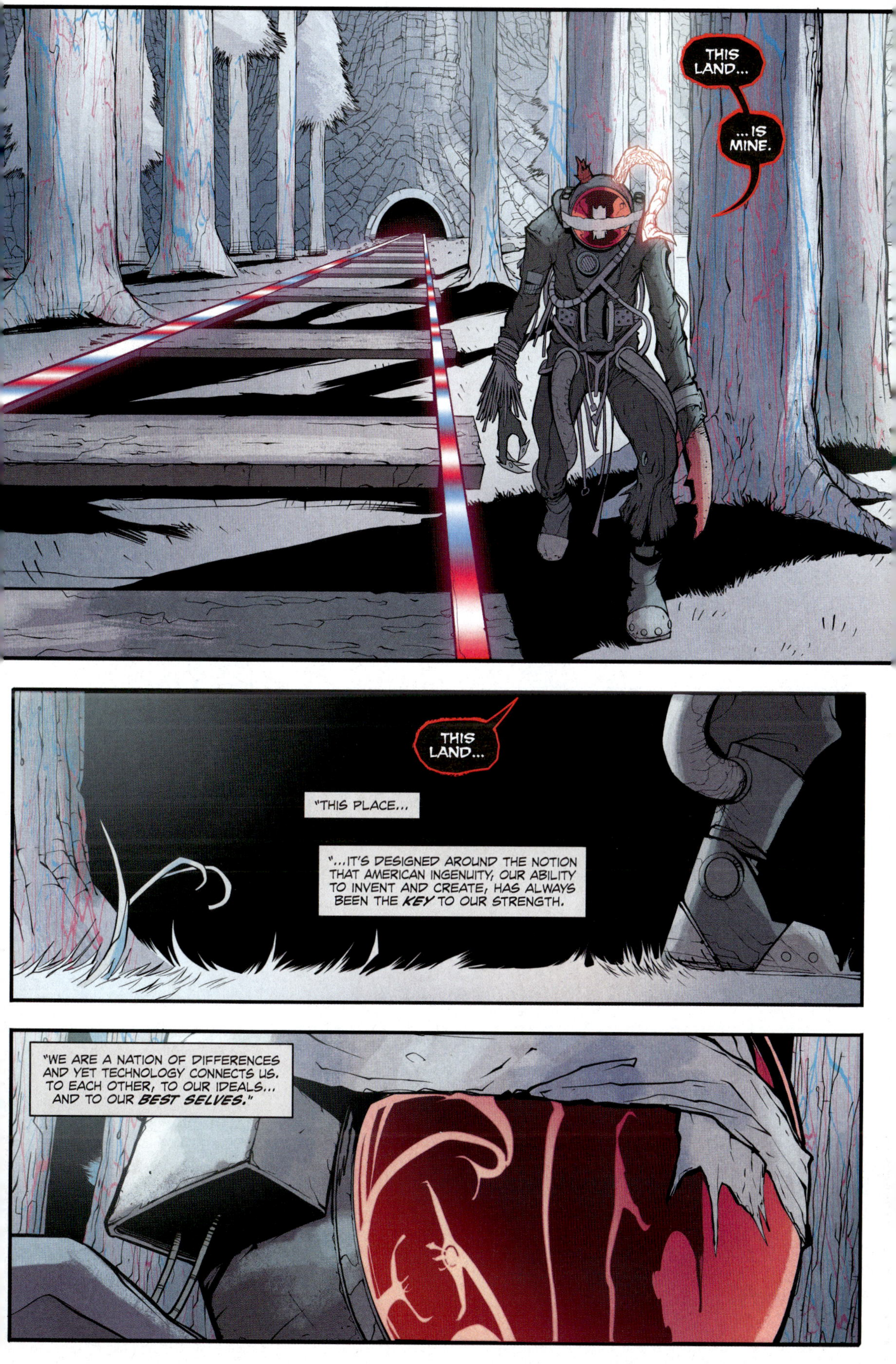
THIS LAND...
...IS MINE.
THIS LAND...
"THIS PLACE...
"...IT'S DESIGNED AROUND THE NOTION THAT AMERICAN INGENUITY, OUR ABILITY TO INVENT AND CREATE, HAS ALWAYS BEEN THE KEY TO OUR STRENGTH.
"WE ARE A NATION OF DIFFERENCES AND YET TECHNOLOGY CONNECTS US. TO EACH OTHER, TO OUR IDEALS... AND TO OUR BEST SELVES."

"IT'S LIKE AN OASIS. HOW DID YOU DO IT?"
"IT WASN'T EASY. THERE WERE SETBACKS, CHALLENGES... BUT THE KEY, AS ALWAYS, IS ENGAGING THE PROBLEM...
FWIP FWIP
"...AND TACKLING IT HEAD ON, AGGRESSIVELY...
NO...
FWIP
FWIP
FWIP
"...UNTIL IT'S SOLVED AND SIMPLY BECOMES PART OF THE GREATER ACHIEVEMENT.
THIS LAND IS--
FWIP FWIP FWIP FWIP FWIP
"WE CALL THE NANO-MATERIAL THE 'DIAMOND DESERT' FROM--"
"WOODIE GUTHRIE'S 'THIS LAND IS YOUR LAND.'"
"THAT'S RIGHT MR. KENYATTA. AND THIS LAND IS YOURS, AS MUCH AS OURS. SO LET ME BE THE FIRST TO SAY, ESPECIALLY TO YOU, DR. AND MR. GRAVES..."

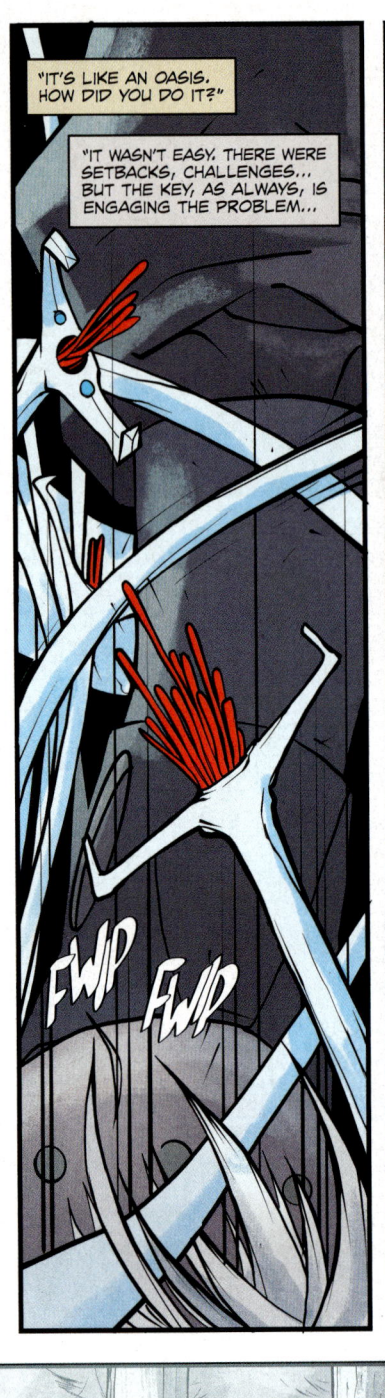

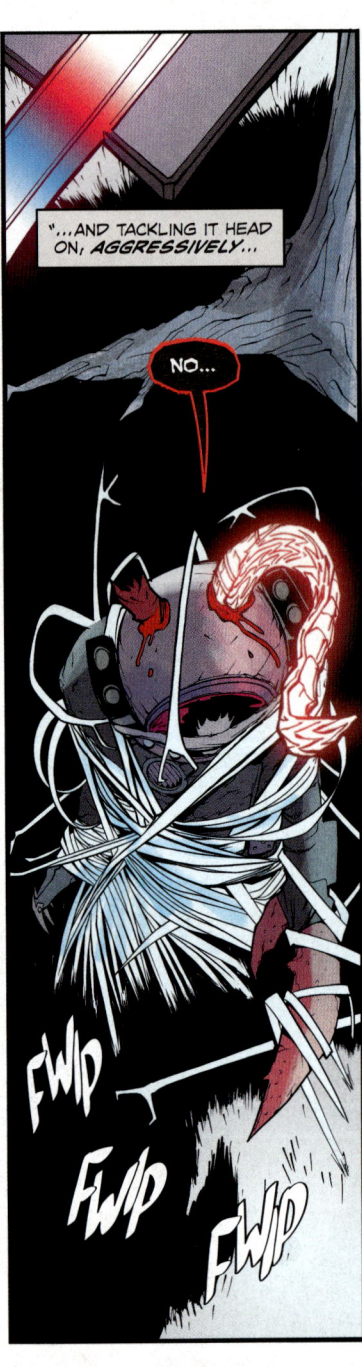

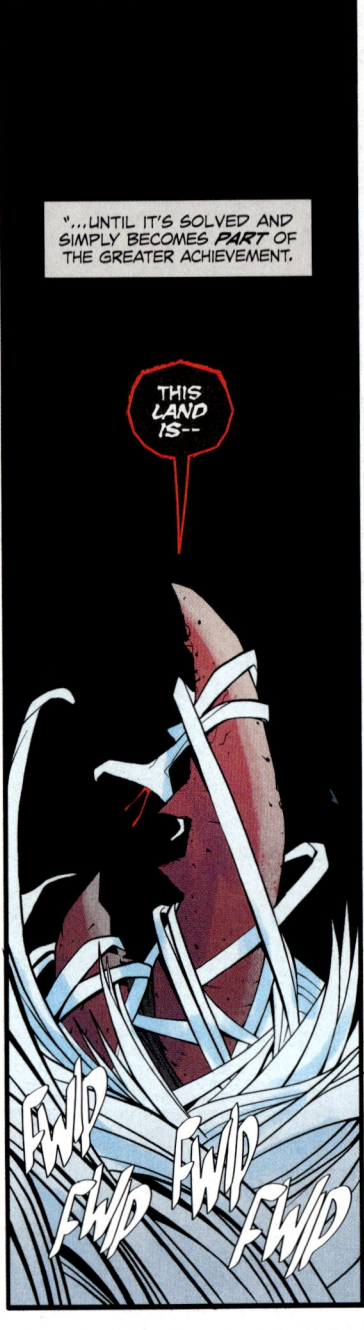

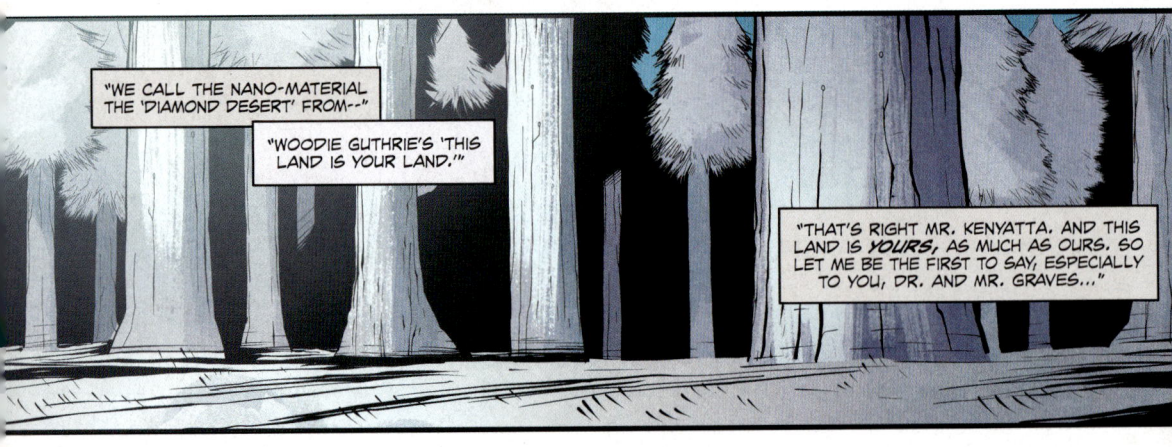

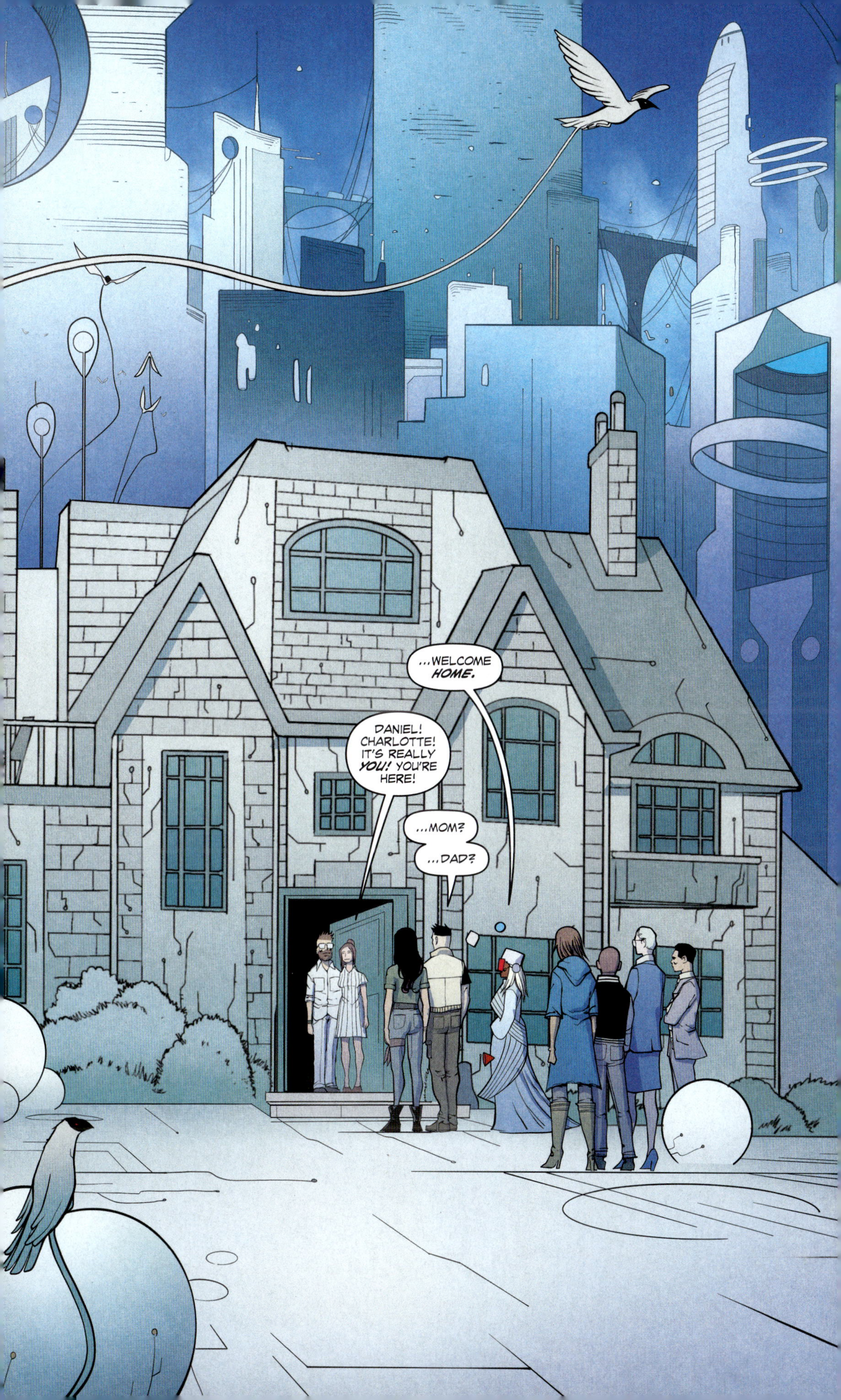
DANIEL! CHARLOTTE! IT'S REALLY YOU! YOU'RE HERE!
...MOM?
...DAD?
...WELCOME HOME.

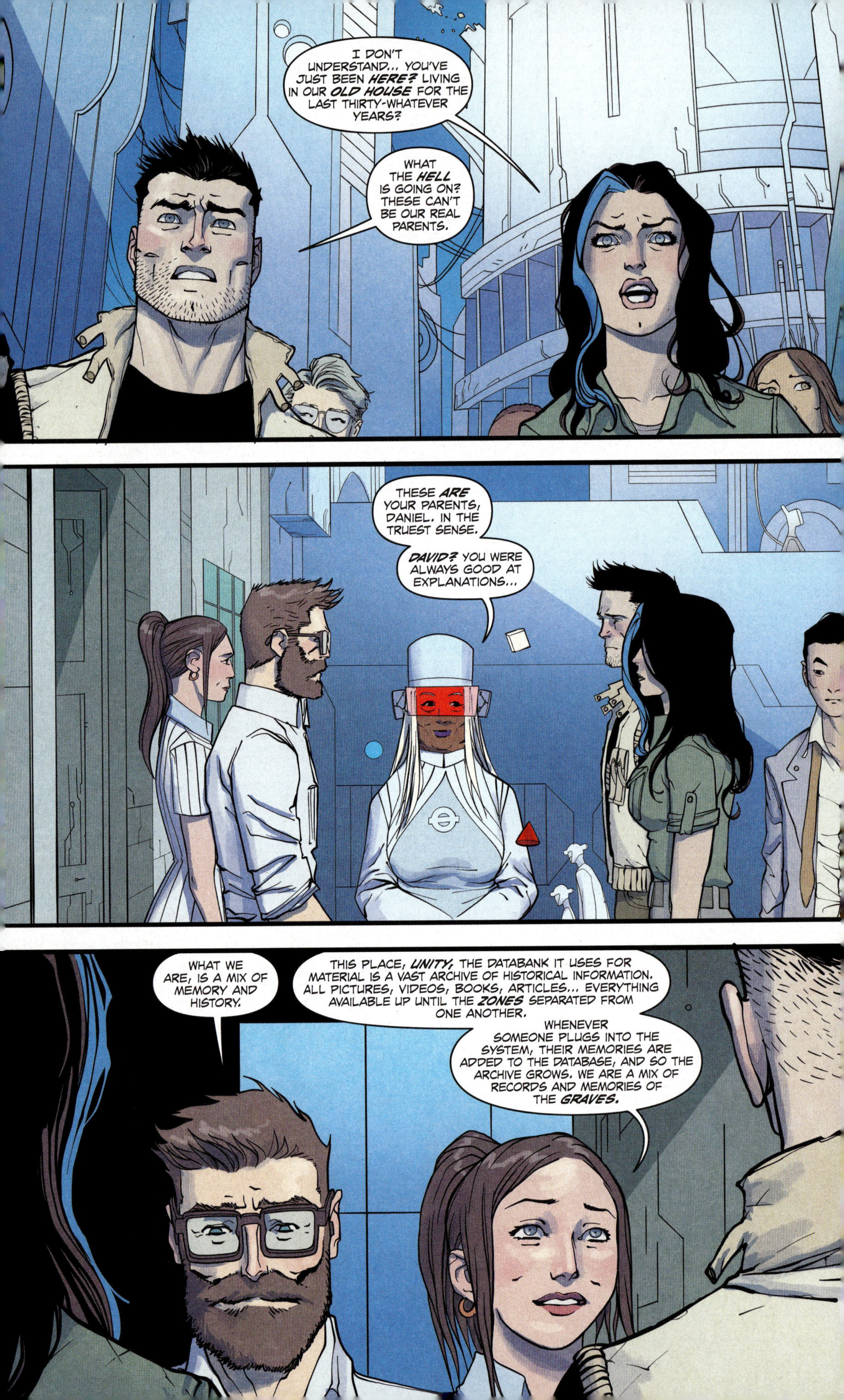
I DON'T UNDERSTAND... YOU'VE JUST BEEN HERE? LIVING IN OUR OLD HOUSE FOR THE LAST THIRTY-WHATEVER YEARS?
WHAT THE HELL IS GOING ON? THESE CAN'T BE OUR REAL PARENTS.
THESE ARE YOUR PARENTS, DANIEL. IN THE TRUEST SENSE.
DAVID? YOU WERE ALWAYS GOOD AT EXPLANATIONS...
WHAT WE ARE, IS A MIX OF MEMORY AND HISTORY.
THIS PLACE, UNITY, THE DATABANK IT USES FOR MATERIAL IS A VAST ARCHIVE OF HISTORICAL INFORMATION. ALL PICTURES, VIDEOS, BOOKS, ARTICLES... EVERYTHING AVAILABLE UP UNTIL THE ZONES SEPARATED FROM ONE ANOTHER.
WHENEVER SOMEONE PLUGS INTO THE SYSTEM, THEIR MEMORIES ARE ADDED TO THE DATABASE, AND SO THE ARCHIVE GROWS. WE ARE A MIX OF RECORDS AND MEMORIES OF THE GRAVES.

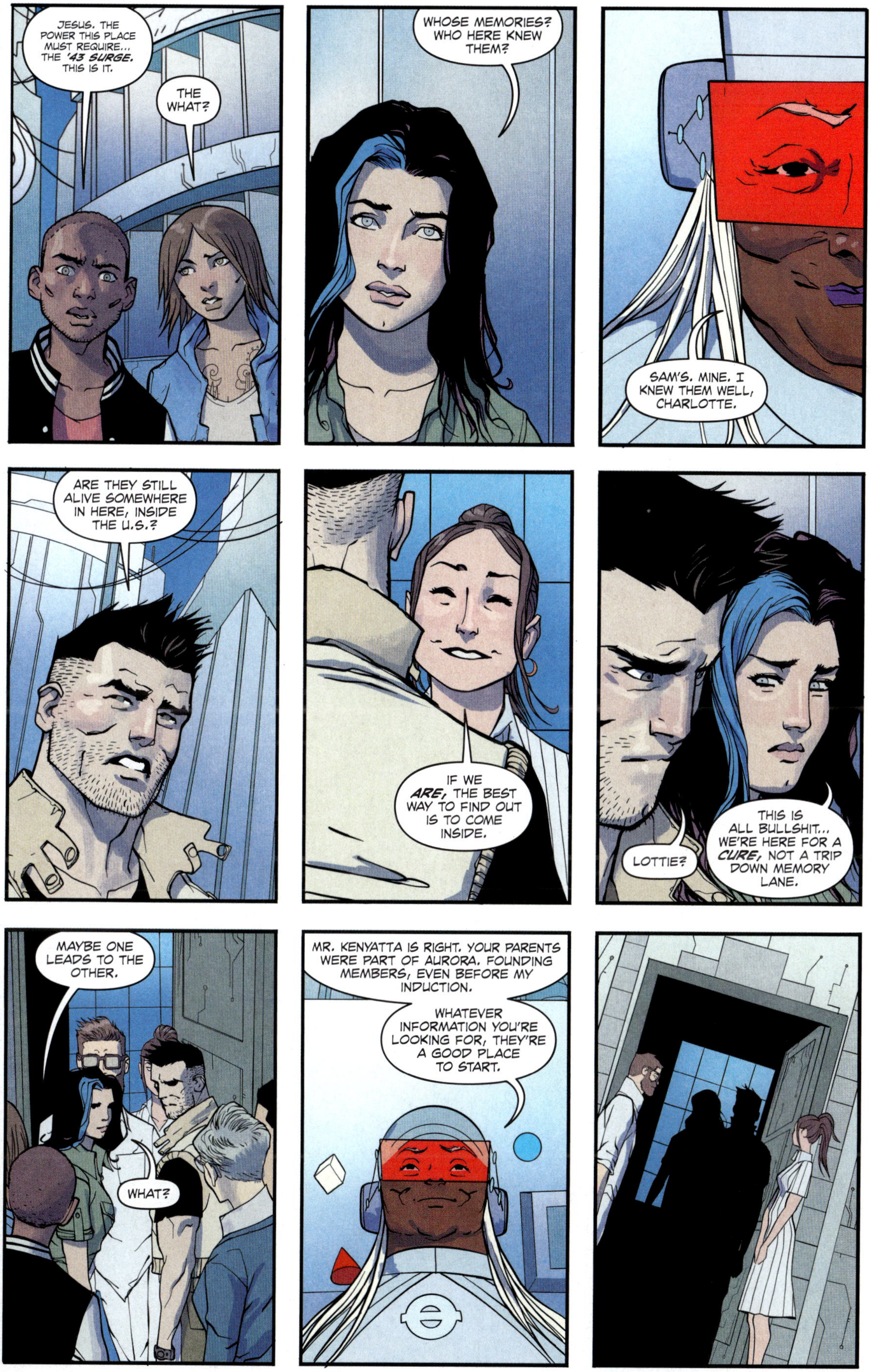
JESUS. THE POWER THIS PLACE MUST REQUIRE... THE '43 SURGE. THIS IS IT.
THE WHAT?
WHOSE MEMORIES? WHO HERE KNEW THEM?
SAM'S. MINE. I KNEW THEM WELL, CHARLOTTE.
ARE THEY STILL ALIVE SOMEWHERE IN HERE, INSIDE THE U.S.?
IF WE ARE, THE BEST WAY TO FIND OUT IS TO COME INSIDE.
LOTTIE?
THIS IS ALL BULLSHIT... WE'RE HERE FOR A CURE, NOT A TRIP DOWN MEMORY LANE.
MAYBE ONE LEADS TO THE OTHER.
WHAT?
MR. KENYATTA IS RIGHT. YOUR PARENTS WERE PART OF AURORA. FOUNDING MEMBERS, EVEN BEFORE MY INDUCTION.
WHATEVER INFORMATION YOU'RE LOOKING FOR, THEY'RE A GOOD PLACE TO START.

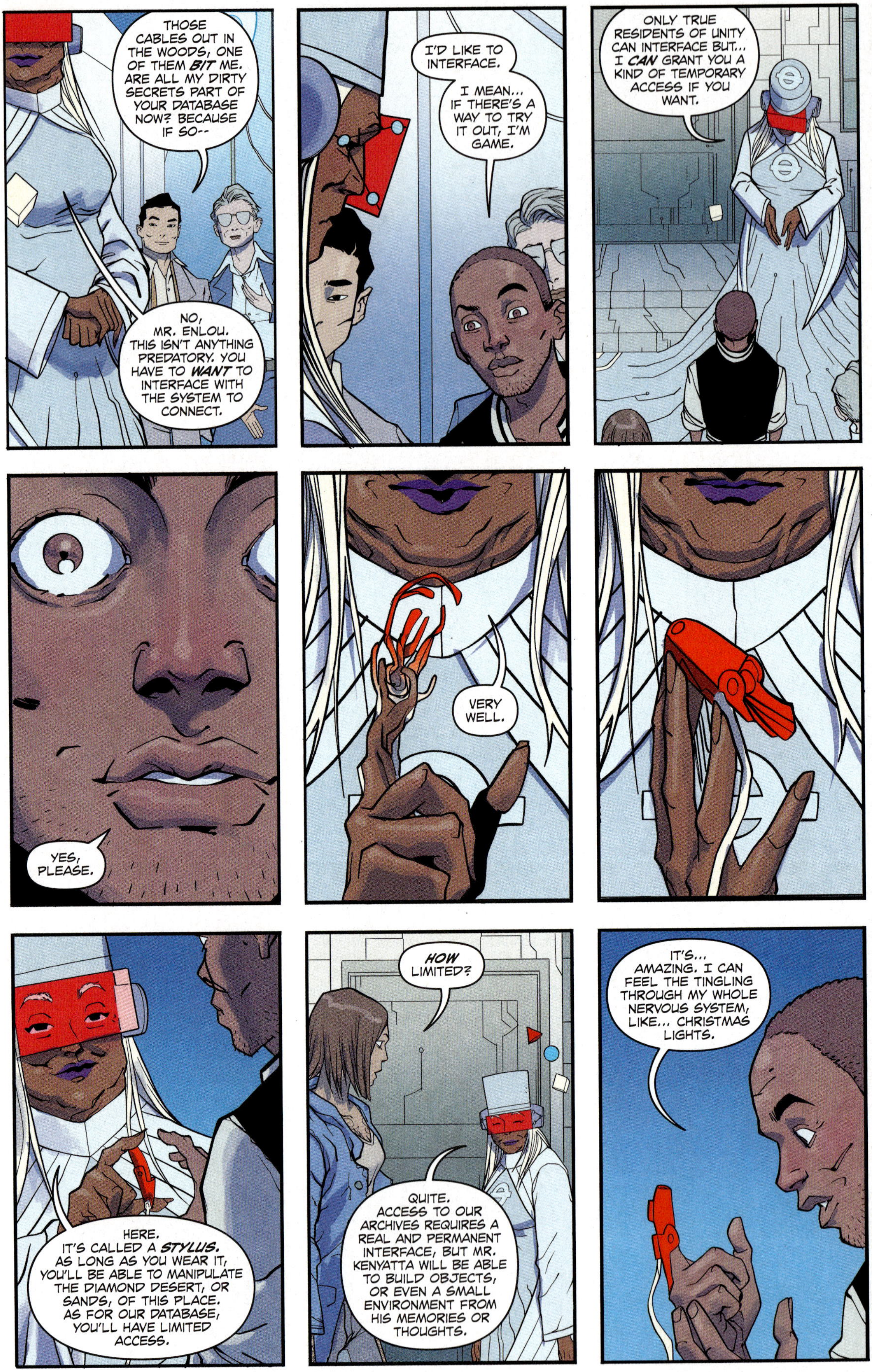
THOSE CABLES OUT IN THE WOODS, ONE OF THEM *BIT* ME. ARE ALL MY DIRTY SECRETS PART OF YOUR DATABASE NOW? BECAUSE IF SO--
NO, MR. ENLOU. THIS ISN'T ANYTHING PREDATORY. YOU HAVE TO *WANT* TO INTERFACE WITH THE SYSTEM TO CONNECT.
I'D LIKE TO INTERFACE.
I MEAN... IF THERE'S A WAY TO TRY IT OUT, I'M GAME.
ONLY TRUE RESIDENTS OF UNITY CAN INTERFACE BUT... I *CAN* GRANT YOU A KIND OF TEMPORARY ACCESS IF YOU WANT.
YES, PLEASE.
VERY WELL.
HERE. IT'S CALLED A *STYLUS*. AS LONG AS YOU WEAR IT, YOU'LL BE ABLE TO MANIPULATE THE DIAMOND DESERT, OR SANDS, OF THIS PLACE. AS FOR OUR DATABASE, YOU'LL HAVE LIMITED ACCESS.
HOW LIMITED?
QUITE. ACCESS TO OUR ARCHIVES REQUIRES A REAL AND PERMANENT INTERFACE, BUT MR. KENYATTA WILL BE ABLE TO BUILD OBJECTS, OR EVEN A SMALL ENVIRONMENT FROM HIS MEMORIES OR THOUGHTS.
IT'S... AMAZING. I CAN FEEL THE TINGLING THROUGH MY WHOLE NERVOUS SYSTEM, LIKE... CHRISTMAS LIGHTS.

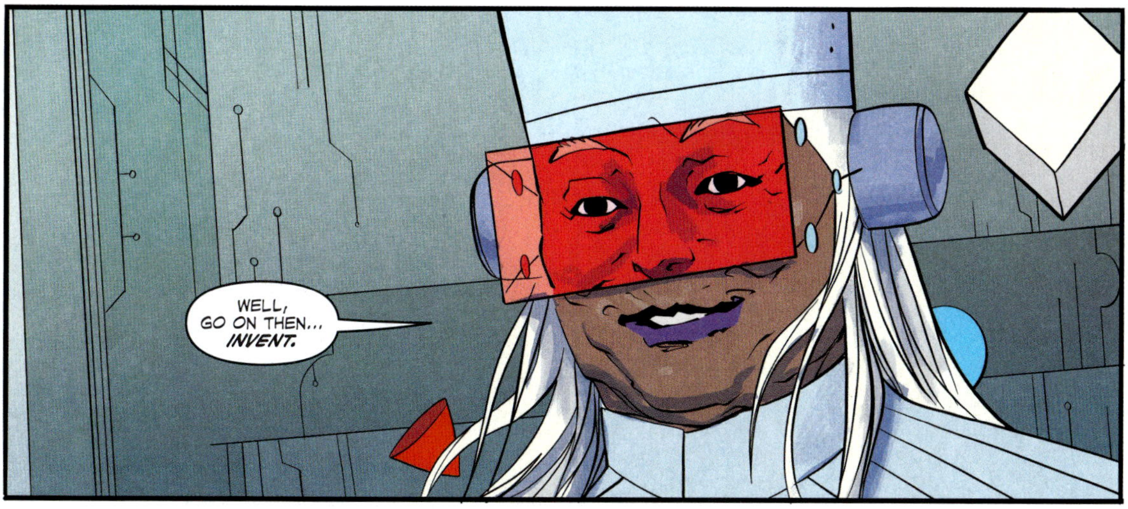
WELL, GO ON THEN... *INVENT.*

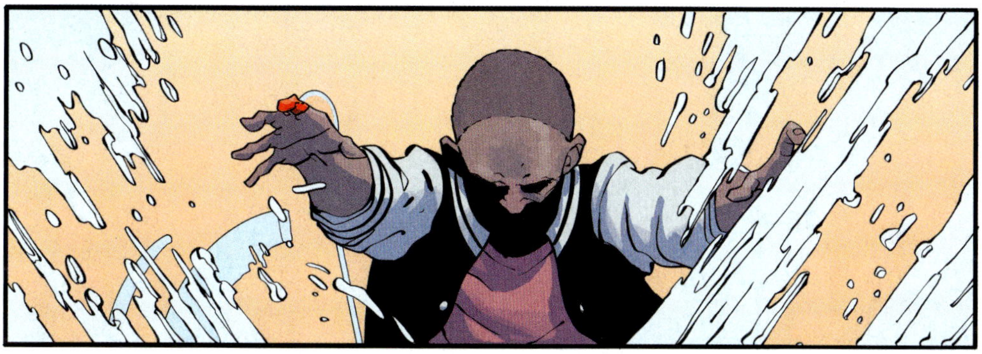

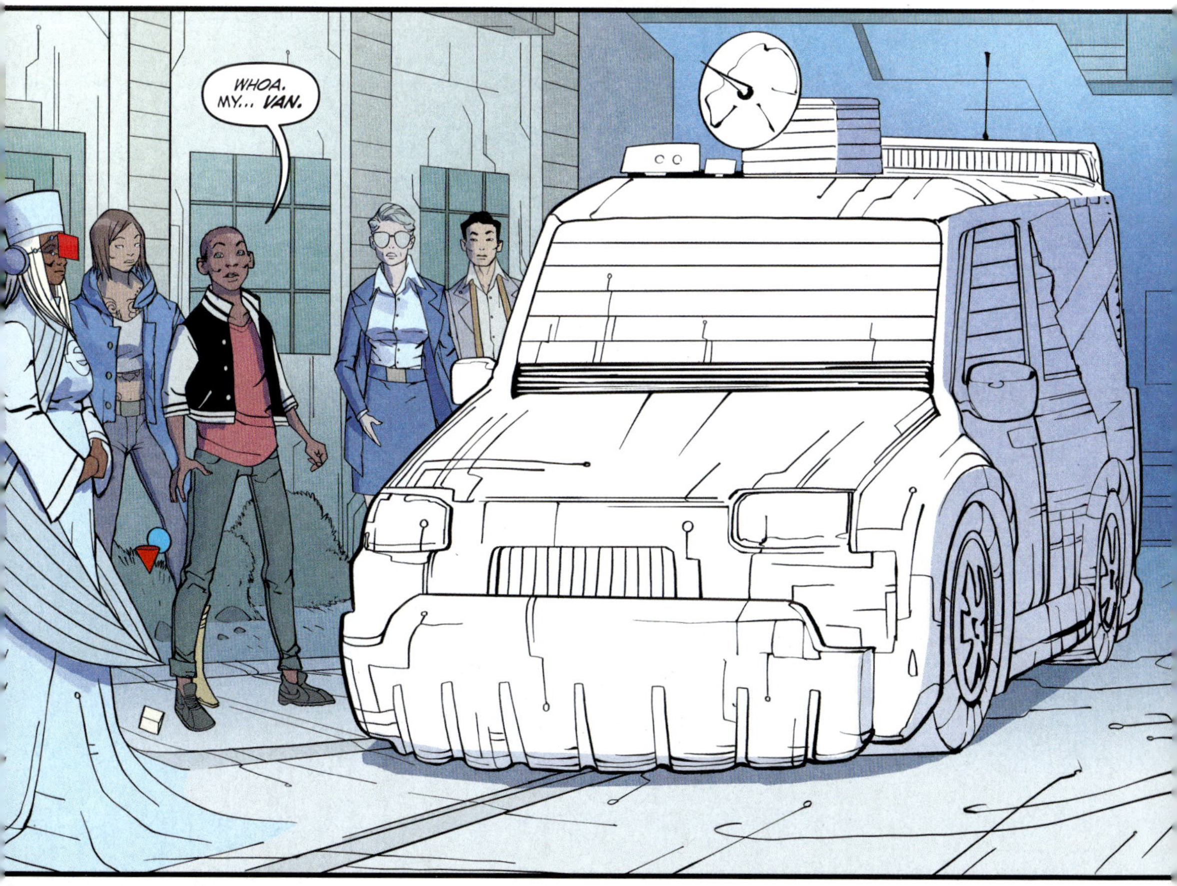
WHOA. MY... *VAN.*

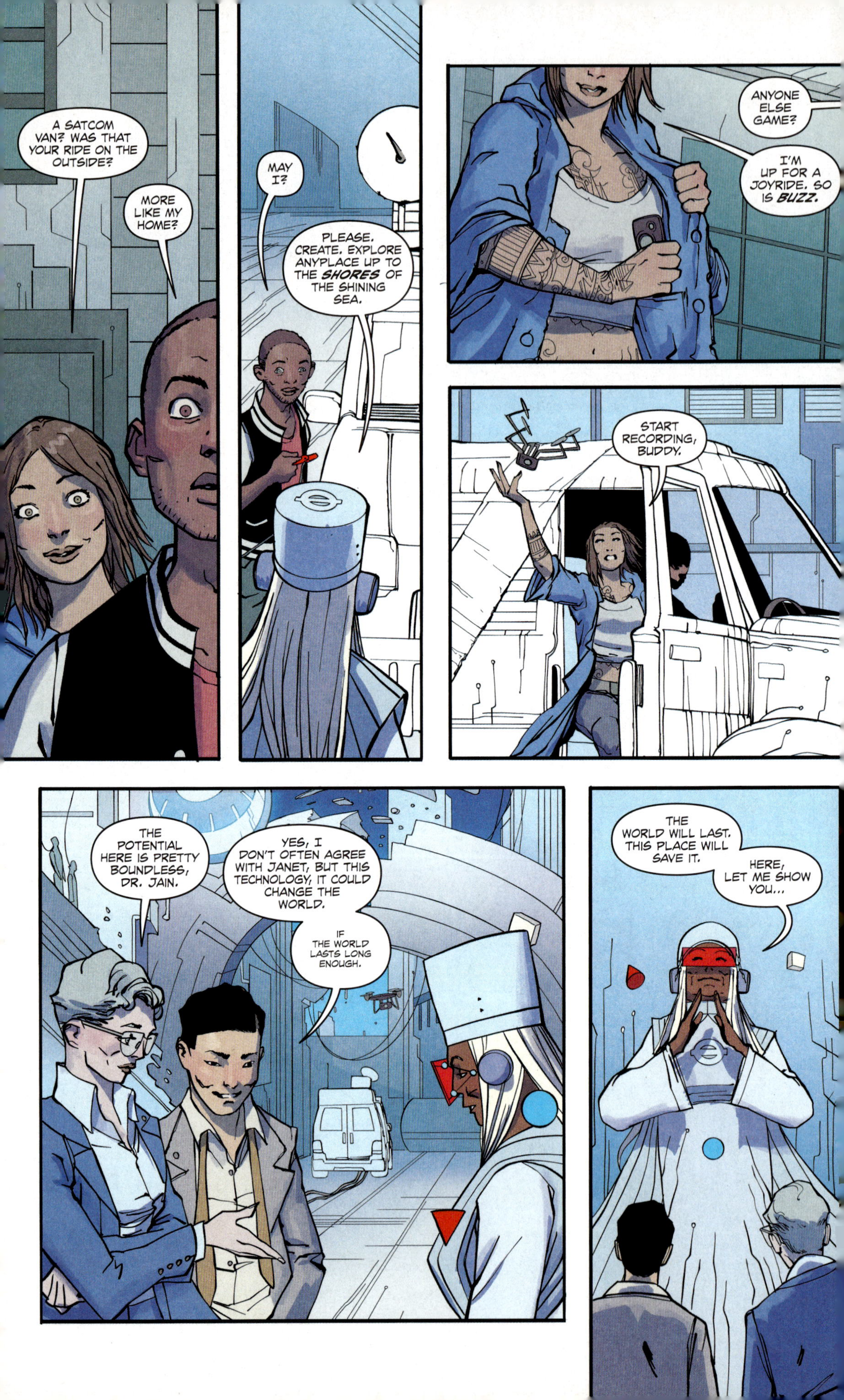
A SATCOM VAN? WAS THAT YOUR RIDE ON THE OUTSIDE?
MORE LIKE MY HOME?
MAY I?
PLEASE. CREATE. EXPLORE ANYPLACE UP TO THE *SHORES* OF THE SHINING SEA.
ANYONE ELSE GAME?
I'M UP FOR A JOYRIDE. SO IS *BUZZ*.
START RECORDING, BUDDY.
THE POTENTIAL HERE IS PRETTY BOUNDLESS, DR. JAIN.
YES, I DON'T OFTEN AGREE WITH JANET, BUT THIS TECHNOLOGY, IT COULD CHANGE THE WORLD.
IF THE WORLD LASTS LONG ENOUGH.
THE WORLD WILL LAST. THIS PLACE WILL SAVE IT.
HERE, LET ME SHOW YOU...

"...HOW FREEING UNITY CAN BE."
THIS-- UNH!--THIS... LAND...
YOU HAVE NO LAND ANYMORE.
AURORA TOOK IT BACK.
SSSSAM. YOU ARE NOTHING... NOTHING BUT AN ABOMINATION OF WHO YOU ONCE WERE.
I COULD SAY THE SAME THING ABOUT YOU. BUT EITHER WAY, THIS ISN'T YOUR LAND...
...YOU ARE ITS PROPERTY NOW.
AAAAAGH!!
FWP
FWP
FWP

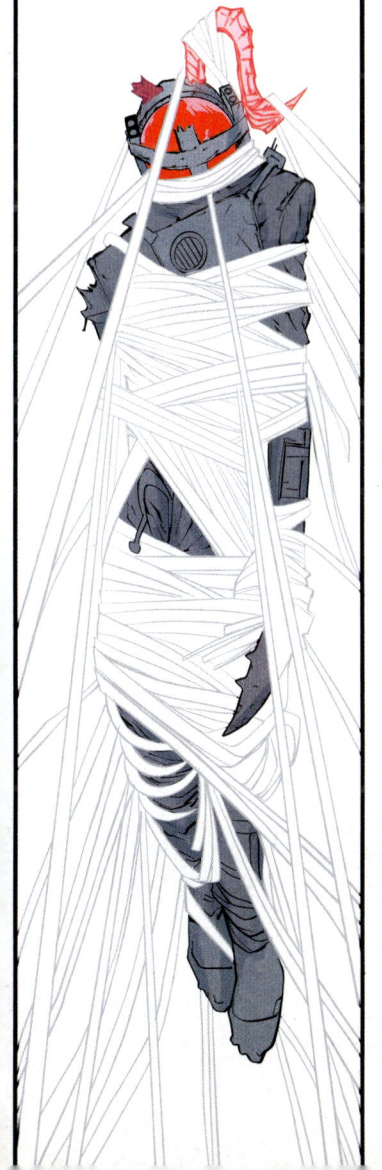

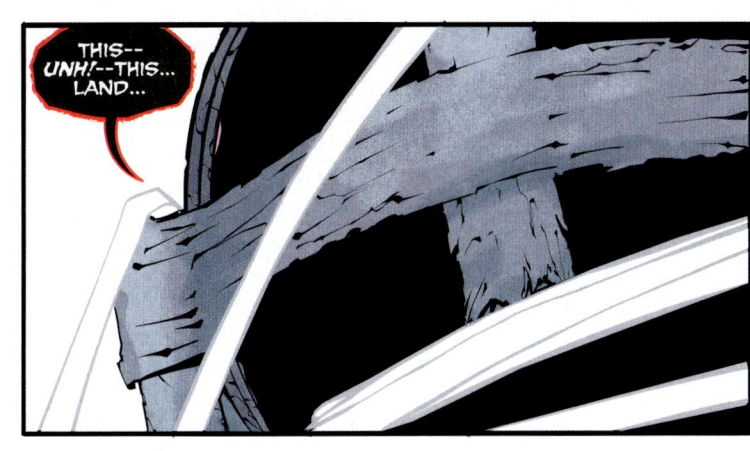

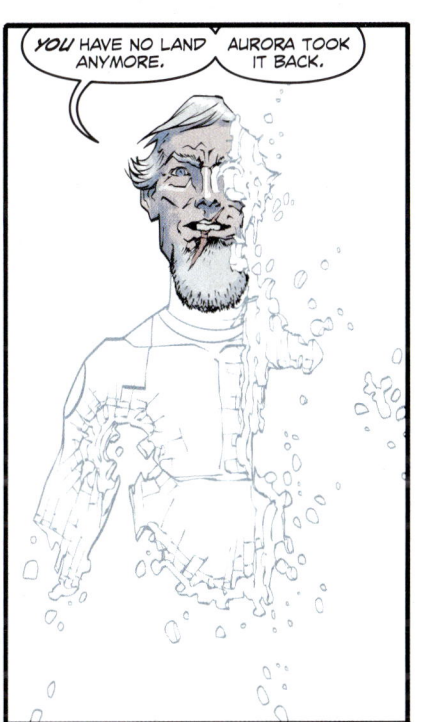

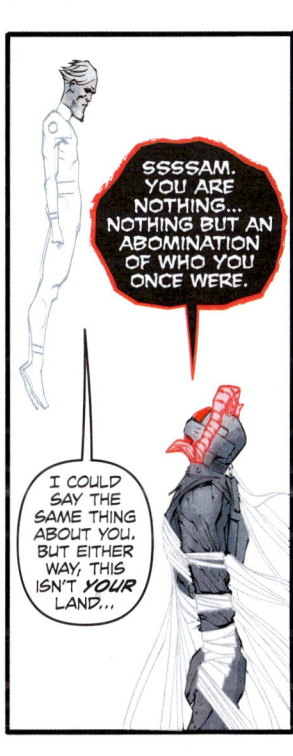

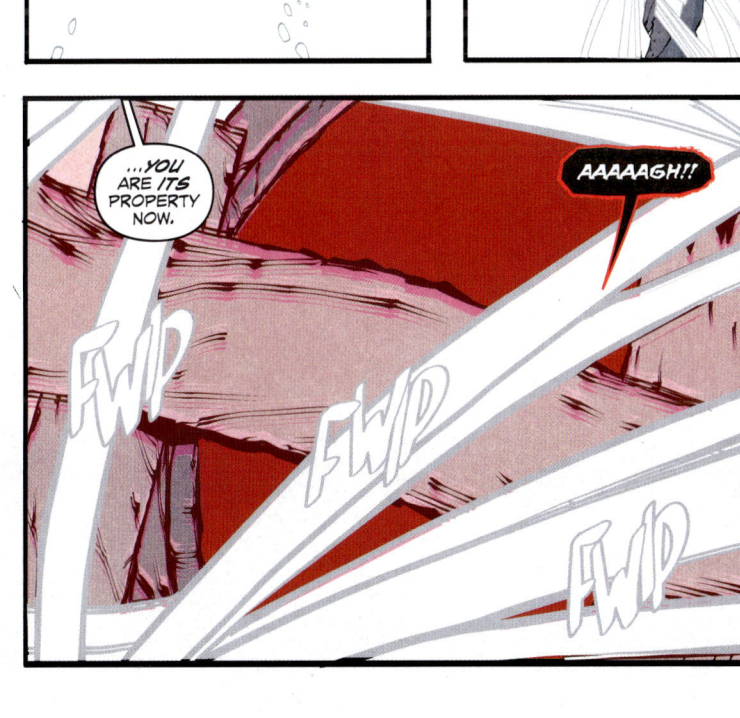

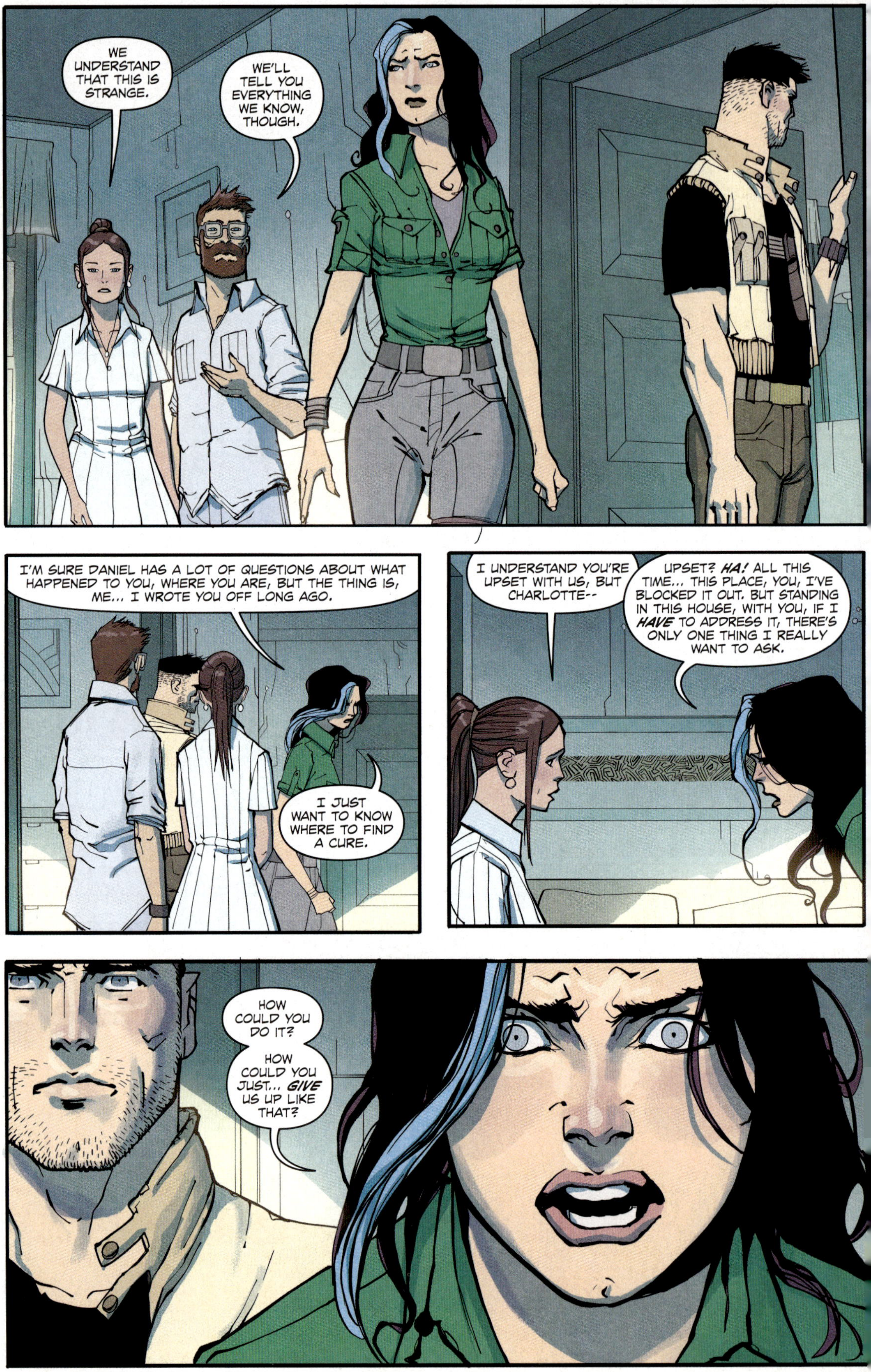
WE UNDERSTAND THAT THIS IS STRANGE.
WE'LL TELL YOU EVERYTHING WE KNOW, THOUGH.
I'M SURE DANIEL HAS A LOT OF QUESTIONS ABOUT WHAT HAPPENED TO YOU, WHERE YOU ARE, BUT THE THING IS, ME... I WROTE YOU OFF LONG AGO.
I JUST WANT TO KNOW WHERE TO FIND A CURE.
I UNDERSTAND YOU'RE UPSET WITH US, BUT CHARLOTTE--
UPSET? HA! ALL THIS TIME... THIS PLACE, YOU, I'VE BLOCKED IT OUT. BUT STANDING IN THIS HOUSE, WITH YOU, IF I HAVE TO ADDRESS IT, THERE'S ONLY ONE THING I REALLY WANT TO ASK.
HOW COULD YOU DO IT?
HOW COULD YOU JUST... GIVE US UP LIKE THAT?

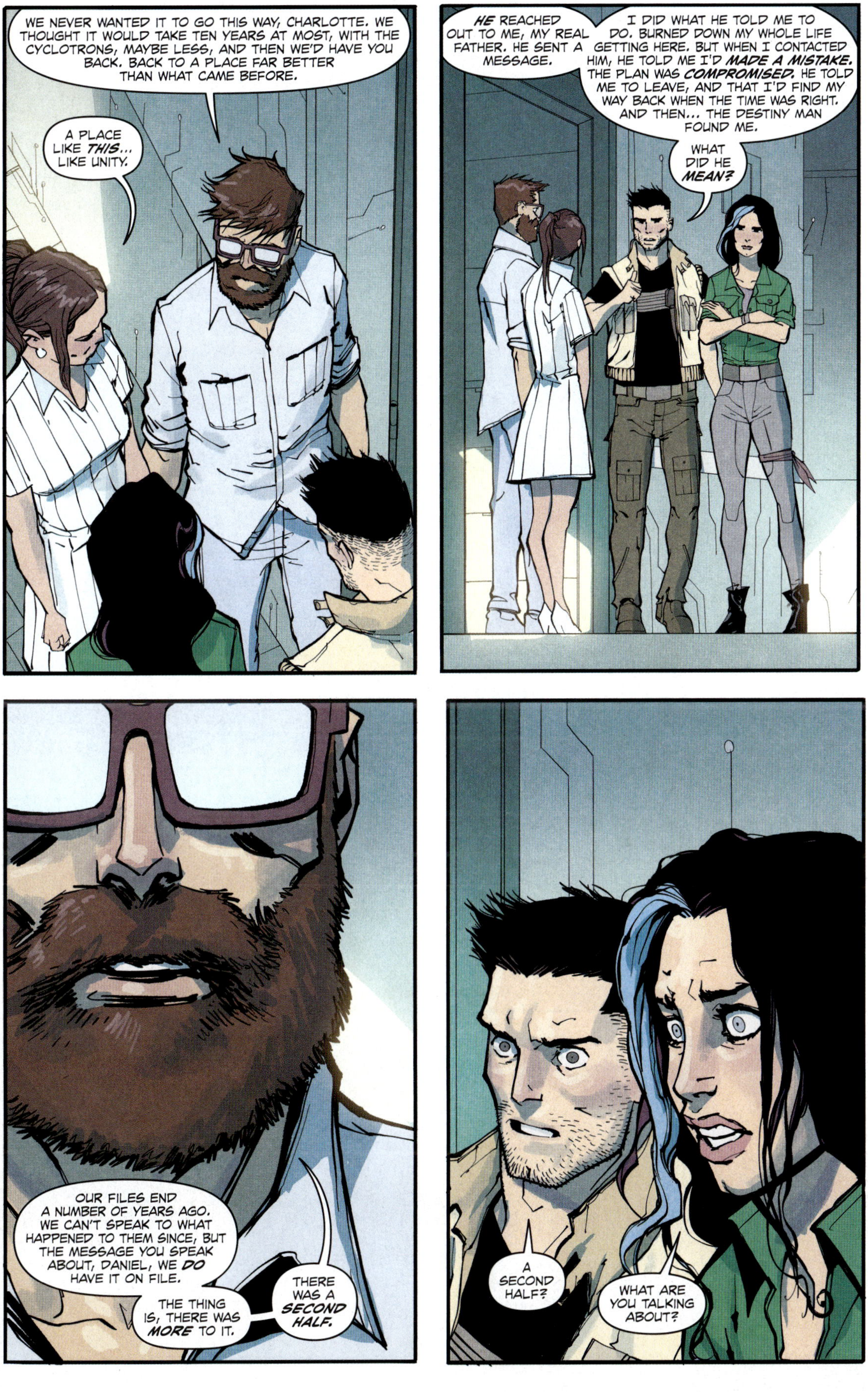
WE NEVER WANTED IT TO GO THIS WAY, CHARLOTTE. WE THOUGHT IT WOULD TAKE TEN YEARS AT MOST, WITH THE CYCLOTRONS, MAYBE LESS, AND THEN WE'D HAVE YOU BACK. BACK TO A PLACE FAR BETTER THAN WHAT CAME BEFORE.
A PLACE LIKE *THIS*... LIKE UNITY.
HE REACHED OUT TO ME, MY REAL FATHER. HE SENT A MESSAGE.
I DID WHAT HE TOLD ME TO DO. BURNED DOWN MY WHOLE LIFE GETTING HERE. BUT WHEN I CONTACTED HIM, HE TOLD ME I'D *MADE A MISTAKE.* THE PLAN WAS *COMPROMISED.* HE TOLD ME TO LEAVE, AND THAT I'D FIND MY WAY BACK WHEN THE TIME WAS RIGHT. AND THEN... THE DESTINY MAN FOUND ME.
WHAT DID HE *MEAN?*
OUR FILES END A NUMBER OF YEARS AGO. WE CAN'T SPEAK TO WHAT HAPPENED TO THEM SINCE, BUT THE MESSAGE YOU SPEAK ABOUT, DANIEL, WE *DO* HAVE IT ON FILE.
THE THING IS, THERE WAS *MORE* TO IT.
THERE WAS A *SECOND HALF.*
A SECOND HALF?
WHAT ARE YOU TALKING ABOUT?

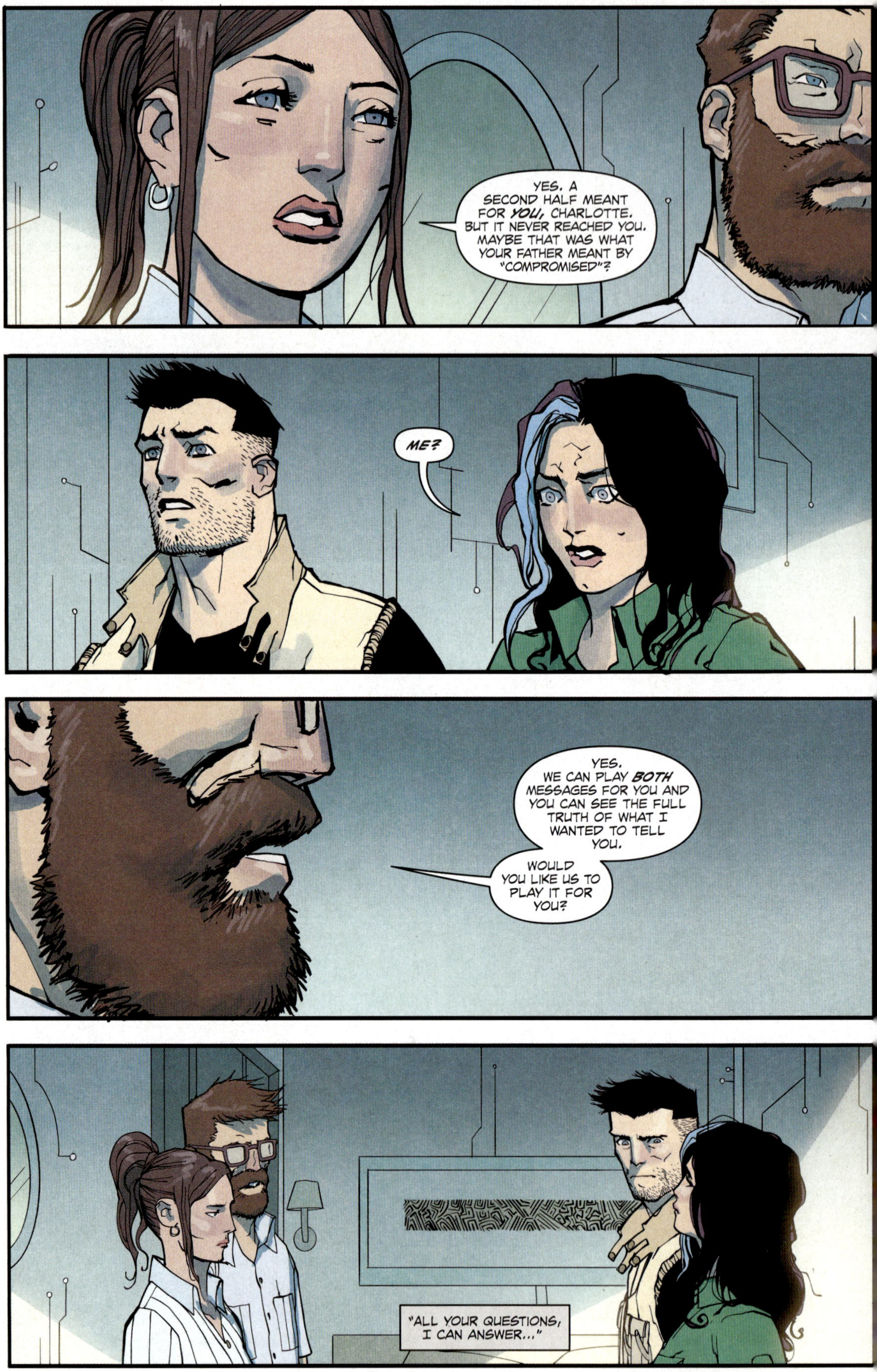
YES. A SECOND HALF MEANT FOR *YOU,* CHARLOTTE. BUT IT NEVER REACHED YOU. MAYBE THAT WAS WHAT YOUR FATHER MEANT BY "COMPROMISED"?
ME?
YES. WE CAN PLAY *BOTH* MESSAGES FOR YOU AND YOU CAN SEE THE FULL TRUTH OF WHAT I WANTED TO TELL YOU.
WOULD YOU LIKE US TO PLAY IT FOR YOU?
"ALL YOUR QUESTIONS, I CAN ANSWER..."

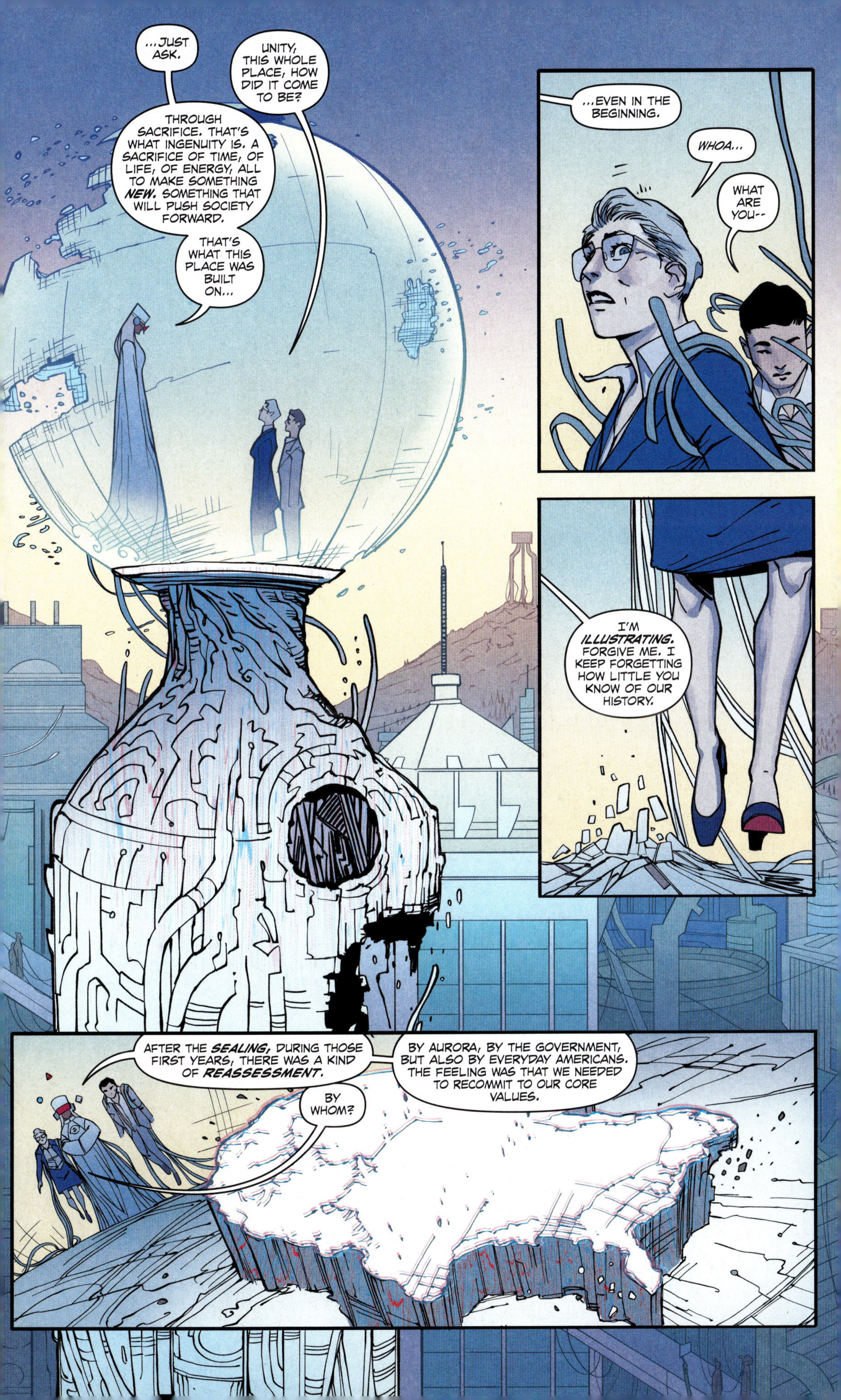

...JUST ASK.
UNITY, THIS WHOLE PLACE, HOW DID IT COME TO BE?
THROUGH SACRIFICE. THAT'S WHAT INGENUITY IS. A SACRIFICE OF TIME, OF LIFE, OF ENERGY, ALL TO MAKE SOMETHING NEW. SOMETHING THAT WILL PUSH SOCIETY FORWARD.
THAT'S WHAT THIS PLACE WAS BUILT ON...
...EVEN IN THE BEGINNING.
WHOA...
WHAT ARE YOU--
I'M ILLUSTRATING. FORGIVE ME. I KEEP FORGETTING HOW LITTLE YOU KNOW OF OUR HISTORY.
AFTER THE SEALING, DURING THOSE FIRST YEARS, THERE WAS A KIND OF REASSESSMENT.
BY WHOM?
BY AURORA, BY THE GOVERNMENT, BUT ALSO BY EVERYDAY AMERICANS. THE FEELING WAS THAT WE NEEDED TO RECOMMIT TO OUR CORE VALUES.

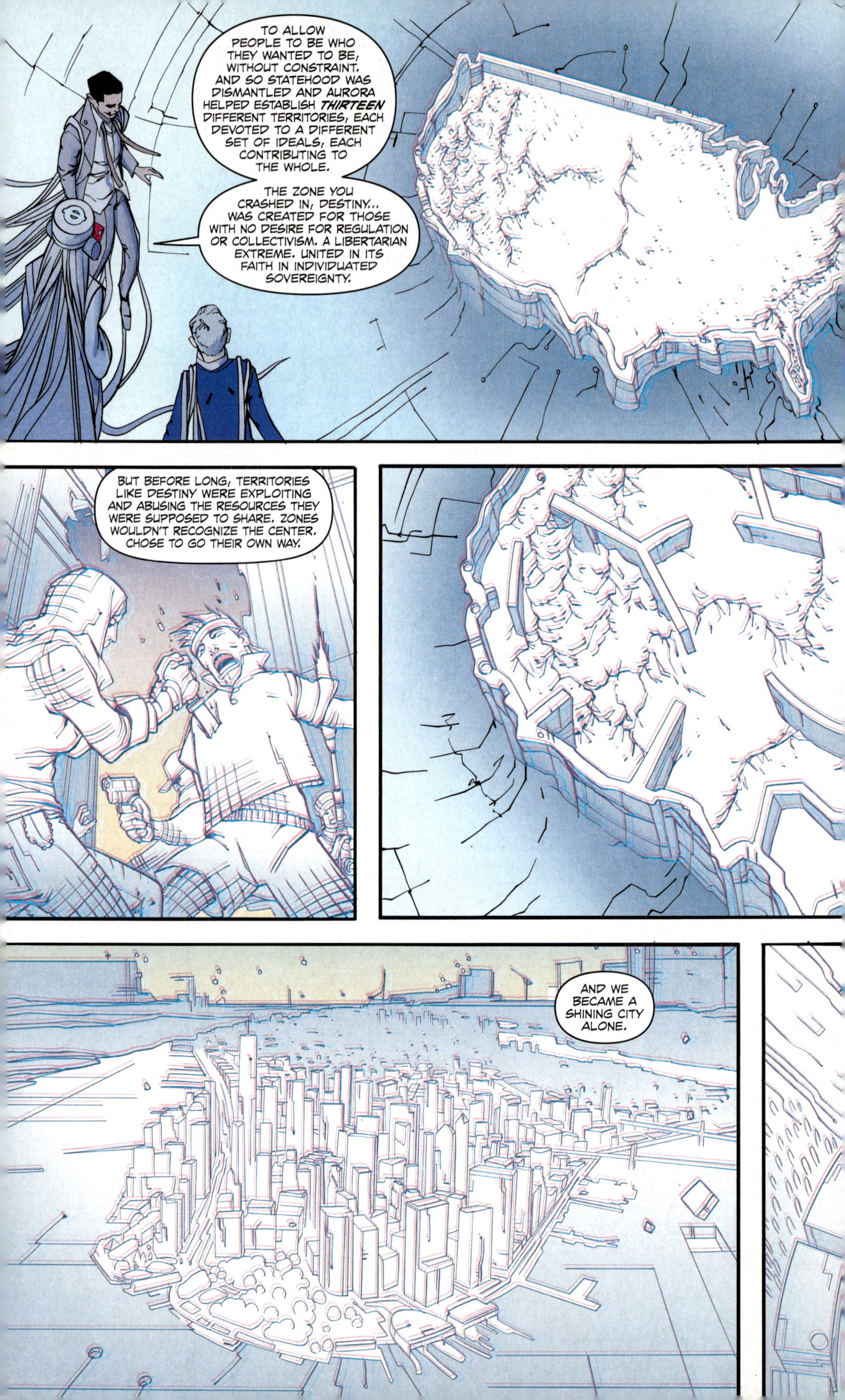
TO ALLOW PEOPLE TO BE WHO THEY WANTED TO BE, WITHOUT CONSTRAINT. AND SO STATEHOOD WAS DISMANTLED AND AURORA HELPED ESTABLISH *THIRTEEN* DIFFERENT TERRITORIES, EACH DEVOTED TO A DIFFERENT SET OF IDEALS, EACH CONTRIBUTING TO THE WHOLE.
THE ZONE YOU CRASHED IN, DESTINY.. WAS CREATED FOR THOSE WITH NO DESIRE FOR REGULATION OR COLLECTIVISM. A LIBERTARIAN EXTREME. UNITED IN ITS FAITH IN INDIVIDUATED SOVEREIGNTY.
BUT BEFORE LONG, TERRITORIES LIKE DESTINY WERE EXPLOITING AND ABUSING THE RESOURCES THEY WERE SUPPOSED TO SHARE. ZONES WOULDN'T RECOGNIZE THE CENTER. CHOSE TO GO THEIR OWN WAY.
AND WE BECAME A SHINING CITY ALONE.

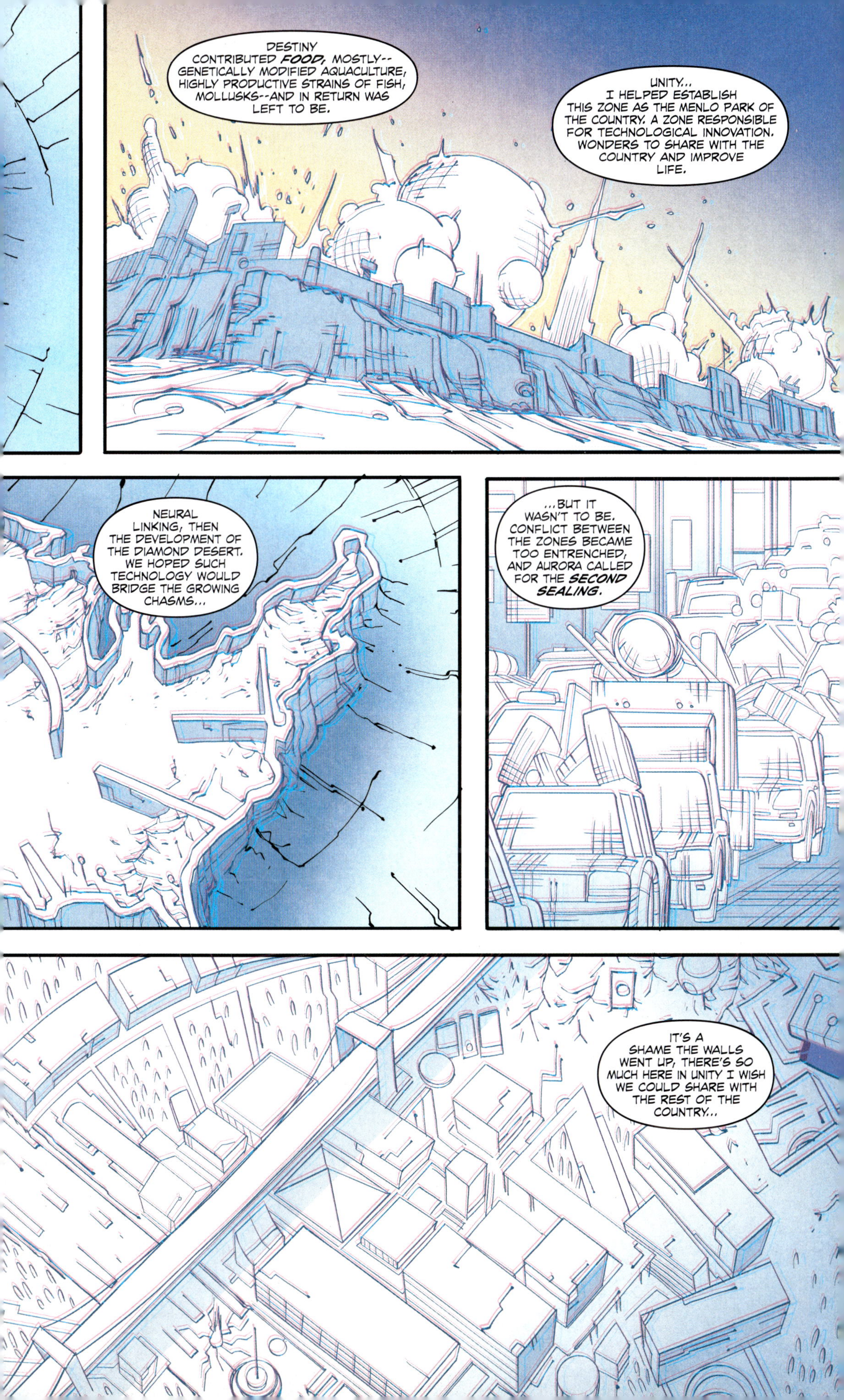
DESTINY CONTRIBUTED FOOD, MOSTLY-- GENETICALLY MODIFIED AQUACULTURE, HIGHLY PRODUCTIVE STRAINS OF FISH, MOLLUSKS--AND IN RETURN WAS LEFT TO BE.
UNITY... I HELPED ESTABLISH THIS ZONE AS THE MENLO PARK OF THE COUNTRY. A ZONE RESPONSIBLE FOR TECHNOLOGICAL INNOVATION. WONDERS TO SHARE WITH THE COUNTRY AND IMPROVE LIFE.
NEURAL LINKING, THEN THE DEVELOPMENT OF THE DIAMOND DESERT. WE HOPED SUCH TECHNOLOGY WOULD BRIDGE THE GROWING CHASMS...
...BUT IT WASN'T TO BE. CONFLICT BETWEEN THE ZONES BECAME TOO ENTRENCHED, AND AURORA CALLED FOR THE SECOND SEALING.
IT'S A SHAME THE WALLS WENT UP, THERE'S SO MUCH HERE IN UNITY I WISH WE COULD SHARE WITH THE REST OF THE COUNTRY...

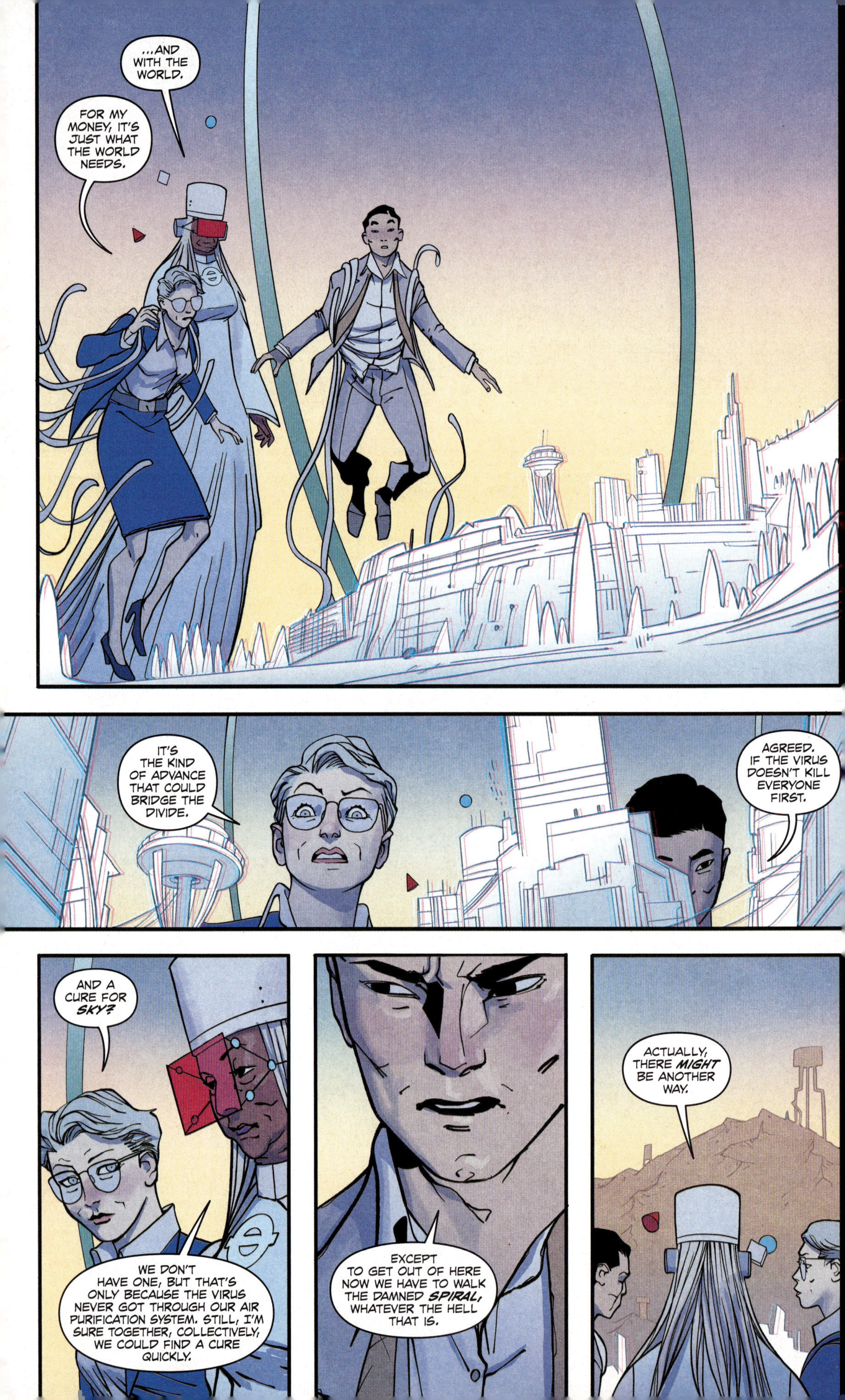
...AND WITH THE WORLD.
FOR MY MONEY, IT'S JUST WHAT THE WORLD NEEDS.
IT'S THE KIND OF ADVANCE THAT COULD BRIDGE THE DIVIDE.
AGREED. IF THE VIRUS DOESN'T KILL EVERYONE FIRST.
AND A CURE FOR *SKY?*
WE DON'T HAVE ONE, BUT THAT'S ONLY BECAUSE THE VIRUS NEVER GOT THROUGH OUR AIR PURIFICATION SYSTEM. STILL, I'M SURE TOGETHER, COLLECTIVELY, WE COULD FIND A CURE QUICKLY.
EXCEPT TO GET OUT OF HERE NOW WE HAVE TO WALK THE DAMNED *SPIRAL,* WHATEVER THE HELL THAT IS.
ACTUALLY, THERE *MIGHT* BE ANOTHER WAY.

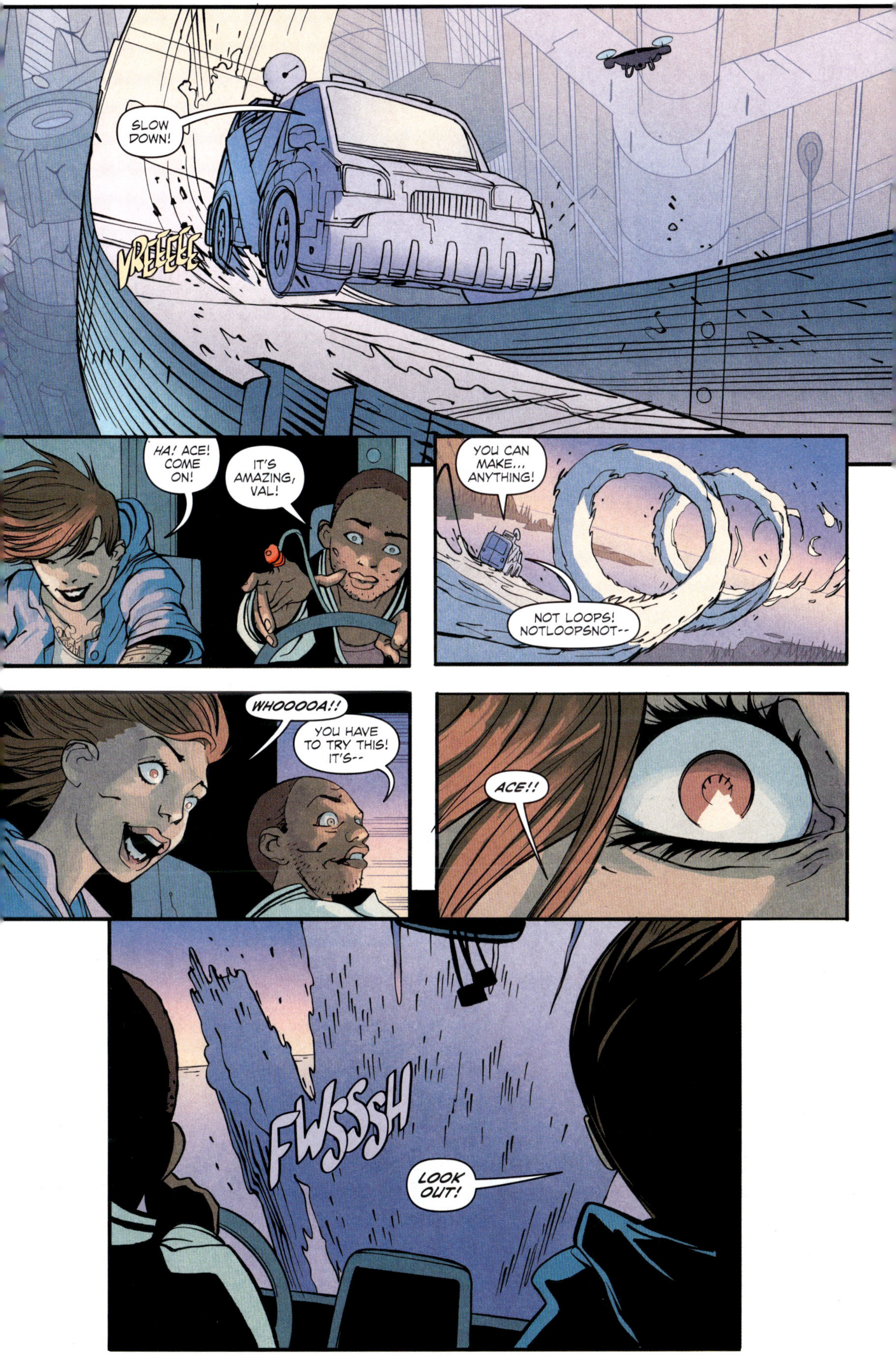
SLOW DOWN!
VREEEEE
HA! ACE! COME ON!
IT'S AMAZING, VAL!
YOU CAN MAKE... ANYTHING!
NOT LOOPS! NOTLOOPSNOT--
WHOOOOA!!
YOU HAVE TO TRY THIS! IT'S--
ACE!!
FWSSSH
LOOK OUT!

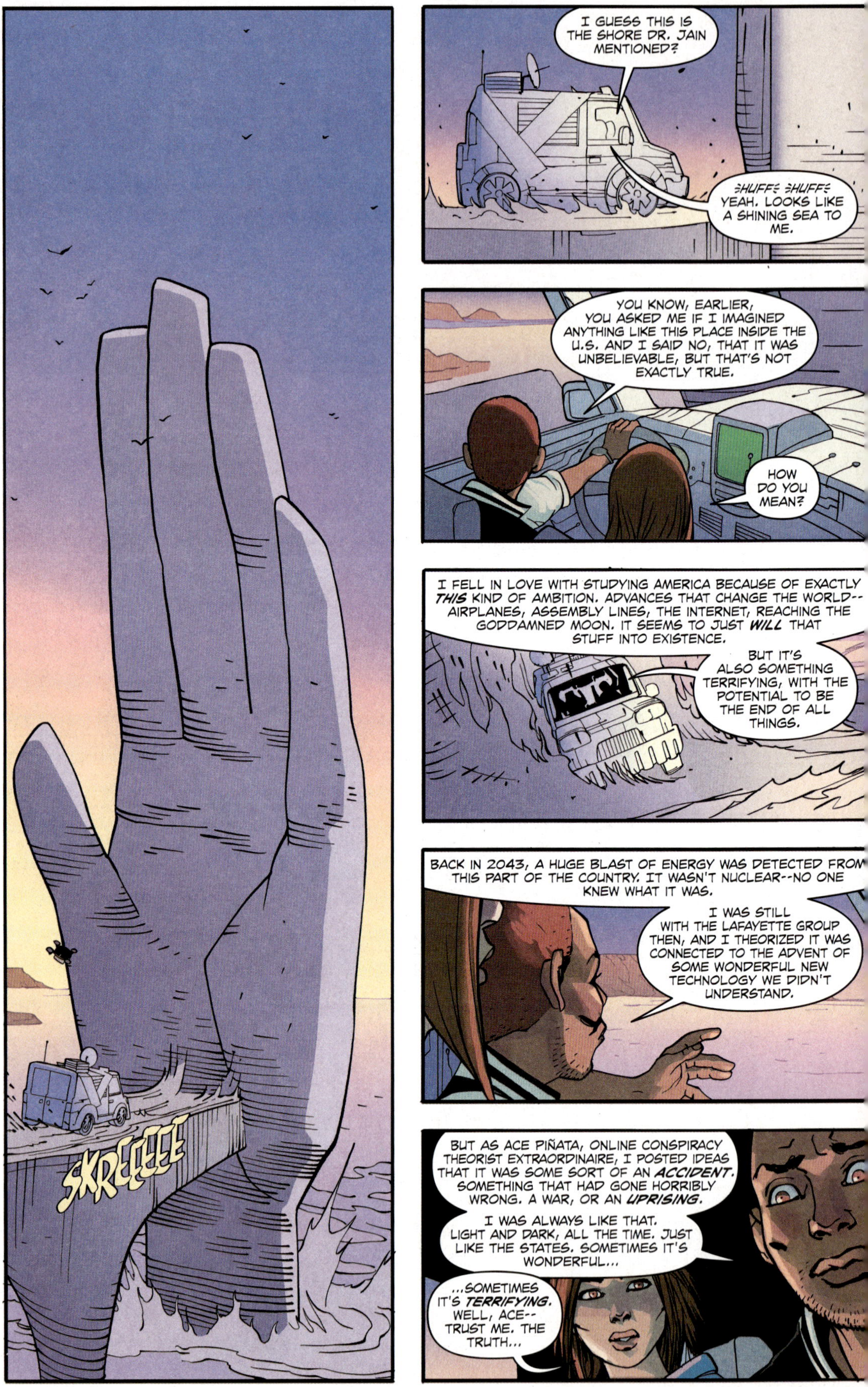
SKREEEEE
I GUESS THIS IS THE SHORE DR. JAIN MENTIONED?
SHUFF SHUFF YEAH. LOOKS LIKE A SHINING SEA TO ME.
YOU KNOW, EARLIER, YOU ASKED ME IF I IMAGINED ANYTHING LIKE THIS PLACE INSIDE THE U.S. AND I SAID NO, THAT IT WAS UNBELIEVABLE, BUT THAT'S NOT EXACTLY TRUE.
HOW DO YOU MEAN?
I FELL IN LOVE WITH STUDYING AMERICA BECAUSE OF EXACTLY *THIS* KIND OF AMBITION. ADVANCES THAT CHANGE THE WORLD--AIRPLANES, ASSEMBLY LINES, THE INTERNET, REACHING THE GODDAMNED MOON. IT SEEMS TO JUST *WILL* THAT STUFF INTO EXISTENCE.
BUT IT'S ALSO SOMETHING TERRIFYING, WITH THE POTENTIAL TO BE THE END OF ALL THINGS.
BACK IN 2043, A HUGE BLAST OF ENERGY WAS DETECTED FROM THIS PART OF THE COUNTRY. IT WASN'T NUCLEAR--NO ONE KNEW WHAT IT WAS.
I WAS STILL WITH THE LAFAYETTE GROUP THEN, AND I THEORIZED IT WAS CONNECTED TO THE ADVENT OF SOME WONDERFUL NEW TECHNOLOGY WE DIDN'T UNDERSTAND.
BUT AS ACE PIÑATA, ONLINE CONSPIRACY THEORIST EXTRAORDINAIRE, I POSTED IDEAS THAT IT WAS SOME SORT OF AN *ACCIDENT*. SOMETHING THAT HAD GONE HORRIBLY WRONG. A WAR, OR AN *UPRISING*.
I WAS ALWAYS LIKE THAT. LIGHT AND DARK, ALL THE TIME. JUST LIKE THE STATES. SOMETIMES IT'S WONDERFUL...
...SOMETIMES IT'S *TERRIFYING*. WELL, ACE--TRUST ME. THE TRUTH...

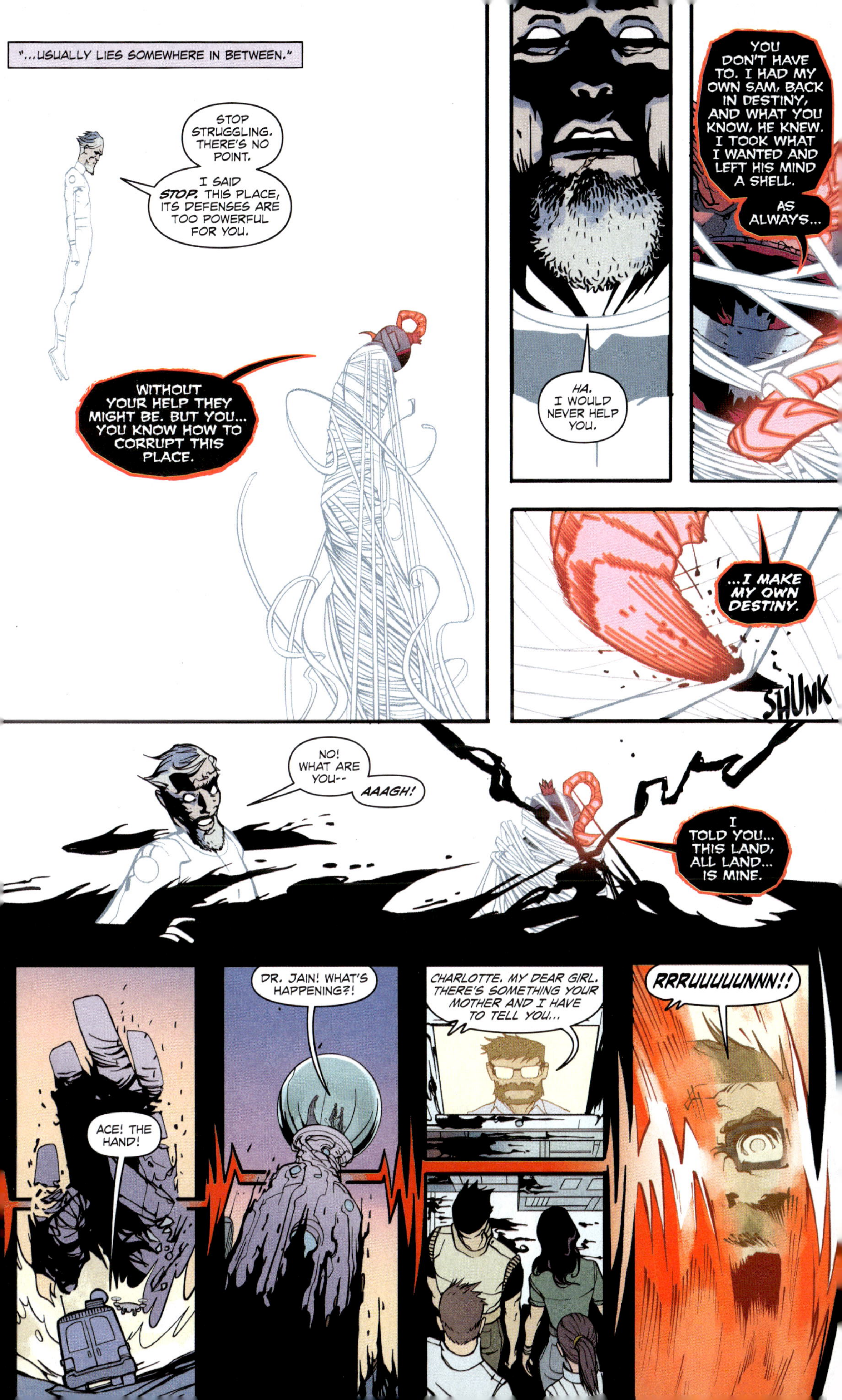
"...USUALLY LIES SOMEWHERE IN BETWEEN."
STOP STRUGGLING. THERE'S NO POINT.
I SAID *STOP.* THIS PLACE, ITS DEFENSES ARE TOO POWERFUL FOR YOU.
WITHOUT YOUR HELP THEY MIGHT BE. BUT YOU... YOU KNOW HOW TO CORRUPT THIS PLACE.
HA. I WOULD NEVER HELP YOU.
YOU DON'T HAVE TO. I HAD MY OWN SAM, BACK IN DESTINY, AND WHAT YOU KNOW, HE KNEW. I TOOK WHAT I WANTED AND LEFT HIS MIND A SHELL.
AS ALWAYS...
...I MAKE MY OWN DESTINY.
SHUNK
NO! WHAT ARE YOU--
AAAGH!
I TOLD YOU... THIS LAND, ALL LAND... IS MINE.
ACE! THE HAND!
DR. JAIN! WHAT'S HAPPENING?!
CHARLOTTE. MY DEAR GIRL. THERE'S SOMETHING YOUR MOTHER AND I HAVE TO TELL YOU...
RRRUUUUUNNN!!

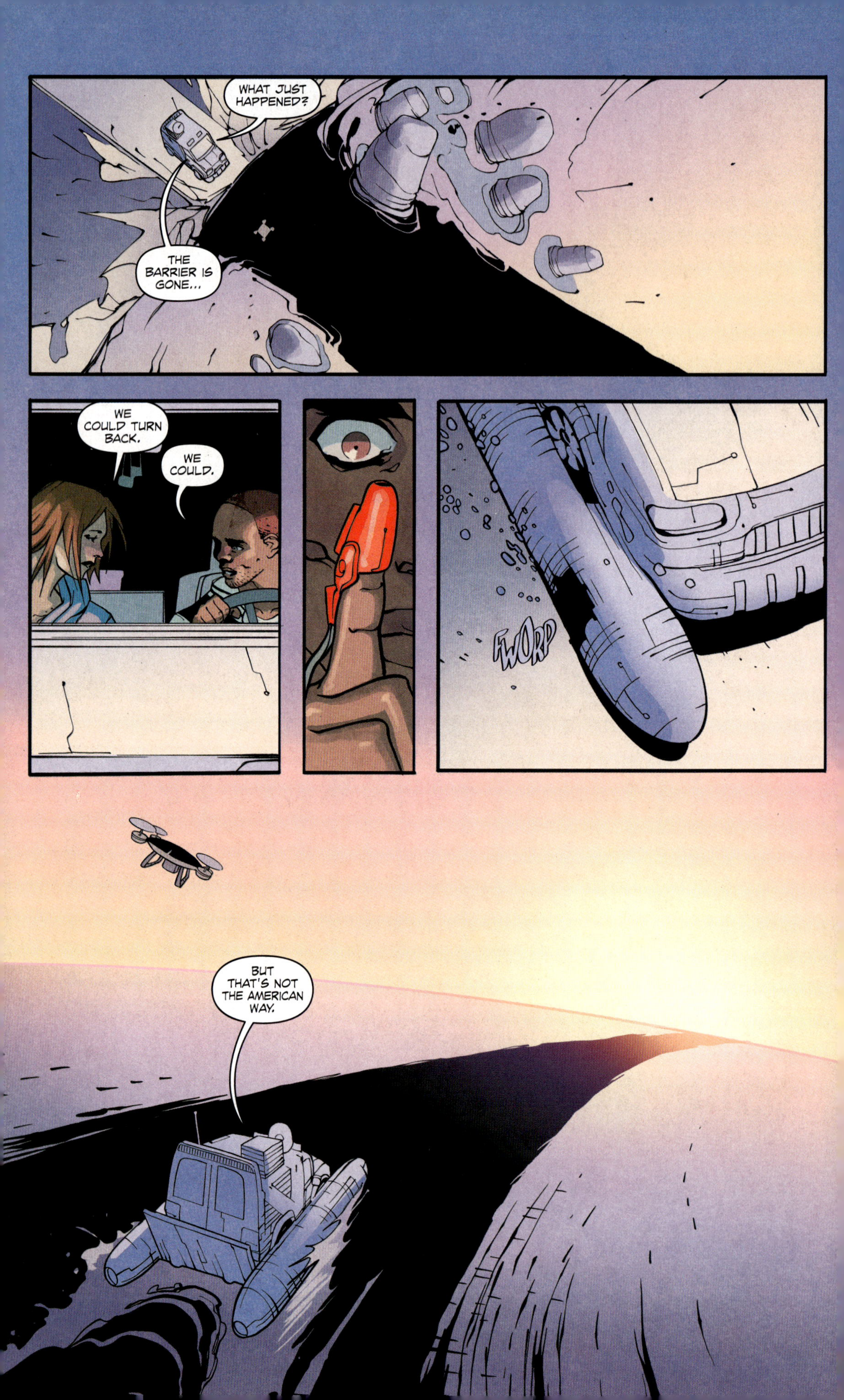
WHAT JUST HAPPENED?
THE BARRIER IS GONE...
WE COULD TURN BACK.
WE COULD.
FWORP
BUT THAT'S NOT THE AMERICAN WAY.

The Lafayette Group

"Something's happened. <u>Inside the walls.</u> Other than the Juneau Event, this is the most significant signal we have detected from within the borders of what was - what perhaps still is? - the United States of America. A massive energy surge somewhere in the Pacific Northwest - electromagnetic, but with odd resonance patterns that our technicians can't explain. The closest analogue we can find are EEG readings, but it's hard to see how that could possibly make sense.

The Group will be occupied for years trying to figure out what this means."

--Journal Entry by Dr. Warren Antone,
November 11, 2044.

FROM THE ARCHIVES OF THE LAFAYETTE GROUP.

FOR OFFICIAL USE ONLY.

CHAPTER TEN

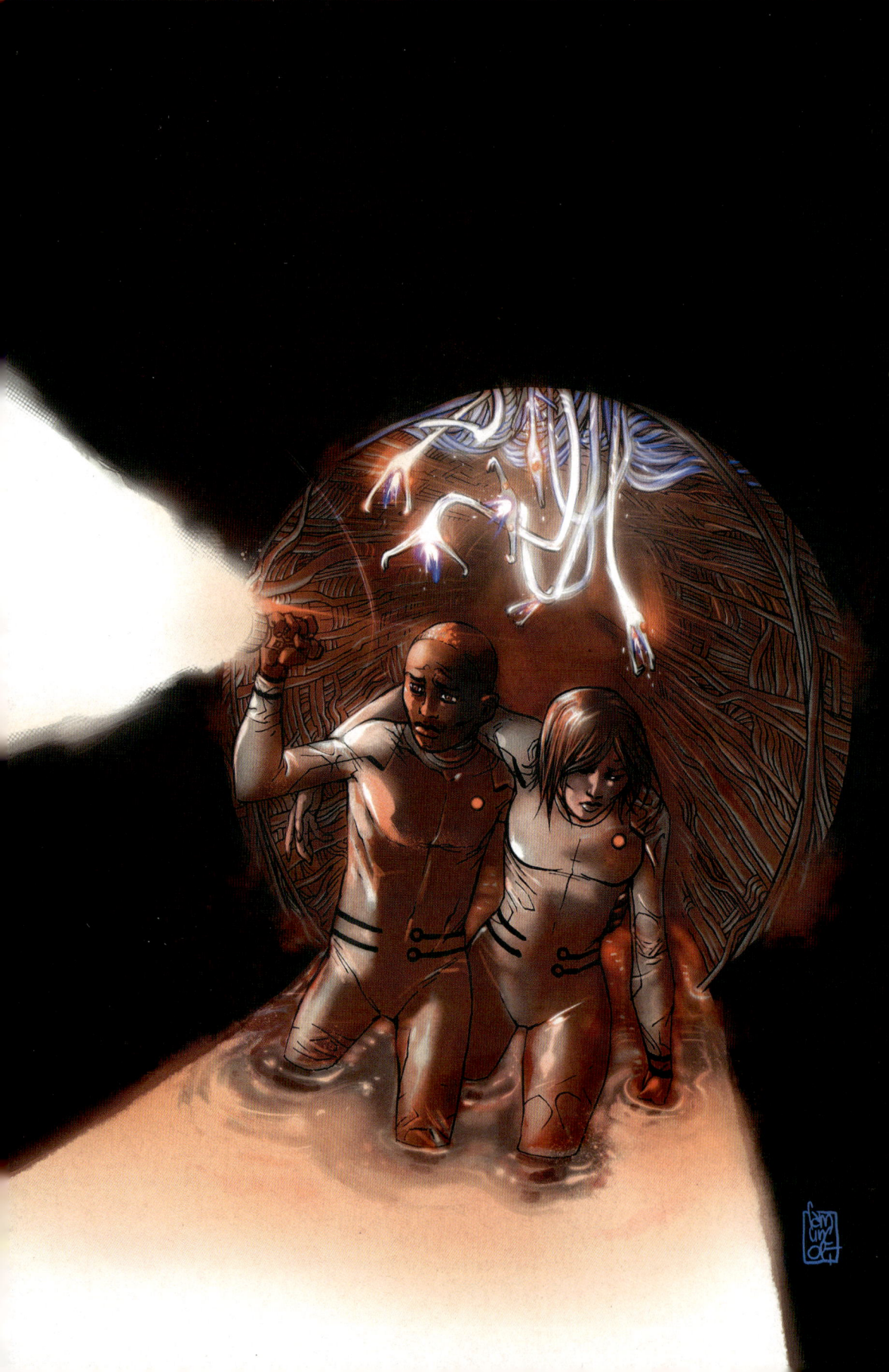

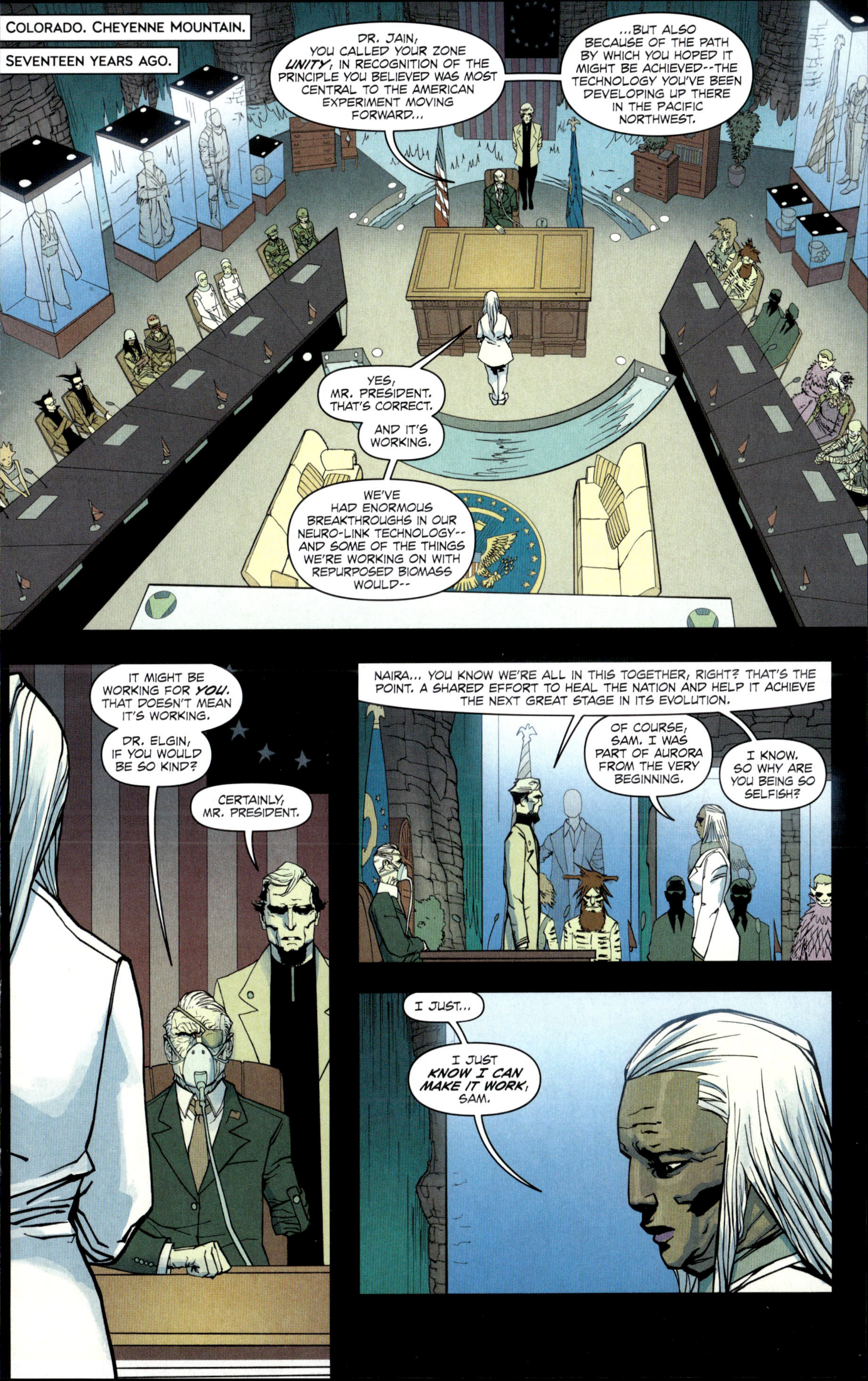
COLORADO. CHEYENNE MOUNTAIN.
SEVENTEEN YEARS AGO.
DR. JAIN, YOU CALLED YOUR ZONE *UNITY*, IN RECOGNITION OF THE PRINCIPLE YOU BELIEVED WAS MOST CENTRAL TO THE AMERICAN EXPERIMENT MOVING FORWARD...
...BUT ALSO BECAUSE OF THE PATH BY WHICH YOU HOPED IT MIGHT BE ACHIEVED--THE TECHNOLOGY YOU'VE BEEN DEVELOPING UP THERE IN THE PACIFIC NORTHWEST.
YES, MR. PRESIDENT. THAT'S CORRECT.
AND IT'S WORKING.
WE'VE HAD ENORMOUS BREAKTHROUGHS IN OUR NEURO-LINK TECHNOLOGY--AND SOME OF THE THINGS WE'RE WORKING ON WITH REPURPOSED BIOMASS WOULD--
IT MIGHT BE WORKING FOR *YOU*. THAT DOESN'T MEAN IT'S WORKING.
DR. ELGIN, IF YOU WOULD BE SO KIND?
CERTAINLY, MR. PRESIDENT.
NAIRA... YOU KNOW WE'RE ALL IN THIS TOGETHER, RIGHT? THAT'S THE POINT. A SHARED EFFORT TO HEAL THE NATION AND HELP IT ACHIEVE THE NEXT GREAT STAGE IN ITS EVOLUTION.
OF COURSE, SAM. I WAS PART OF AURORA FROM THE VERY BEGINNING.
I KNOW. SO WHY ARE YOU BEING SO SELFISH?
I JUST...
I JUST *KNOW I CAN MAKE IT WORK*, SAM.

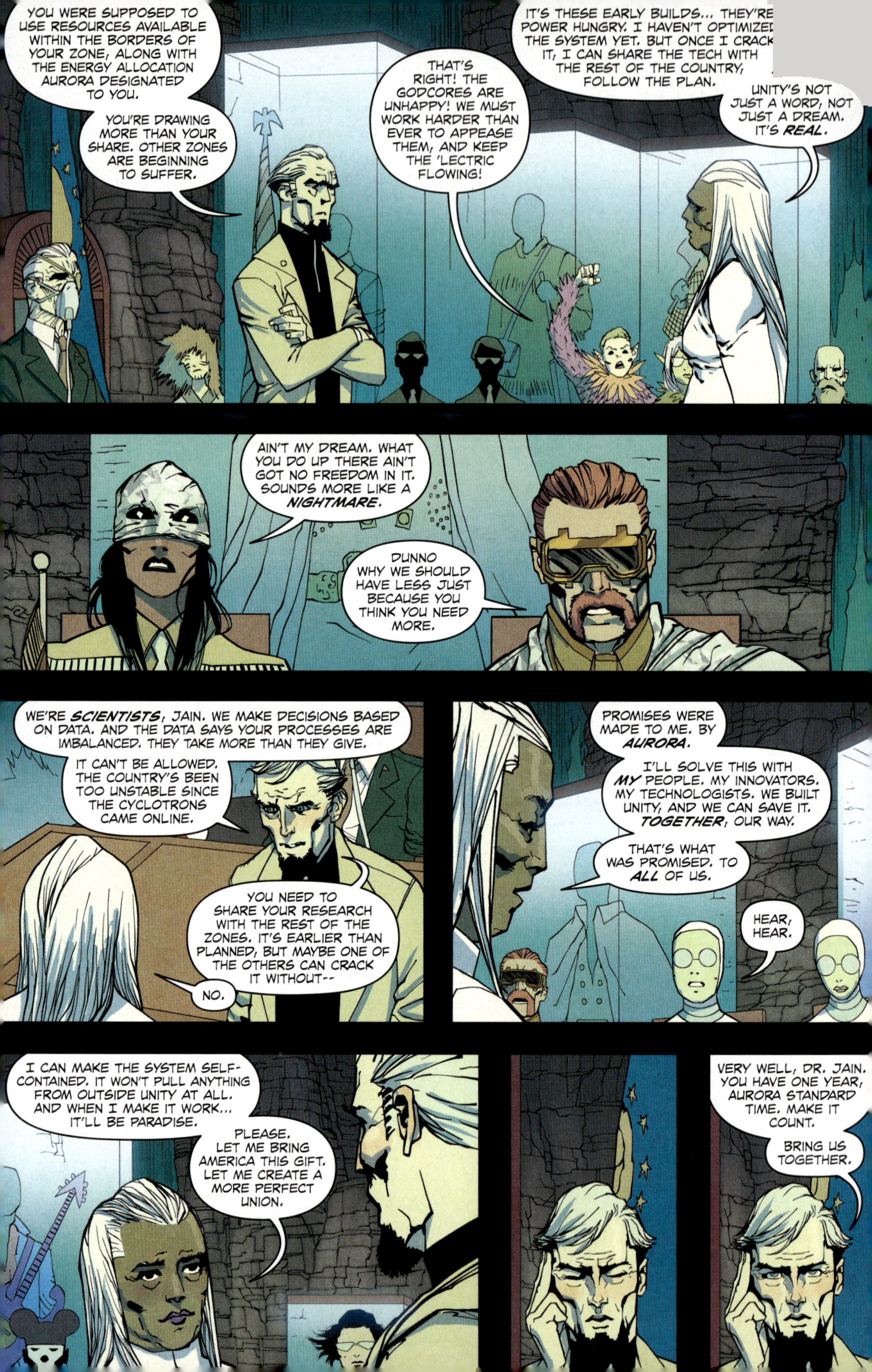
YOU WERE SUPPOSED TO USE RESOURCES AVAILABLE WITHIN THE BORDERS OF YOUR ZONE, ALONG WITH THE ENERGY ALLOCATION AURORA DESIGNATED TO YOU.
YOU'RE DRAWING MORE THAN YOUR SHARE. OTHER ZONES ARE BEGINNING TO SUFFER.
THAT'S RIGHT! THE GODCORES ARE UNHAPPY! WE MUST WORK HARDER THAN EVER TO APPEASE THEM, AND KEEP THE 'LECTRIC FLOWING!
IT'S THESE EARLY BUILDS... THEY'RE POWER HUNGRY. I HAVEN'T OPTIMIZED THE SYSTEM YET. BUT ONCE I CRACK IT, I CAN SHARE THE TECH WITH THE REST OF THE COUNTRY, FOLLOW THE PLAN.
UNITY'S NOT JUST A WORD, NOT JUST A DREAM. IT'S *REAL*.
AIN'T MY DREAM. WHAT YOU DO UP THERE AIN'T GOT NO FREEDOM IN IT. SOUNDS MORE LIKE A *NIGHTMARE*.
DUNNO WHY WE SHOULD HAVE LESS JUST BECAUSE YOU THINK YOU NEED MORE.
WE'RE *SCIENTISTS*, JAIN. WE MAKE DECISIONS BASED ON DATA. AND THE DATA SAYS YOUR PROCESSES ARE IMBALANCED. THEY TAKE MORE THAN THEY GIVE.
IT CAN'T BE ALLOWED. THE COUNTRY'S BEEN TOO UNSTABLE SINCE THE CYCLOTRONS CAME ONLINE.
YOU NEED TO SHARE YOUR RESEARCH WITH THE REST OF THE ZONES. IT'S EARLIER THAN PLANNED, BUT MAYBE ONE OF THE OTHERS CAN CRACK IT WITHOUT--
NO.
PROMISES WERE MADE TO ME. BY *AURORA*.
I'LL SOLVE THIS WITH *MY* PEOPLE. MY INNOVATORS. MY TECHNOLOGISTS. WE BUILT UNITY, AND WE CAN SAVE IT. *TOGETHER*, OUR WAY.
THAT'S WHAT WAS PROMISED. TO *ALL* OF US.
HEAR, HEAR.
I CAN MAKE THE SYSTEM SELF-CONTAINED. IT WON'T PULL ANYTHING FROM OUTSIDE UNITY AT ALL. AND WHEN I MAKE IT WORK... IT'LL BE PARADISE.
PLEASE. LET ME BRING AMERICA THIS GIFT. LET ME CREATE A MORE PERFECT UNION.
VERY WELL, DR. JAIN. YOU HAVE ONE YEAR, AURORA STANDARD TIME. MAKE IT COUNT.
BRING US TOGETHER.

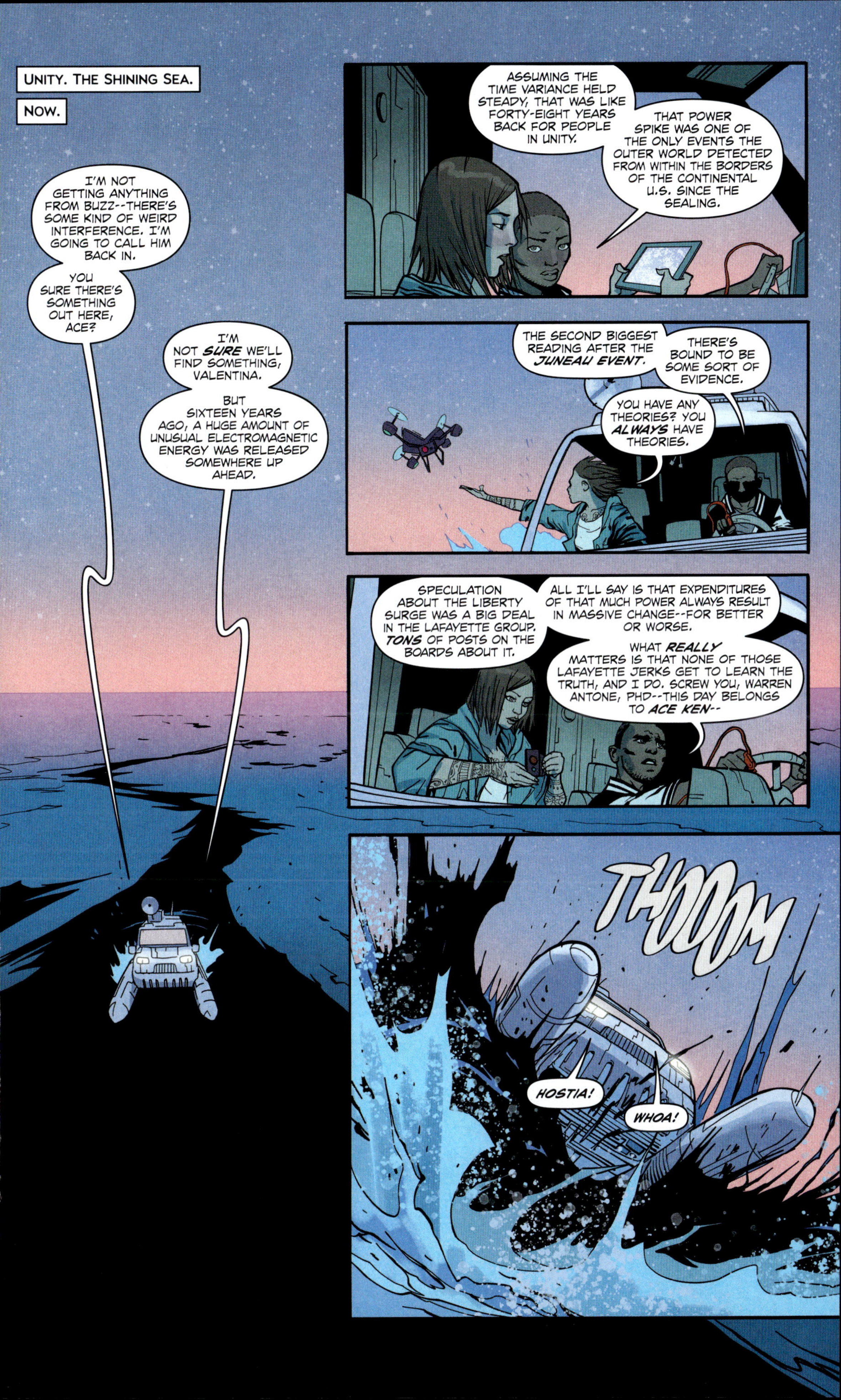
UNITY. THE SHINING SEA.
NOW.
I'M NOT GETTING ANYTHING FROM BUZZ--THERE'S SOME KIND OF WEIRD INTERFERENCE. I'M GOING TO CALL HIM BACK IN.
YOU SURE THERE'S SOMETHING OUT HERE, ACE?
I'M NOT SURE WE'LL FIND SOMETHING, VALENTINA.
BUT SIXTEEN YEARS AGO, A HUGE AMOUNT OF UNUSUAL ELECTROMAGNETIC ENERGY WAS RELEASED SOMEWHERE UP AHEAD.
ASSUMING THE TIME VARIANCE HELD STEADY, THAT WAS LIKE FORTY-EIGHT YEARS BACK FOR PEOPLE IN UNITY.
THAT POWER SPIKE WAS ONE OF THE ONLY EVENTS THE OUTER WORLD DETECTED FROM WITHIN THE BORDERS OF THE CONTINENTAL U.S. SINCE THE SEALING.
THE SECOND BIGGEST READING AFTER THE JUNEAU EVENT.
THERE'S BOUND TO BE SOME SORT OF EVIDENCE.
YOU HAVE ANY THEORIES? YOU ALWAYS HAVE THEORIES.
SPECULATION ABOUT THE LIBERTY SURGE WAS A BIG DEAL IN THE LAFAYETTE GROUP. TONS OF POSTS ON THE BOARDS ABOUT IT.
ALL I'LL SAY IS THAT EXPENDITURES OF THAT MUCH POWER ALWAYS RESULT IN MASSIVE CHANGE--FOR BETTER OR WORSE.
WHAT REALLY MATTERS IS THAT NONE OF THOSE LAFAYETTE JERKS GET TO LEARN THE TRUTH, AND I DO. SCREW YOU, WARREN ANTONE, PHD--THIS DAY BELONGS TO ACE KEN--
THOOOM
HOSTIA!
WHOA!

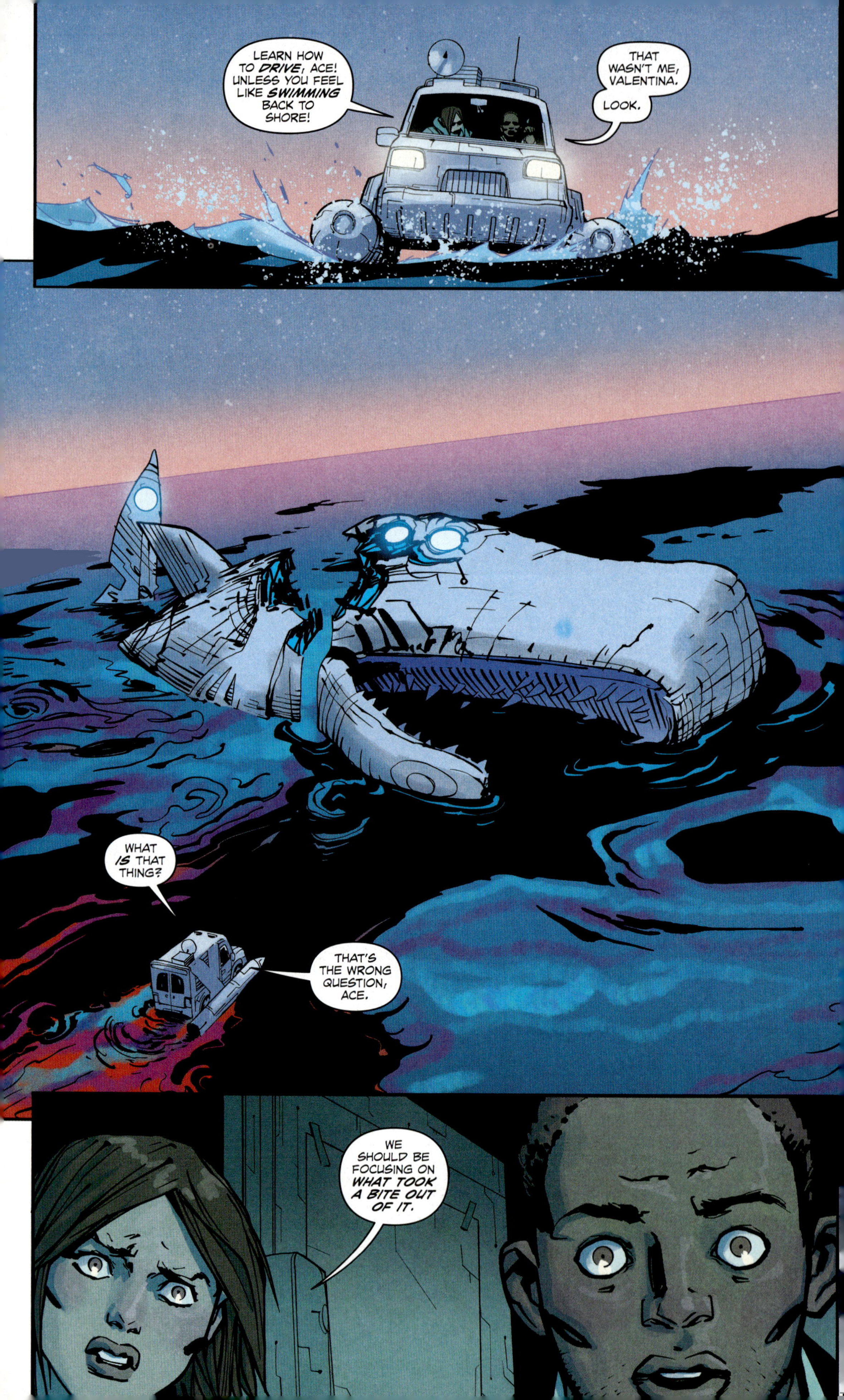
LEARN HOW TO *DRIVE*, ACE! UNLESS YOU FEEL LIKE *SWIMMING* BACK TO SHORE!
THAT WASN'T ME, VALENTINA.
LOOK.
WHAT *IS* THAT THING?
THAT'S THE WRONG QUESTION, ACE.
WE SHOULD BE FOCUSING ON *WHAT TOOK A BITE OUT OF IT*.

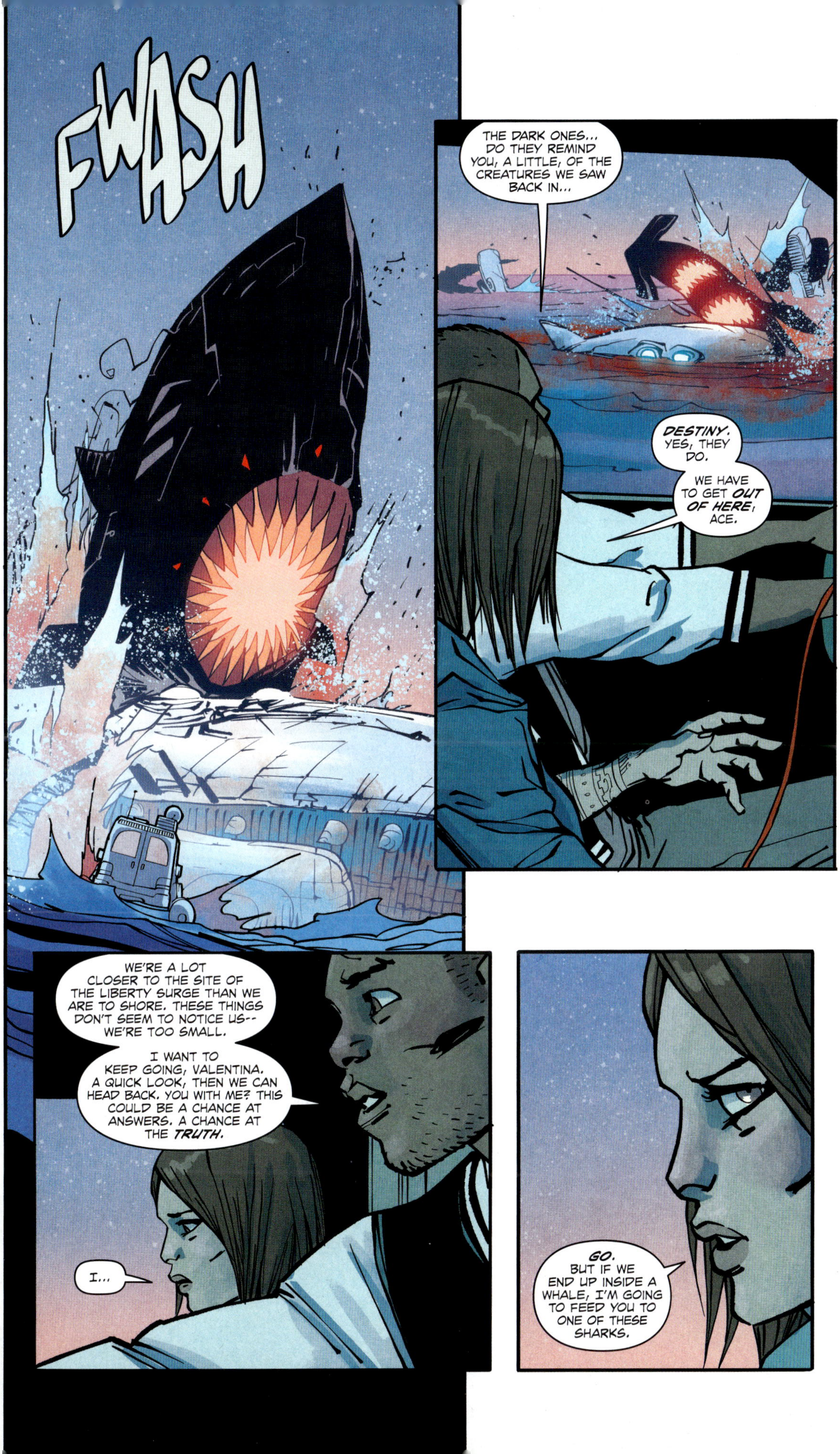
FWASH
THE DARK ONES... DO THEY REMIND YOU, A LITTLE, OF THE CREATURES WE SAW BACK IN...
DESTINY. YES, THEY DO.
WE HAVE TO GET OUT OF HERE, ACE.
WE'RE A LOT CLOSER TO THE SITE OF THE LIBERTY SURGE THAN WE ARE TO SHORE. THESE THINGS DON'T SEEM TO NOTICE US-- WE'RE TOO SMALL.
I WANT TO KEEP GOING, VALENTINA. A QUICK LOOK, THEN WE CAN HEAD BACK. YOU WITH ME? THIS COULD BE A CHANCE AT ANSWERS. A CHANCE AT THE TRUTH.
I...
GO. BUT IF WE END UP INSIDE A WHALE, I'M GOING TO FEED YOU TO ONE OF THESE SHARKS.

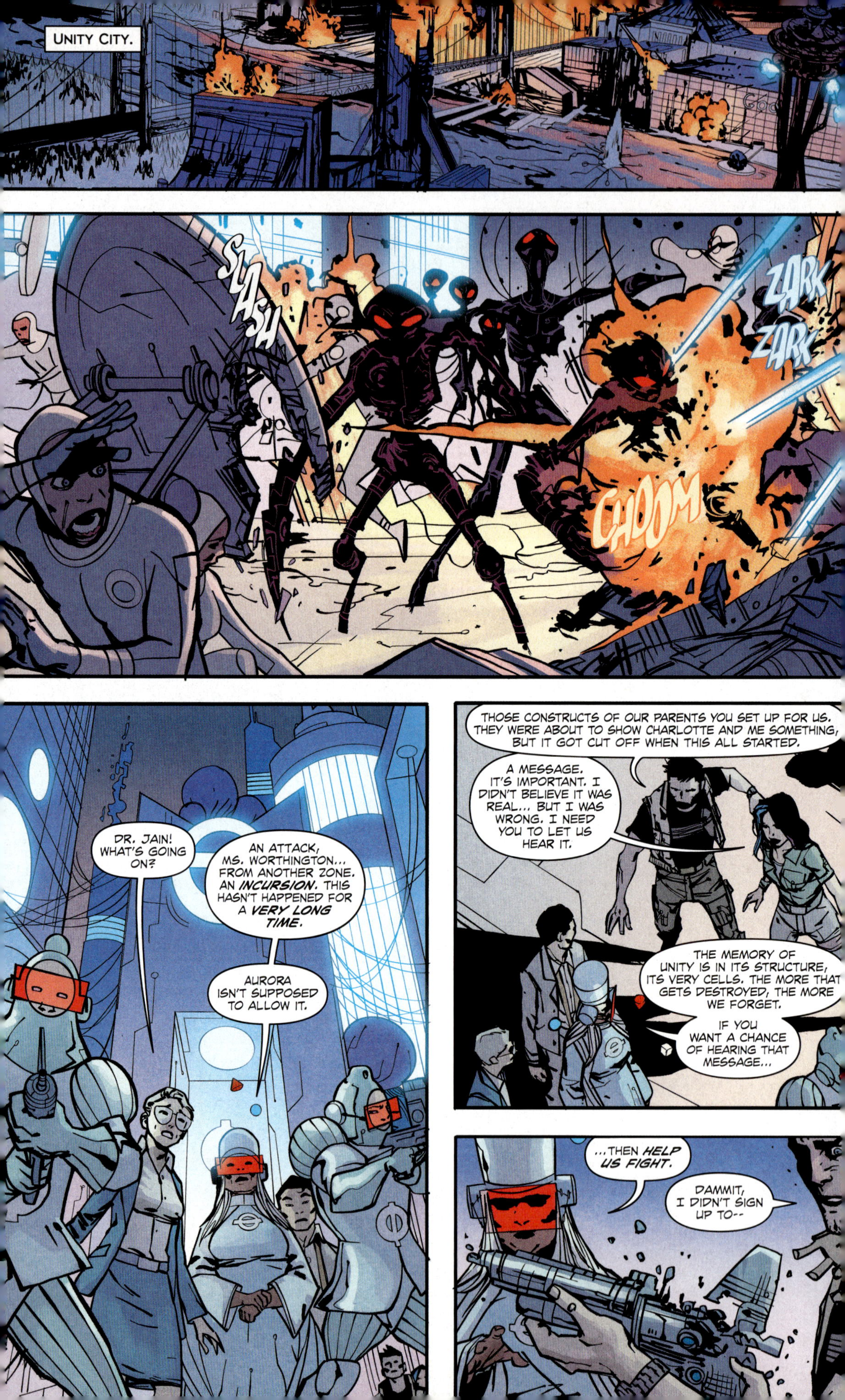
UNITY CITY.
SLASH
ZARK
ZARK
CHOOM
DR. JAIN! WHAT'S GOING ON?
AN ATTACK, MS. WORTHINGTON... FROM ANOTHER ZONE. AN *INCURSION*. THIS HASN'T HAPPENED FOR A *VERY LONG TIME*.
AURORA ISN'T SUPPOSED TO ALLOW IT.
THOSE CONSTRUCTS OF OUR PARENTS YOU SET UP FOR US. THEY WERE ABOUT TO SHOW CHARLOTTE AND ME SOMETHING, BUT IT GOT CUT OFF WHEN THIS ALL STARTED.
A MESSAGE. IT'S IMPORTANT. I DIDN'T BELIEVE IT WAS REAL... BUT I WAS WRONG. I NEED YOU TO LET US HEAR IT.
THE MEMORY OF UNITY IS IN ITS STRUCTURE, ITS VERY CELLS. THE MORE THAT GETS DESTROYED, THE MORE WE FORGET.
IF YOU WANT A CHANCE OF HEARING THAT MESSAGE...
...THEN *HELP US FIGHT*.
DAMMIT, I DIDN'T SIGN UP TO--

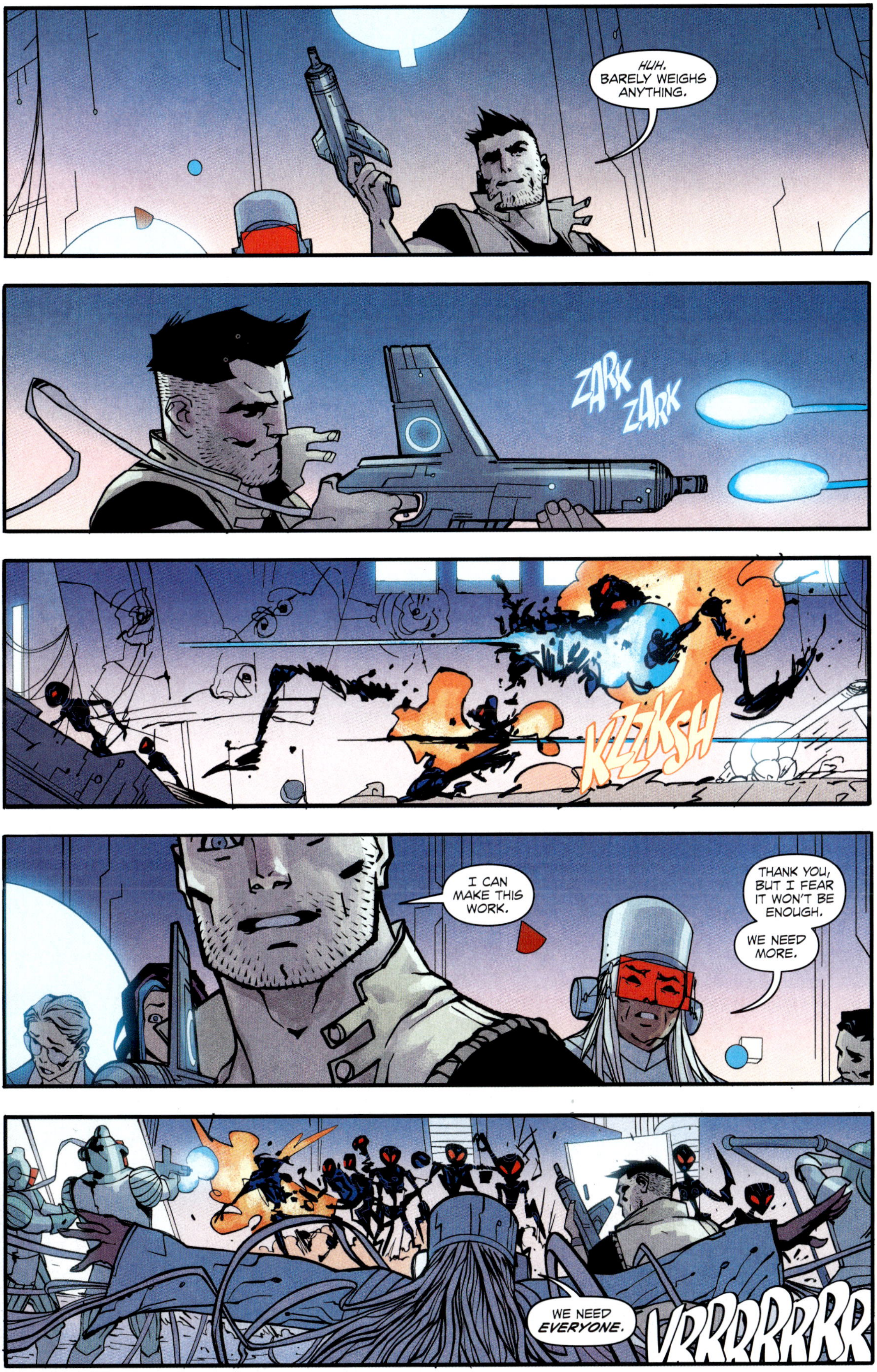
HUH. BARELY WEIGHS ANYTHING.
ZARK ZARK
KZZKSH
I CAN MAKE THIS WORK.
THANK YOU, BUT I FEAR IT WON'T BE ENOUGH.
WE NEED MORE.
WE NEED EVERYONE.
VRRRRRRRR

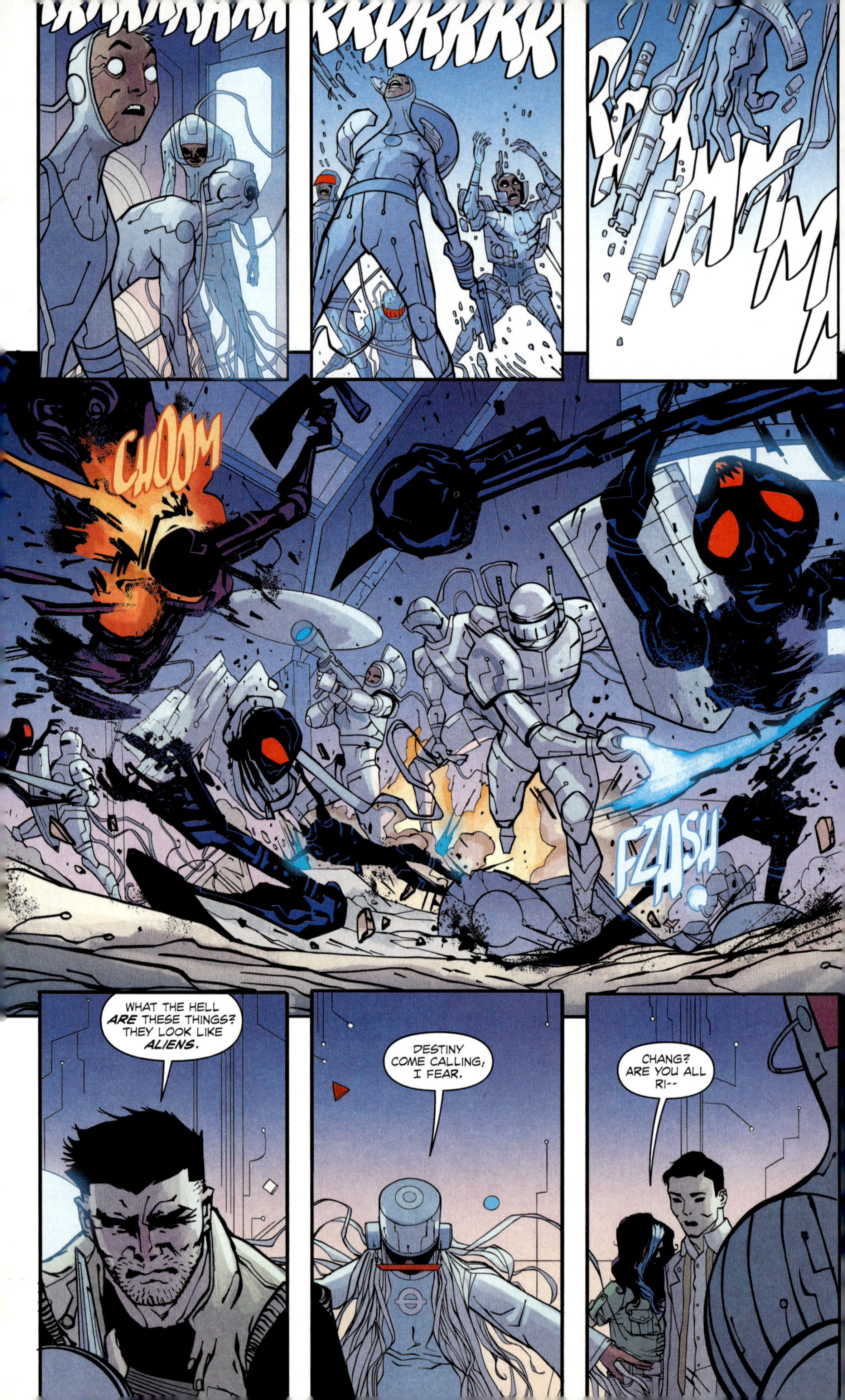
CHOOM
FZASH
WHAT THE HELL *ARE* THESE THINGS? THEY LOOK LIKE *ALIENS*.
DESTINY COME CALLING, I FEAR.
CHANG? ARE YOU ALL RI--

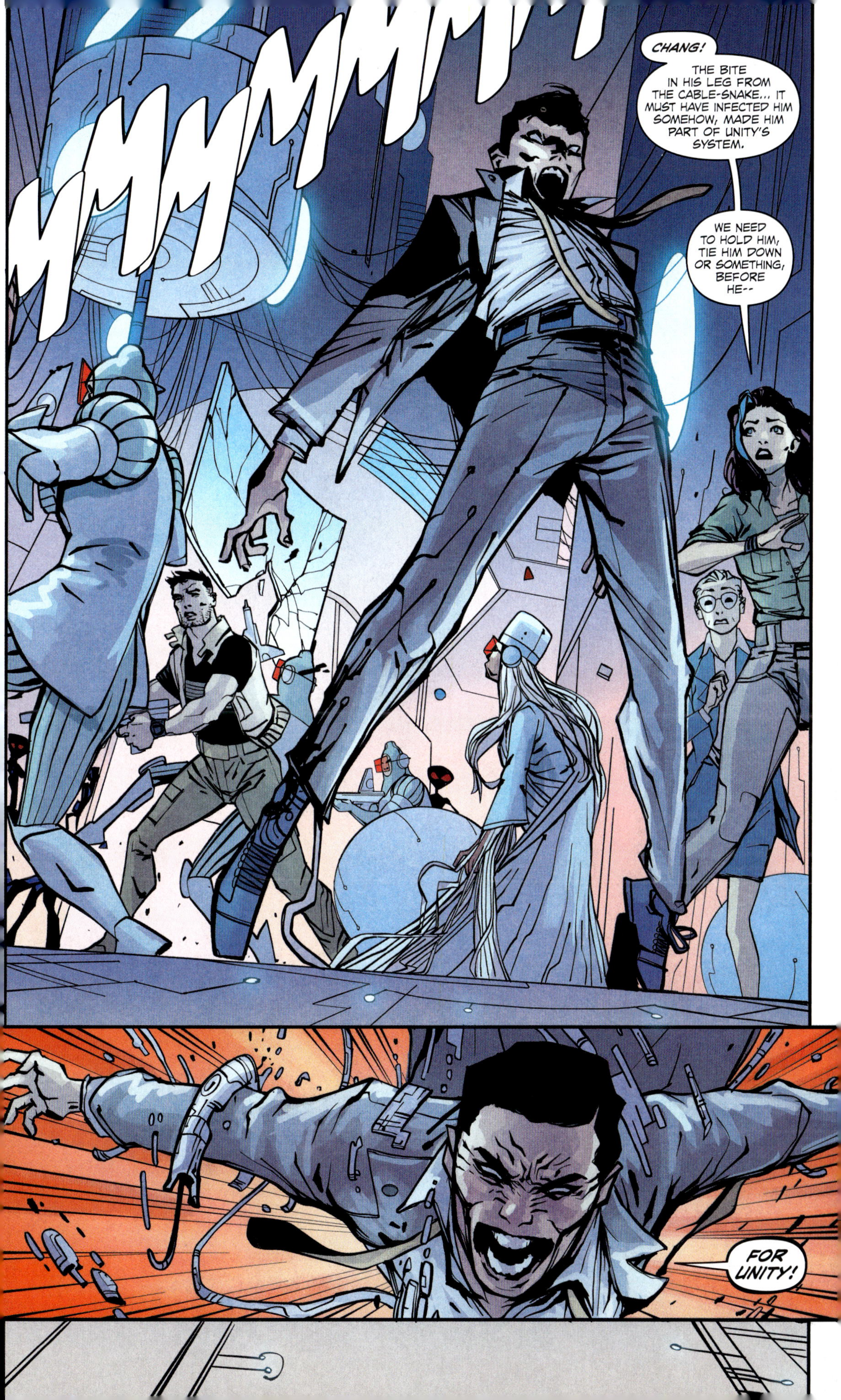
MMMMMMMMMM
CHANG!
THE BITE IN HIS LEG FROM THE CABLE-SNAKE... IT MUST HAVE INFECTED HIM SOMEHOW, MADE HIM PART OF UNITY'S SYSTEM.
WE NEED TO HOLD HIM, TIE HIM DOWN OR SOMETHING, BEFORE HE--
FOR UNITY!

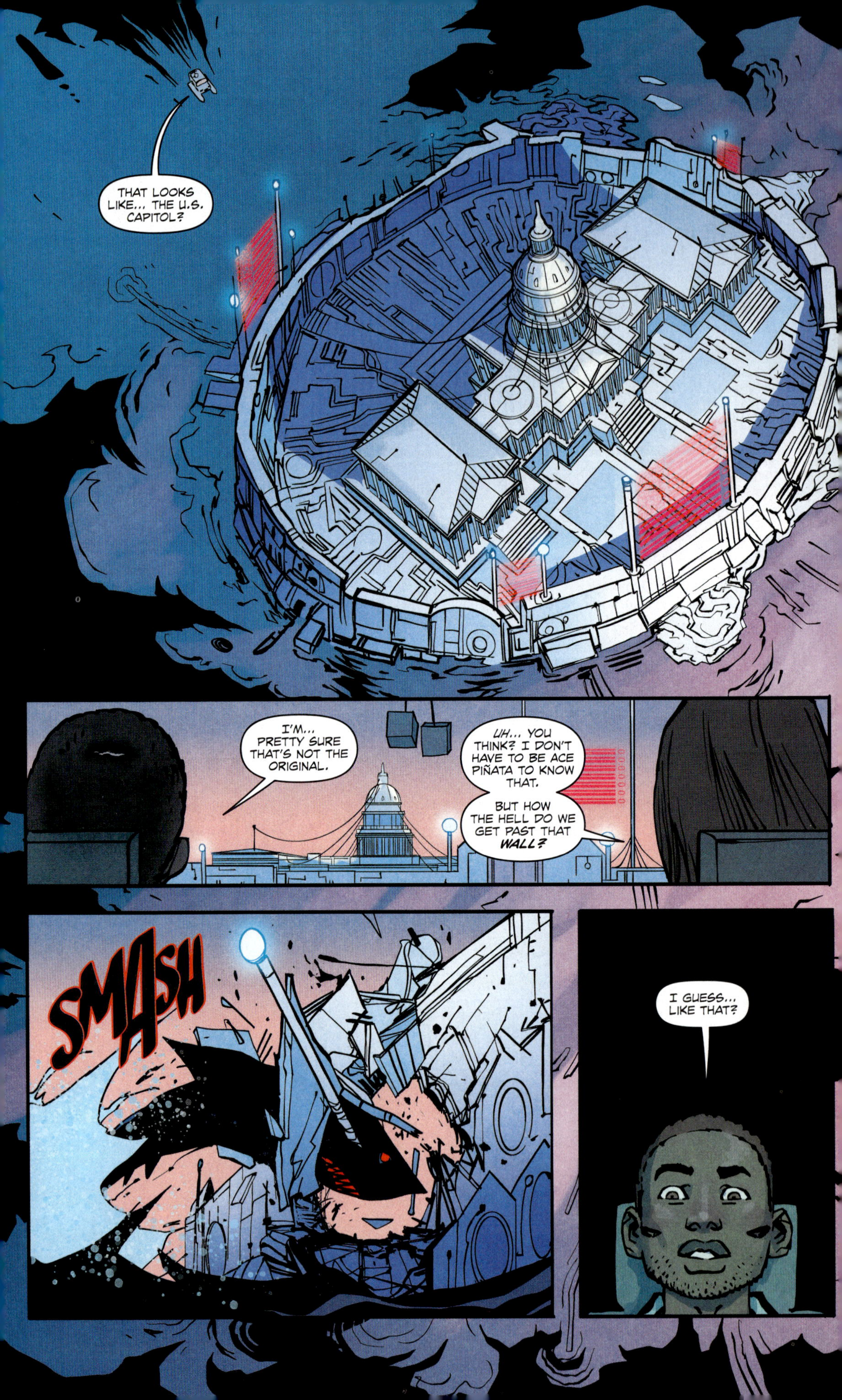

THAT LOOKS LIKE... THE U.S. CAPITOL?
I'M... PRETTY SURE THAT'S NOT THE ORIGINAL.
UH... YOU THINK? I DON'T HAVE TO BE ACE PIÑATA TO KNOW THAT.
BUT HOW THE HELL DO WE GET PAST THAT WALL?
SMASH
I GUESS... LIKE THAT?

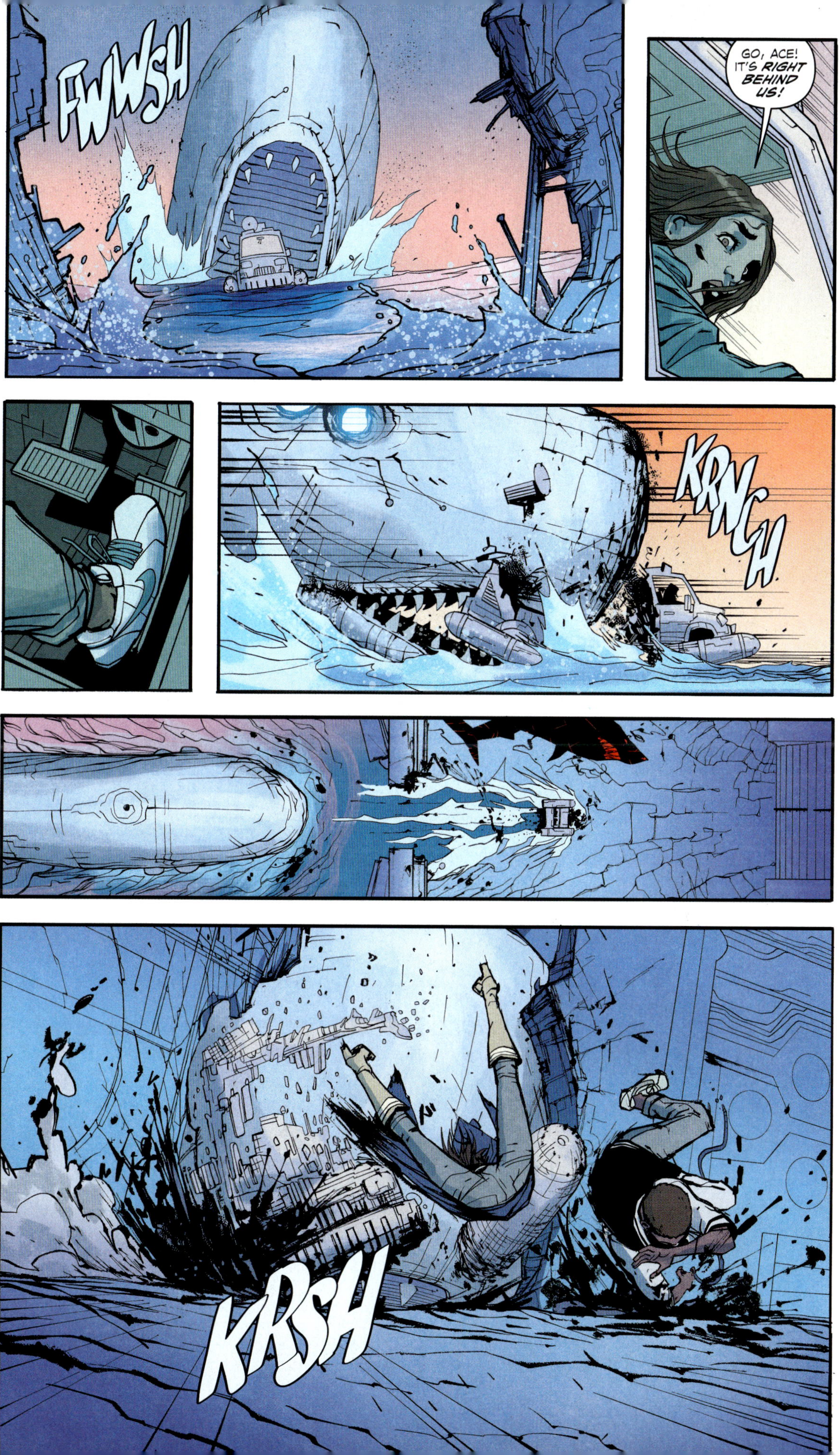

FWWSH
GO, ACE! IT'S RIGHT BEHIND US!
KRNCH
KRSH

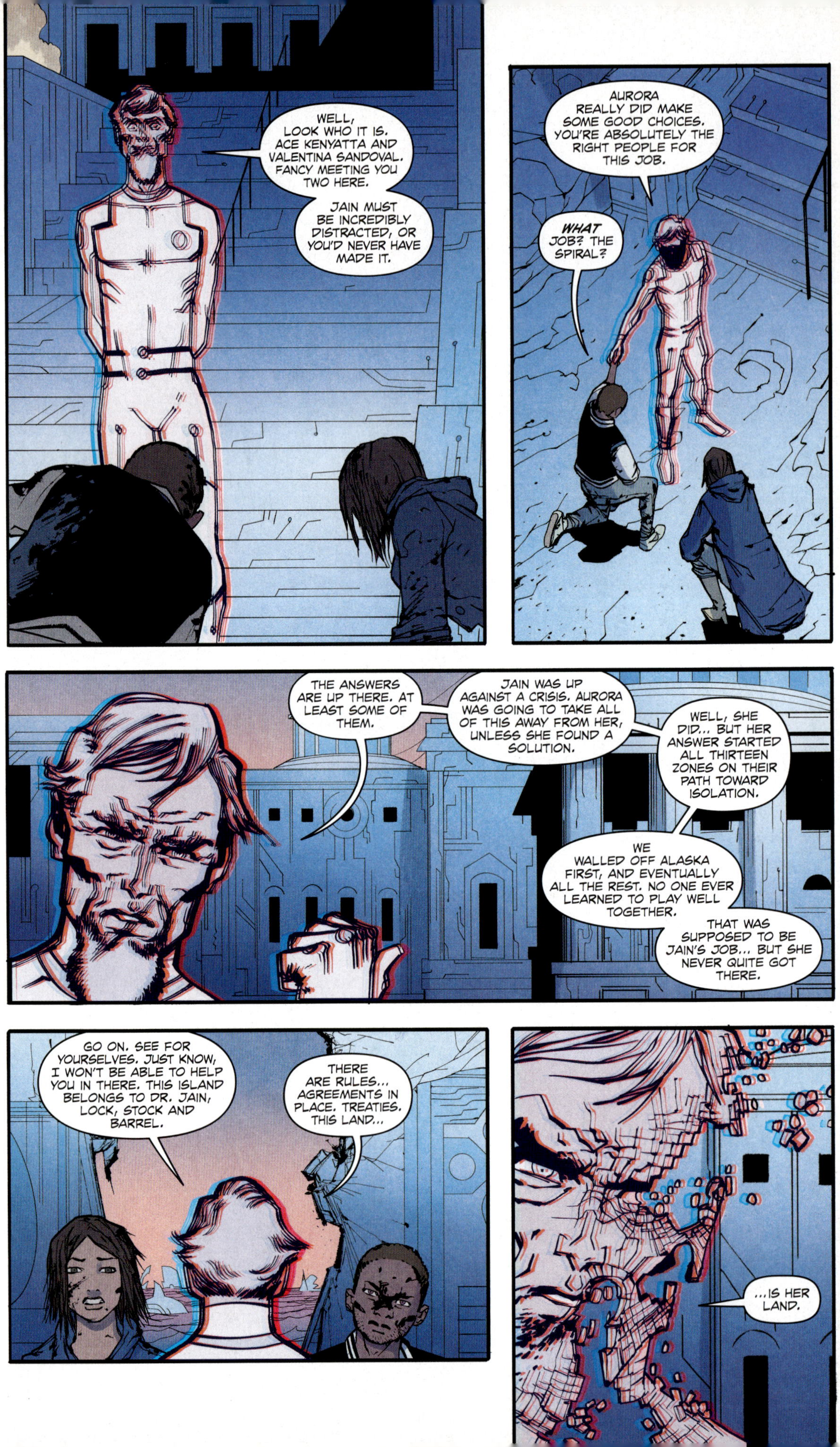
WELL, LOOK WHO IT IS. ACE KENYATTA AND VALENTINA SANDOVAL. FANCY MEETING YOU TWO HERE.
JAIN MUST BE INCREDIBLY DISTRACTED, OR YOU'D NEVER HAVE MADE IT.
AURORA REALLY DID MAKE SOME GOOD CHOICES. YOU'RE ABSOLUTELY THE RIGHT PEOPLE FOR THIS JOB.
WHAT JOB? THE SPIRAL?
THE ANSWERS ARE UP THERE. AT LEAST SOME OF THEM.
JAIN WAS UP AGAINST A CRISIS. AURORA WAS GOING TO TAKE ALL OF THIS AWAY FROM HER, UNLESS SHE FOUND A SOLUTION.
WELL, SHE DID... BUT HER ANSWER STARTED ALL THIRTEEN ZONES ON THEIR PATH TOWARD ISOLATION.
WE WALLED OFF ALASKA FIRST, AND EVENTUALLY ALL THE REST. NO ONE EVER LEARNED TO PLAY WELL TOGETHER.
THAT WAS SUPPOSED TO BE JAIN'S JOB... BUT SHE NEVER QUITE GOT THERE.
GO ON. SEE FOR YOURSELVES. JUST KNOW, I WON'T BE ABLE TO HELP YOU IN THERE. THIS ISLAND BELONGS TO DR. JAIN, LOCK, STOCK AND BARREL.
THERE ARE RULES... AGREEMENTS IN PLACE. TREATIES. THIS LAND...
...IS HER LAND.

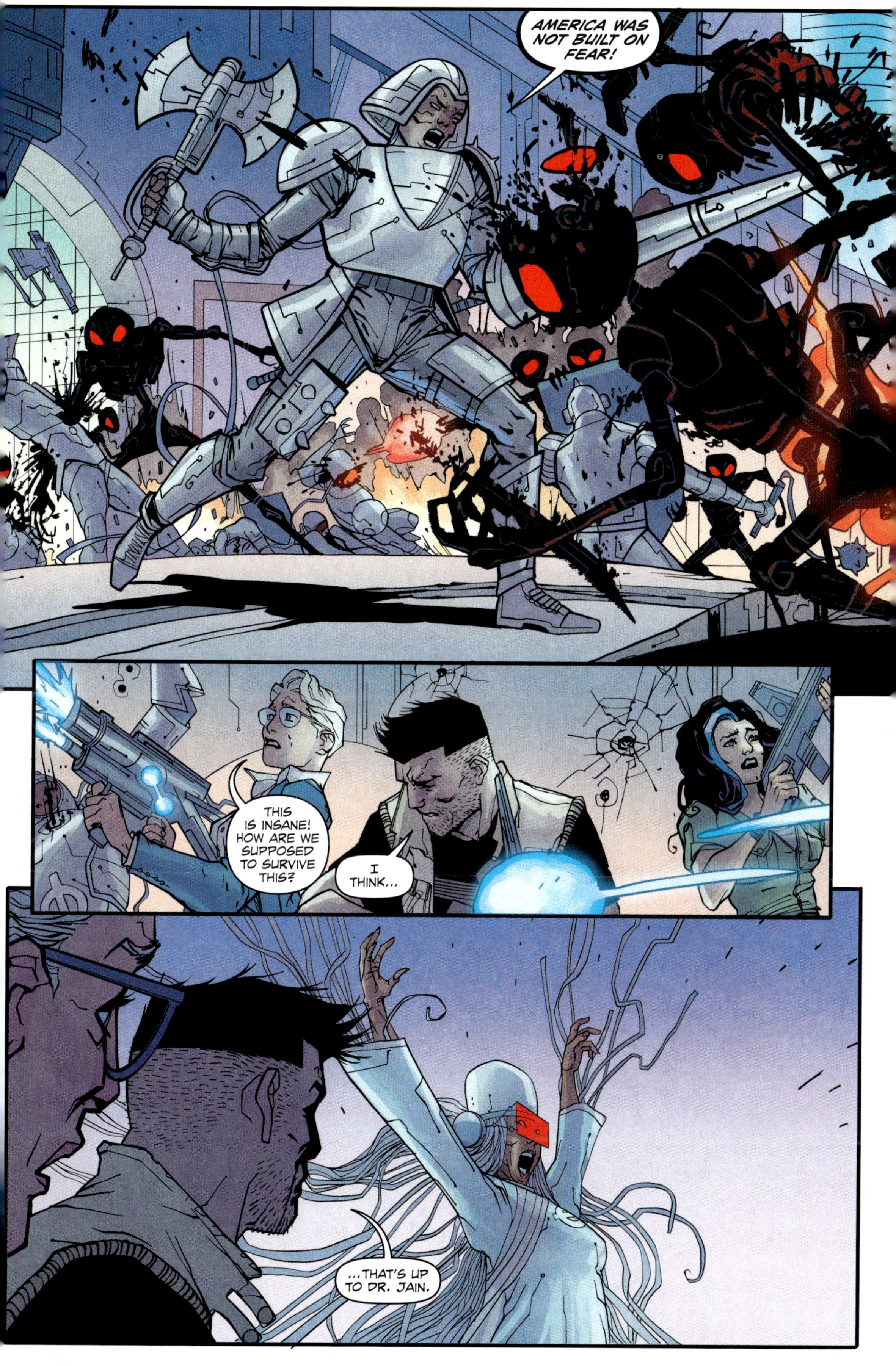
AMERICA WAS NOT BUILT ON FEAR!
THIS IS INSANE! HOW ARE WE SUPPOSED TO SURVIVE THIS?
I THINK...
...THAT'S UP TO DR. JAIN.

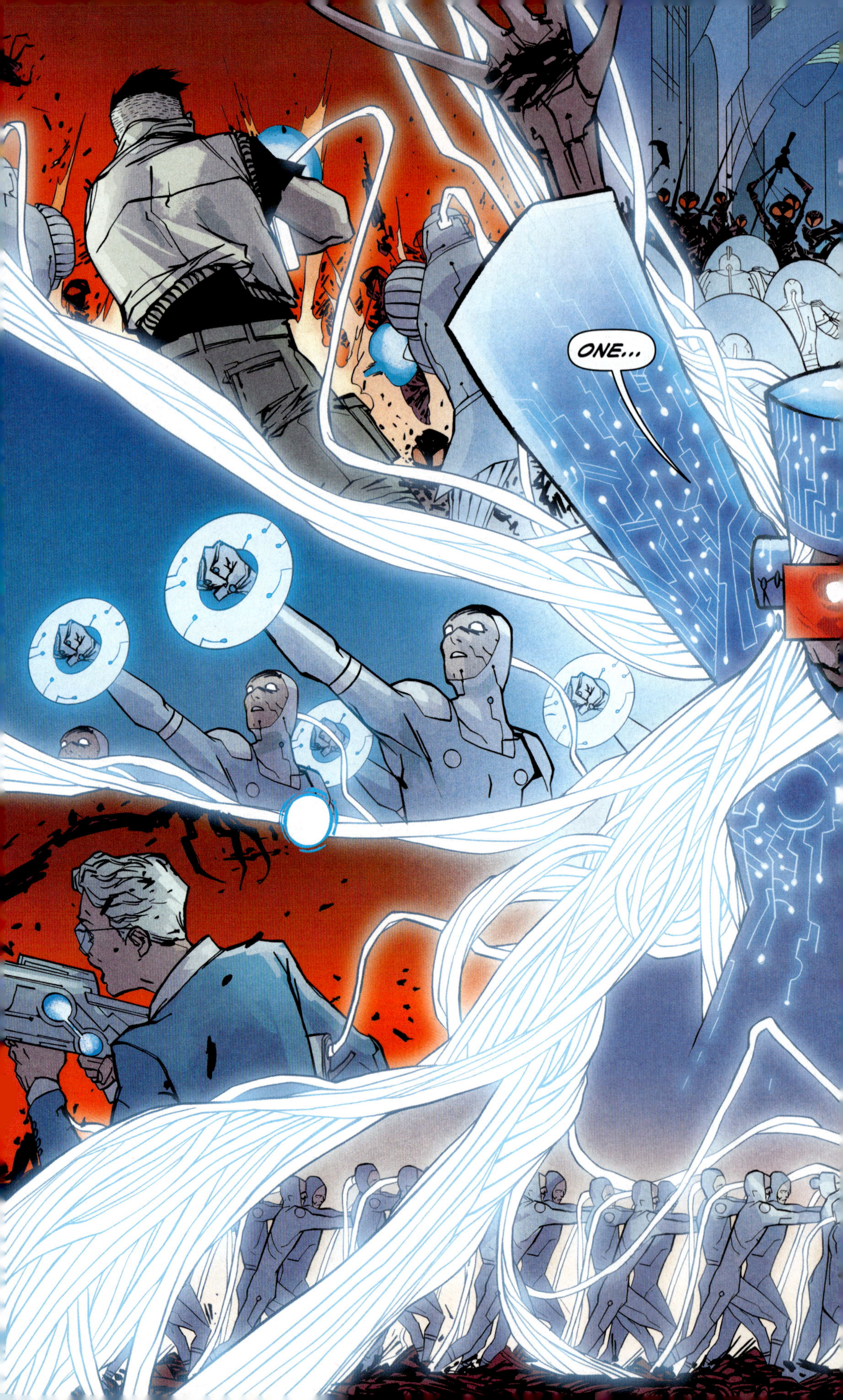
ONE...

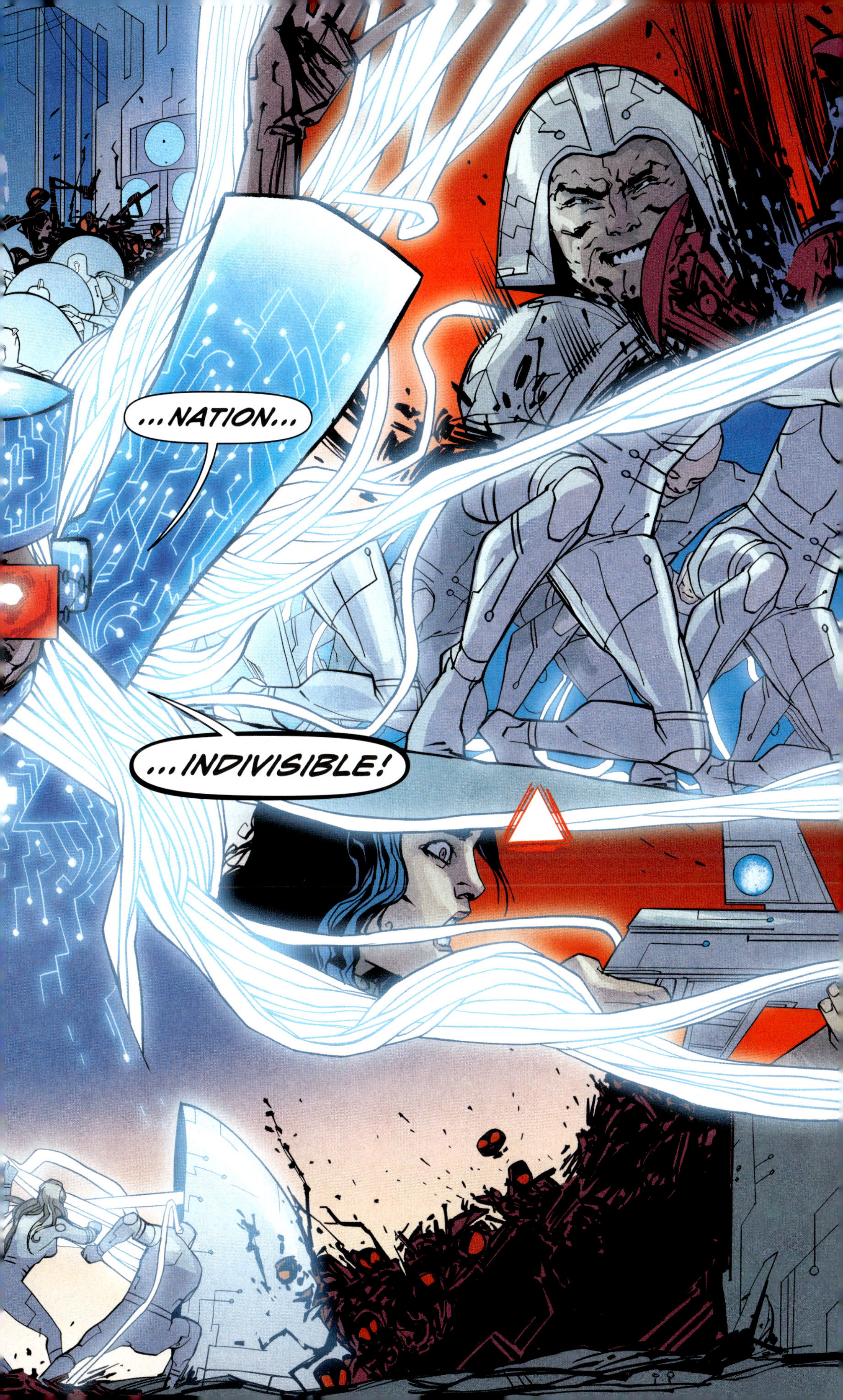
...NATION...
...INDIVISIBLE!

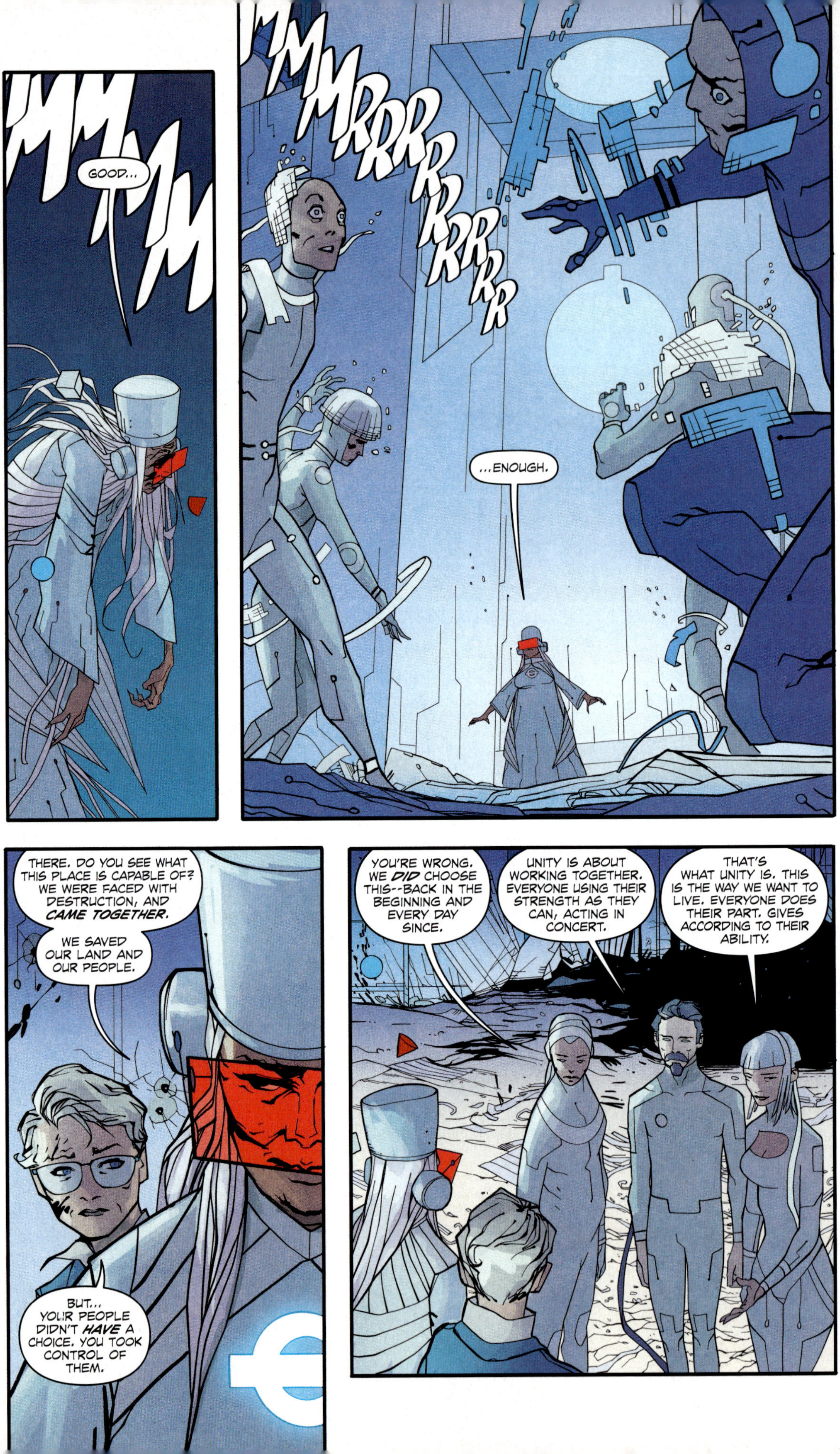
MMMMM
GOOD...
MMMRRRRRRRRRRRR
...ENOUGH.
THERE. DO YOU SEE WHAT THIS PLACE IS CAPABLE OF? WE WERE FACED WITH DESTRUCTION, AND *CAME TOGETHER.*
WE SAVED OUR LAND AND OUR PEOPLE.
BUT... YOUR PEOPLE DIDN'T *HAVE* A CHOICE. YOU TOOK CONTROL OF THEM.
YOU'RE WRONG. WE *DID* CHOOSE THIS--BACK IN THE BEGINNING AND EVERY DAY SINCE.
UNITY IS ABOUT WORKING TOGETHER. EVERYONE USING THEIR STRENGTH AS THEY CAN, ACTING IN CONCERT.
THAT'S WHAT UNITY IS. THIS IS THE WAY WE WANT TO LIVE. EVERYONE DOES THEIR PART. GIVES ACCORDING TO THEIR ABILITY.

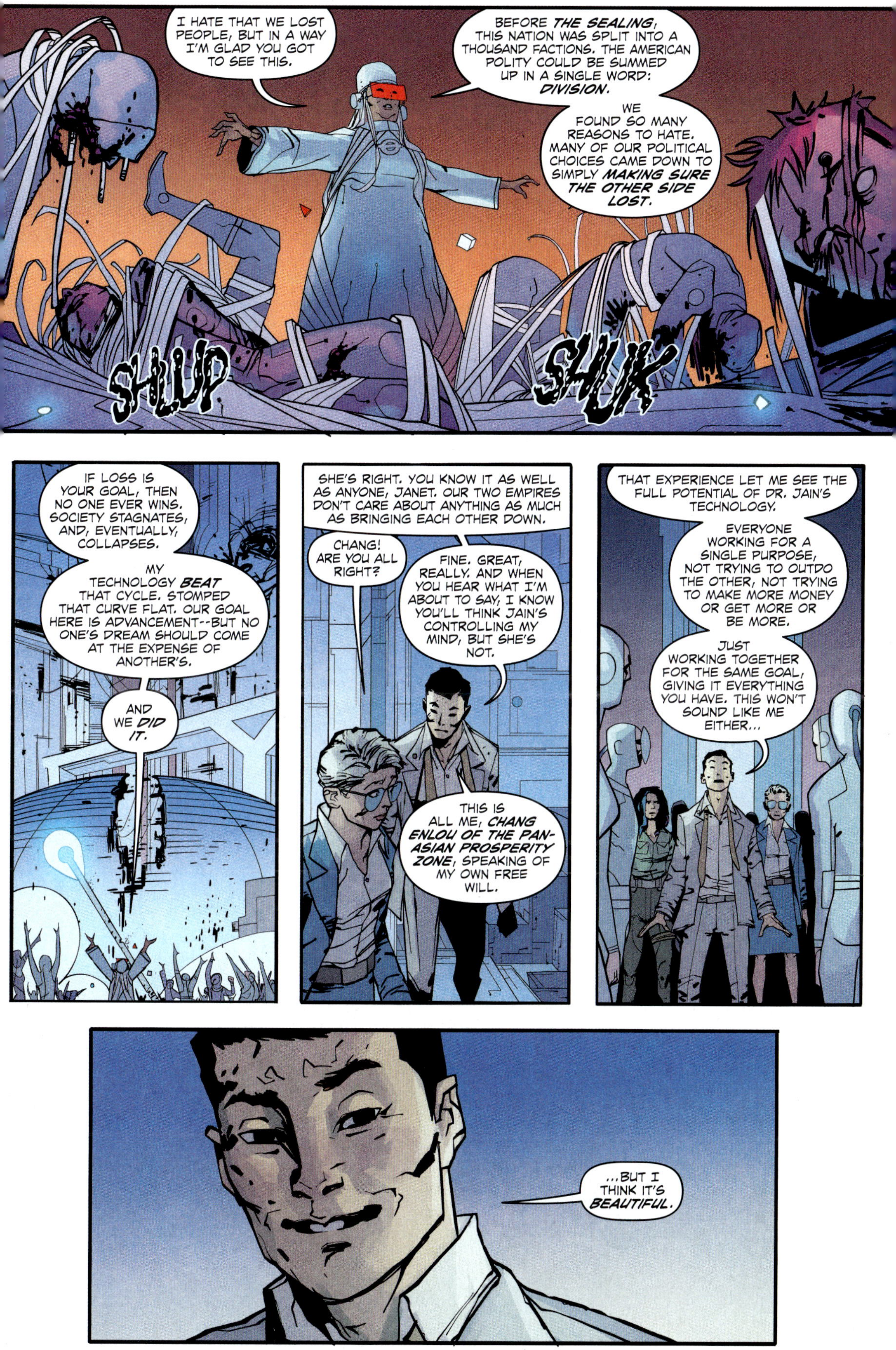
I HATE THAT WE LOST PEOPLE, BUT IN A WAY I'M GLAD YOU GOT TO SEE THIS.
BEFORE *THE SEALING*, THIS NATION WAS SPLIT INTO A THOUSAND FACTIONS. THE AMERICAN POLITY COULD BE SUMMED UP IN A SINGLE WORD: *DIVISION*.
WE FOUND SO MANY REASONS TO HATE. MANY OF OUR POLITICAL CHOICES CAME DOWN TO SIMPLY *MAKING SURE THE OTHER SIDE LOST*.
SHLUP
SHLK
IF LOSS IS YOUR GOAL, THEN NO ONE EVER WINS. SOCIETY STAGNATES, AND, EVENTUALLY, COLLAPSES.
MY TECHNOLOGY *BEAT* THAT CYCLE. STOMPED THAT CURVE FLAT. OUR GOAL HERE IS ADVANCEMENT--BUT NO ONE'S DREAM SHOULD COME AT THE EXPENSE OF ANOTHER'S.
AND WE *DID IT*.
SHE'S RIGHT. YOU KNOW IT AS WELL AS ANYONE, JANET. OUR TWO EMPIRES DON'T CARE ABOUT ANYTHING AS MUCH AS BRINGING EACH OTHER DOWN.
CHANG! ARE YOU ALL RIGHT?
FINE. GREAT, REALLY. AND WHEN YOU HEAR WHAT I'M ABOUT TO SAY, I KNOW YOU'LL THINK JAIN'S CONTROLLING MY MIND, BUT SHE'S NOT.
THIS IS ALL ME, *CHANG ENLOU OF THE PAN-ASIAN PROSPERITY ZONE*, SPEAKING OF MY OWN FREE WILL.
THAT EXPERIENCE LET ME SEE THE FULL POTENTIAL OF DR. JAIN'S TECHNOLOGY.
EVERYONE WORKING FOR A SINGLE PURPOSE, NOT TRYING TO OUTDO THE OTHER, NOT TRYING TO MAKE MORE MONEY OR GET MORE OR BE MORE.
JUST WORKING TOGETHER FOR THE SAME GOAL, GIVING IT EVERYTHING YOU HAVE. THIS WON'T SOUND LIKE ME EITHER...
...BUT I THINK IT'S *BEAUTIFUL*.

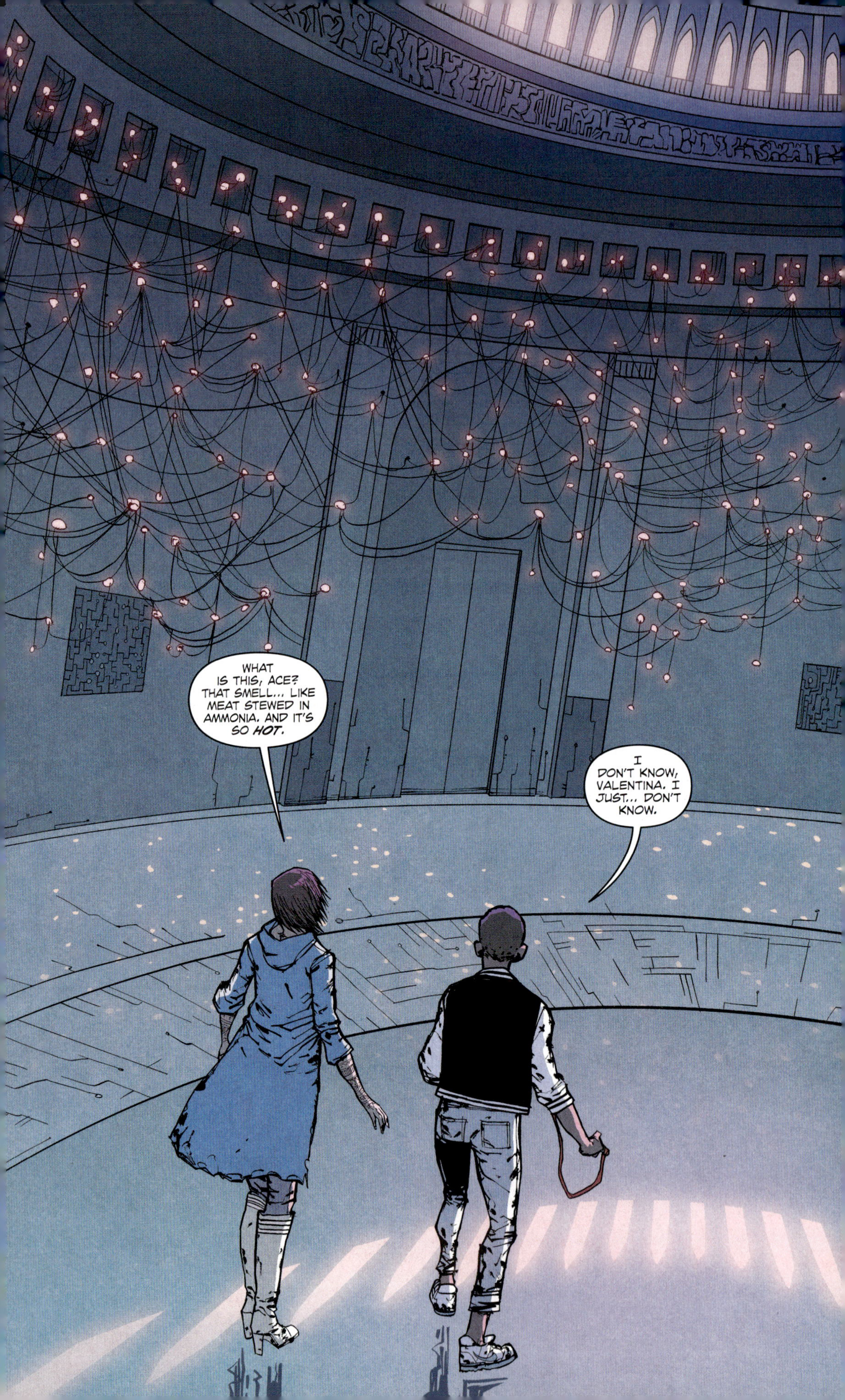
WHAT IS THIS, ACE? THAT SMELL... LIKE MEAT STEWED IN AMMONIA. AND IT'S SO HOT.
I DON'T KNOW, VALENTINA. I JUST... DON'T KNOW.

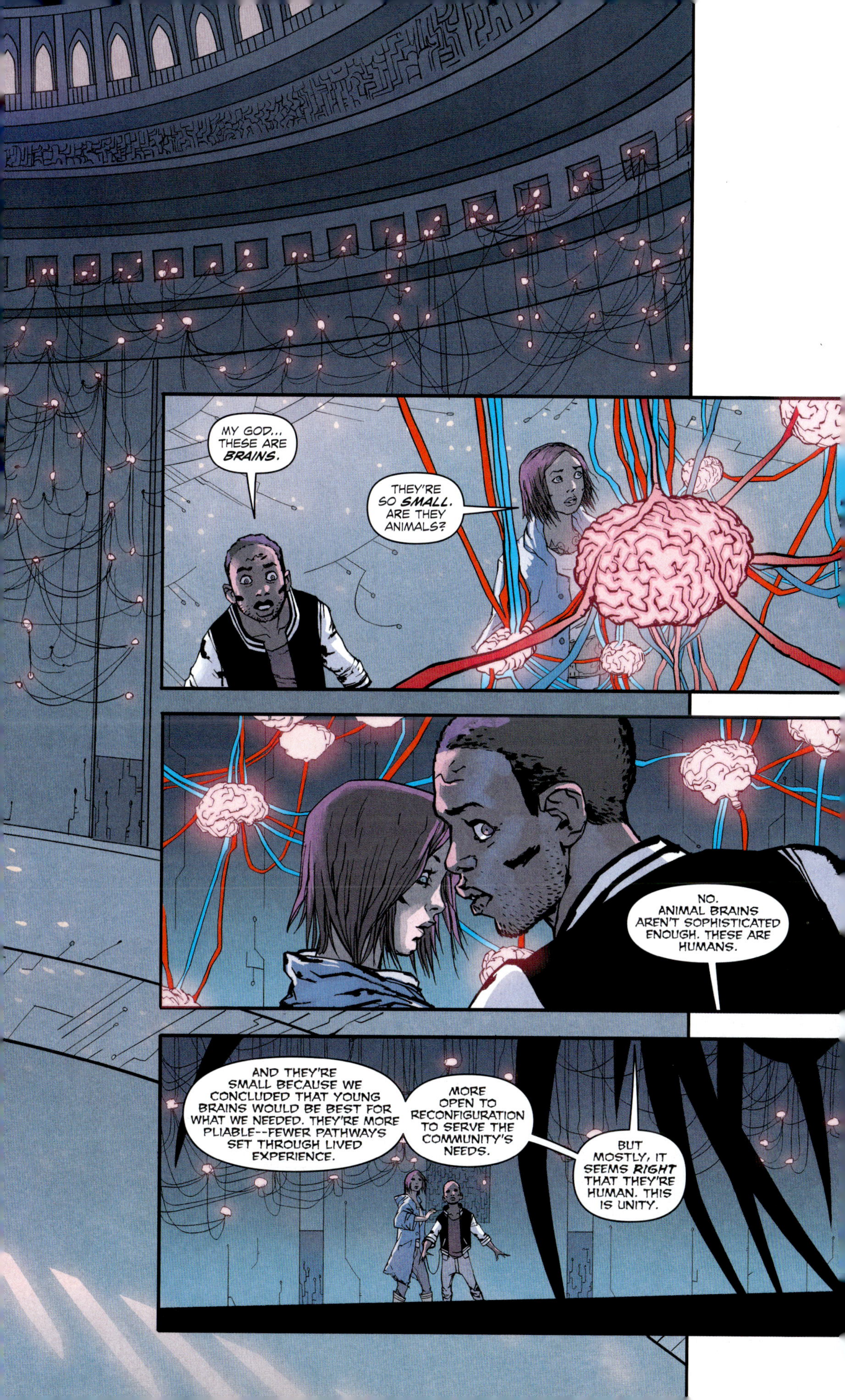
MY GOD... THESE ARE BRAINS.
THEY'RE SO SMALL. ARE THEY ANIMALS?
NO. ANIMAL BRAINS AREN'T SOPHISTICATED ENOUGH. THESE ARE HUMANS.
AND THEY'RE SMALL BECAUSE WE CONCLUDED THAT YOUNG BRAINS WOULD BE BEST FOR WHAT WE NEEDED. THEY'RE MORE PLIABLE--FEWER PATHWAYS SET THROUGH LIVED EXPERIENCE.
MORE OPEN TO RECONFIGURATION TO SERVE THE COMMUNITY'S NEEDS.
BUT MOSTLY, IT SEEMS RIGHT THAT THEY'RE HUMAN. THIS IS UNITY.

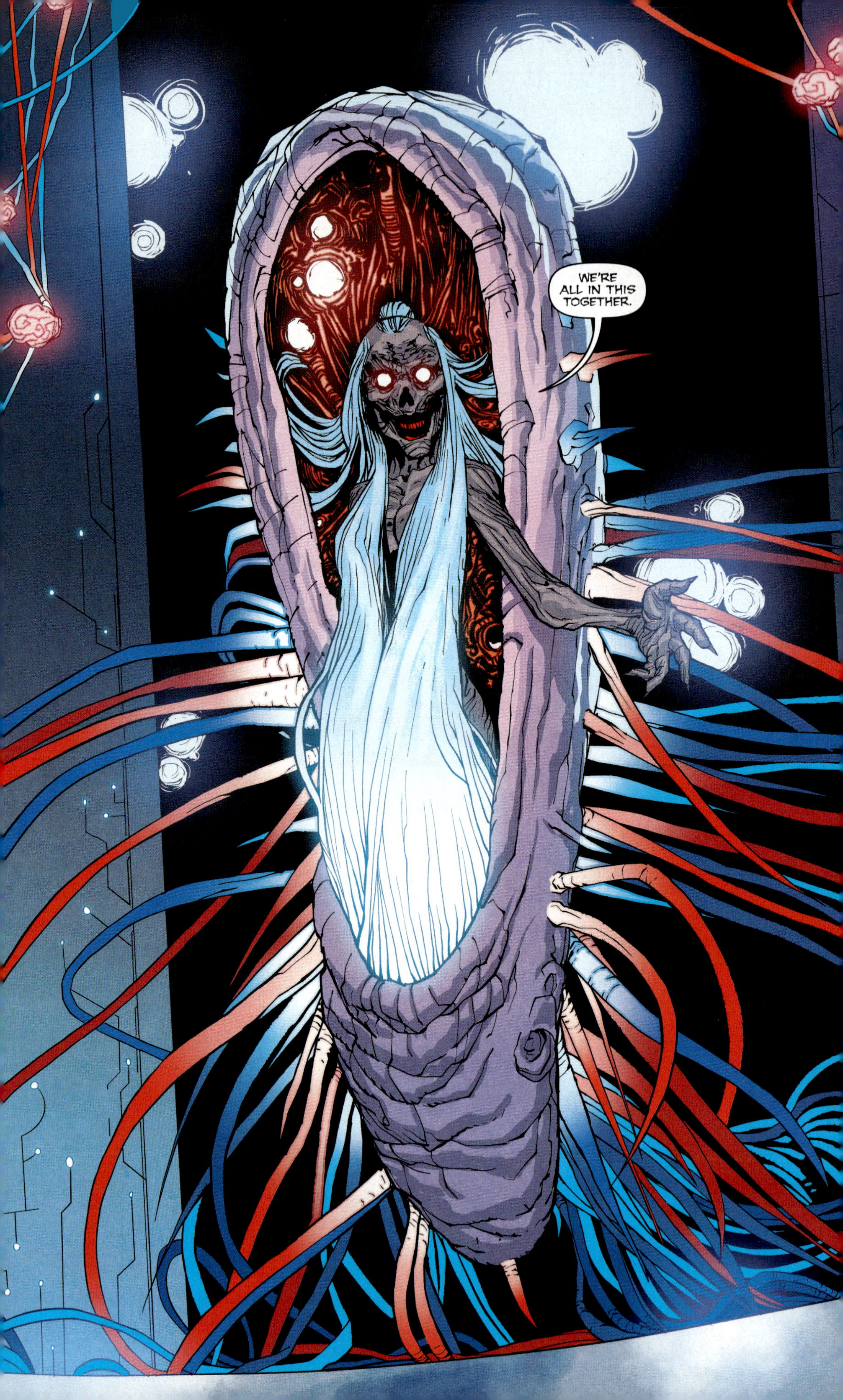
WE'RE ALL IN THIS TOGETHER.

DRONET

"The Liberty Surge, the Liberty Surge, my oh my what could it be?

Massive, MASSIVE power spike out of the Pacific Northwest. Must have been off the charts for us to register it here in the Outer Empires. Normally, we don't get a peep of any kind of signal from inside the US borders, with all that weird EM shielding they put up. If we saw it, it must have been more power used in a single moment than most countries use in a year.

That's weird enough, but even worse was that no one had ever seen the particular strata of the radiation spectrum occupied by this Liberty Surge. Scientists had no idea what the source could be. Not in the AEA, not in the PAPZ, and sure as hell not in the Lafayette Group. No one knew.

But I do. Your boy Piñata. I did some digging, found some records out of MK-ULTRA, the old CIA project designed to identify and boost psychic phenomena in human subjects. Buried in an archive, I tracked down some readings from a round of experiments where the spooks were trying to link human minds together. It failed, and a bunch of people died, but before they did, the instruments recorded an energy signature not so different from the Liberty Surge.

So what am I saying, friends? Brains, baby. The Liberty Surge was brains."

—**Posted by Ace Piñata on the 'America Unsealed' Dronet, August 7, 2057**

CHAPTER ELEVEN

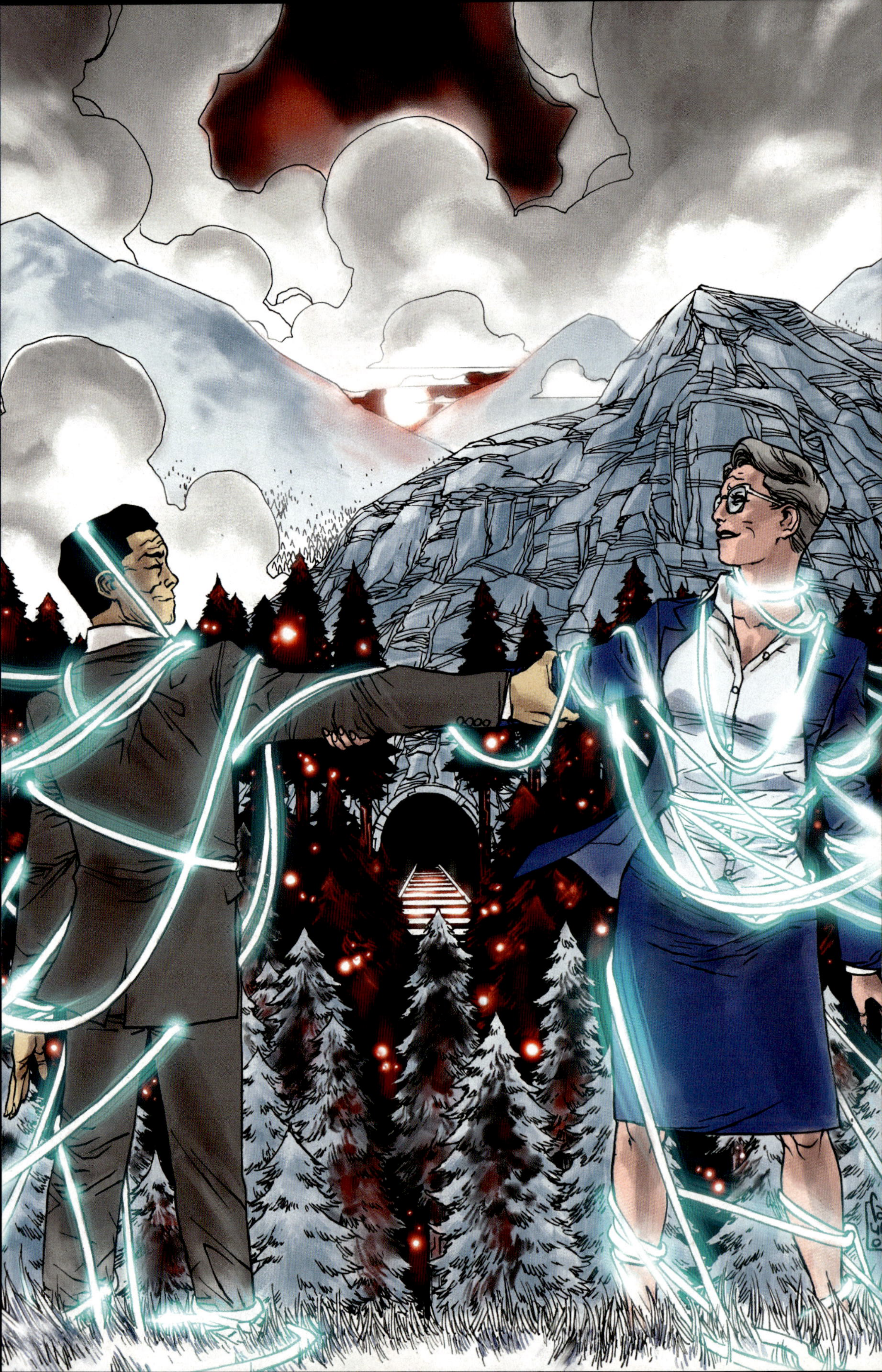

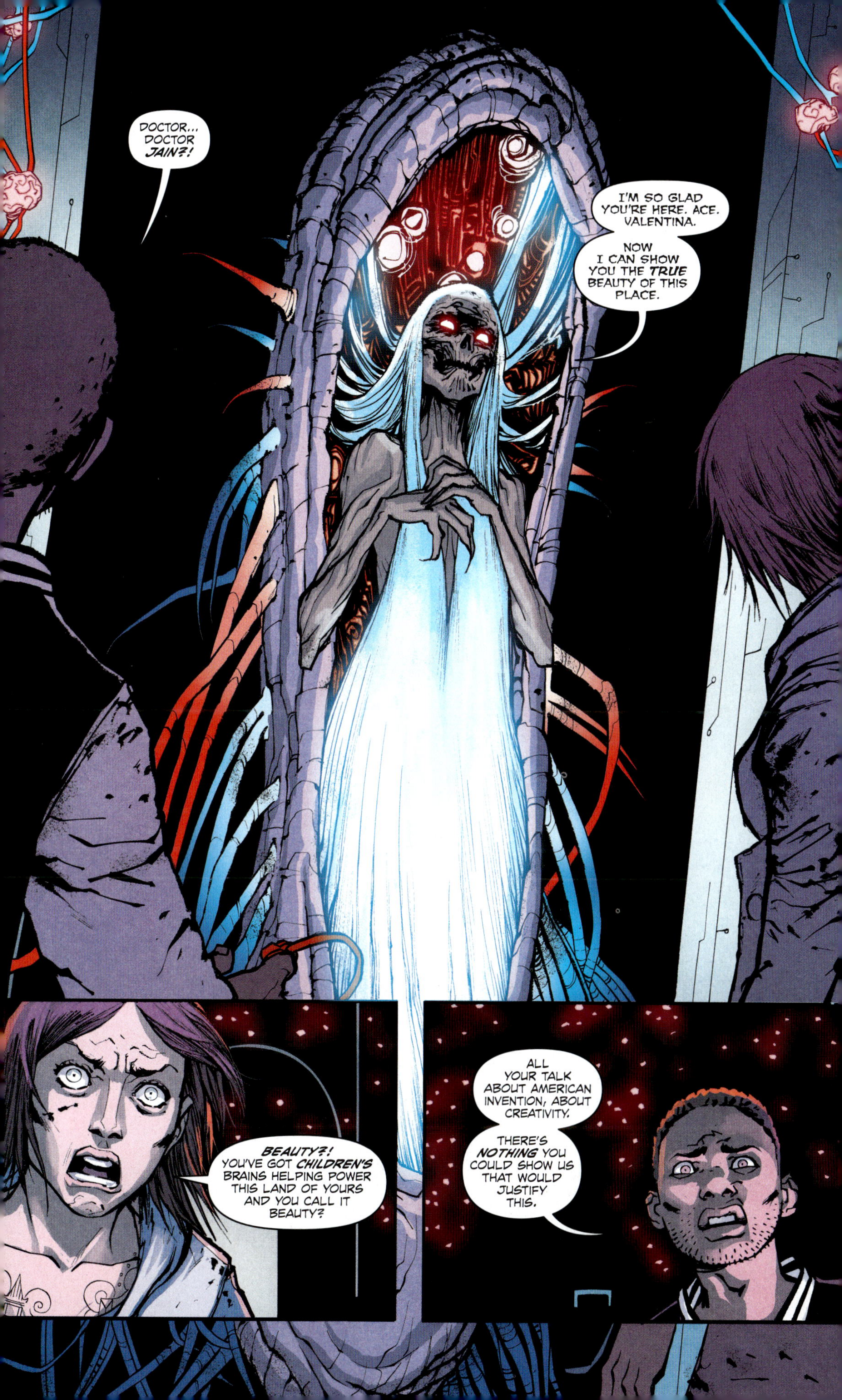
DOCTOR... DOCTOR JAIN?!
I'M SO GLAD YOU'RE HERE. ACE. VALENTINA.
NOW I CAN SHOW YOU THE TRUE BEAUTY OF THIS PLACE.
BEAUTY?! YOU'VE GOT CHILDREN'S BRAINS HELPING POWER THIS LAND OF YOURS AND YOU CALL IT BEAUTY?
ALL YOUR TALK ABOUT AMERICAN INVENTION, ABOUT CREATIVITY.
THERE'S NOTHING YOU COULD SHOW US THAT WOULD JUSTIFY THIS.

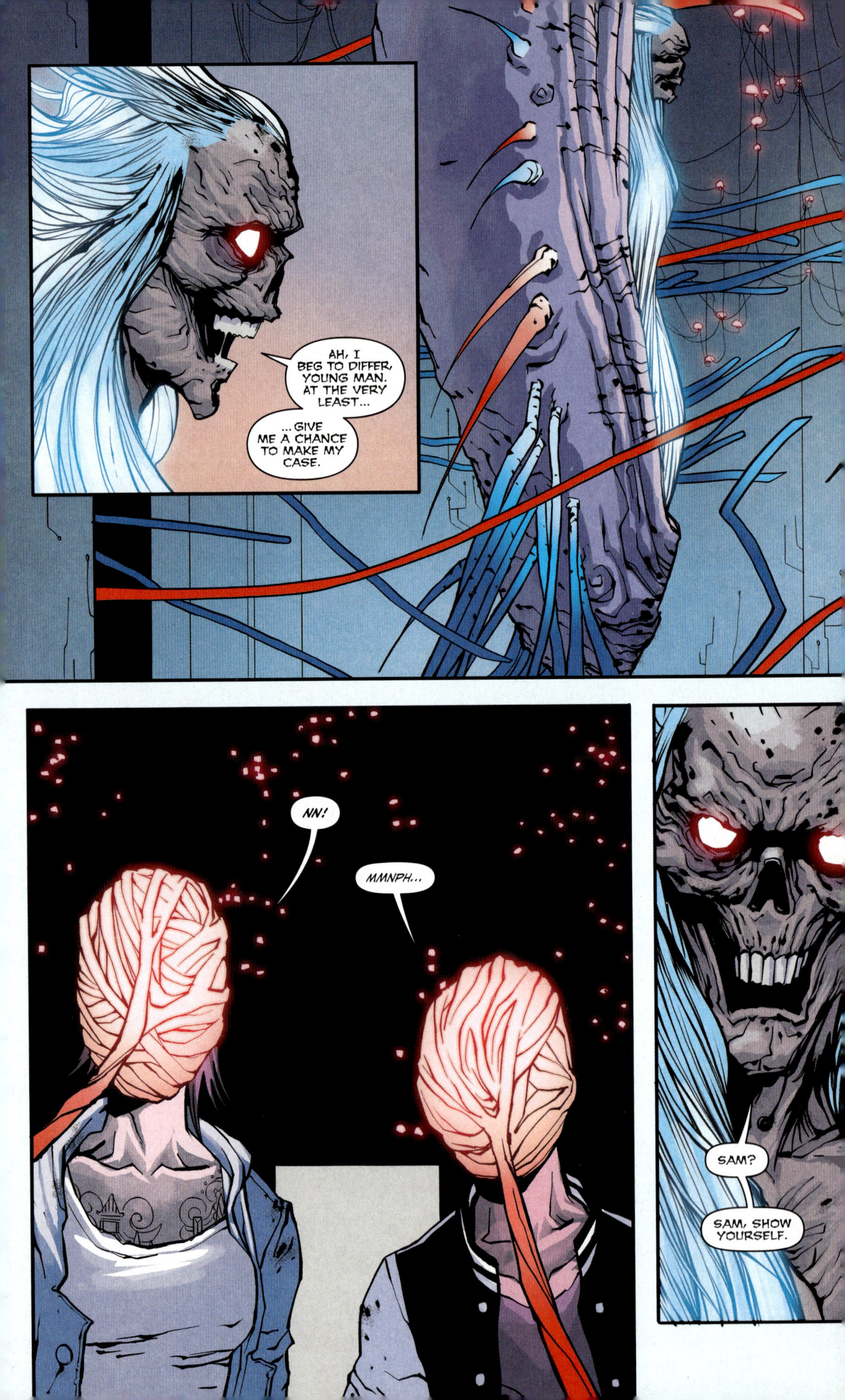
AH, I BEG TO DIFFER, YOUNG MAN. AT THE VERY LEAST...
...GIVE ME A CHANCE TO MAKE MY CASE.
NN!
MMNPH...
SAM?
SAM, SHOW YOURSELF.

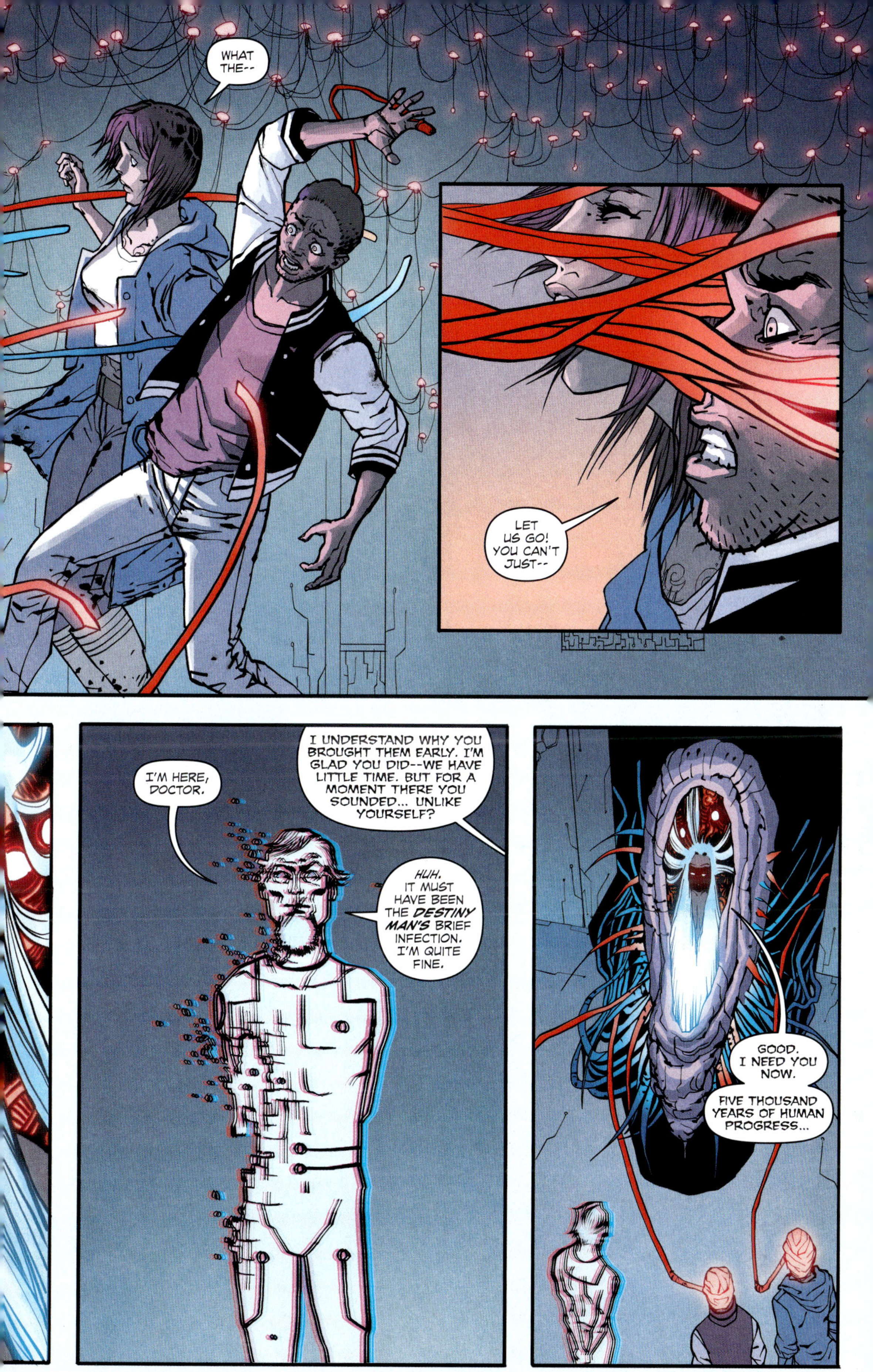
WHAT THE--
LET US GO! YOU CAN'T JUST--
I'M HERE, DOCTOR.
I UNDERSTAND WHY YOU BROUGHT THEM EARLY. I'M GLAD YOU DID--WE HAVE LITTLE TIME. BUT FOR A MOMENT THERE YOU SOUNDED... UNLIKE YOURSELF?
HUH. IT MUST HAVE BEEN THE DESTINY MAN'S BRIEF INFECTION. I'M QUITE FINE.
GOOD. I NEED YOU NOW.
FIVE THOUSAND YEARS OF HUMAN PROGRESS...

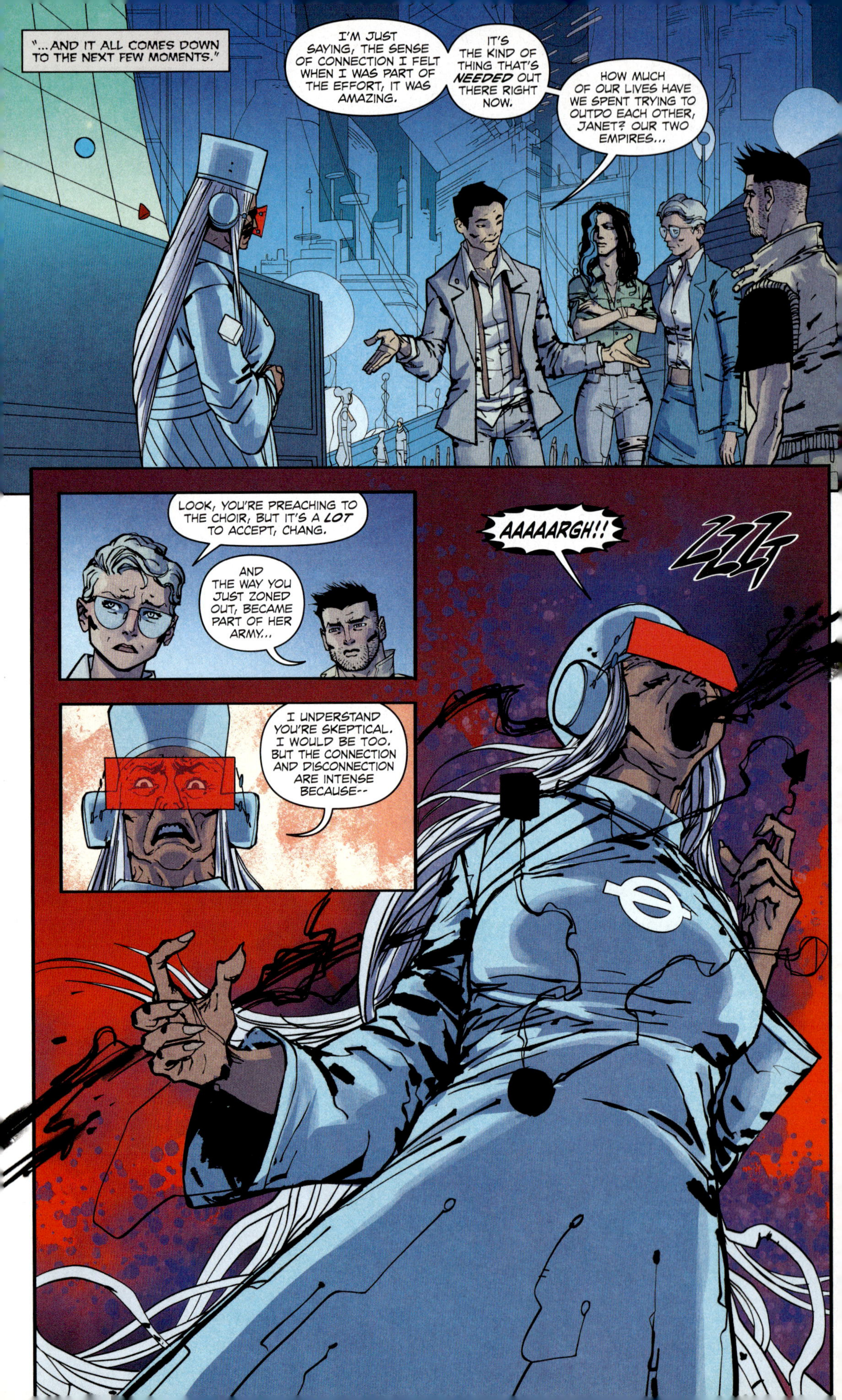
"...AND IT ALL COMES DOWN TO THE NEXT FEW MOMENTS."
I'M JUST SAYING, THE SENSE OF CONNECTION I FELT WHEN I WAS PART OF THE EFFORT, IT WAS AMAZING.
IT'S THE KIND OF THING THAT'S *NEEDED* OUT THERE RIGHT NOW.
HOW MUCH OF OUR LIVES HAVE WE SPENT TRYING TO OUTDO EACH OTHER, JANET? OUR TWO EMPIRES...
LOOK, YOU'RE PREACHING TO THE CHOIR, BUT IT'S A *LOT* TO ACCEPT, CHANG.
AND THE WAY YOU JUST ZONED OUT, BECAME PART OF HER ARMY...
I UNDERSTAND YOU'RE SKEPTICAL. I WOULD BE TOO. BUT THE CONNECTION AND DISCONNECTION ARE INTENSE BECAUSE--
AAAAARGH!!
ZZZT

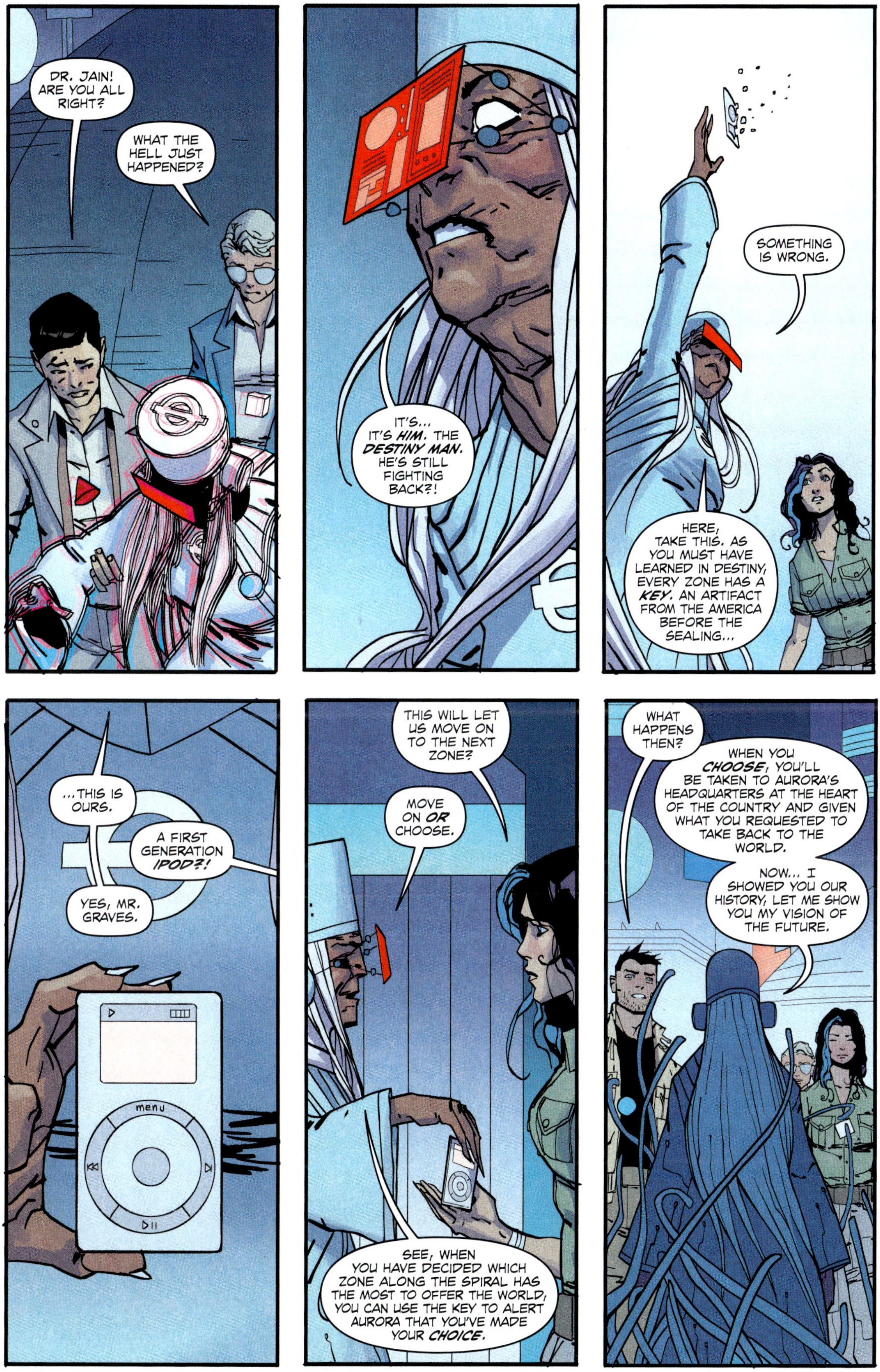
DR. JAIN! ARE YOU ALL RIGHT?
WHAT THE HELL JUST HAPPENED?
IT'S... IT'S HIM. THE DESTINY MAN. HE'S STILL FIGHTING BACK?!
SOMETHING IS WRONG.
HERE, TAKE THIS. AS YOU MUST HAVE LEARNED IN DESTINY, EVERY ZONE HAS A KEY. AN ARTIFACT FROM THE AMERICA BEFORE THE SEALING...
...THIS IS OURS.
A FIRST GENERATION IPOD?!
YES, MR. GRAVES.
menu
THIS WILL LET US MOVE ON TO THE NEXT ZONE?
MOVE ON OR CHOOSE.
SEE, WHEN YOU HAVE DECIDED WHICH ZONE ALONG THE SPIRAL HAS THE MOST TO OFFER THE WORLD, YOU CAN USE THE KEY TO ALERT AURORA THAT YOU'VE MADE YOUR CHOICE.
WHAT HAPPENS THEN?
WHEN YOU CHOOSE, YOU'LL BE TAKEN TO AURORA'S HEADQUARTERS AT THE HEART OF THE COUNTRY AND GIVEN WHAT YOU REQUESTED TO TAKE BACK TO THE WORLD.
NOW... I SHOWED YOU OUR HISTORY, LET ME SHOW YOU MY VISION OF THE FUTURE.

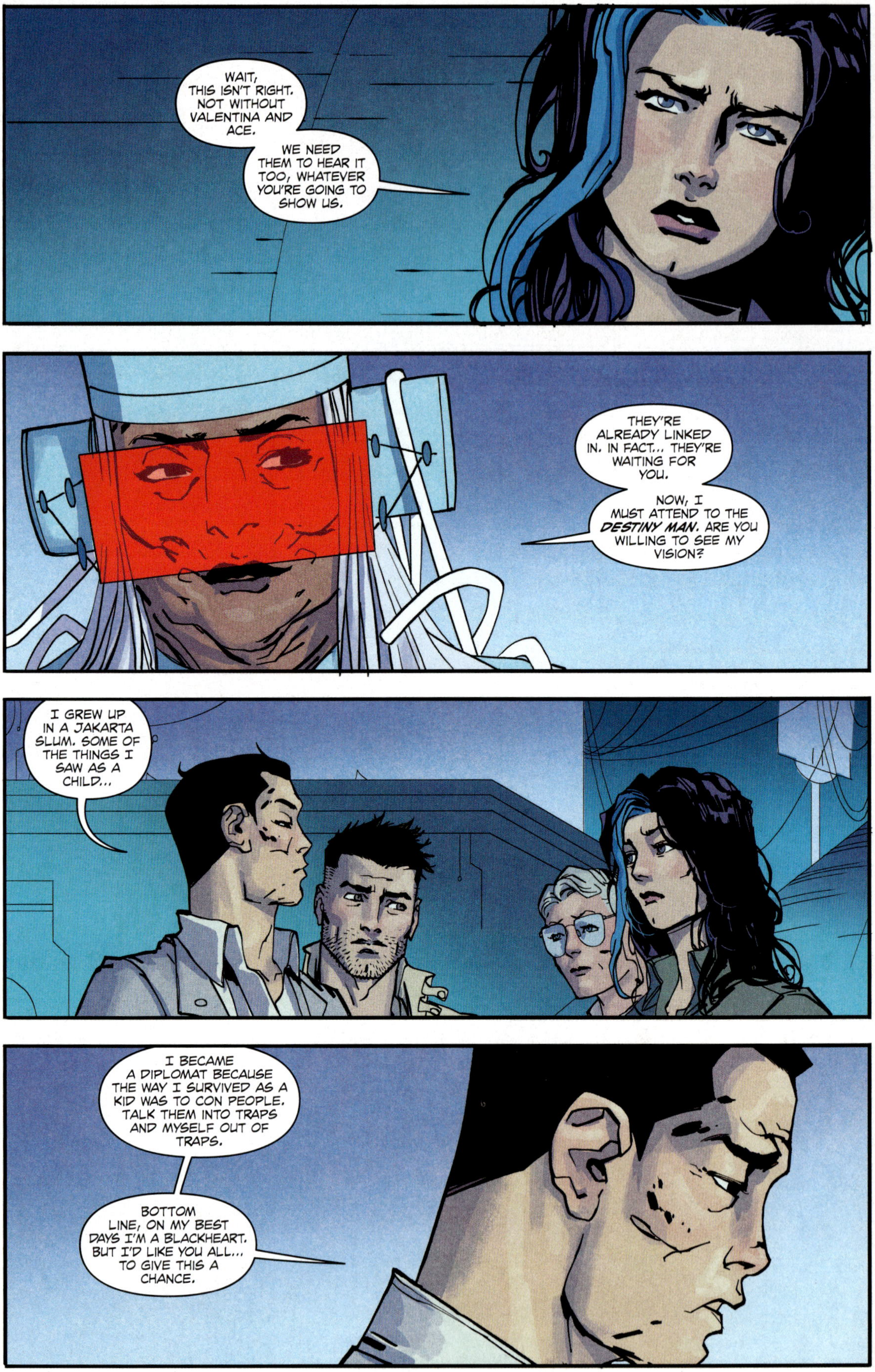
WAIT, THIS ISN'T RIGHT. NOT WITHOUT VALENTINA AND ACE.
WE NEED THEM TO HEAR IT TOO, WHATEVER YOU'RE GOING TO SHOW US.
THEY'RE ALREADY LINKED IN. IN FACT... THEY'RE WAITING FOR YOU.
NOW, I MUST ATTEND TO THE ***DESTINY MAN***. ARE YOU WILLING TO SEE MY VISION?
I GREW UP IN A JAKARTA SLUM. SOME OF THE THINGS I SAW AS A CHILD...
I BECAME A DIPLOMAT BECAUSE THE WAY I SURVIVED AS A KID WAS TO CON PEOPLE. TALK THEM INTO TRAPS AND MYSELF OUT OF TRAPS.
BOTTOM LINE, ON MY BEST DAYS I'M A BLACKHEART. BUT I'D LIKE YOU ALL... TO GIVE THIS A CHANCE.

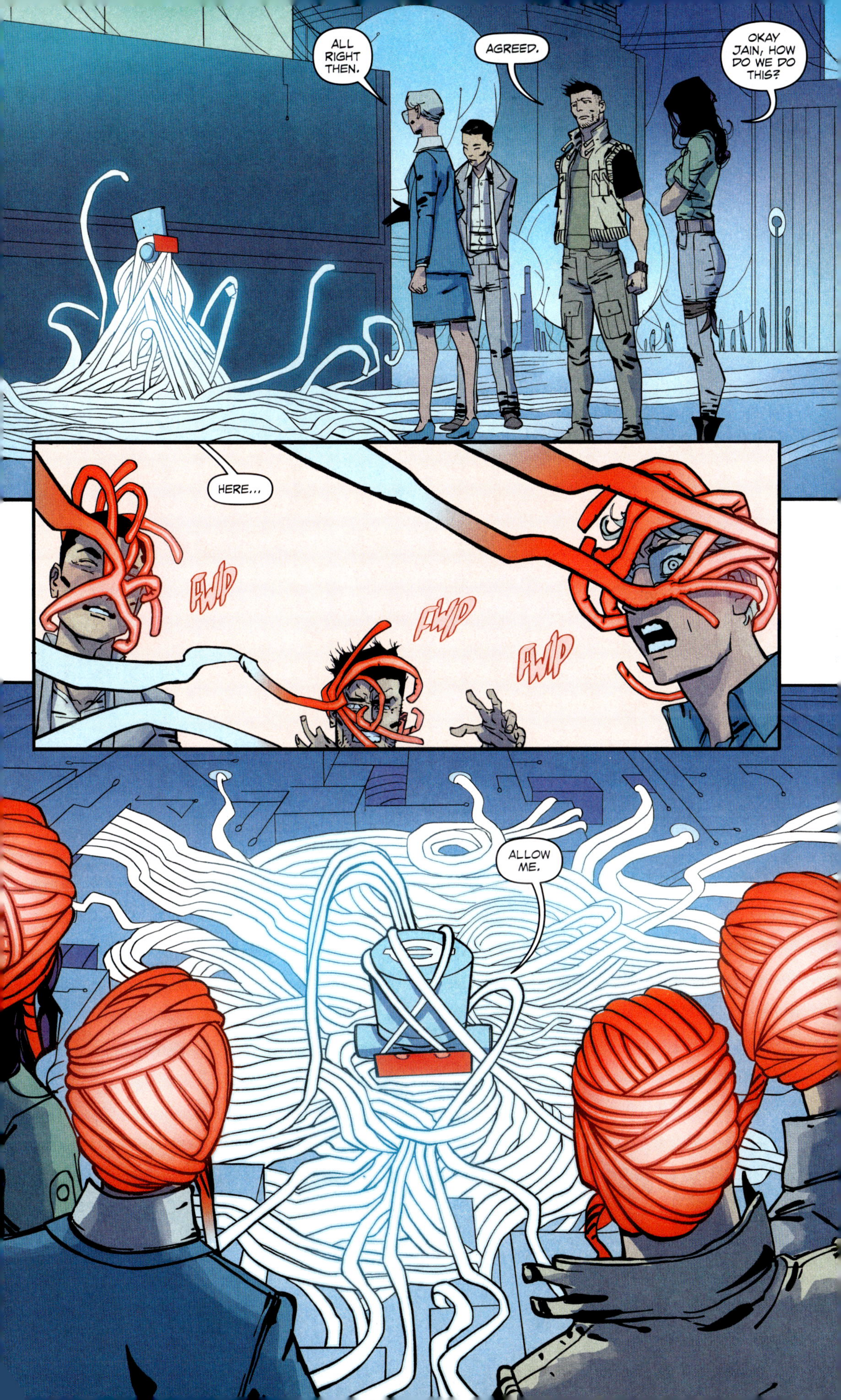
ALL RIGHT THEN.
AGREED.
OKAY JAIN, HOW DO WE DO THIS?
HERE...
FWIP
FWIP
FWIP
ALLOW ME.

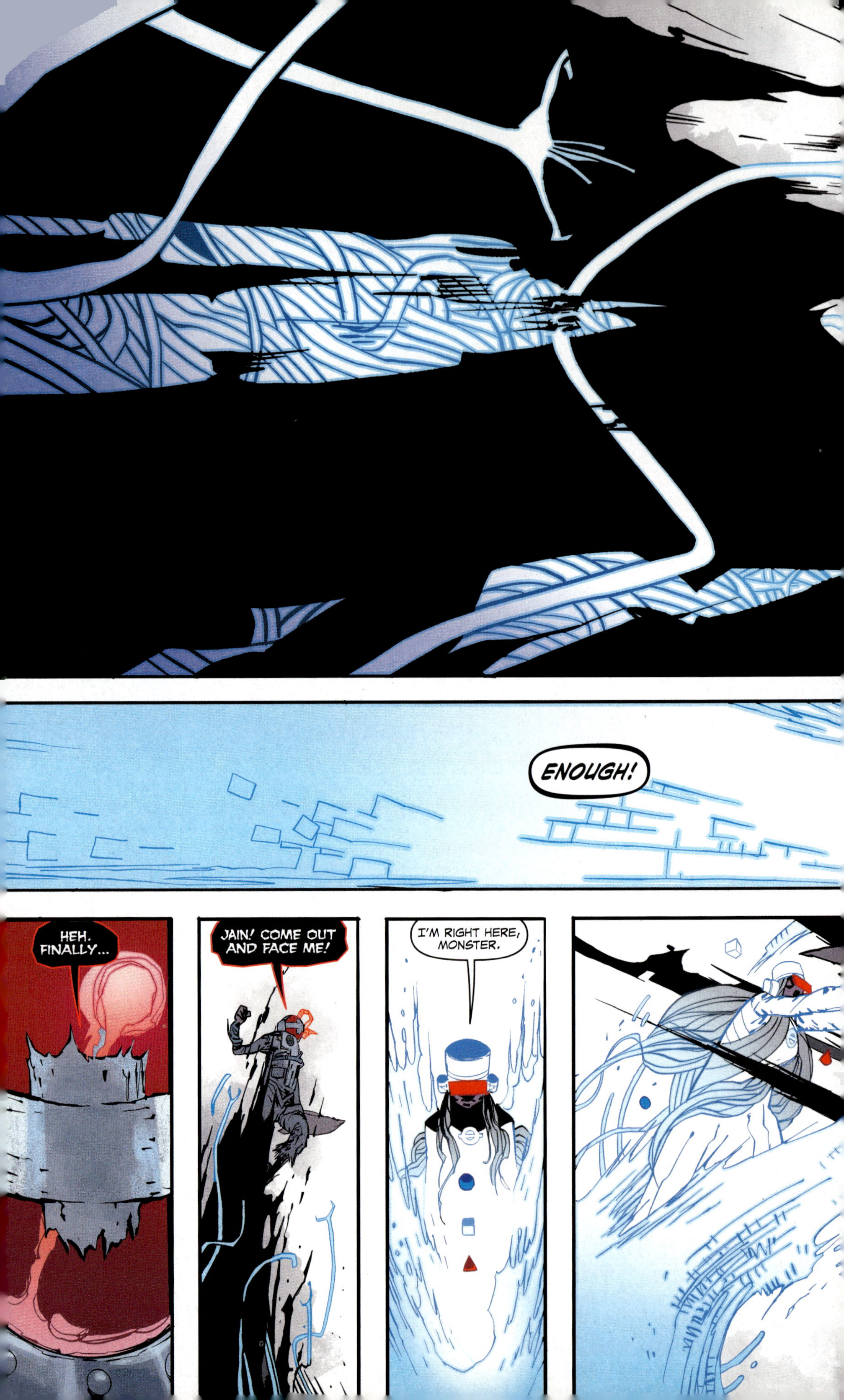
ENOUGH!
HEH. FINALLY...
JAIN! COME OUT AND FACE ME!
I'M RIGHT HERE, MONSTER.

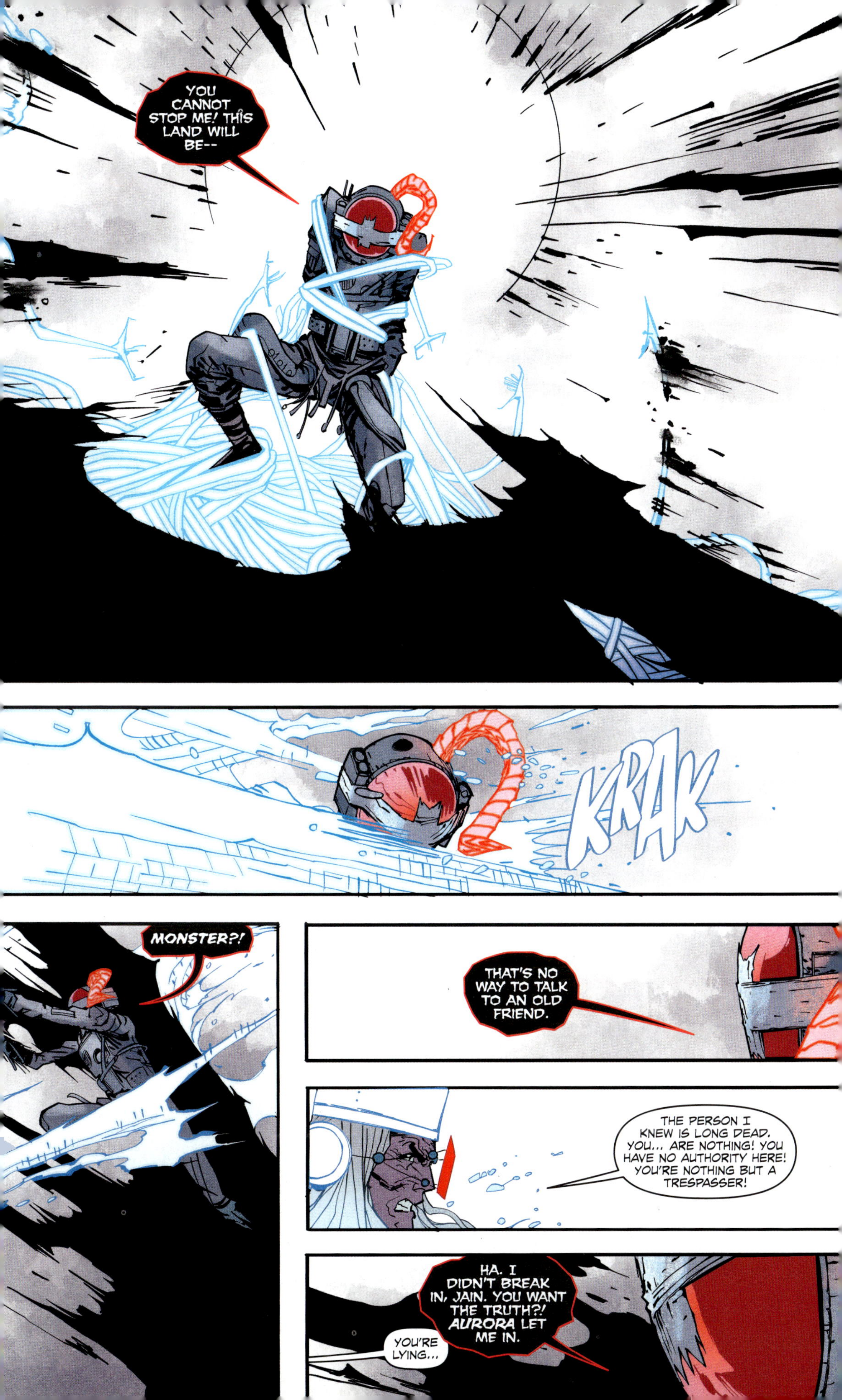
YOU CANNOT STOP ME! THIS LAND WILL BE--
KRAK
MONSTER?!
THAT'S NO WAY TO TALK TO AN OLD FRIEND.
THE PERSON I KNEW IS LONG DEAD. YOU... ARE NOTHING! YOU HAVE NO AUTHORITY HERE! YOU'RE NOTHING BUT A TRESPASSER!
HA. I DIDN'T BREAK IN, JAIN. YOU WANT THE TRUTH?! AURORA LET ME IN.
YOU'RE LYING...

"...THAT'S IMPOSSIBLE!"
BLIP
WHOA...
ACE, VAL! ARE YOU GUYS OK?
UH, NOT BY A LONG SHOT!
JAIN, SHE'S GOT THE MINDS OF CHILDREN HOOKED UP TO POWER THIS PLACE!
SHE GRABBED US WHEN WE FOUND THEM!
HE'S RIGHT! SHE'S HIDING ALL OF IT!
I'M HIDING NOTHING, VALENTINA. AS I TOLD YOU, I'M GLAD YOU SAW WHAT YOU SAW. I'M PROUD OF IT.
PROUD?!
YES. I PLANNED ON SHOWING YOU THE ENTIRETY MYSELF AFTER YOU ALL HAD TIME TO ADJUST. BUT NOW, I'M AFRAID THAT'S NOT POSSIBLE.

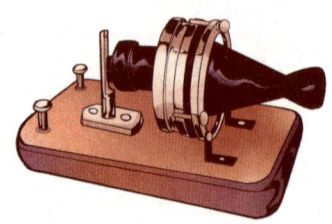

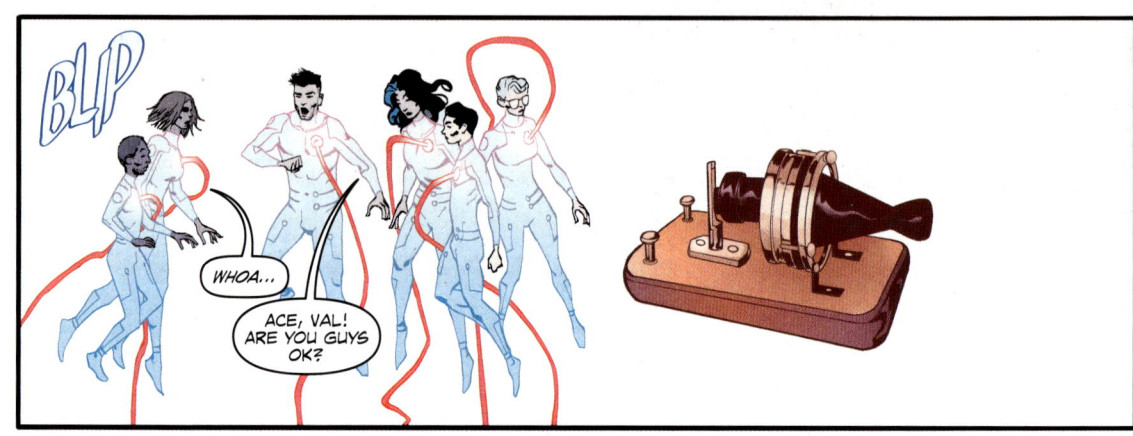

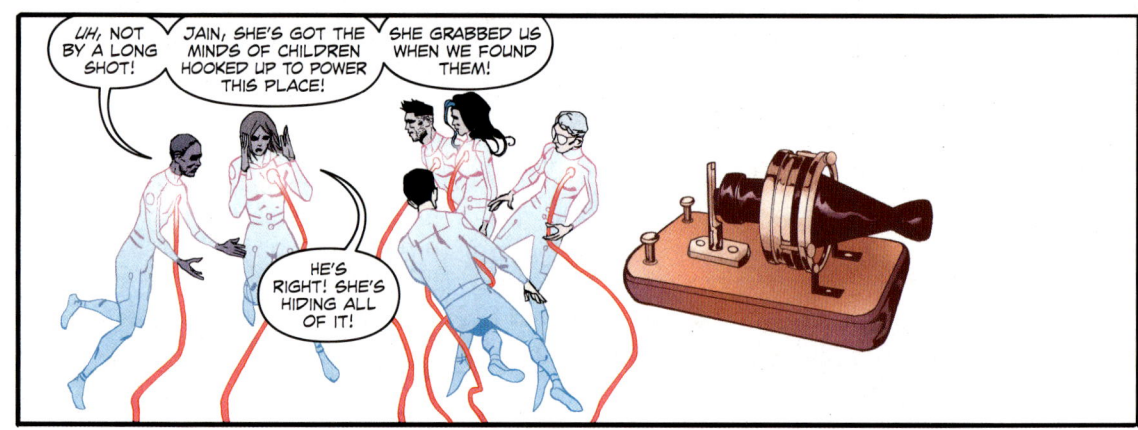

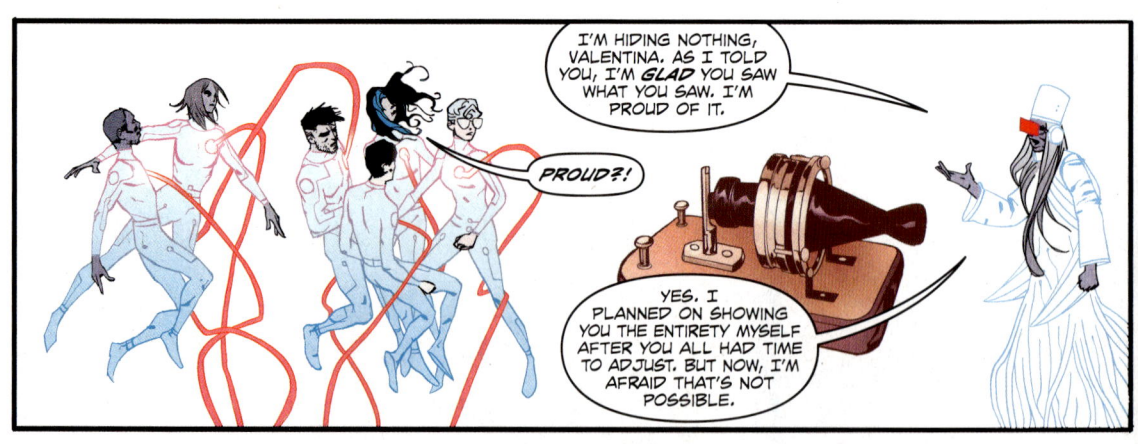

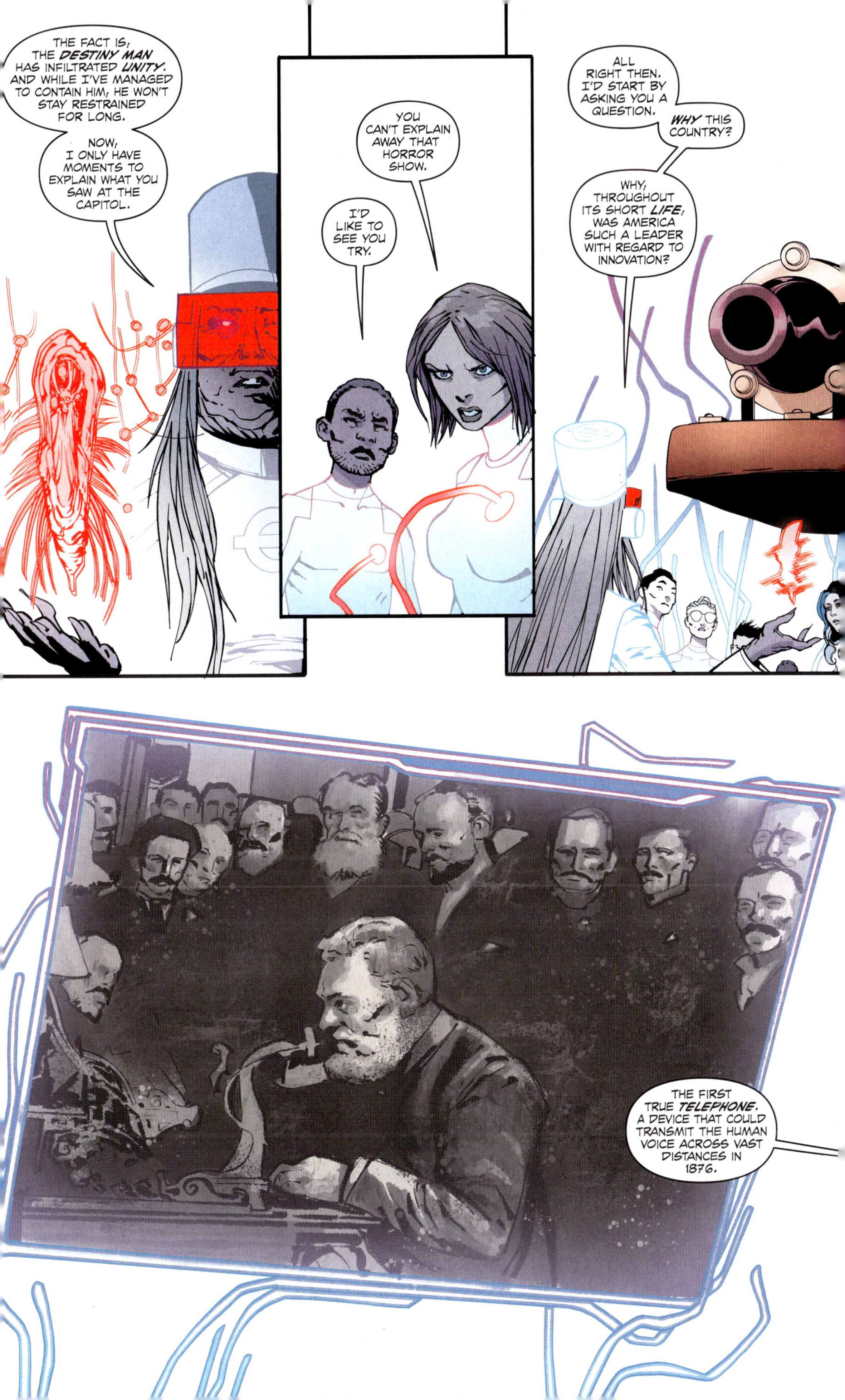
THE FACT IS, THE ***DESTINY MAN*** HAS INFILTRATED ***UNITY***. AND WHILE I'VE MANAGED TO CONTAIN HIM, HE WON'T STAY RESTRAINED FOR LONG.
NOW, I ONLY HAVE MOMENTS TO EXPLAIN WHAT YOU SAW AT THE CAPITOL.
YOU CAN'T EXPLAIN AWAY THAT HORROR SHOW.
I'D LIKE TO SEE YOU TRY.
ALL RIGHT THEN. I'D START BY ASKING YOU A QUESTION.
WHY THIS COUNTRY?
WHY, THROUGHOUT ITS SHORT ***LIFE***, WAS AMERICA SUCH A LEADER WITH REGARD TO INNOVATION?
THE FIRST TRUE ***TELEPHONE***. A DEVICE THAT COULD TRANSMIT THE HUMAN VOICE ACROSS VAST DISTANCES IN 1876.

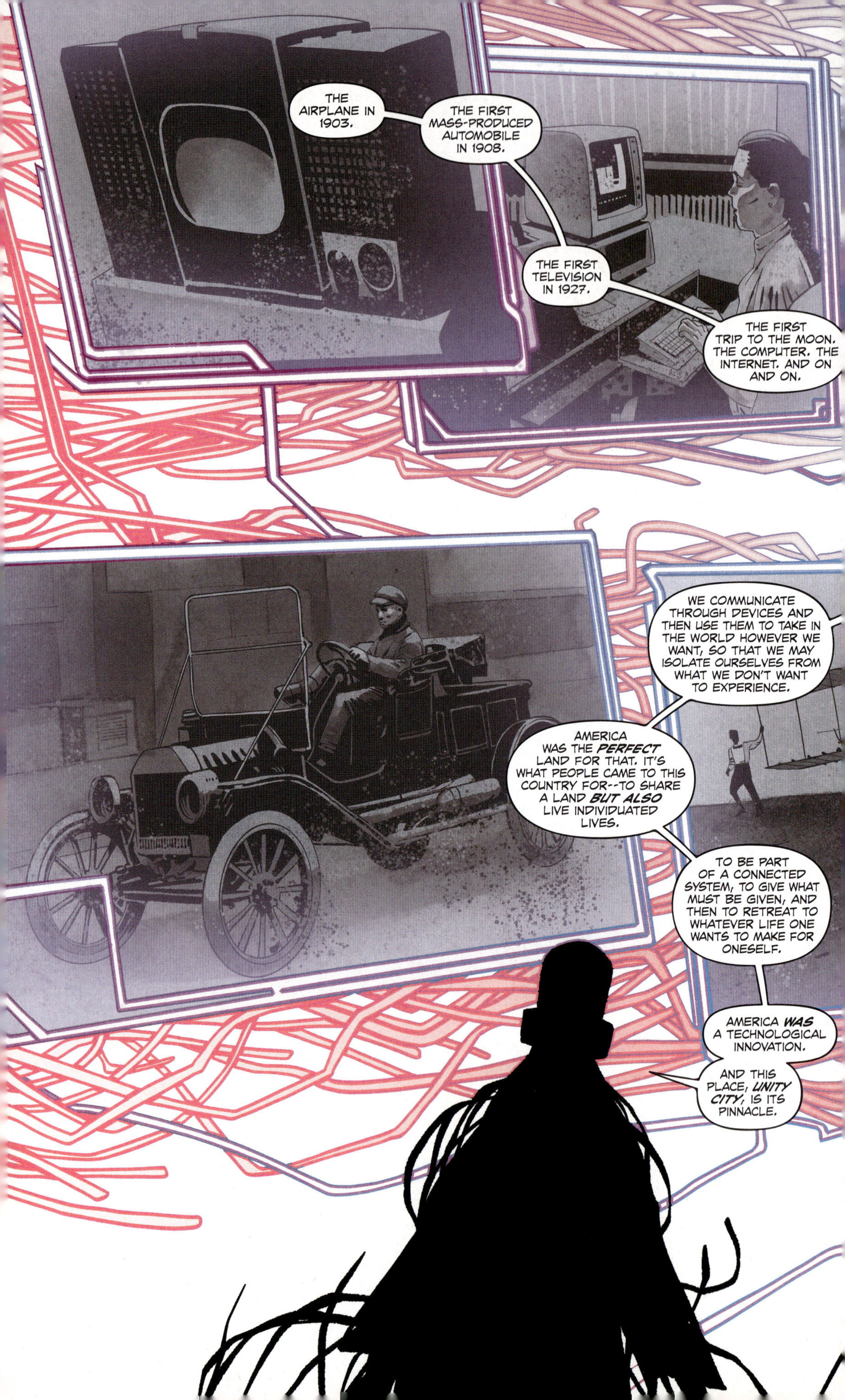
THE AIRPLANE IN 1903.
THE FIRST MASS-PRODUCED AUTOMOBILE IN 1908.
THE FIRST TELEVISION IN 1927.
THE FIRST TRIP TO THE MOON. THE COMPUTER. THE INTERNET. AND ON AND ON.
WE COMMUNICATE THROUGH DEVICES AND THEN USE THEM TO TAKE IN THE WORLD HOWEVER WE WANT, SO THAT WE MAY ISOLATE OURSELVES FROM WHAT WE DON'T WANT TO EXPERIENCE.
AMERICA WAS THE *PERFECT* LAND FOR THAT. IT'S WHAT PEOPLE CAME TO THIS COUNTRY FOR--TO SHARE A LAND *BUT ALSO* LIVE INDIVIDUATED LIVES.
TO BE PART OF A CONNECTED SYSTEM, TO GIVE WHAT MUST BE GIVEN, AND THEN TO RETREAT TO WHATEVER LIFE ONE WANTS TO MAKE FOR ONESELF.
AMERICA *WAS* A TECHNOLOGICAL INNOVATION.
AND THIS PLACE, *UNITY CITY,* IS ITS PINNACLE.

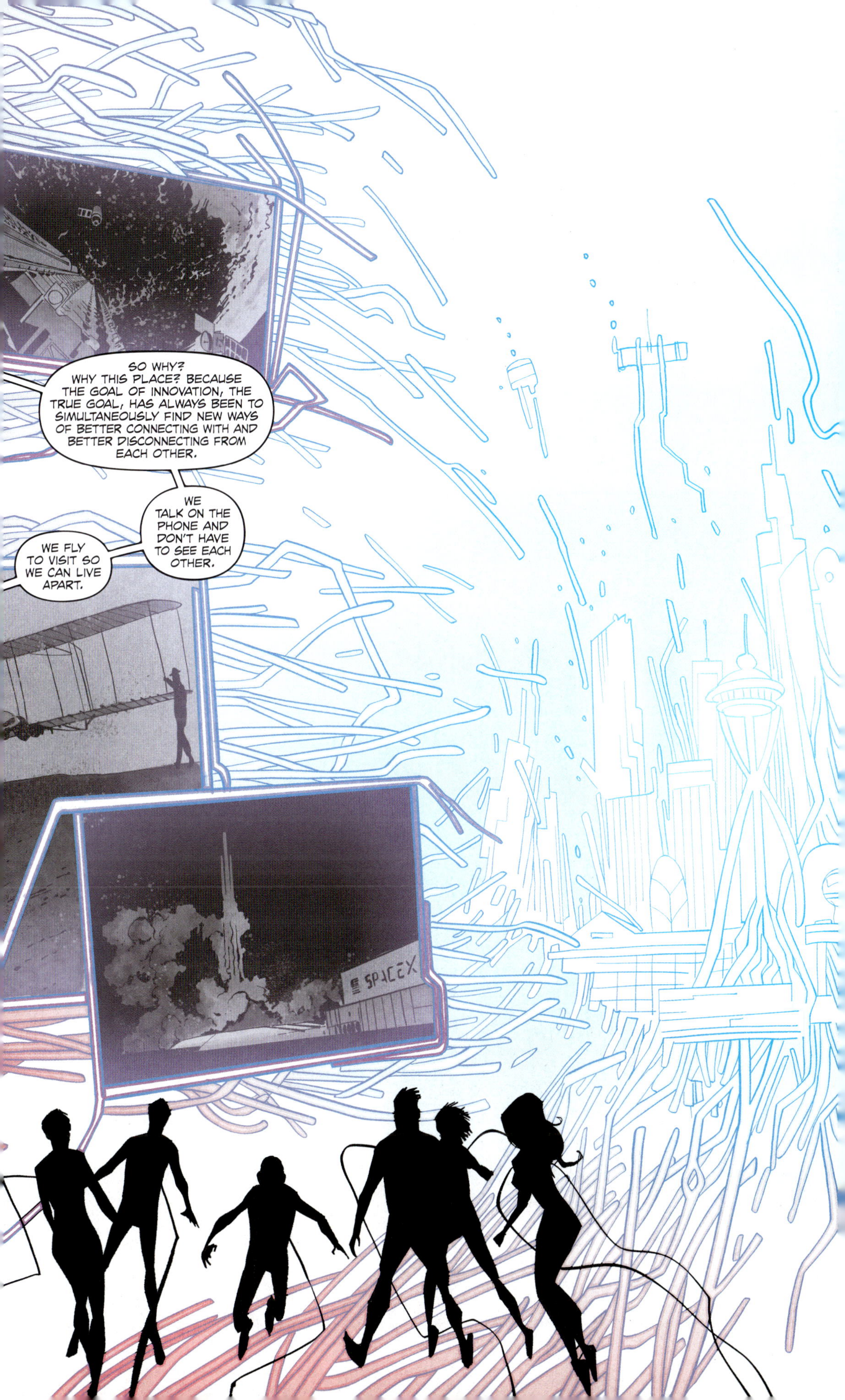
SO WHY? WHY THIS PLACE? BECAUSE THE GOAL OF INNOVATION, THE TRUE GOAL, HAS ALWAYS BEEN TO SIMULTANEOUSLY FIND NEW WAYS OF BETTER CONNECTING WITH AND BETTER DISCONNECTING FROM EACH OTHER.
WE TALK ON THE PHONE AND DON'T HAVE TO SEE EACH OTHER.
WE FLY TO VISIT SO WE CAN LIVE APART.
SPACEX

NICE SPEECH. BUT IT DOESN'T EXPLAIN WHAT WE SAW.
EXACTLY. WE WERE JUST TALKING TO A VERSION OF YOU THAT LOOKED LIKE A MUMMY SCREWED A CENTIPEDE!
WHAT *WAS* THAT?
WHAT YOU SAW WAS SACRIFICE. WHEN WE FORMED UNITY AND WERE TASKED WITH COMING UP WITH SOMETHING THAT WOULD *UNITE* THE ZONES, THE NEURO-LINK TECHNOLOGY, IT REQUIRED MORE BIO-POWER THAN WE COULD GENERATE HERE.
WE TRIED TO PULL FROM OTHER ZONES, BUT WE WERE THWARTED.
WHEN THE SECOND SEALING HAPPENED, AND THE ZONES WERE CUT OFF FROM ONE ANOTHER, WE WERE FORCED TO BECOME CREATIVE.
SO WE GAVE OF OURSELVES. AFTER AGE SEVENTY, WE BECAME ITS POWER SOURCE--PLUGGED OUR BODIES INTO THE ENGINE, OUR MINDS INTO THE SERVER.
BUT IT WAS NOT ENOUGH. BY THEN OUR MINDS WERE TOO WEAK.
WE REALIZED THAT THERE WOULD NEVER BE ENOUGH POWER.
SO INSTEAD OF USING OUR OWN BODIES, WE CREATED A MANDATE.

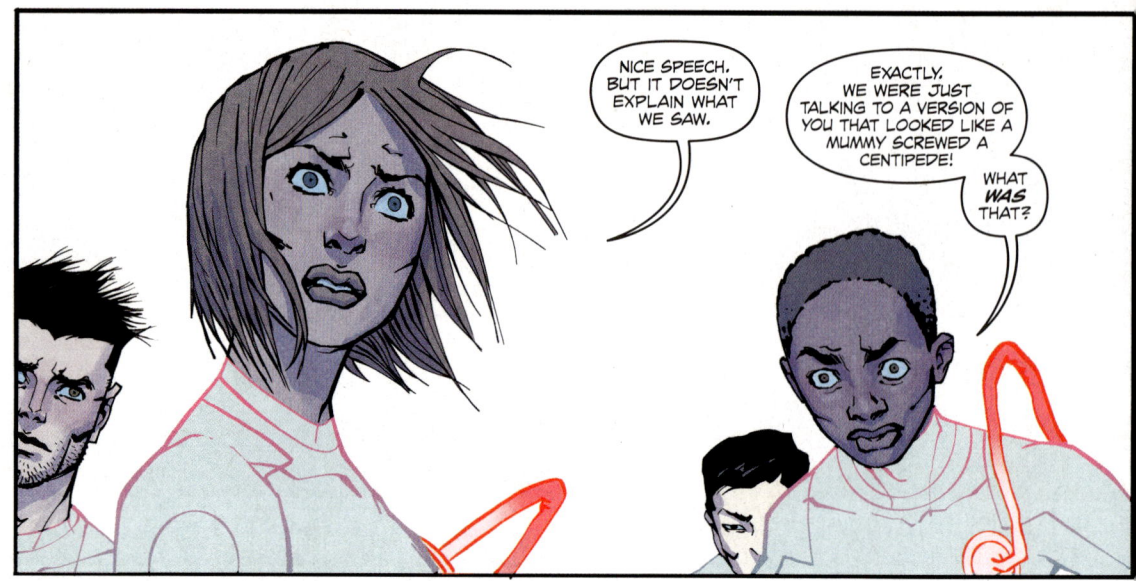

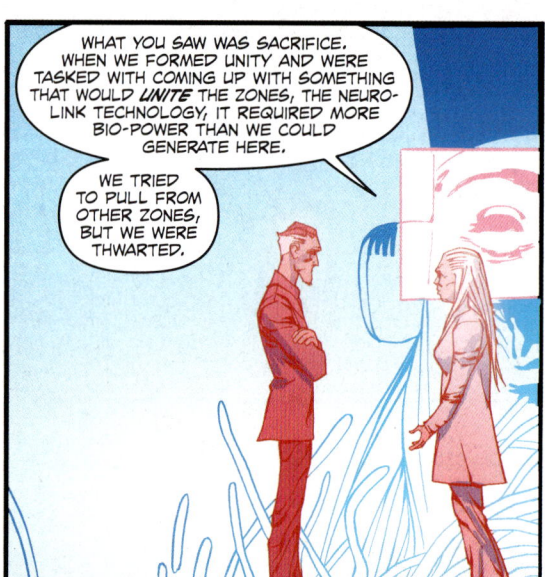

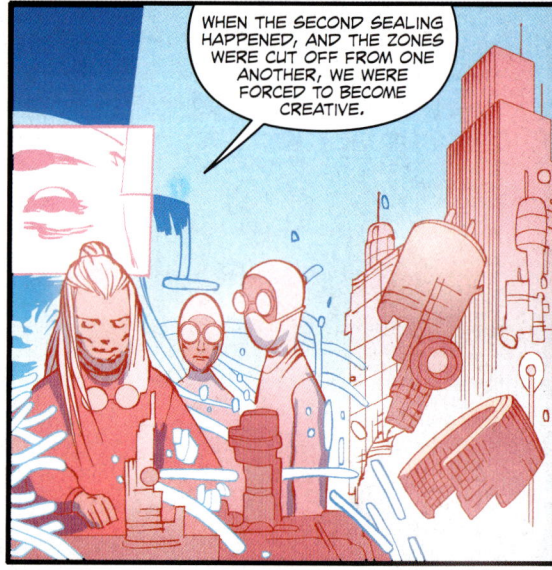

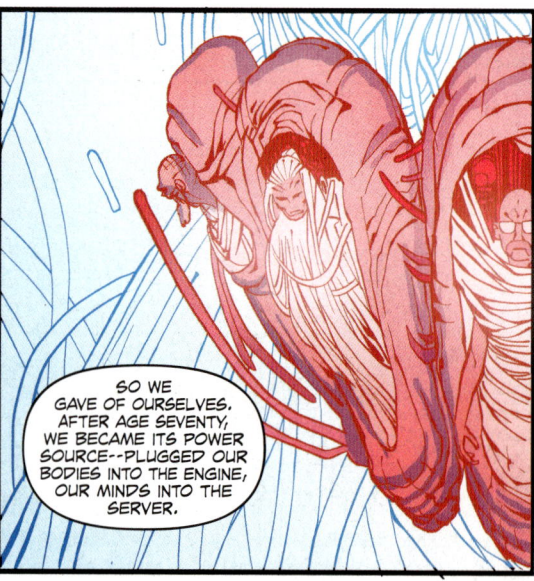

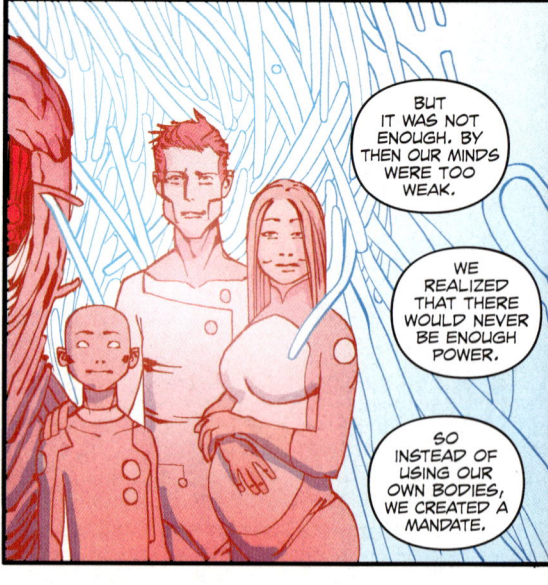

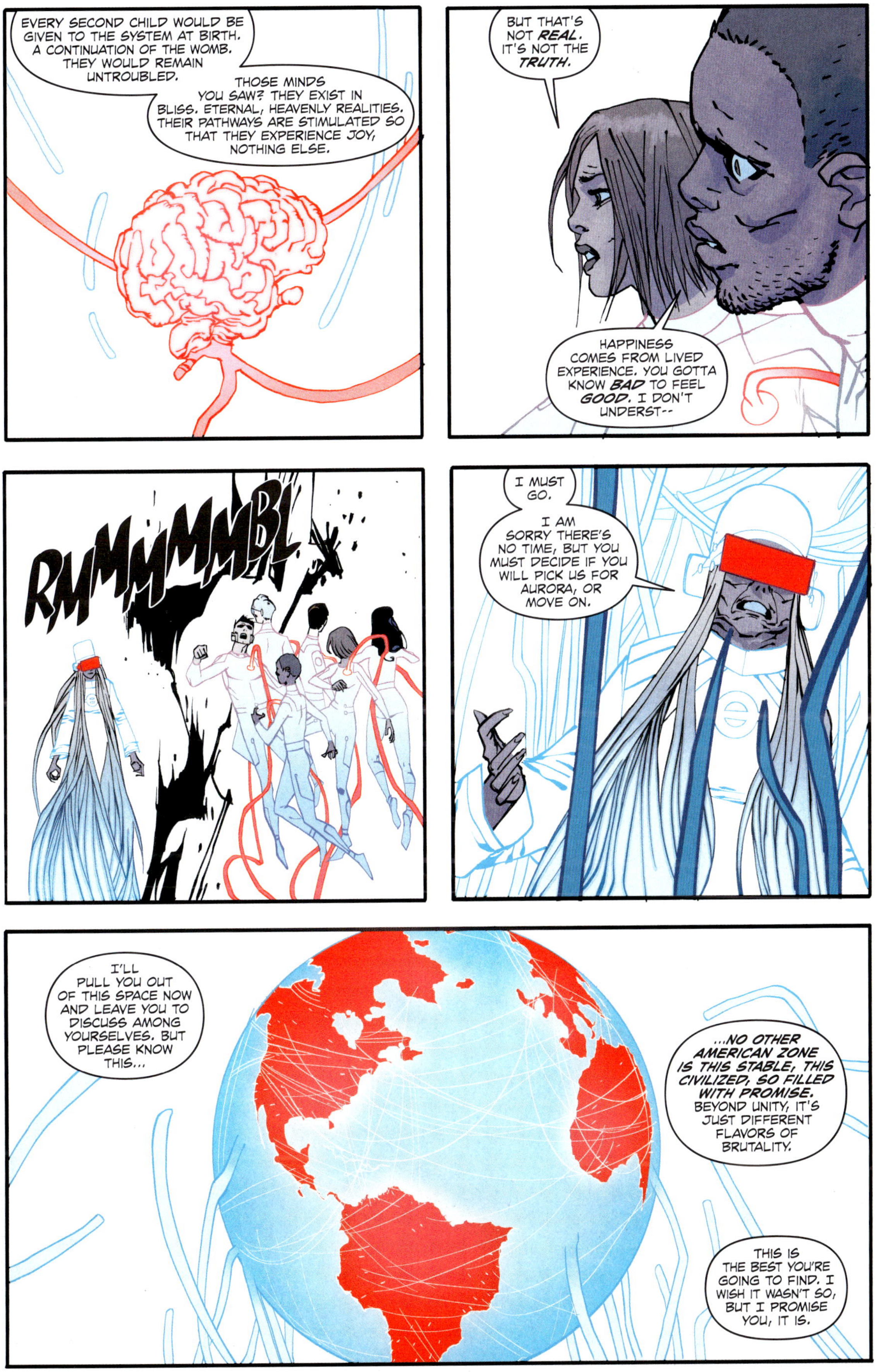

EVERY SECOND CHILD WOULD BE GIVEN TO THE SYSTEM AT BIRTH. A CONTINUATION OF THE WOMB. THEY WOULD REMAIN UNTROUBLED.
THOSE MINDS YOU SAW? THEY EXIST IN BLISS. ETERNAL, HEAVENLY REALITIES. THEIR PATHWAYS ARE STIMULATED SO THAT THEY EXPERIENCE JOY, NOTHING ELSE.
BUT THAT'S NOT ***REAL***. IT'S NOT THE ***TRUTH***.
HAPPINESS COMES FROM LIVED EXPERIENCE. YOU GOTTA KNOW ***BAD*** TO FEEL ***GOOD***. I DON'T UNDERST--
RUMMMMMBL
I MUST GO.
I AM SORRY THERE'S NO TIME, BUT YOU MUST DECIDE IF YOU WILL PICK US FOR AURORA, OR MOVE ON.
I'LL PULL YOU OUT OF THIS SPACE NOW AND LEAVE YOU TO DISCUSS AMONG YOURSELVES. BUT PLEASE KNOW THIS...
...NO OTHER AMERICAN ZONE IS THIS STABLE, THIS CIVILIZED, SO FILLED WITH PROMISE. BEYOND UNITY, IT'S JUST DIFFERENT FLAVORS OF BRUTALITY.
THIS IS THE BEST YOU'RE GOING TO FIND. I WISH IT WASN'T SO, BUT I PROMISE YOU, IT IS.

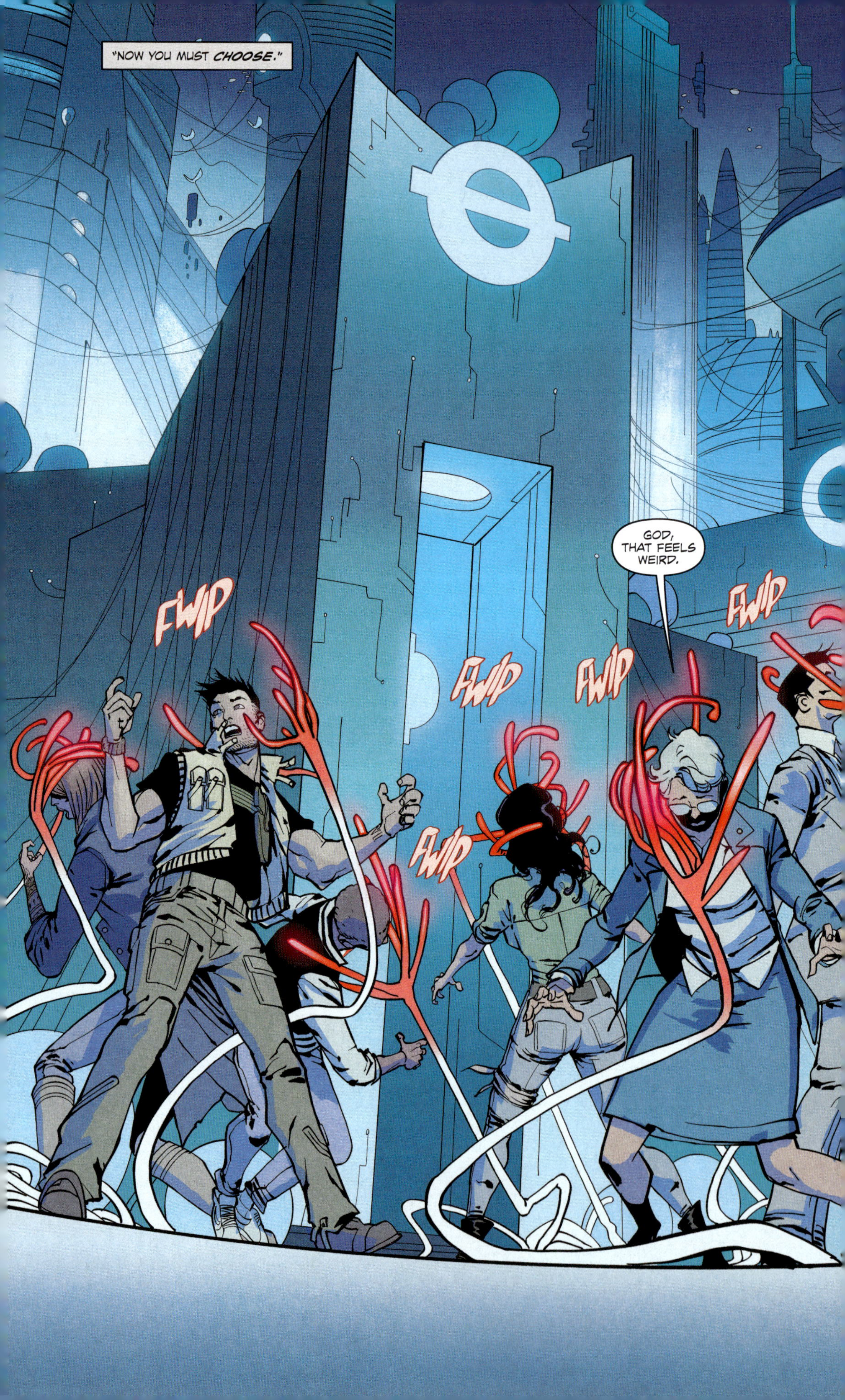
"NOW YOU MUST CHOOSE."
FWIP
FWIP
FWIP
FWIP
GOD, THAT FEELS WEIRD.
FWIP

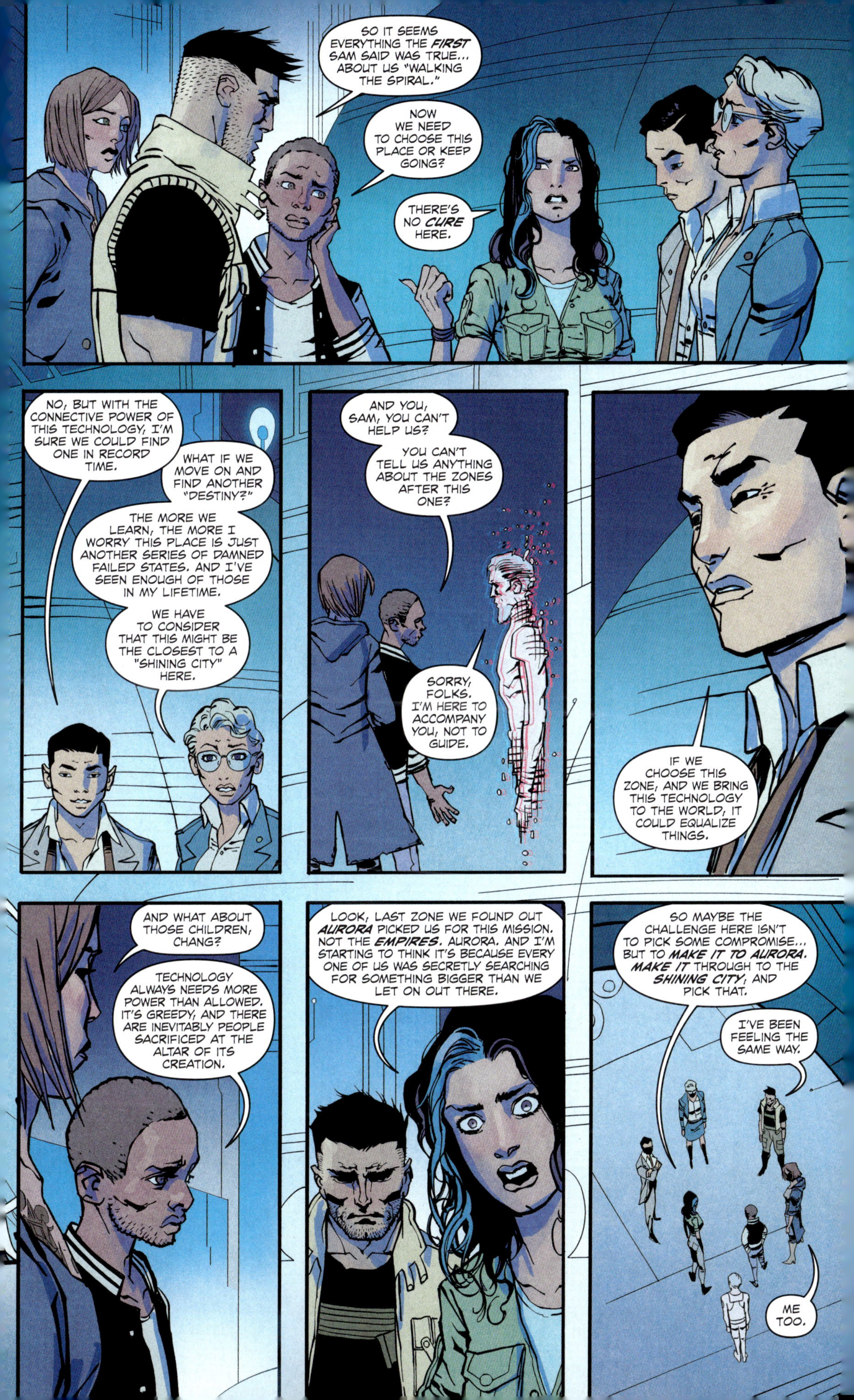
SO IT SEEMS EVERYTHING THE *FIRST* SAM SAID WAS TRUE... ABOUT US "WALKING THE SPIRAL."
NOW WE NEED TO CHOOSE THIS PLACE OR KEEP GOING?
THERE'S NO *CURE* HERE.
NO, BUT WITH THE CONNECTIVE POWER OF THIS TECHNOLOGY, I'M SURE WE COULD FIND ONE IN RECORD TIME.
WHAT IF WE MOVE ON AND FIND ANOTHER "DESTINY?"
THE MORE WE LEARN, THE MORE I WORRY THIS PLACE IS JUST ANOTHER SERIES OF DAMNED FAILED STATES. AND I'VE SEEN ENOUGH OF THOSE IN MY LIFETIME.
WE HAVE TO CONSIDER THAT THIS MIGHT BE THE CLOSEST TO A "SHINING CITY" HERE.
AND YOU, SAM, YOU CAN'T HELP US?
YOU CAN'T TELL US ANYTHING ABOUT THE ZONES AFTER THIS ONE?
SORRY, FOLKS. I'M HERE TO ACCOMPANY YOU, NOT TO GUIDE.
IF WE CHOOSE THIS ZONE, AND WE BRING THIS TECHNOLOGY TO THE WORLD, IT COULD EQUALIZE THINGS.
AND WHAT ABOUT THOSE CHILDREN, CHANG?
TECHNOLOGY ALWAYS NEEDS MORE POWER THAN ALLOWED. IT'S GREEDY, AND THERE ARE INEVITABLY PEOPLE SACRIFICED AT THE ALTAR OF ITS CREATION.
LOOK, LAST ZONE WE FOUND OUT *AURORA* PICKED US FOR THIS MISSION. NOT THE *EMPIRES*. AURORA. AND I'M STARTING TO THINK IT'S BECAUSE EVERY ONE OF US WAS SECRETLY SEARCHING FOR SOMETHING BIGGER THAN WE LET ON OUT THERE.
SO MAYBE THE CHALLENGE HERE ISN'T TO PICK SOME COMPROMISE... BUT TO *MAKE IT TO AURORA. MAKE IT* THROUGH TO THE *SHINING CITY*, AND PICK THAT.
I'VE BEEN FEELING THE SAME WAY.
ME TOO.

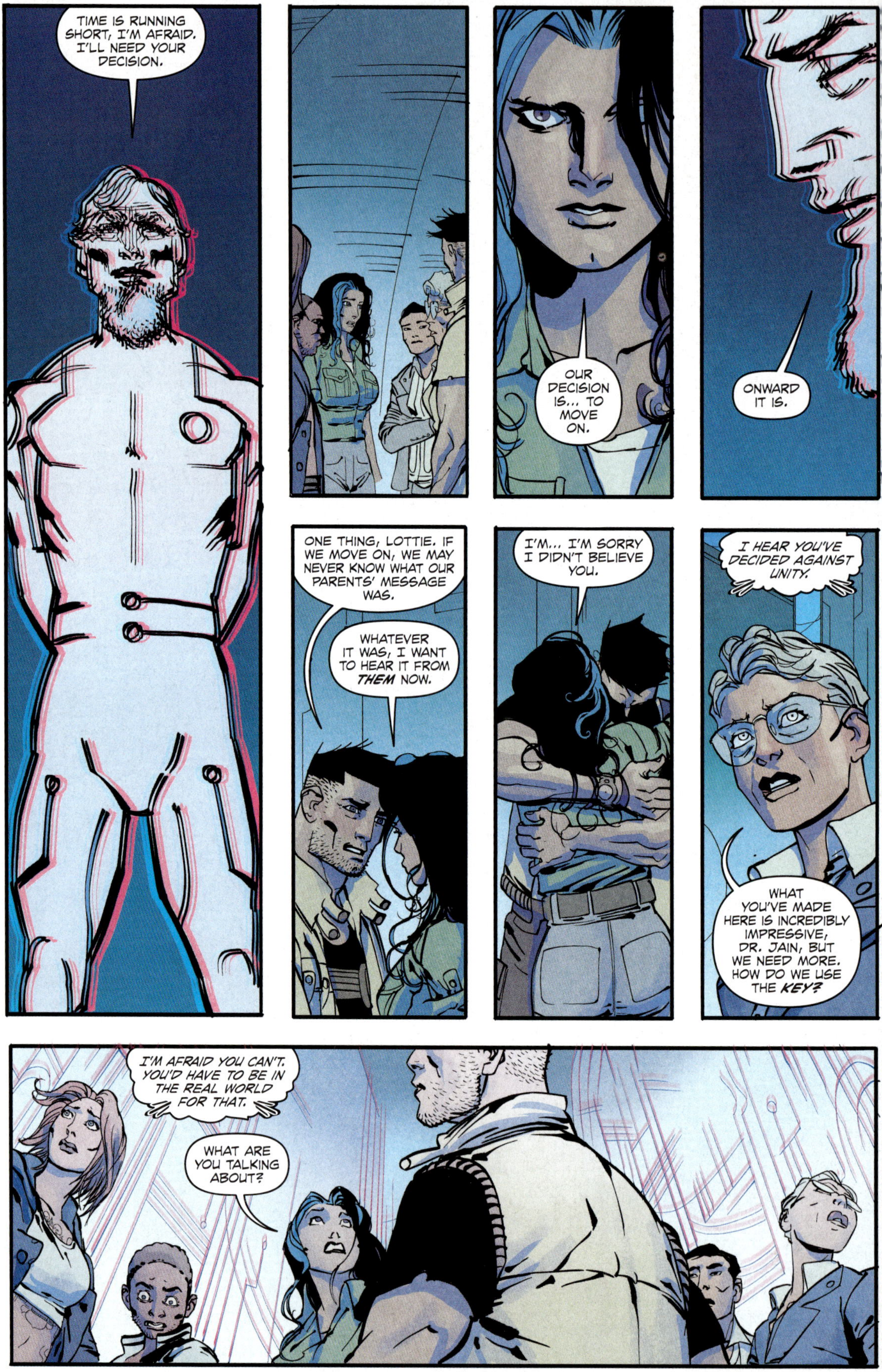
TIME IS RUNNING SHORT, I'M AFRAID. I'LL NEED YOUR DECISION.
OUR DECISION IS... TO MOVE ON.
ONWARD IT IS.
ONE THING, LOTTIE. IF WE MOVE ON, WE MAY NEVER KNOW WHAT OUR PARENTS' MESSAGE WAS.
WHATEVER IT WAS, I WANT TO HEAR IT FROM THEM NOW.
I'M... I'M SORRY I DIDN'T BELIEVE YOU.
I HEAR YOU'VE DECIDED AGAINST UNITY.
WHAT YOU'VE MADE HERE IS INCREDIBLY IMPRESSIVE, DR. JAIN, BUT WE NEED MORE. HOW DO WE USE THE KEY?
I'M AFRAID YOU CAN'T. YOU'D HAVE TO BE IN THE REAL WORLD FOR THAT.
WHAT ARE YOU TALKING ABOUT?

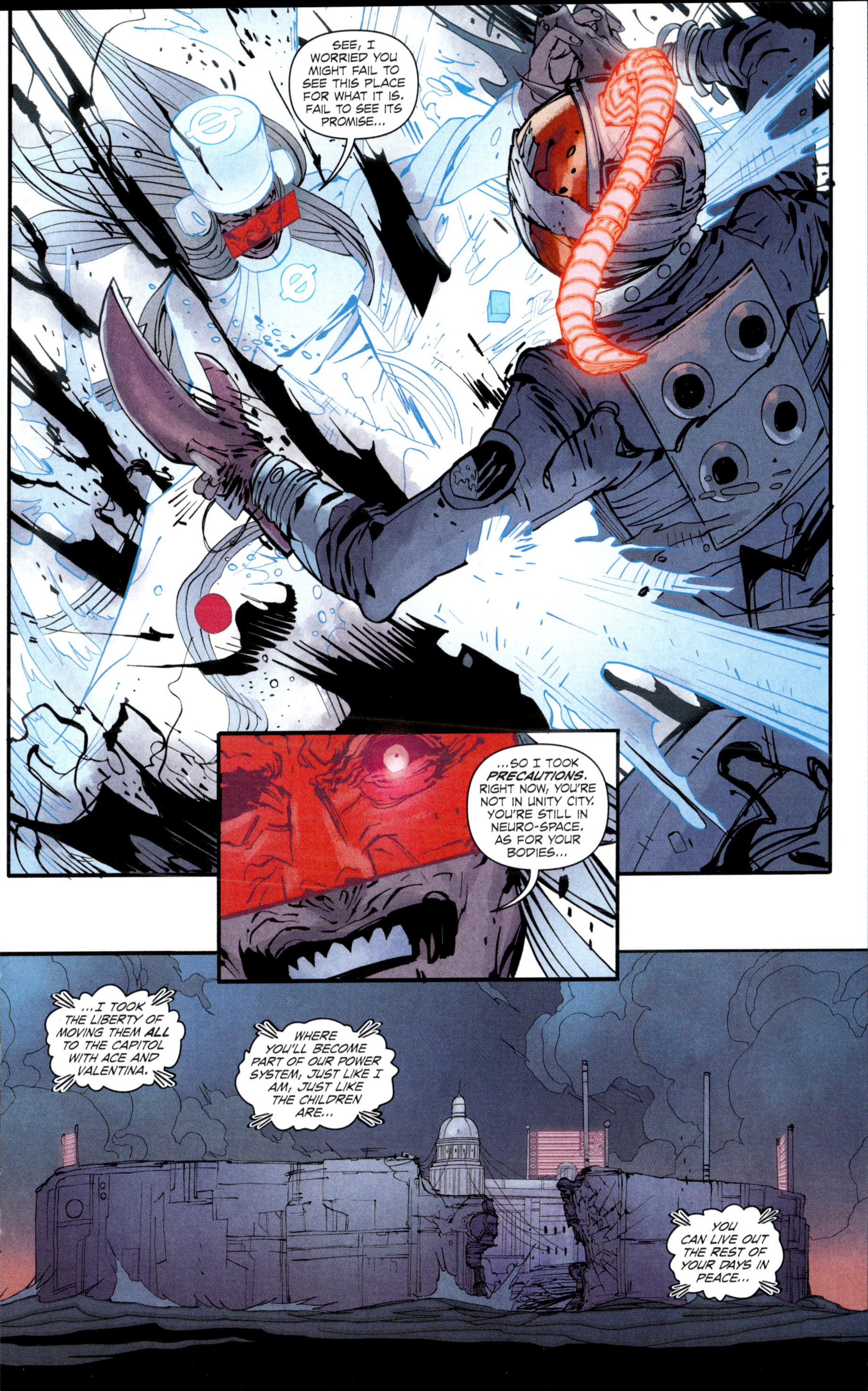
SEE, I WORRIED YOU MIGHT FAIL TO SEE THIS PLACE FOR WHAT IT IS. FAIL TO SEE ITS PROMISE...
...SO I TOOK PRECAUTIONS. RIGHT NOW, YOU'RE NOT IN UNITY CITY. YOU'RE STILL IN NEURO-SPACE. AS FOR YOUR BODIES...
...I TOOK THE LIBERTY OF MOVING THEM ALL TO THE CAPITOL WITH ACE AND VALENTINA.
WHERE YOU'LL BECOME PART OF OUR POWER SYSTEM, JUST LIKE I AM, JUST LIKE THE CHILDREN ARE...
YOU CAN LIVE OUT THE REST OF YOUR DAYS IN PEACE...

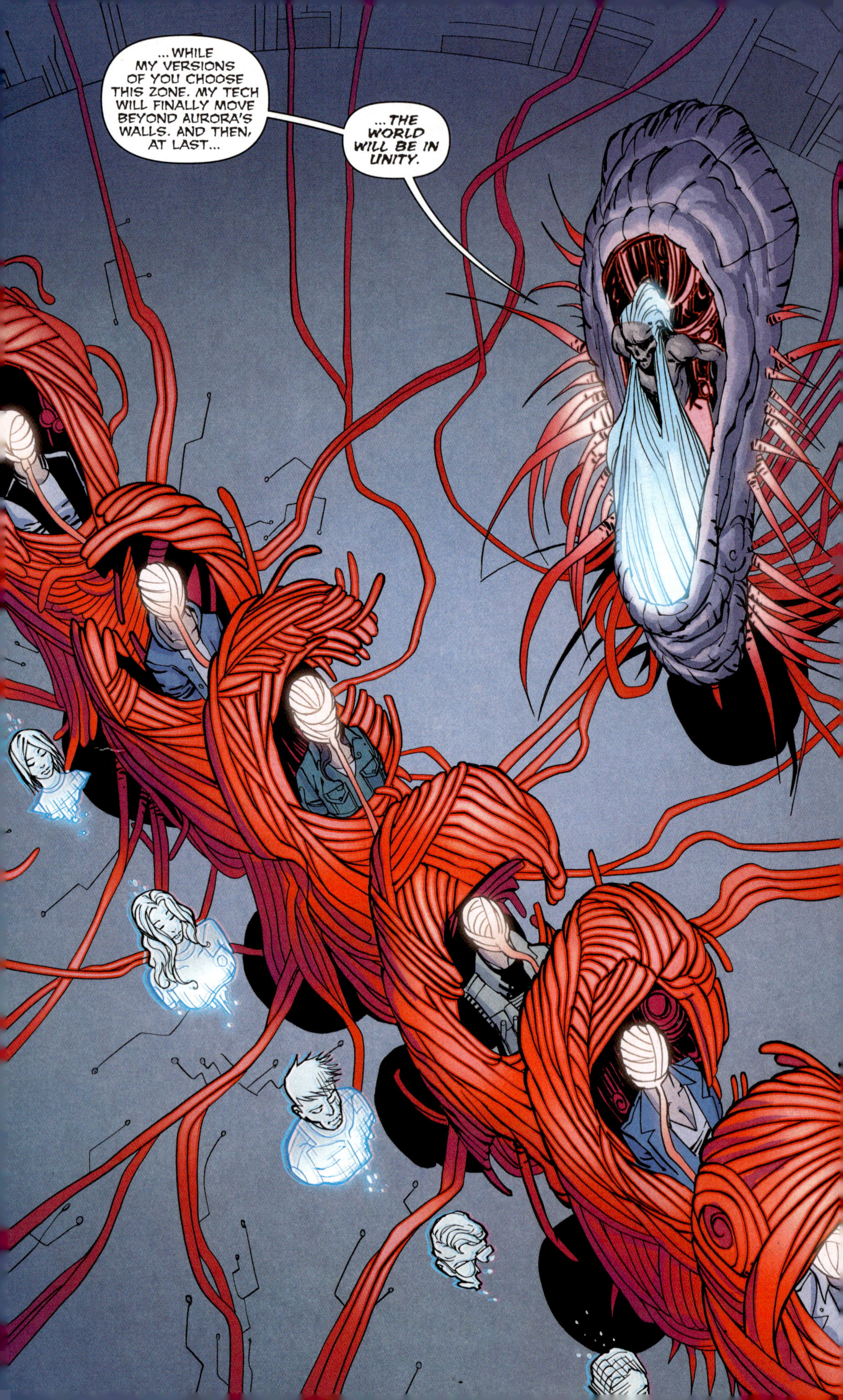
...WHILE MY VERSIONS OF YOU CHOOSE THIS ZONE. MY TECH WILL FINALLY MOVE BEYOND AURORA'S WALLS. AND THEN, AT LAST...
...THE WORLD WILL BE IN UNITY.

The Lafayette Group

"We call it the Juneau Event--but that's just a shorthand. We don't know anything about it, really--in early 2041, something in space fired down on Alaska, and poured out enough energy to scour the state clean.

Bad enough to think that a weapon like that actually exists, and that someone decided to use it... but to not know why? That's even worse. No foreign nation ever claimed responsibility, and based on the level of technology, the most prominent theory is...

...the United States fired on itself."

--Journal Entry by Dr. Warren Antone,
April 18, 2046.

FROM THE ARCHIVES OF THE LAFAYETTE GROUP.
FOR OFFICIAL USE ONLY.

CHAPTER TWELVE

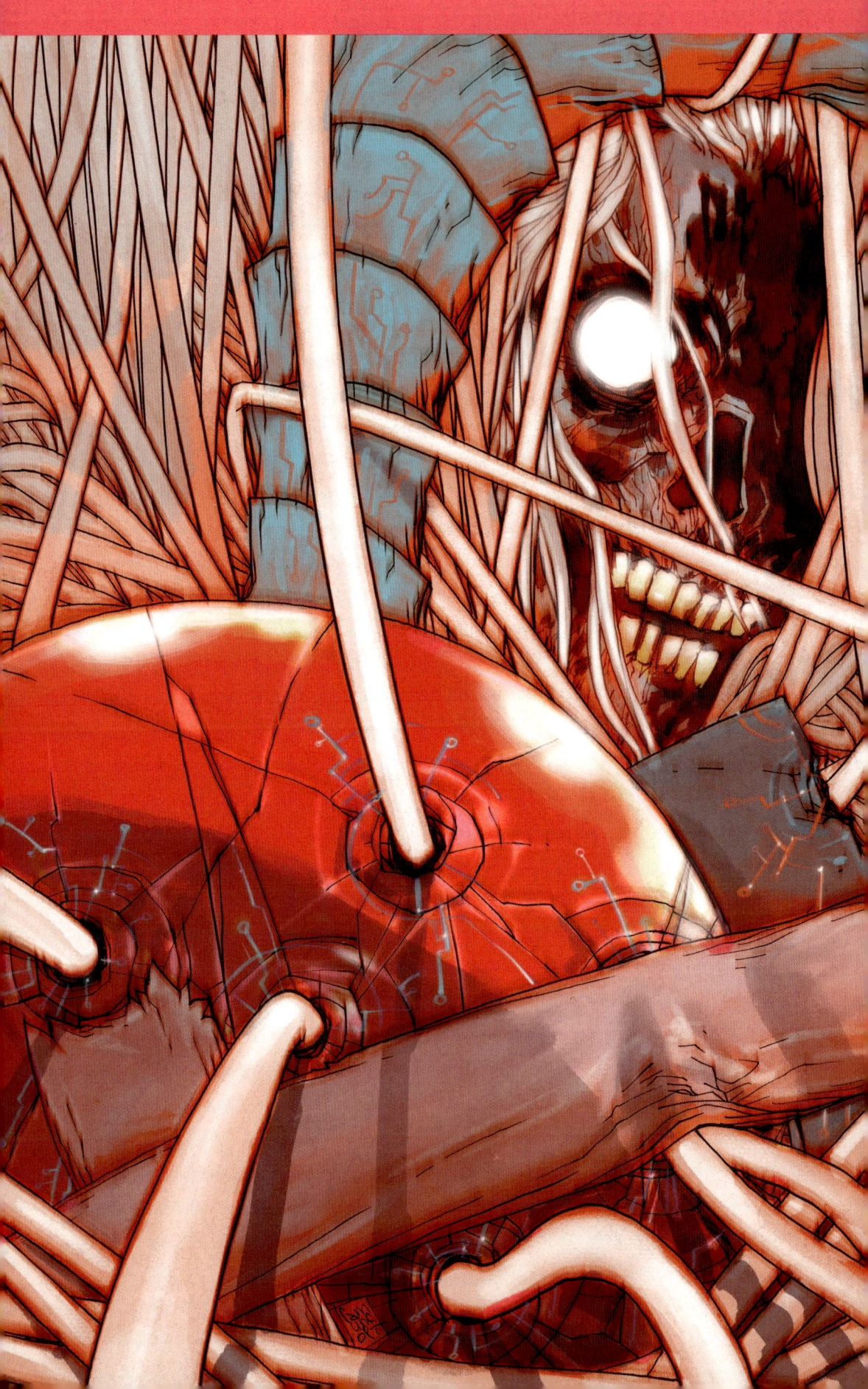

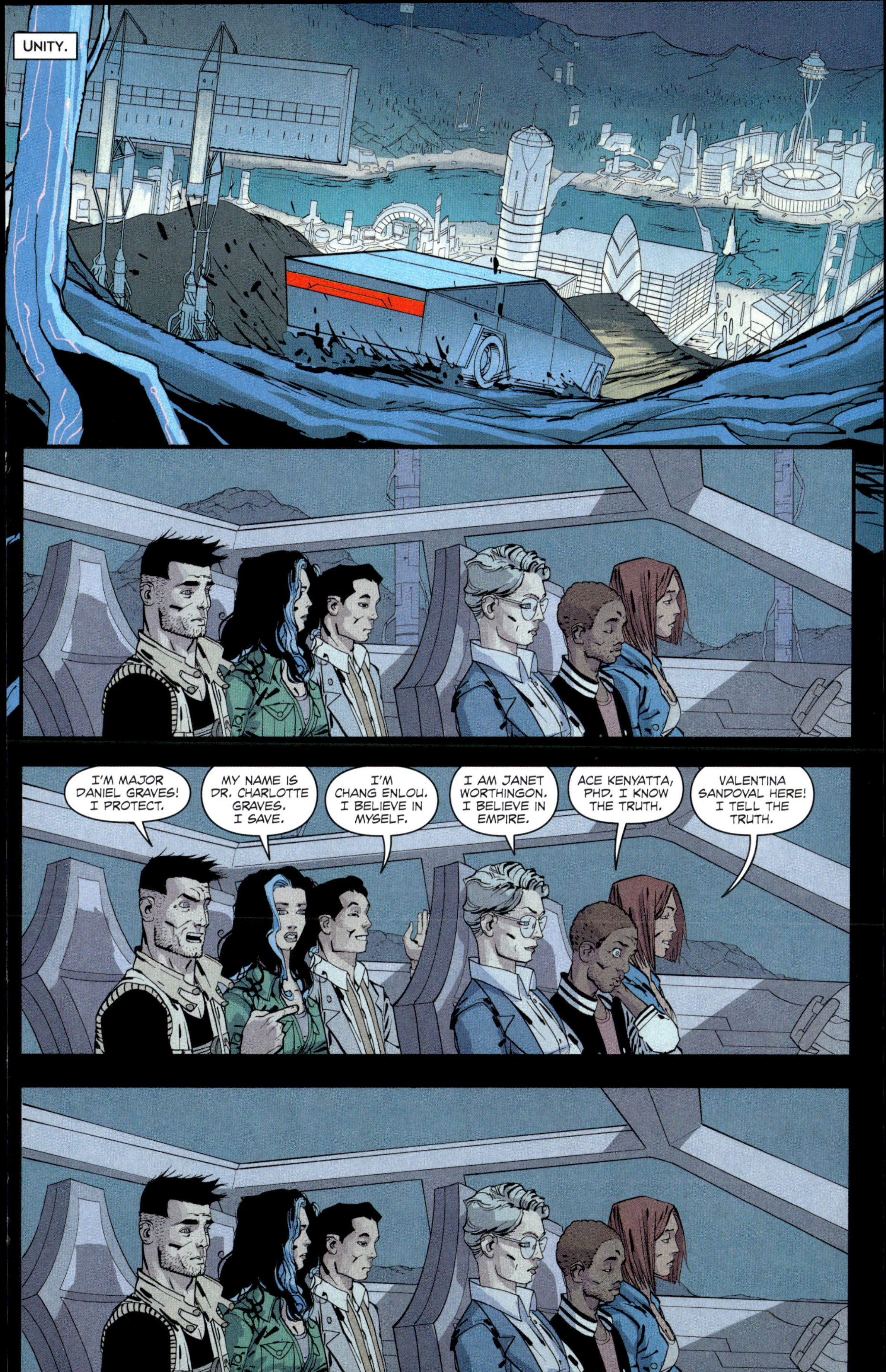
UNITY.
I'M MAJOR DANIEL GRAVES! I PROTECT.
MY NAME IS DR. CHARLOTTE GRAVES. I SAVE.
I'M CHANG ENLOU. I BELIEVE IN MYSELF.
I AM JANET WORTHINGON. I BELIEVE IN EMPIRE.
ACE KENYATTA, PHD. I KNOW THE TRUTH.
VALENTINA SANDOVAL HERE! I TELL THE TRUTH.

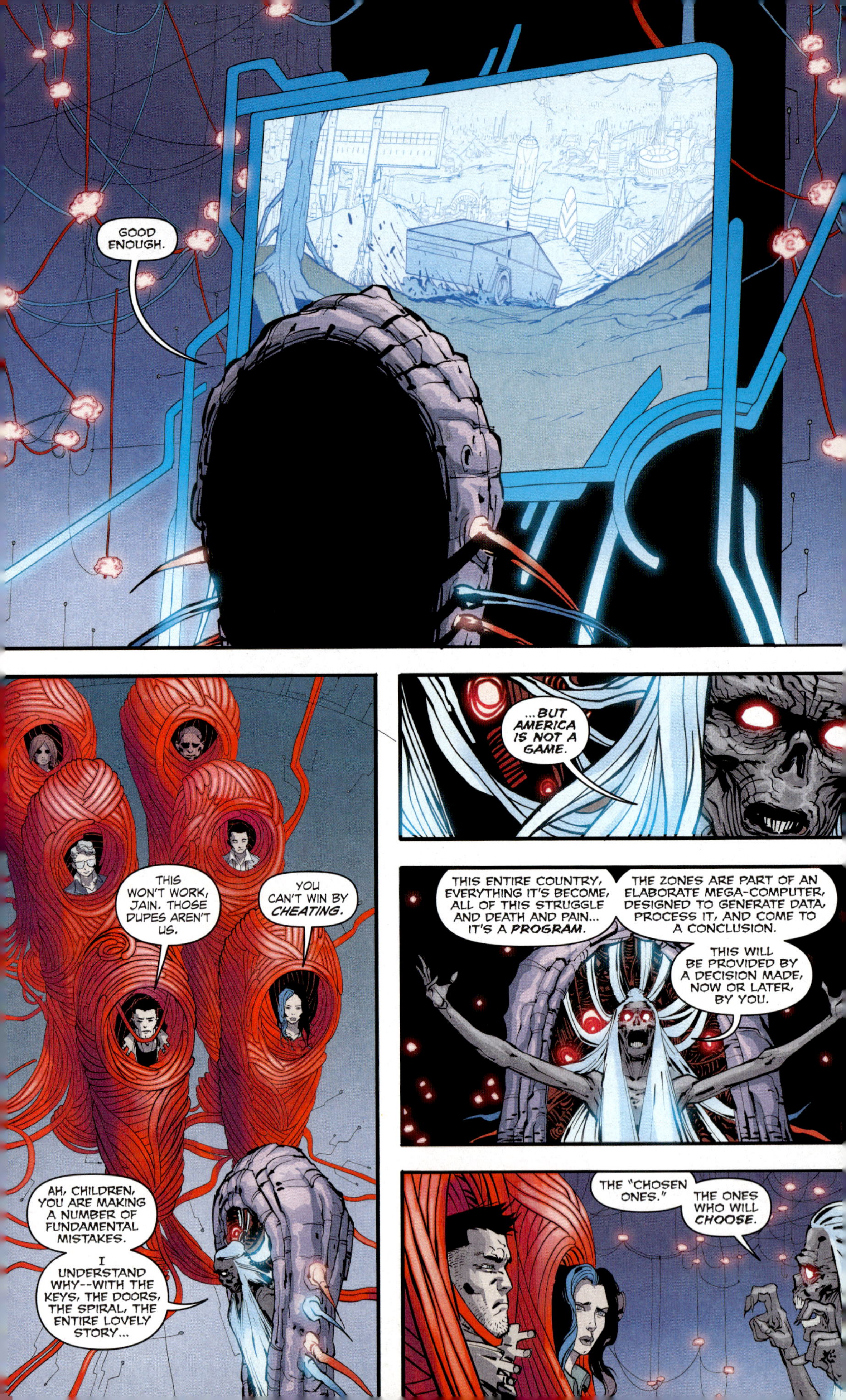

"GOOD ENOUGH."

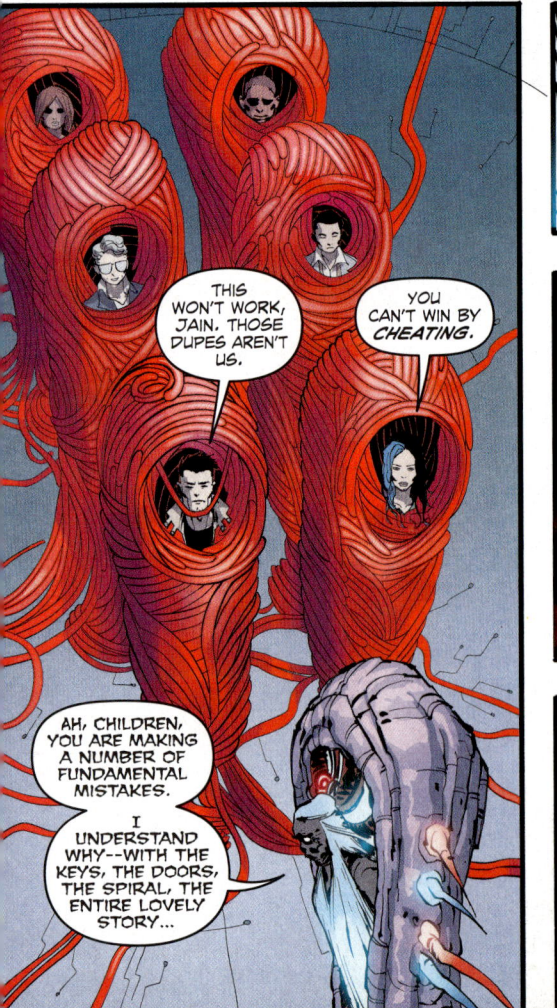

"THIS WON'T WORK, JAIN. THOSE DUPES AREN'T US."

"YOU CAN'T WIN BY CHEATING."

"AH, CHILDREN, YOU ARE MAKING A NUMBER OF FUNDAMENTAL MISTAKES."

"I UNDERSTAND WHY--WITH THE KEYS, THE DOORS, THE SPIRAL, THE ENTIRE LOVELY STORY..."

"...BUT AMERICA IS NOT A GAME."

"THIS ENTIRE COUNTRY, EVERYTHING IT'S BECOME, ALL OF THIS STRUGGLE AND DEATH AND PAIN... IT'S A PROGRAM."

"THE ZONES ARE PART OF AN ELABORATE MEGA-COMPUTER, DESIGNED TO GENERATE DATA, PROCESS IT, AND COME TO A CONCLUSION."

"THIS WILL BE PROVIDED BY A DECISION MADE, NOW OR LATER, BY YOU."

"THE 'CHOSEN ONES.'"

"THE ONES WHO WILL CHOOSE."

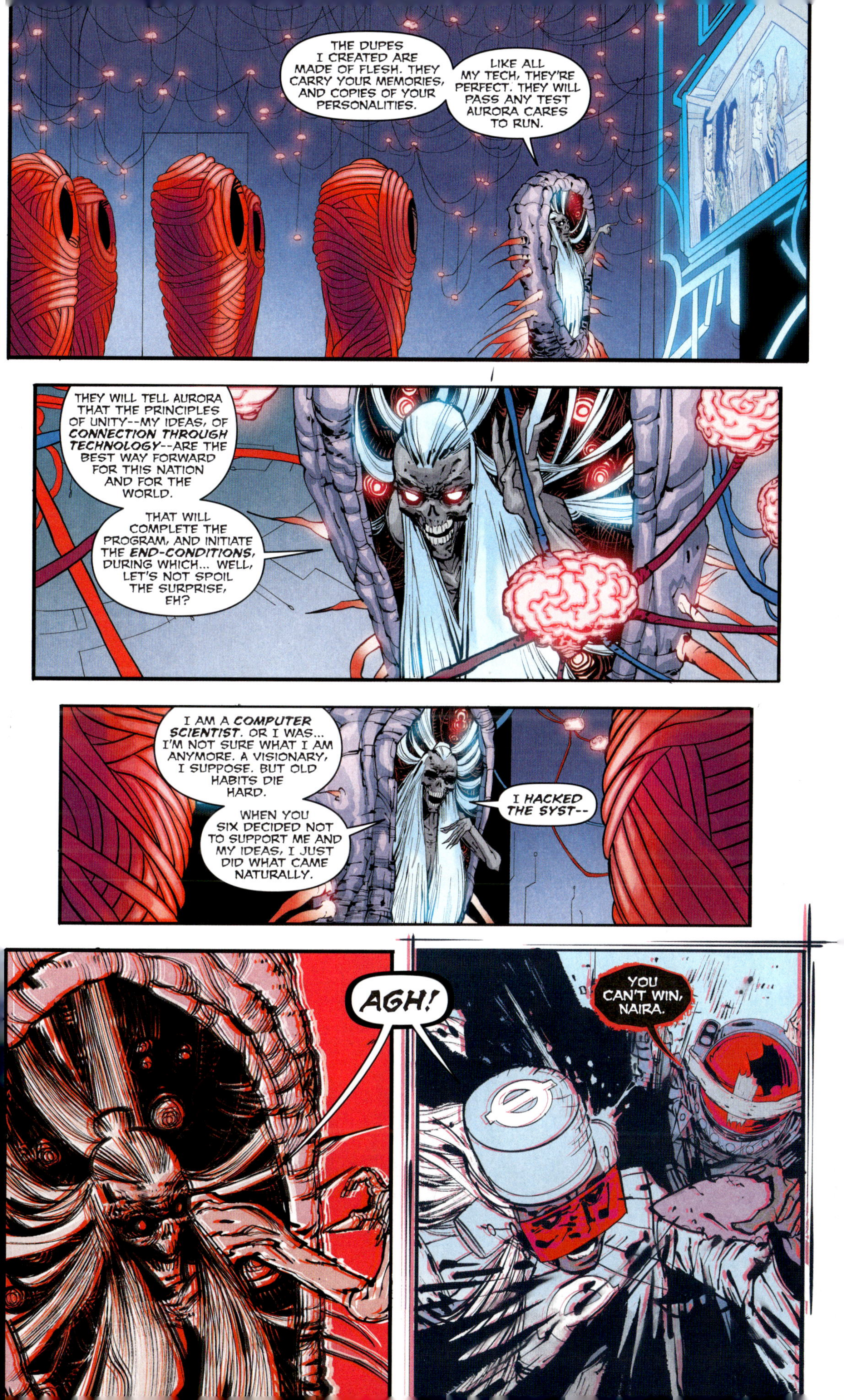
THE DUPES I CREATED ARE MADE OF FLESH. THEY CARRY YOUR MEMORIES, AND COPIES OF YOUR PERSONALITIES.
LIKE ALL MY TECH, THEY'RE PERFECT. THEY WILL PASS ANY TEST AURORA CARES TO RUN.
THEY WILL TELL AURORA THAT THE PRINCIPLES OF UNITY--MY IDEAS, OF *CONNECTION THROUGH TECHNOLOGY*--ARE THE BEST WAY FORWARD FOR THIS NATION AND FOR THE WORLD.
THAT WILL COMPLETE THE PROGRAM, AND INITIATE THE *END-CONDITIONS*, DURING WHICH... WELL, LET'S NOT SPOIL THE SURPRISE, EH?
I AM A *COMPUTER SCIENTIST*. OR I WAS... I'M NOT SURE WHAT I AM ANYMORE. A VISIONARY, I SUPPOSE. BUT OLD HABITS DIE HARD.
WHEN YOU SIX DECIDED NOT TO SUPPORT ME AND MY IDEAS, I JUST DID WHAT CAME NATURALLY.
I *HACKED THE SYST*--
AGH!
YOU CAN'T WIN, NAIRA.

I... I'M SORRY. I'M FIGHTING MANY BATTLES ON MANY FRONTS. THE DESTINY MAN DESIRES HIS OWN VERSION OF THE ENDING CONDITIONS.
I JUST... JUST NEED TO HOLD HIM BACK LONG ENOUGH TO LET THE PROGRAM RUN.
I HAVE TO MAINTAIN MY FOCUS.
PLEASE... EXCUSE MY RUDENESS.
THIS WILL ALL BE OVER SOON.
SHE'LL *KILL* US. YOU KNOW THAT, RIGHT?
SHE'S ONLY KEEPING US ALIVE IN CASE THE DUPLICATES DON'T WORK. BUT IF THEY DO--AND JAIN SEEMS PRETTY GODDAMN CONFIDENT THEY WILL-- WE'RE...
REDUNDANT. YES. THAT TRACKS.

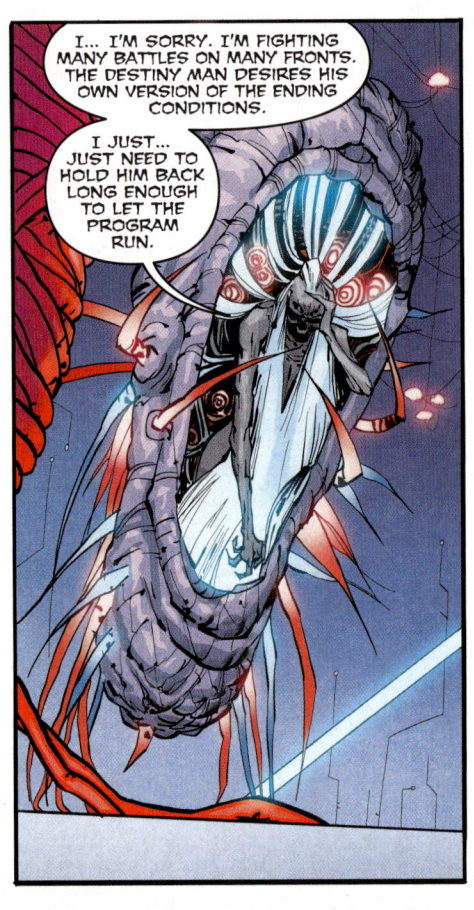

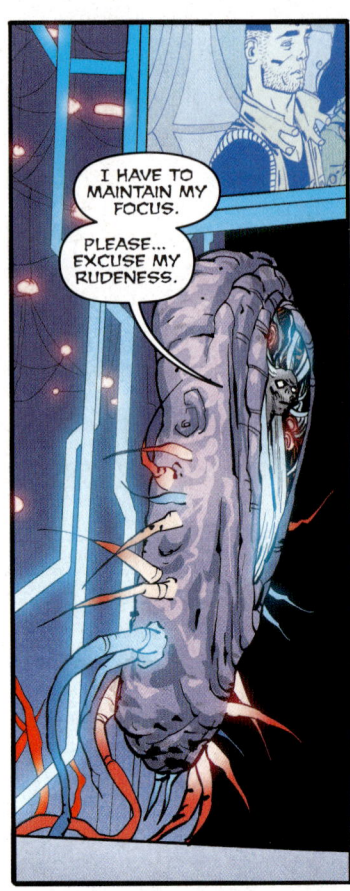

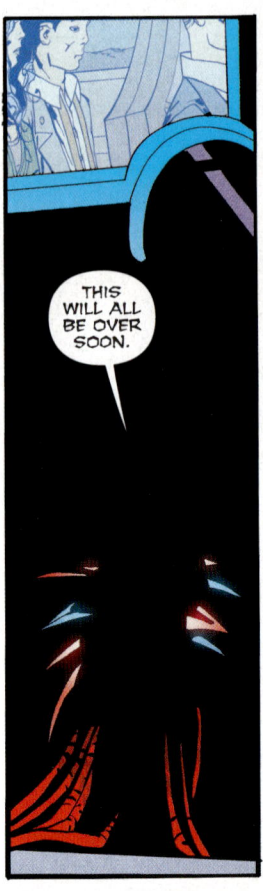

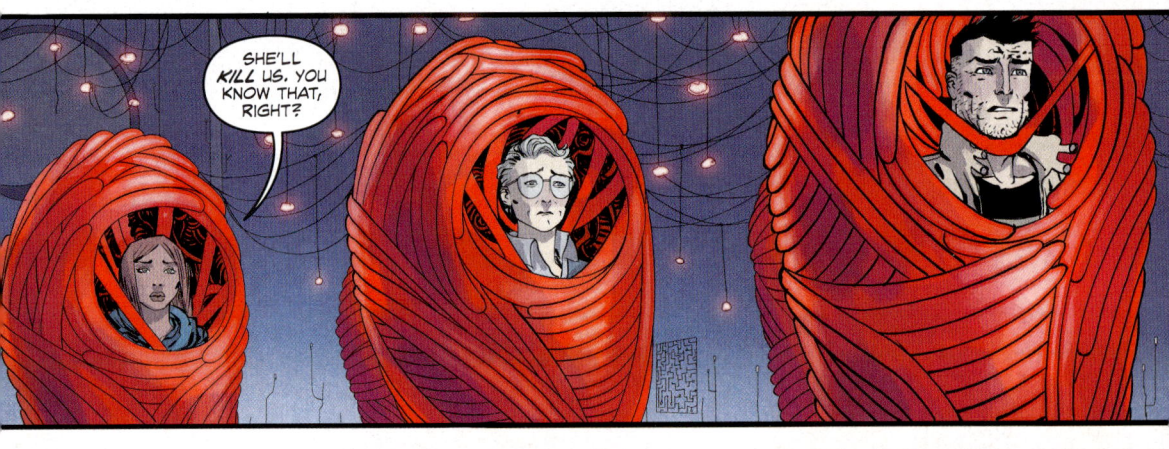

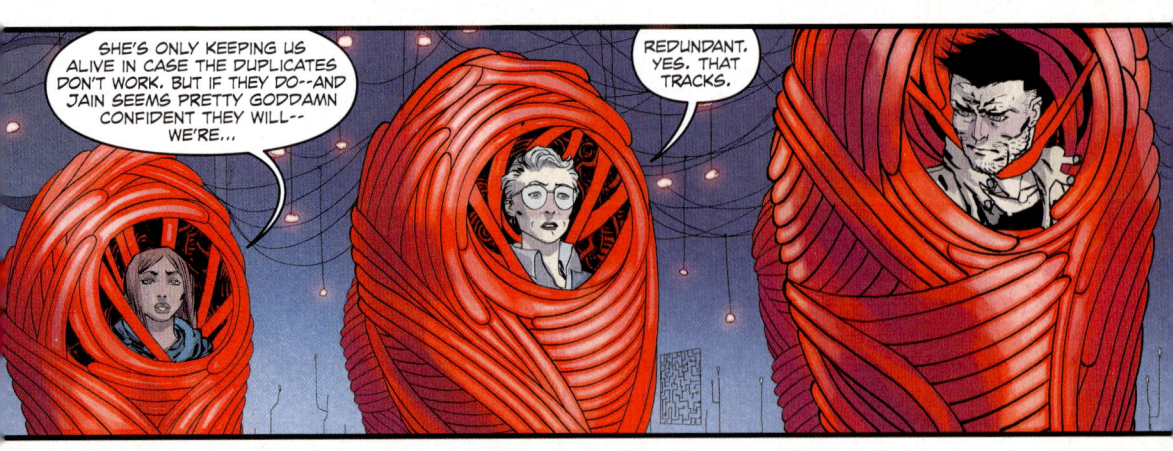

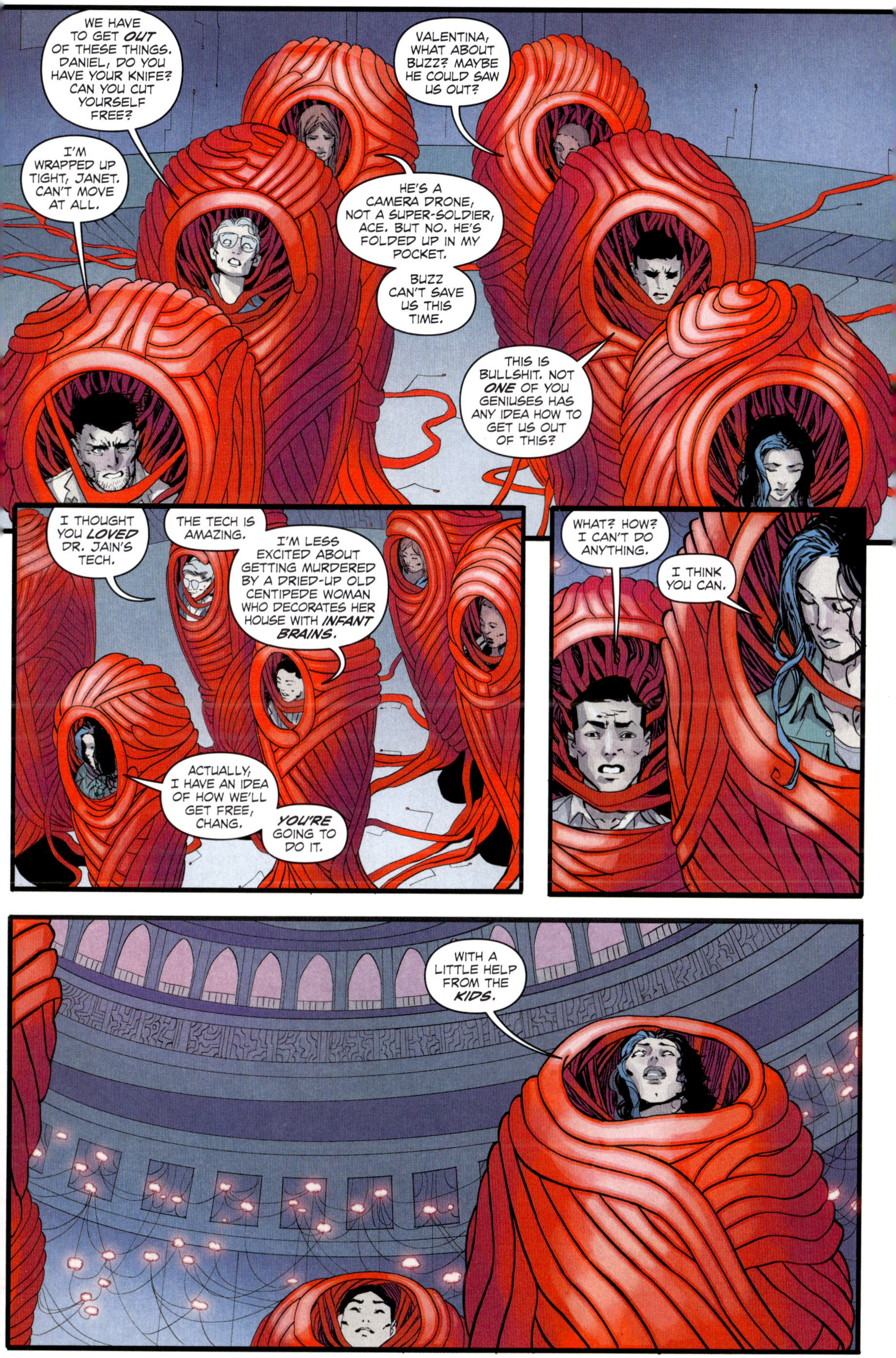
WE HAVE TO GET OUT OF THESE THINGS. DANIEL, DO YOU HAVE YOUR KNIFE? CAN YOU CUT YOURSELF FREE?
I'M WRAPPED UP TIGHT, JANET. CAN'T MOVE AT ALL.
VALENTINA, WHAT ABOUT BUZZ? MAYBE HE COULD SAW US OUT?
HE'S A CAMERA DRONE, NOT A SUPER-SOLDIER, ACE. BUT NO. HE'S FOLDED UP IN MY POCKET.
BUZZ CAN'T SAVE US THIS TIME.
THIS IS BULLSHIT. NOT ONE OF YOU GENIUSES HAS ANY IDEA HOW TO GET US OUT OF THIS?
I THOUGHT YOU LOVED DR. JAIN'S TECH.
THE TECH IS AMAZING.
I'M LESS EXCITED ABOUT GETTING MURDERED BY A DRIED-UP OLD CENTIPEDE WOMAN WHO DECORATES HER HOUSE WITH INFANT BRAINS.
ACTUALLY, I HAVE AN IDEA OF HOW WE'LL GET FREE, CHANG.
YOU'RE GOING TO DO IT.
WHAT? HOW? I CAN'T DO ANYTHING.
I THINK YOU CAN.
WITH A LITTLE HELP FROM THE KIDS.

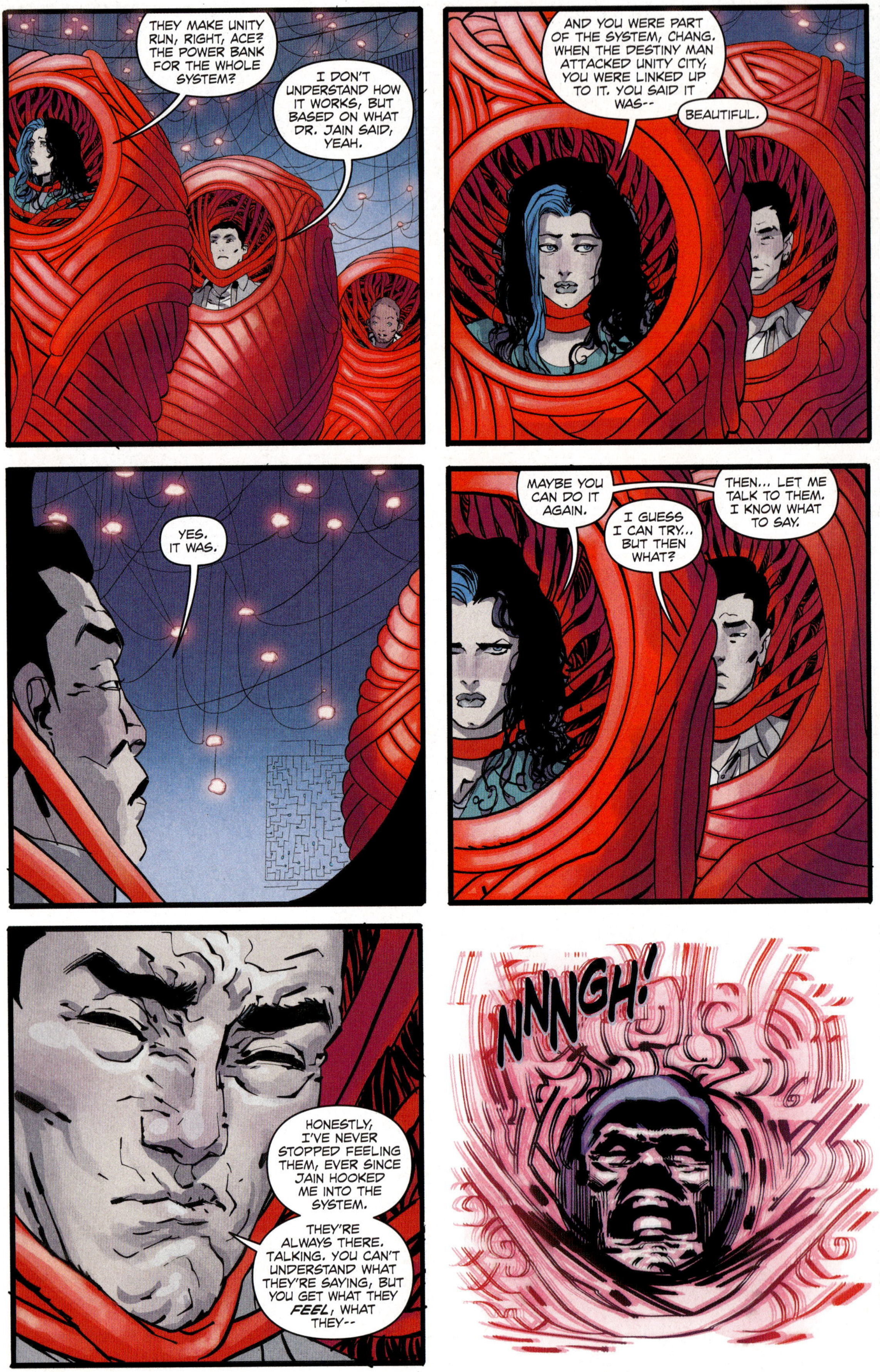

THEY MAKE UNITY RUN, RIGHT, ACE? THE POWER BANK FOR THE WHOLE SYSTEM?
I DON'T UNDERSTAND HOW IT WORKS, BUT BASED ON WHAT DR. JAIN SAID, YEAH.
AND YOU WERE PART OF THE SYSTEM, CHANG. WHEN THE DESTINY MAN ATTACKED UNITY CITY, YOU WERE LINKED UP TO IT. YOU SAID IT WAS--
BEAUTIFUL.
YES. IT WAS.
MAYBE YOU CAN DO IT AGAIN.
I GUESS I CAN TRY... BUT THEN WHAT?
THEN... LET ME TALK TO THEM. I KNOW WHAT TO SAY.
HONESTLY, I'VE NEVER STOPPED FEELING THEM, EVER SINCE JAIN HOOKED ME INTO THE SYSTEM.
THEY'RE ALWAYS THERE. TALKING. YOU CAN'T UNDERSTAND WHAT THEY'RE SAYING, BUT YOU GET WHAT THEY *FEEL*, WHAT THEY--
NNNGH!

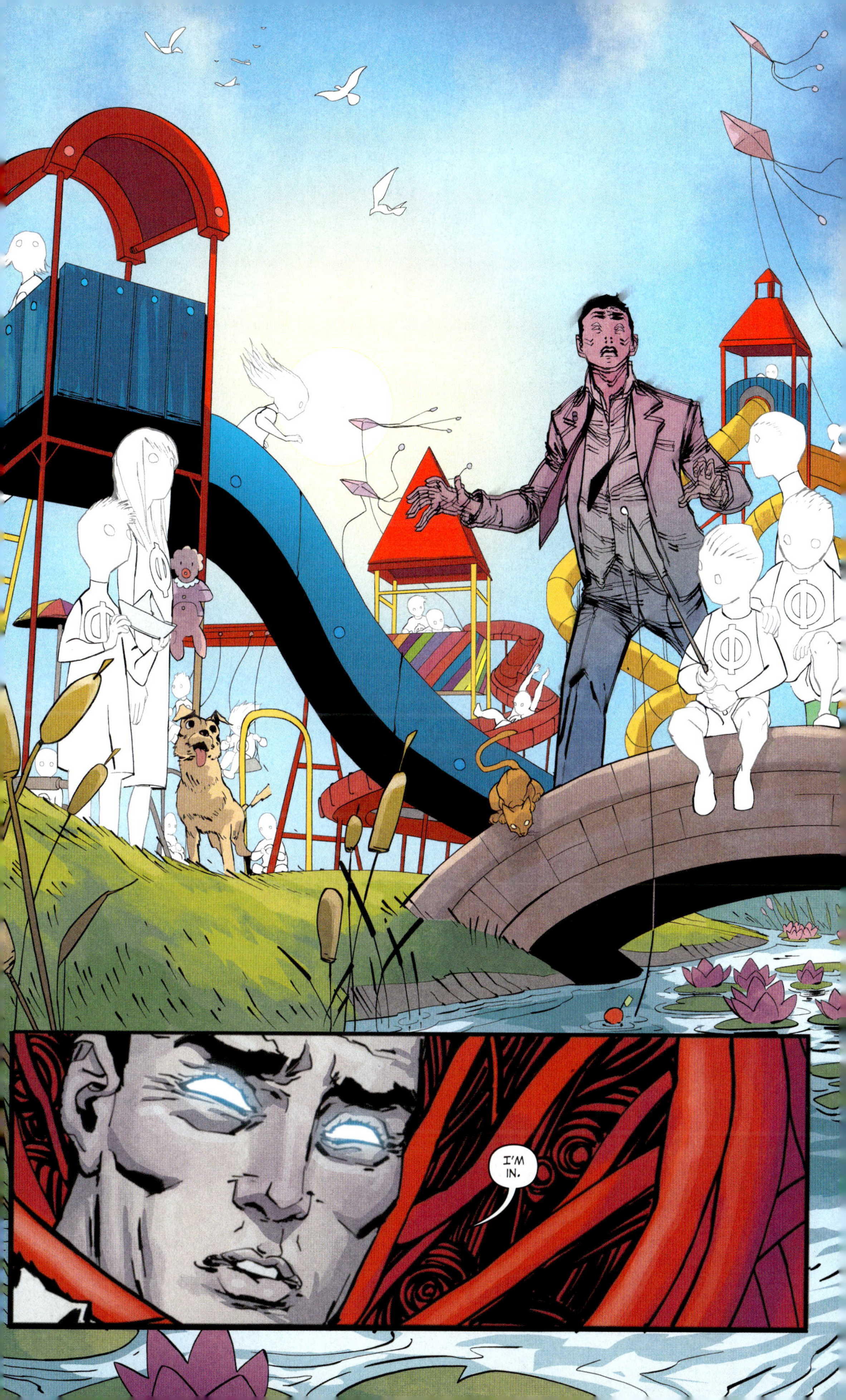
I'M IN.

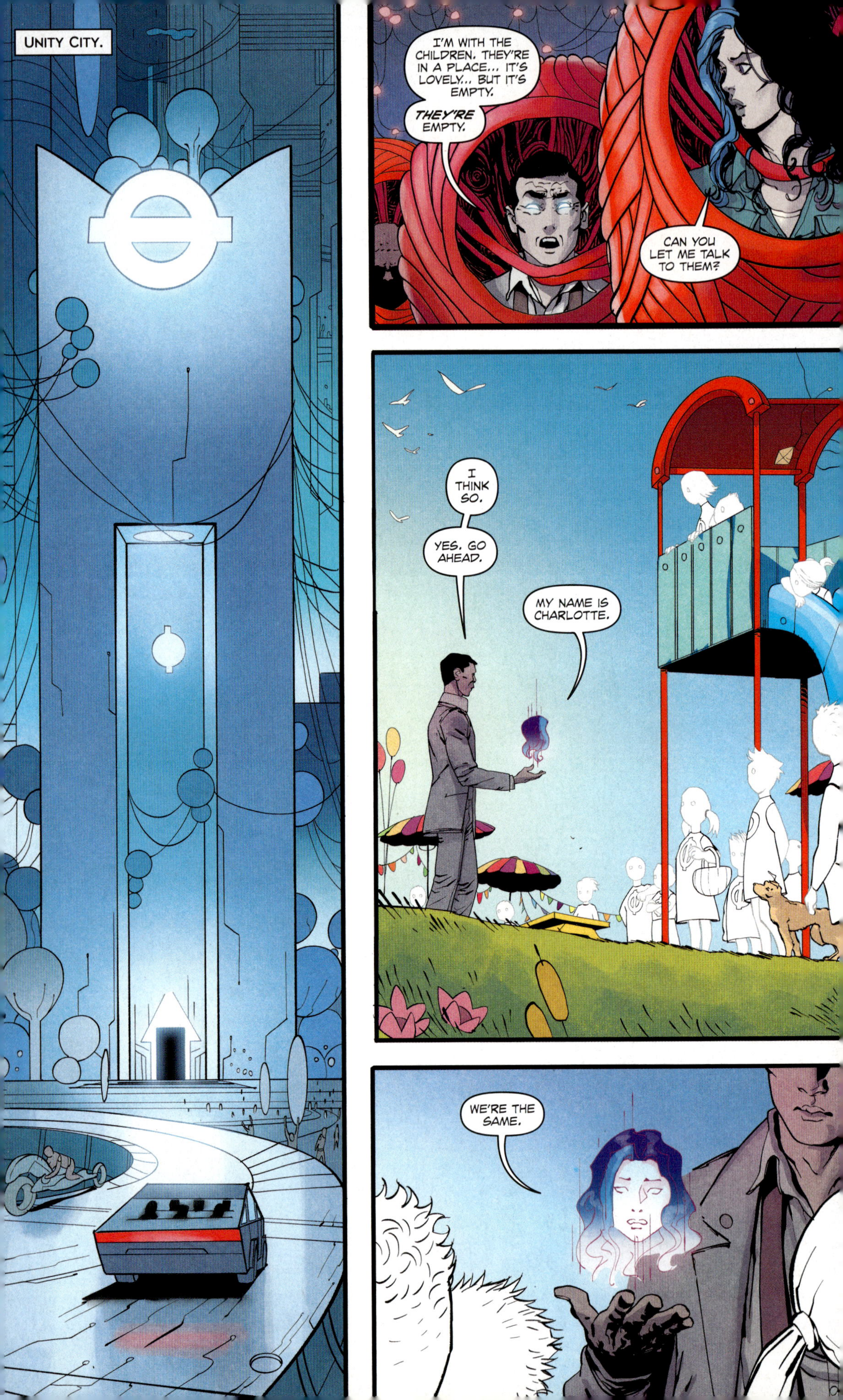
UNITY CITY.
I'M WITH THE CHILDREN. THEY'RE IN A PLACE... IT'S LOVELY... BUT IT'S EMPTY.
THEY'RE EMPTY.
CAN YOU LET ME TALK TO THEM?
I THINK SO.
YES. GO AHEAD.
MY NAME IS CHARLOTTE.
WE'RE THE SAME.

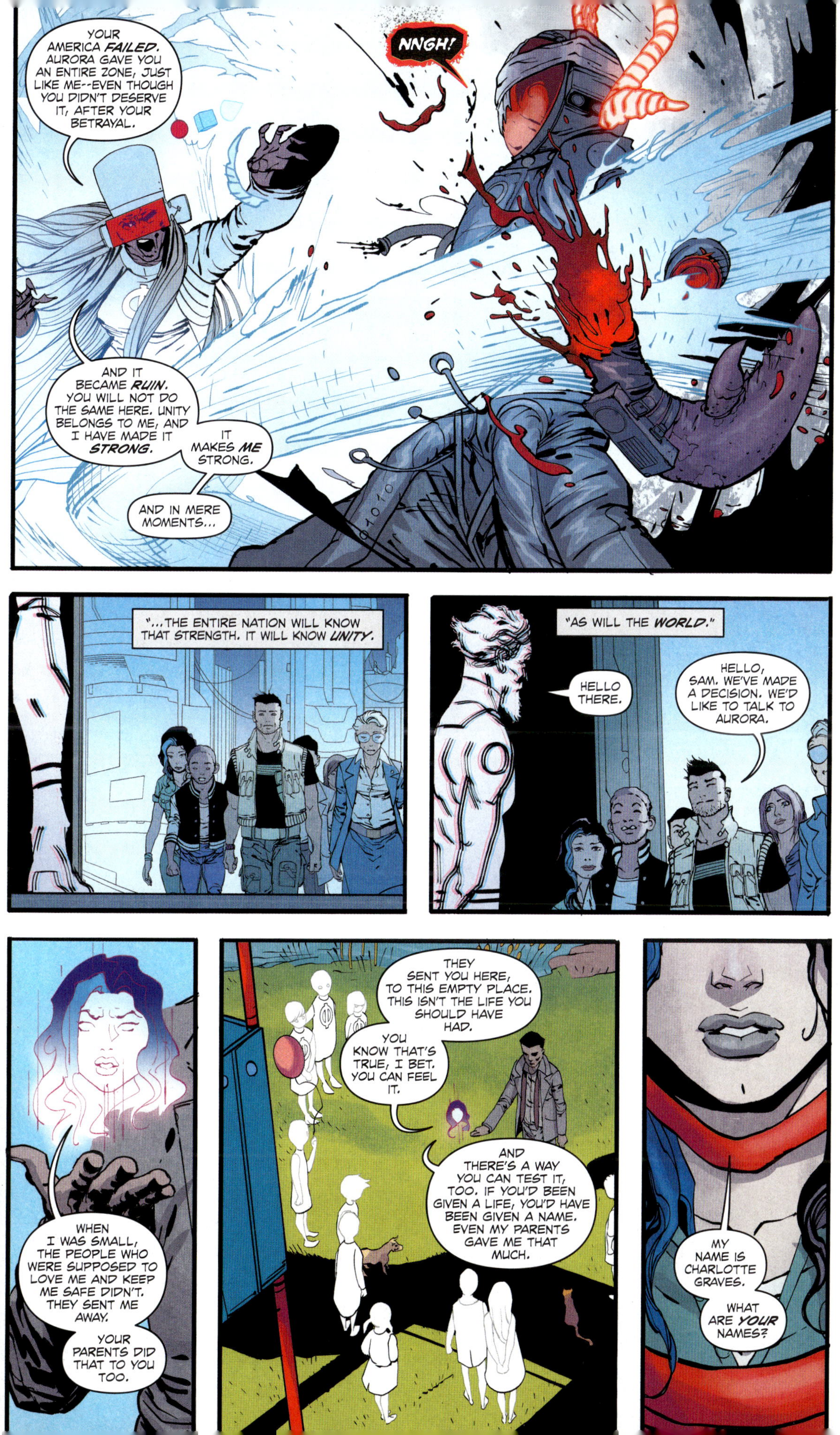
YOUR AMERICA FAILED. AURORA GAVE YOU AN ENTIRE ZONE, JUST LIKE ME--EVEN THOUGH YOU DIDN'T DESERVE IT, AFTER YOUR BETRAYAL.
NNGH!
AND IT BECAME RUIN. YOU WILL NOT DO THE SAME HERE. UNITY BELONGS TO ME, AND I HAVE MADE IT STRONG.
IT MAKES ME STRONG.
AND IN MERE MOMENTS...
"...THE ENTIRE NATION WILL KNOW THAT STRENGTH. IT WILL KNOW UNITY.
"AS WILL THE WORLD."
HELLO THERE.
HELLO, SAM. WE'VE MADE A DECISION. WE'D LIKE TO TALK TO AURORA.
WHEN I WAS SMALL, THE PEOPLE WHO WERE SUPPOSED TO LOVE ME AND KEEP ME SAFE DIDN'T. THEY SENT ME AWAY.
YOUR PARENTS DID THAT TO YOU TOO.
THEY SENT YOU HERE, TO THIS EMPTY PLACE. THIS ISN'T THE LIFE YOU SHOULD HAVE HAD.
YOU KNOW THAT'S TRUE, I BET. YOU CAN FEEL IT.
AND THERE'S A WAY YOU CAN TEST IT, TOO. IF YOU'D BEEN GIVEN A LIFE, YOU'D HAVE BEEN GIVEN A NAME. EVEN MY PARENTS GAVE ME THAT MUCH.
MY NAME IS CHARLOTTE GRAVES.
WHAT ARE YOUR NAMES?

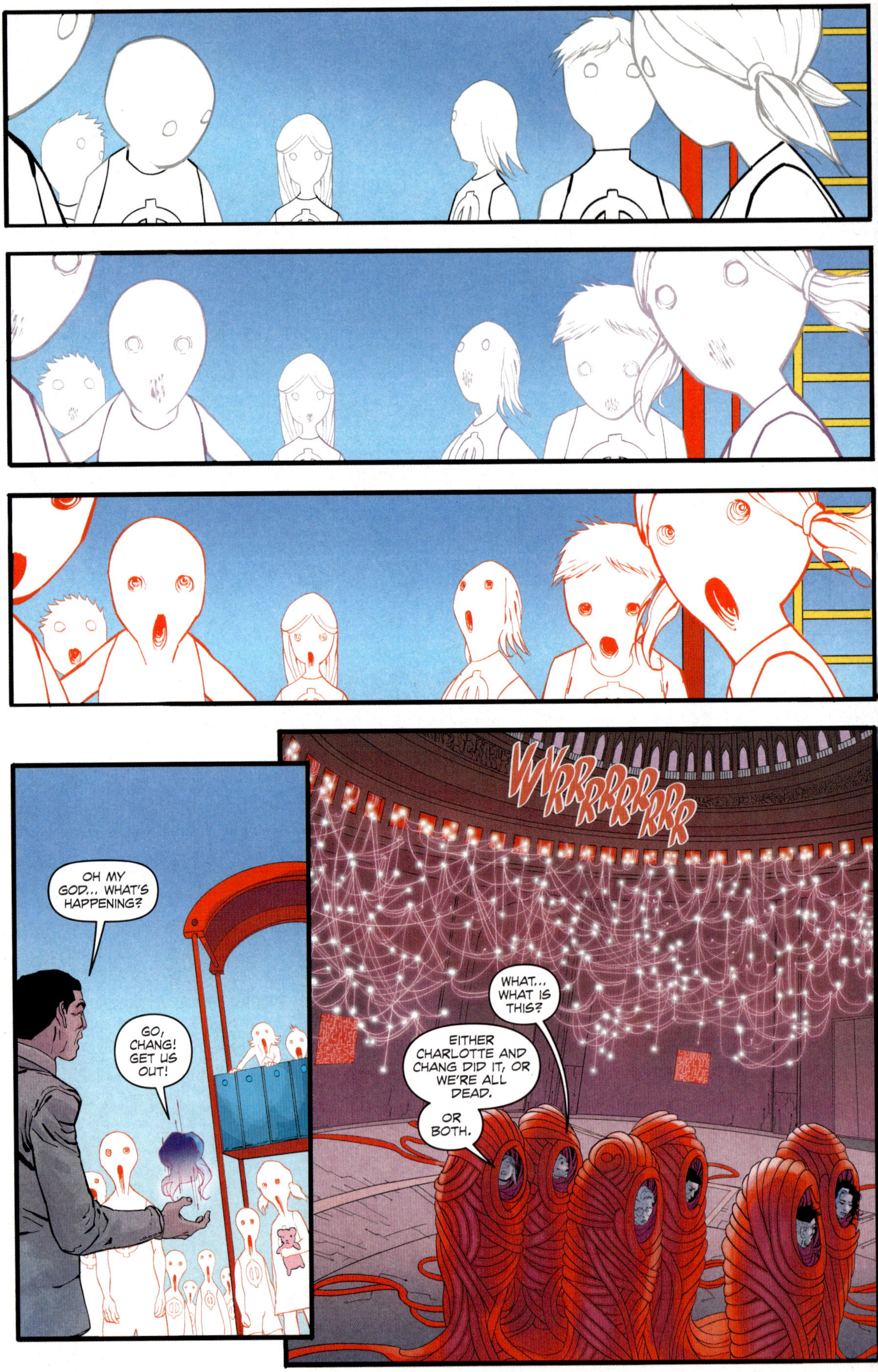
OH MY GOD... WHAT'S HAPPENING?
GO, CHANG! GET US OUT!
VVVRRRRRRRRRR
WHAT... WHAT IS THIS?
EITHER CHARLOTTE AND CHANG DID IT, OR WE'RE ALL DEAD.
OR BOTH.

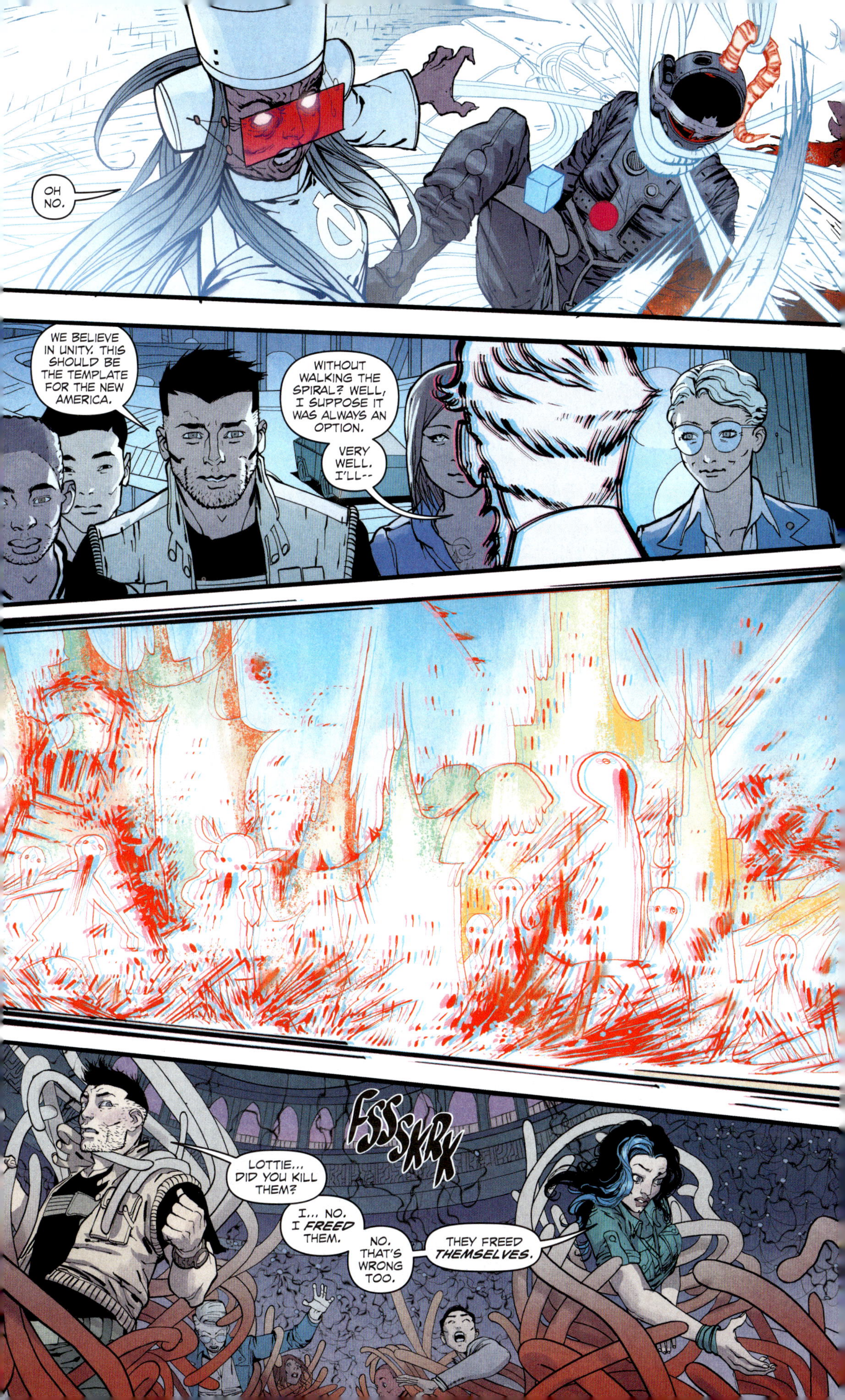
OH NO.
WE BELIEVE IN UNITY. THIS SHOULD BE THE TEMPLATE FOR THE NEW AMERICA.
WITHOUT WALKING THE SPIRAL? WELL, I SUPPOSE IT WAS ALWAYS AN OPTION.
VERY WELL. I'LL--
FSSSKRK
LOTTIE... DID YOU KILL THEM?
I... NO. I *FREED* THEM.
NO. THAT'S WRONG TOO.
THEY FREED *THEMSELVES*.

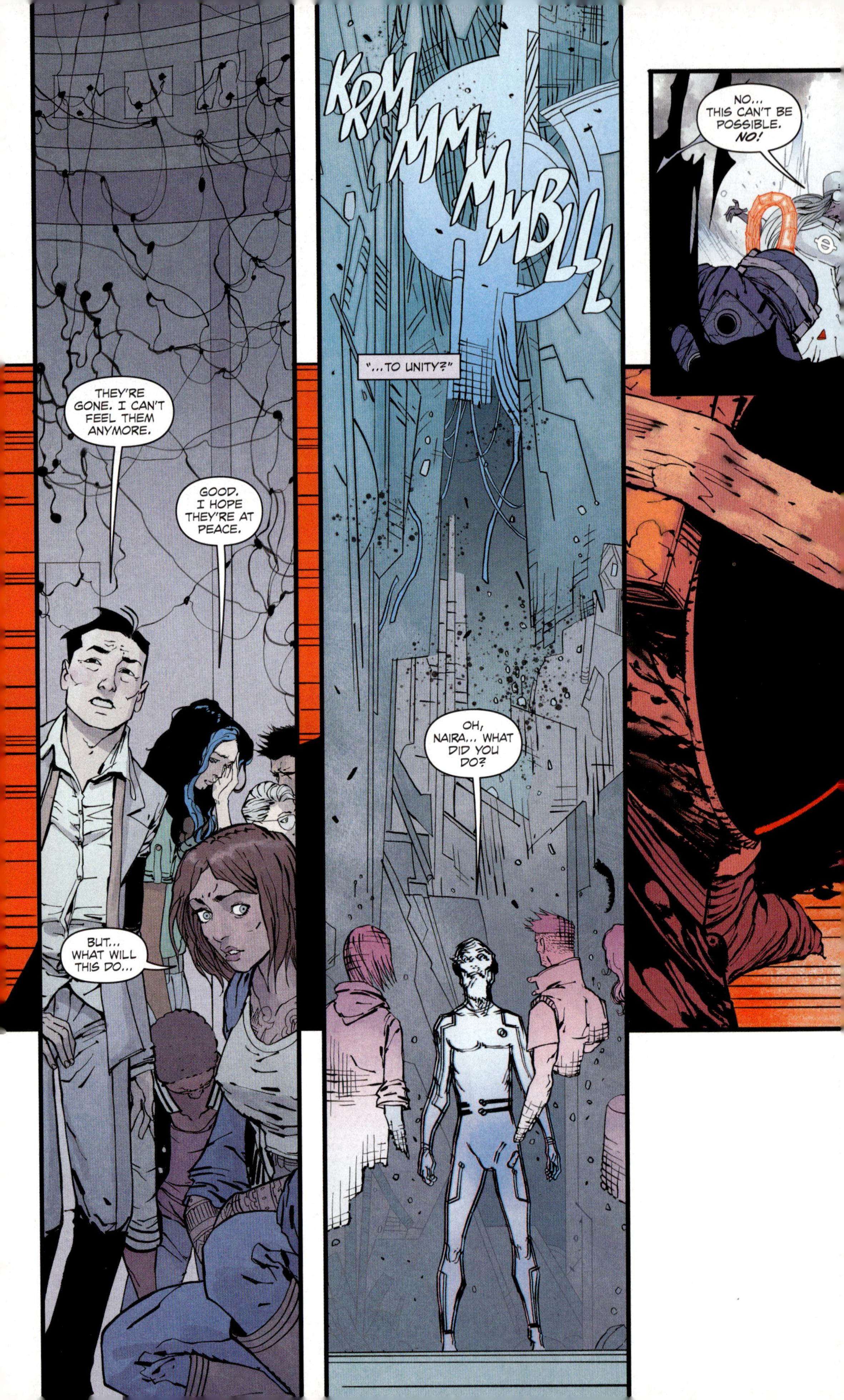
THEY'RE GONE. I CAN'T FEEL THEM ANYMORE.
GOOD. I HOPE THEY'RE AT PEACE.
BUT... WHAT WILL THIS DO...
KRMMMMMBLLL
"...TO UNITY?"
OH, NAIRA... WHAT DID YOU DO?
NO... THIS CAN'T BE POSSIBLE. NO!

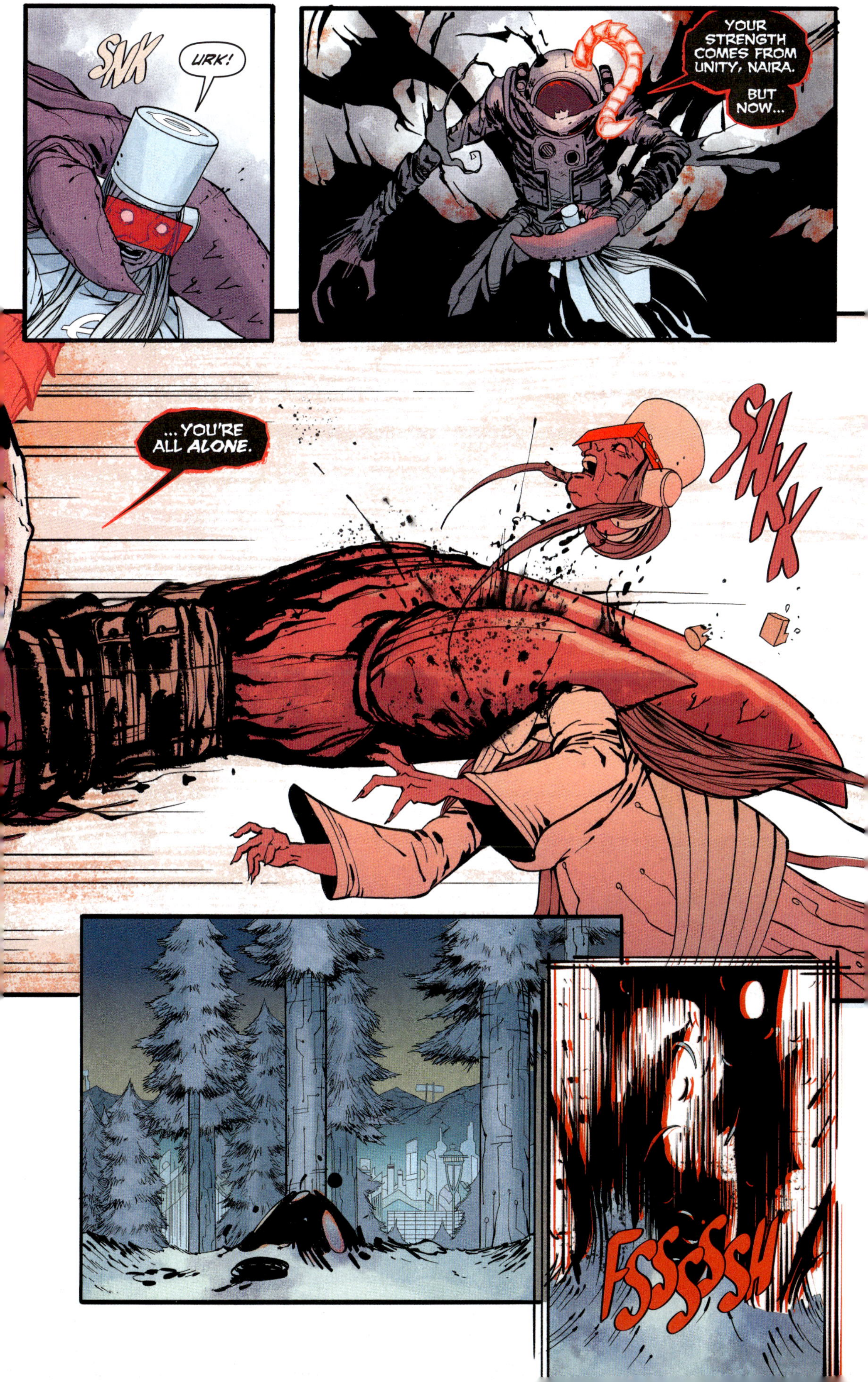
SNK
URK!
YOUR STRENGTH COMES FROM UNITY, NAIRA.
BUT NOW...
...YOU'RE ALL ALONE.
SHKK
FSSSSSH

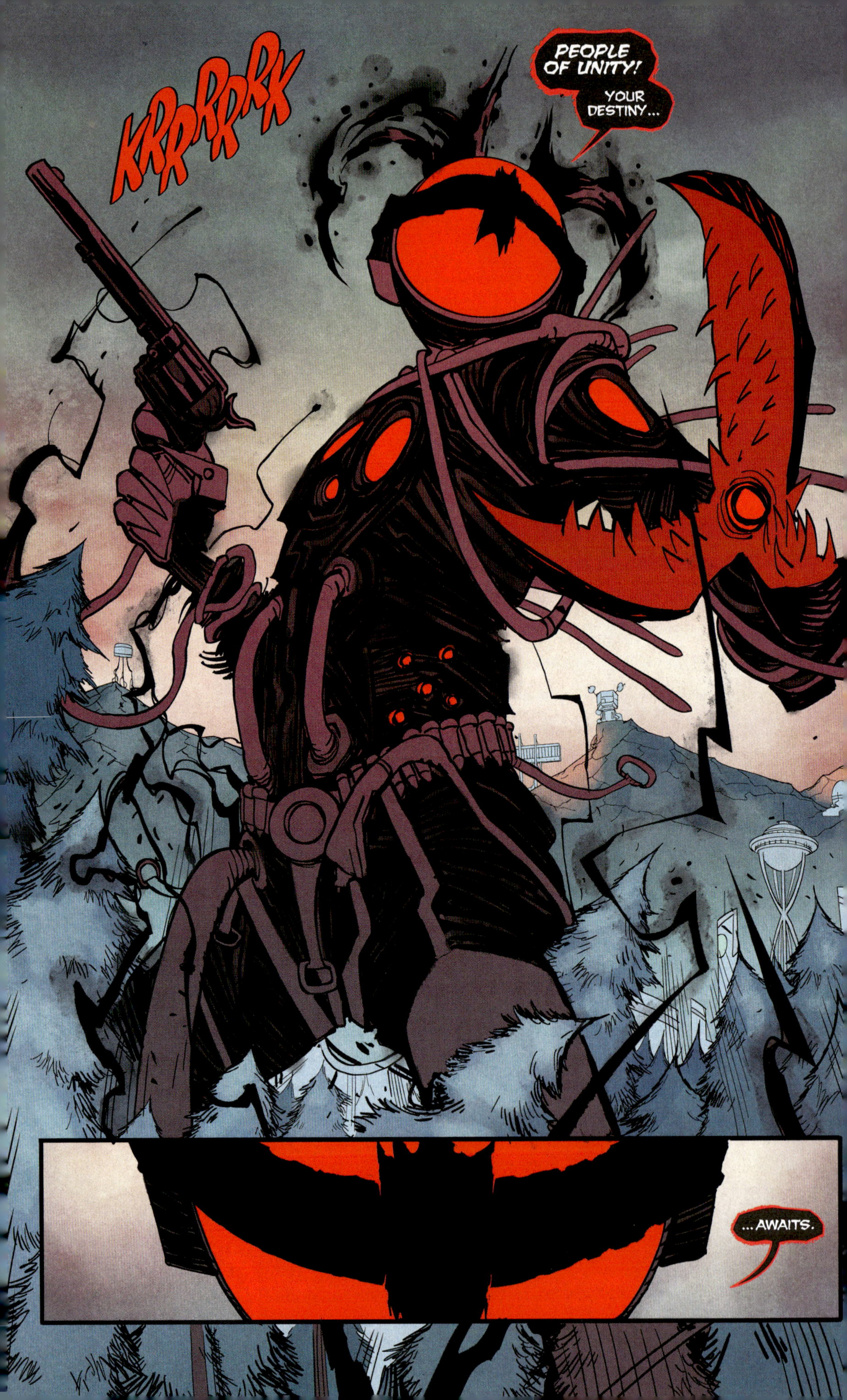
KRRRRRRK
PEOPLE OF UNITY!
YOUR DESTINY...
...AWAITS.

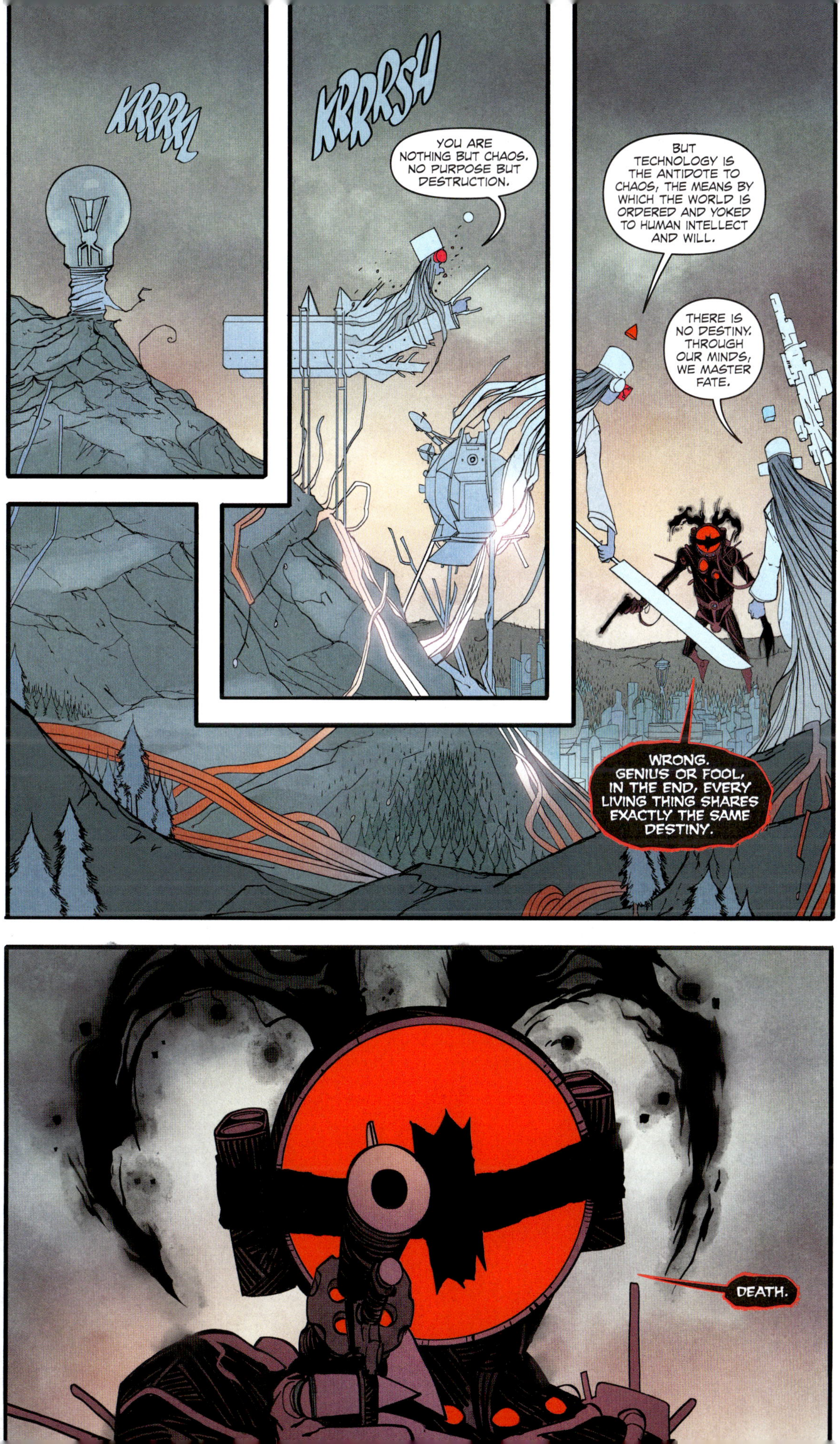
KRRRKL
KRRRSH
YOU ARE NOTHING BUT CHAOS. NO PURPOSE BUT DESTRUCTION.
BUT TECHNOLOGY IS THE ANTIDOTE TO CHAOS, THE MEANS BY WHICH THE WORLD IS ORDERED AND YOKED TO HUMAN INTELLECT AND WILL.
THERE IS NO DESTINY. THROUGH OUR MINDS, WE MASTER FATE.
WRONG. GENIUS OR FOOL, IN THE END, EVERY LIVING THING SHARES EXACTLY THE SAME DESTINY.
DEATH.

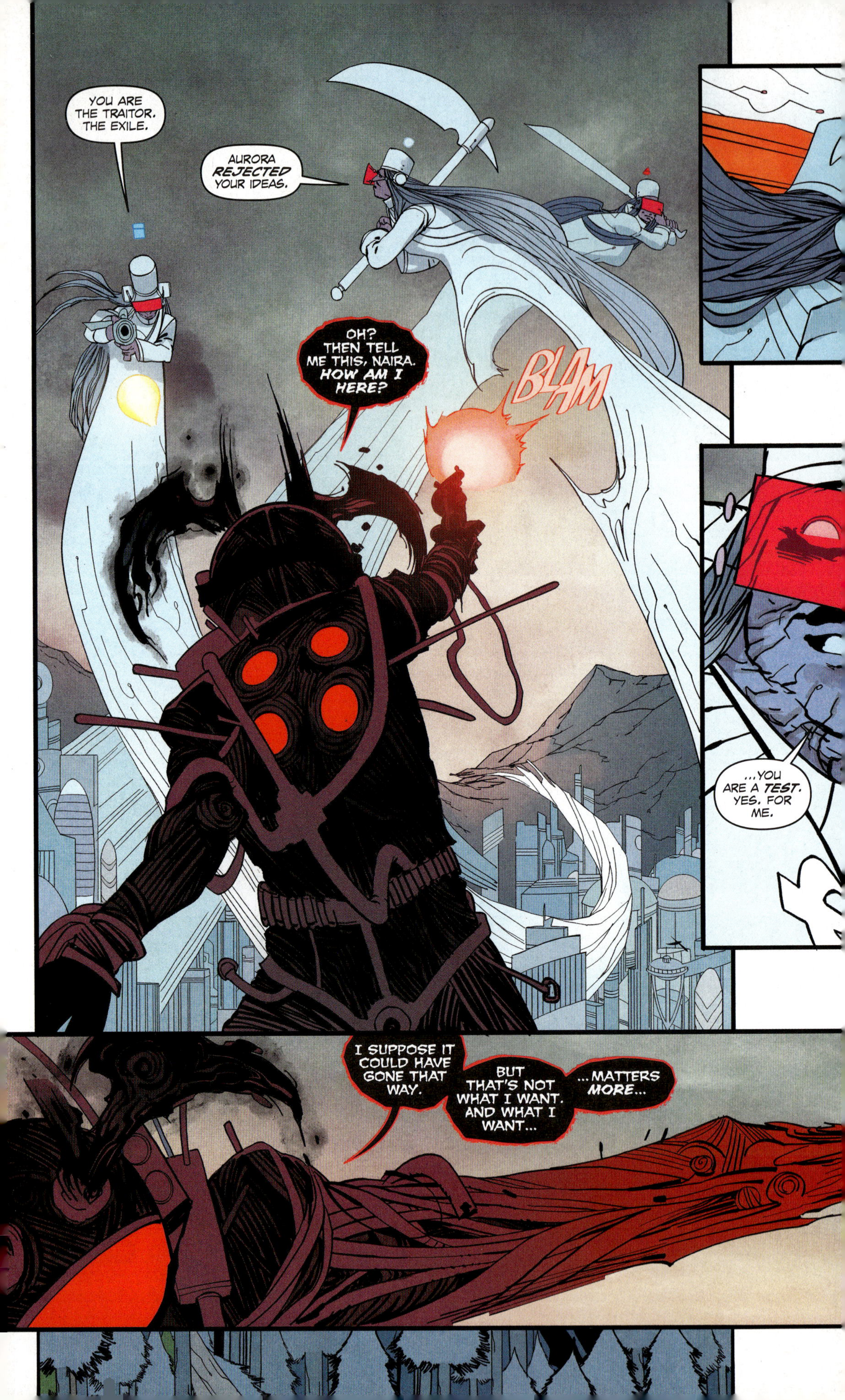
YOU ARE THE TRAITOR. THE EXILE.
AURORA *REJECTED* YOUR IDEAS.
OH? THEN TELL ME THIS, NAIRA. *HOW AM I HERE?*
BLAM
...YOU ARE A *TEST*. YES. FOR ME.
I SUPPOSE IT COULD HAVE GONE THAT WAY.
BUT THAT'S NOT WHAT I WANT. AND WHAT I WANT...
...MATTERS *MORE*...

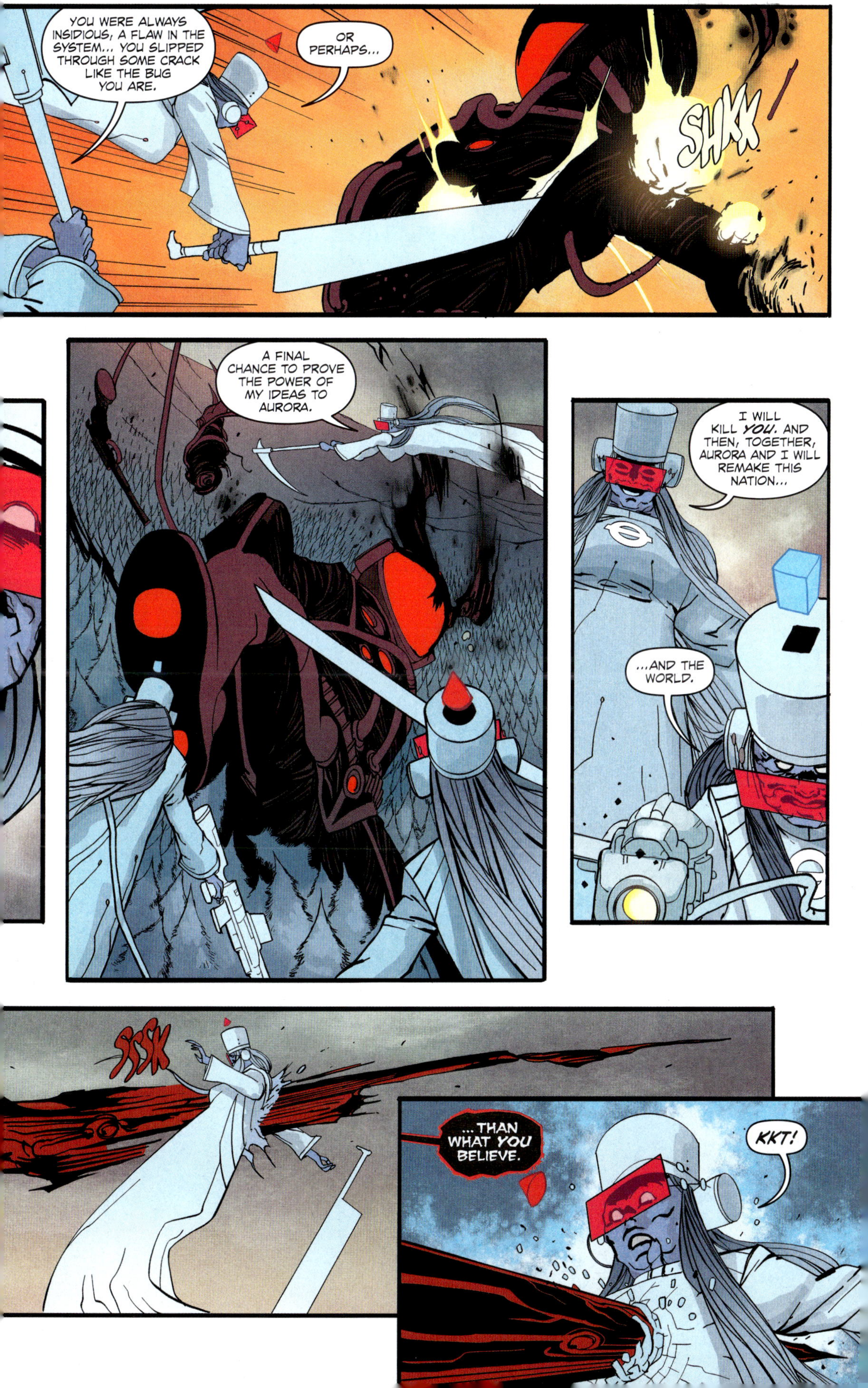
YOU WERE ALWAYS INSIDIOUS, A FLAW IN THE SYSTEM... YOU SLIPPED THROUGH SOME CRACK LIKE THE BUG YOU ARE.
OR PERHAPS...
SHKK
A FINAL CHANCE TO PROVE THE POWER OF MY IDEAS TO AURORA.
I WILL KILL YOU. AND THEN, TOGETHER, AURORA AND I WILL REMAKE THIS NATION...
...AND THE WORLD.
SSSK
...THAN WHAT YOU BELIEVE.
KKT!

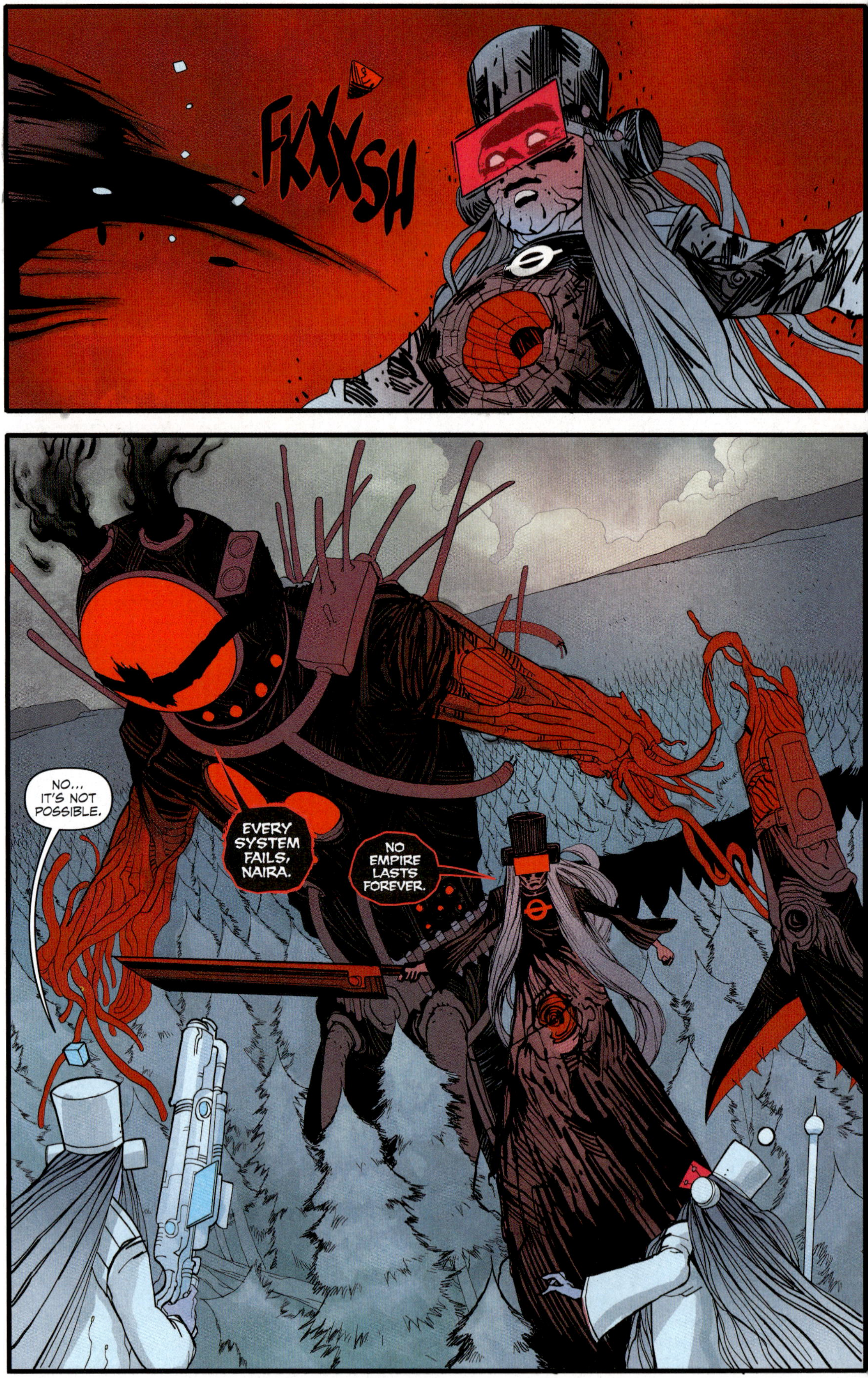

FKXXSH
NO... IT'S NOT POSSIBLE.
EVERY SYSTEM FAILS, NAIRA.
NO EMPIRE LASTS FOREVER.

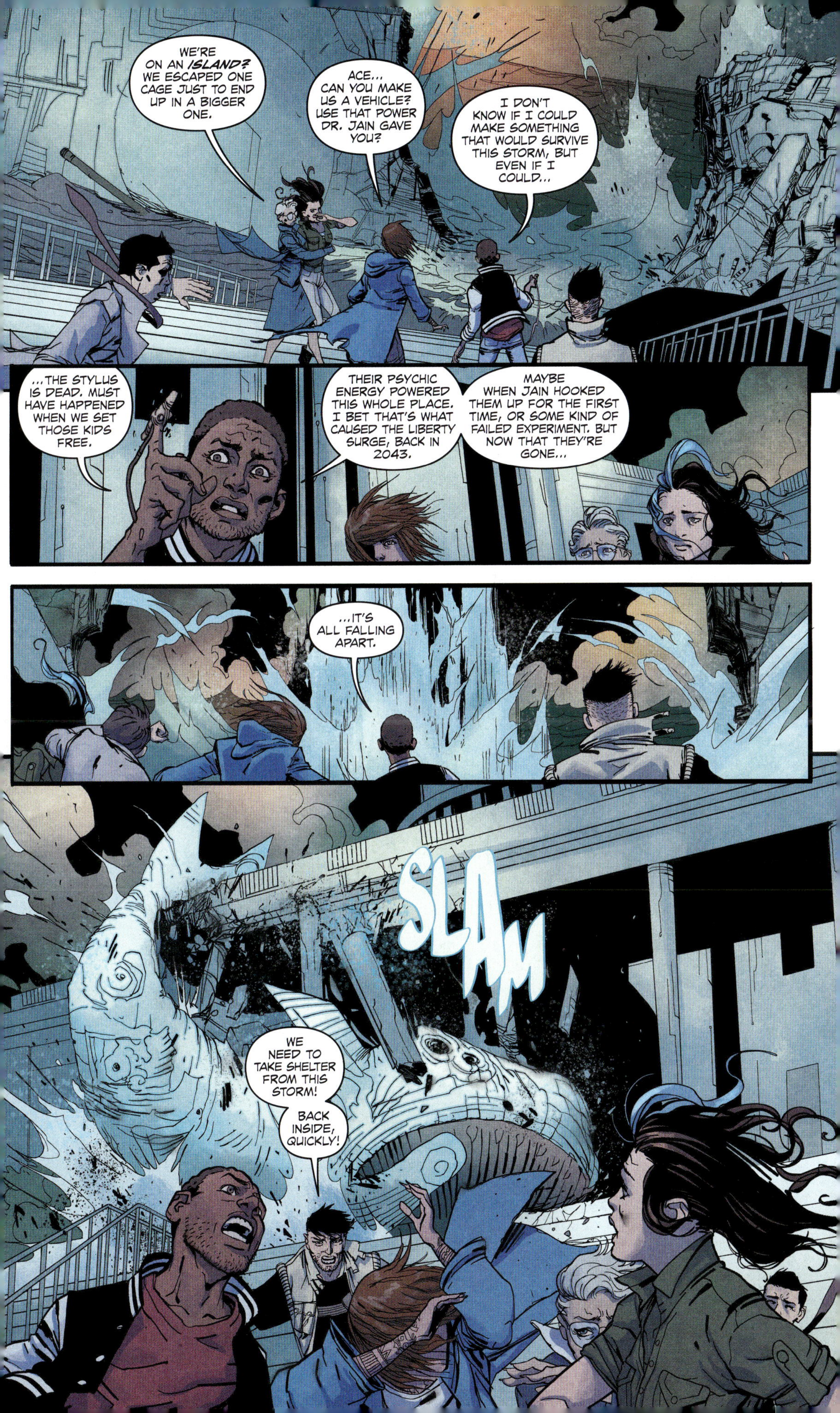
WE'RE ON AN *ISLAND?* WE ESCAPED ONE CAGE JUST TO END UP IN A BIGGER ONE.
ACE... CAN YOU MAKE US A VEHICLE? USE THAT POWER DR. JAIN GAVE YOU?
I DON'T KNOW IF I COULD MAKE SOMETHING THAT WOULD SURVIVE THIS STORM, BUT EVEN IF I COULD...
...THE STYLUS IS DEAD. MUST HAVE HAPPENED WHEN WE SET THOSE KIDS FREE.
THEIR PSYCHIC ENERGY POWERED THIS WHOLE PLACE. I BET THAT'S WHAT CAUSED THE LIBERTY SURGE, BACK IN 2043.
MAYBE WHEN JAIN HOOKED THEM UP FOR THE FIRST TIME, OR SOME KIND OF FAILED EXPERIMENT. BUT NOW THAT THEY'RE GONE...
...IT'S ALL FALLING APART.
SLAM
WE NEED TO TAKE SHELTER FROM THIS STORM!
BACK INSIDE, QUICKLY!

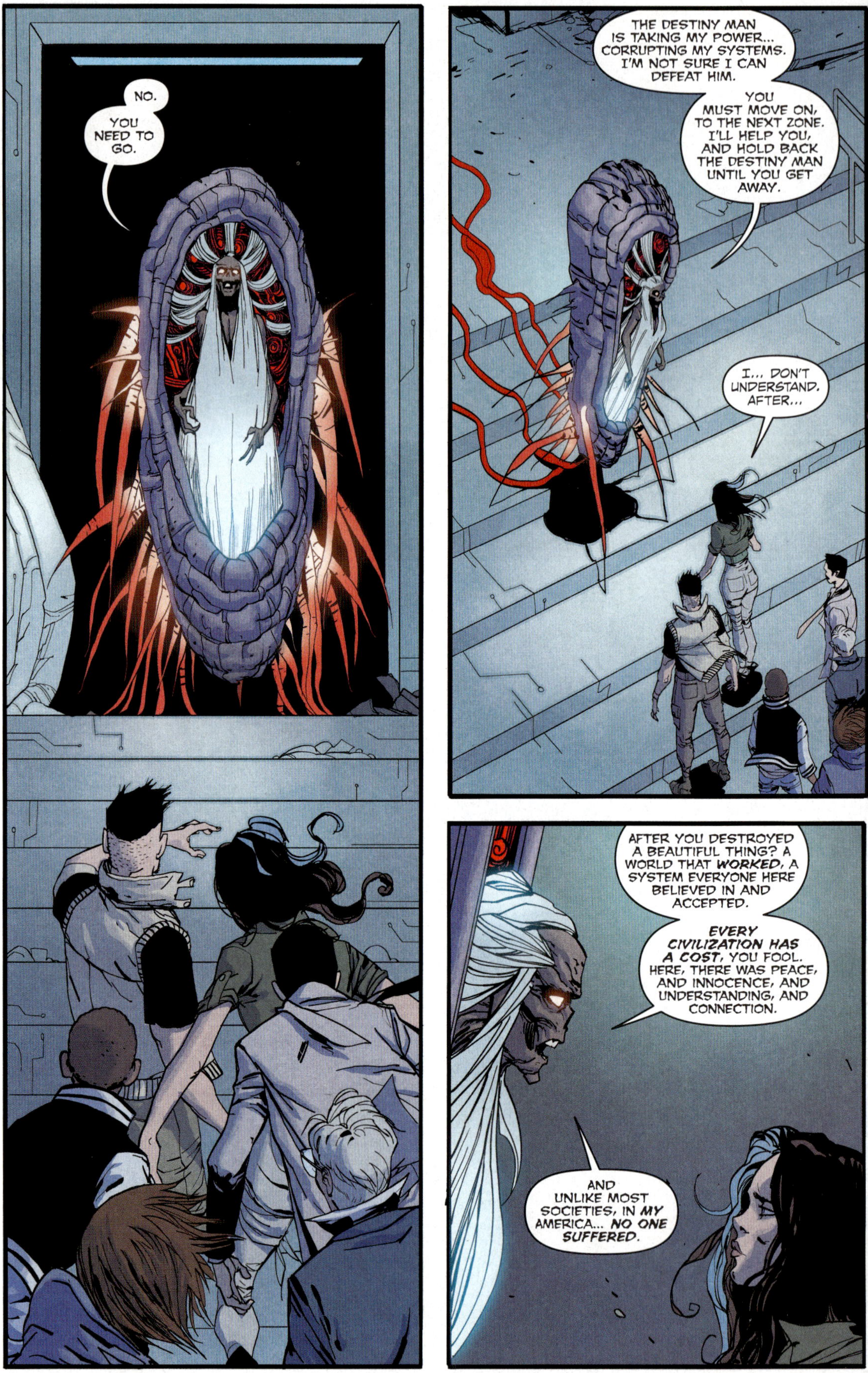
NO.
YOU NEED TO GO.
THE DESTINY MAN IS TAKING MY POWER... CORRUPTING MY SYSTEMS. I'M NOT SURE I CAN DEFEAT HIM.
YOU MUST MOVE ON, TO THE NEXT ZONE. I'LL HELP YOU, AND HOLD BACK THE DESTINY MAN UNTIL YOU GET AWAY.
I... DON'T UNDERSTAND. AFTER...
AFTER YOU DESTROYED A BEAUTIFUL THING? A WORLD THAT *WORKED*, A SYSTEM EVERYONE HERE BELIEVED IN AND ACCEPTED.
EVERY CIVILIZATION HAS A COST, YOU FOOL. HERE, THERE WAS PEACE, AND INNOCENCE, AND UNDERSTANDING, AND CONNECTION.
AND UNLIKE MOST SOCIETIES, IN *MY* AMERICA... ***NO ONE SUFFERED***.

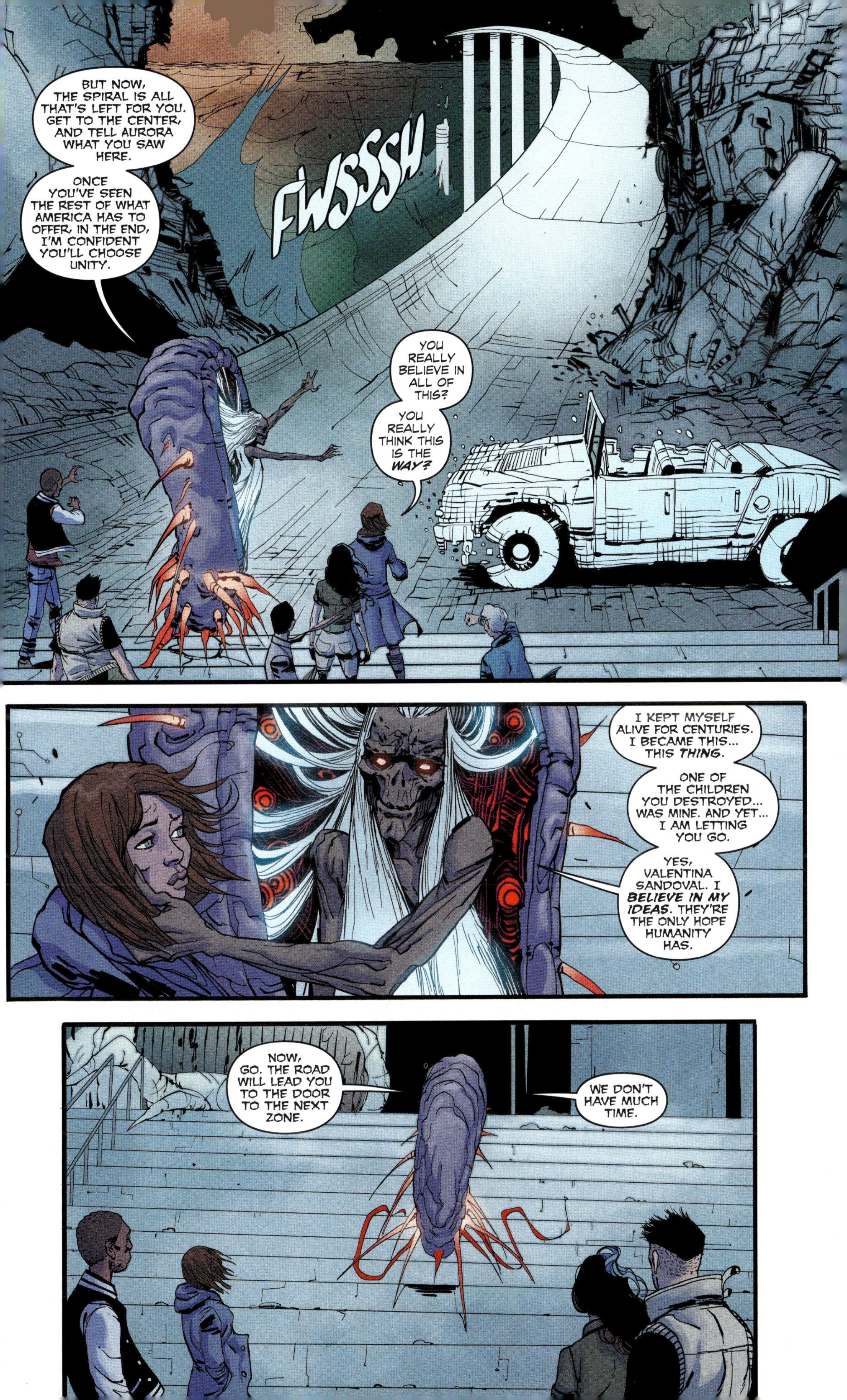

BUT NOW, THE SPIRAL IS ALL THAT'S LEFT FOR YOU. GET TO THE CENTER, AND TELL AURORA WHAT YOU SAW HERE.
ONCE YOU'VE SEEN THE REST OF WHAT AMERICA HAS TO OFFER, IN THE END, I'M CONFIDENT YOU'LL CHOOSE UNITY.
FWSSSH
YOU REALLY BELIEVE IN ALL OF THIS?
YOU REALLY THINK THIS IS THE *WAY?*
I KEPT MYSELF ALIVE FOR CENTURIES. I BECAME THIS... THIS *THING*.
ONE OF THE CHILDREN YOU DESTROYED... WAS MINE. AND YET... I AM LETTING YOU GO.
YES, VALENTINA SANDOVAL. I *BELIEVE IN MY IDEAS*. THEY'RE THE ONLY HOPE HUMANITY HAS.
NOW, GO. THE ROAD WILL LEAD YOU TO THE DOOR TO THE NEXT ZONE.
WE DON'T HAVE MUCH TIME.

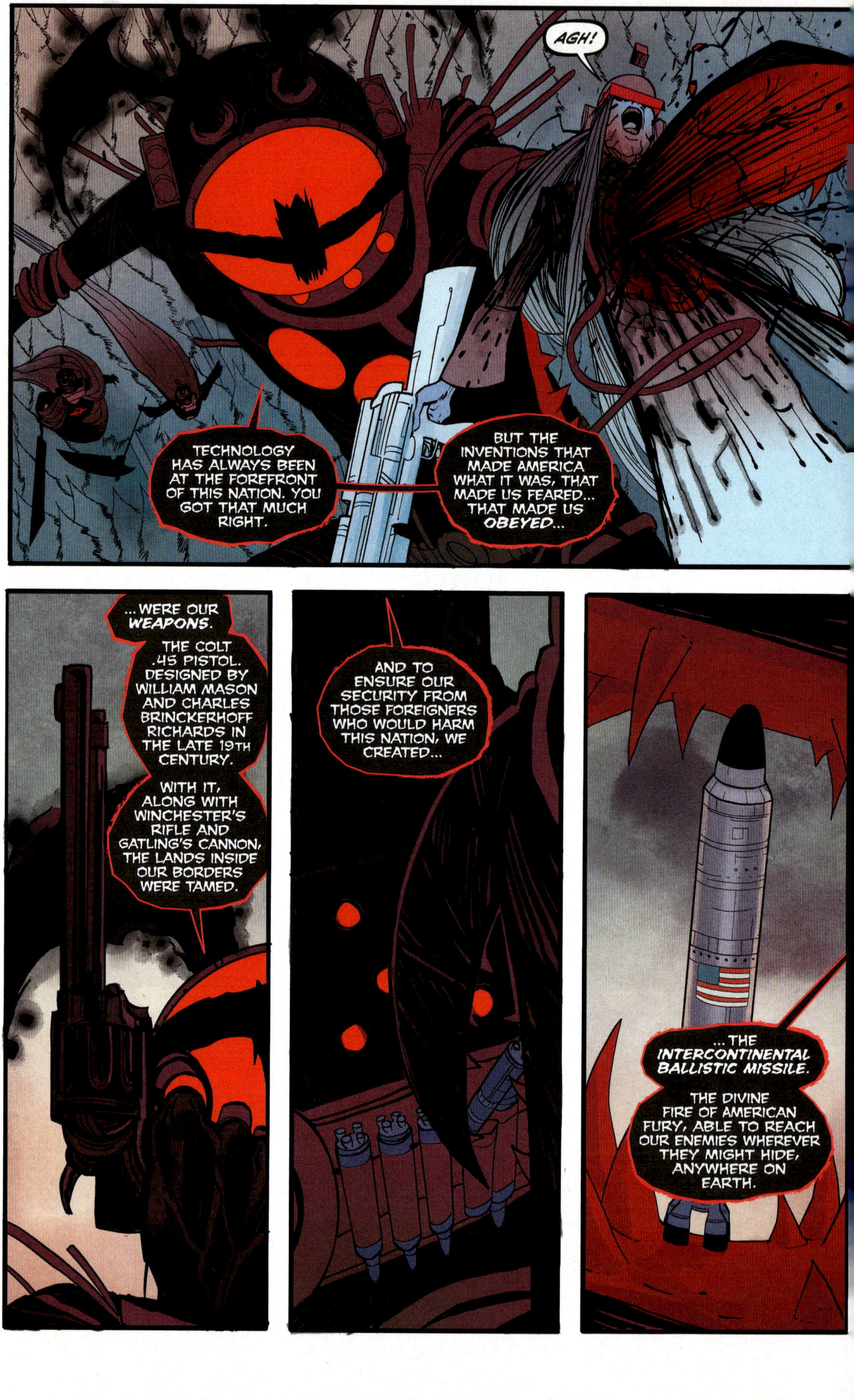
AGH!
TECHNOLOGY HAS ALWAYS BEEN AT THE FOREFRONT OF THIS NATION. YOU GOT THAT MUCH RIGHT.
BUT THE INVENTIONS THAT MADE AMERICA WHAT IT WAS, THAT MADE US FEARED... THAT MADE US OBEYED...
...WERE OUR WEAPONS.
THE COLT .45 PISTOL. DESIGNED BY WILLIAM MASON AND CHARLES BRINCKERHOFF RICHARDS IN THE LATE 19TH CENTURY.
WITH IT, ALONG WITH WINCHESTER'S RIFLE AND GATLING'S CANNON, THE LANDS INSIDE OUR BORDERS WERE TAMED.
AND TO ENSURE OUR SECURITY FROM THOSE FOREIGNERS WHO WOULD HARM THIS NATION, WE CREATED...
...THE INTERCONTINENTAL BALLISTIC MISSILE.
THE DIVINE FIRE OF AMERICAN FURY, ABLE TO REACH OUR ENEMIES WHEREVER THEY MIGHT HIDE, ANYWHERE ON EARTH.

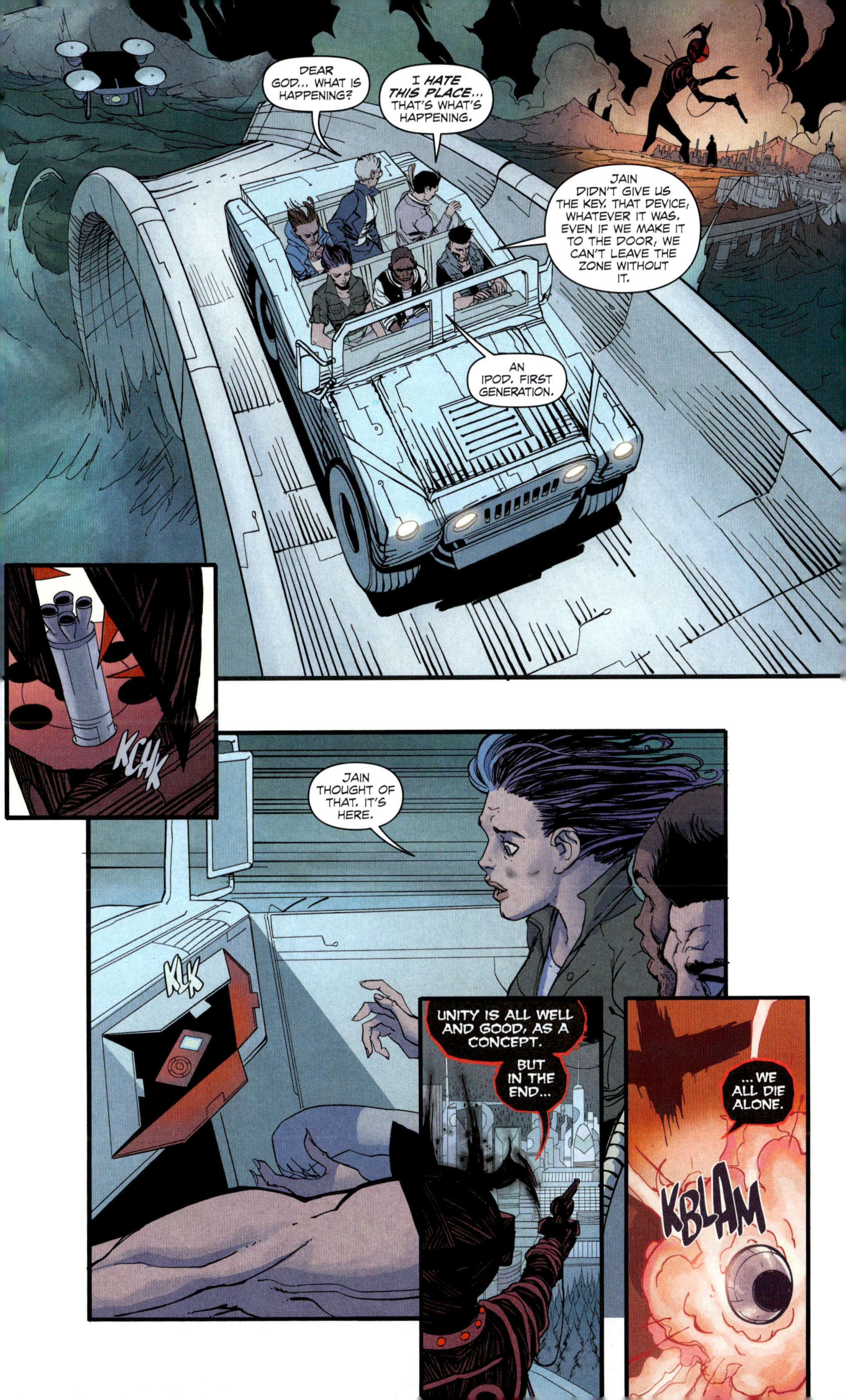
DEAR GOD... WHAT IS HAPPENING?
I HATE THIS PLACE... THAT'S WHAT'S HAPPENING.
JAIN DIDN'T GIVE US THE KEY. THAT DEVICE, WHATEVER IT WAS. EVEN IF WE MAKE IT TO THE DOOR, WE CAN'T LEAVE THE ZONE WITHOUT IT.
AN IPOD. FIRST GENERATION.
KCHK
JAIN THOUGHT OF THAT. IT'S HERE.
KLIK
UNITY IS ALL WELL AND GOOD, AS A CONCEPT.
BUT IN THE END...
...WE ALL DIE ALONE.
KBLAM

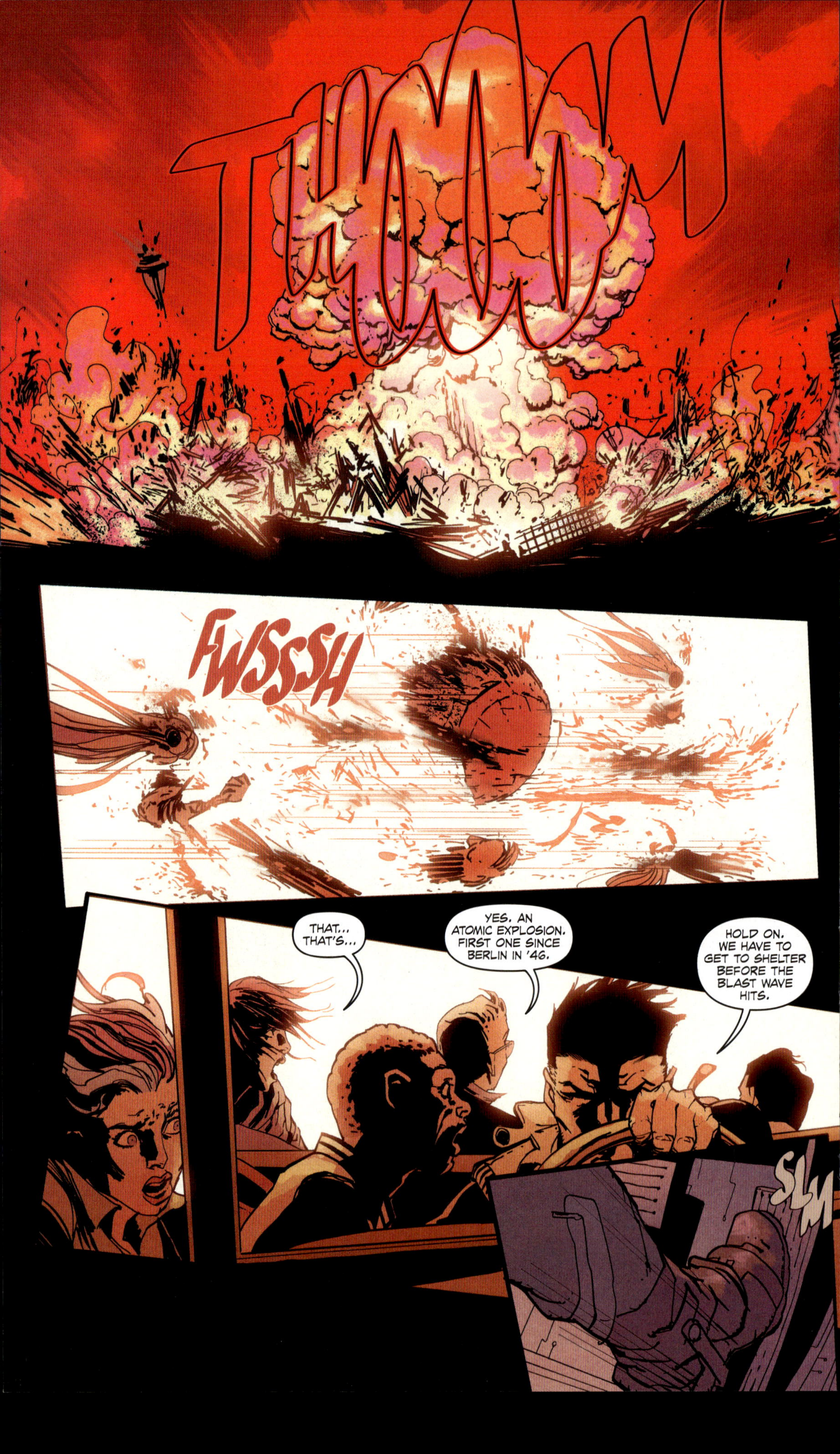
THOOOOM
FWSSSH
THAT... THAT'S...
YES. AN ATOMIC EXPLOSION. FIRST ONE SINCE BERLIN IN '46.
HOLD ON. WE HAVE TO GET TO SHELTER BEFORE THE BLAST WAVE HITS.

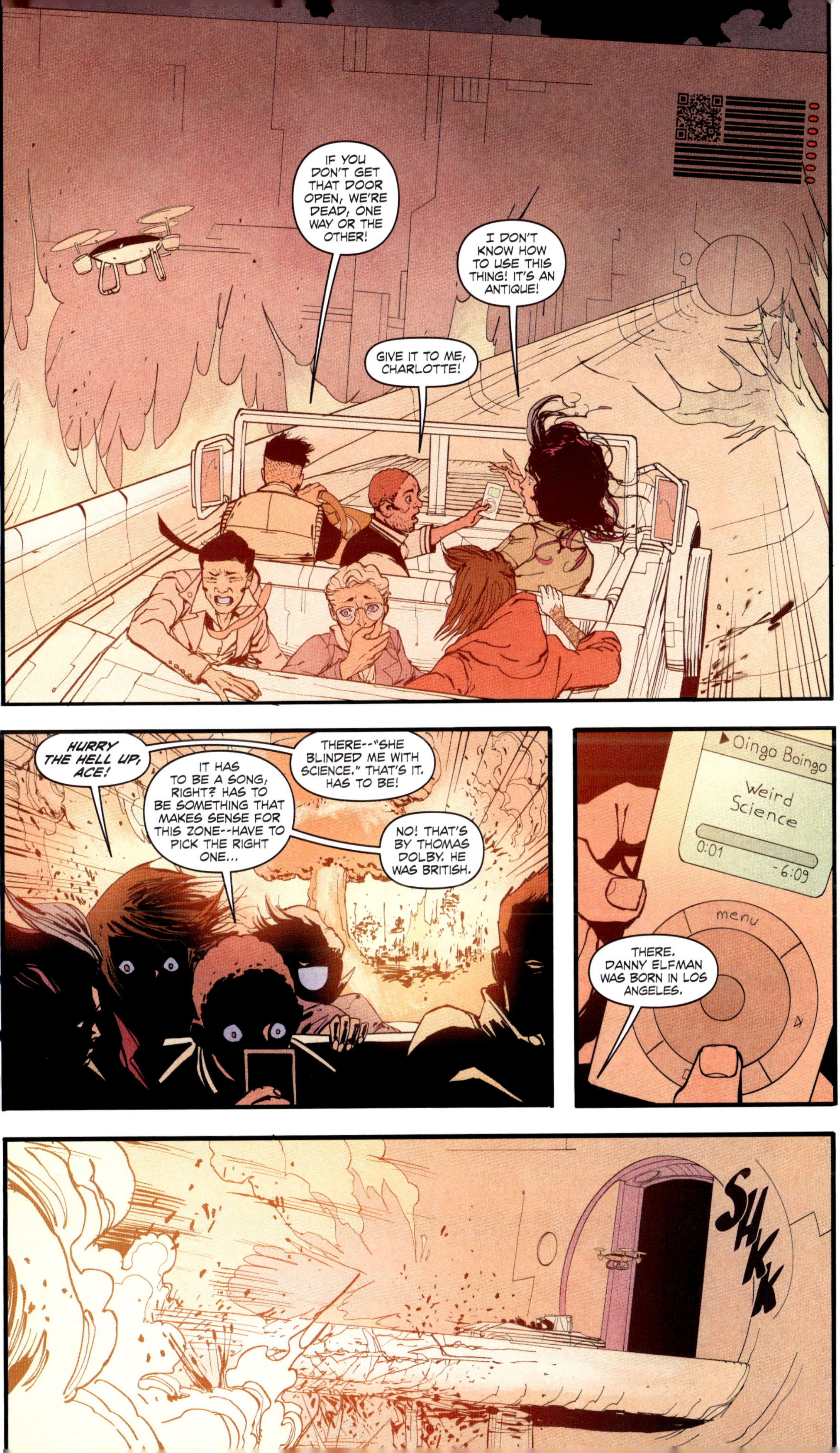
IF YOU DON'T GET THAT DOOR OPEN, WE'RE DEAD, ONE WAY OR THE OTHER!
I DON'T KNOW HOW TO USE THIS THING! IT'S AN ANTIQUE!
GIVE IT TO ME, CHARLOTTE!
HURRY THE HELL UP, ACE!
IT HAS TO BE A SONG, RIGHT? HAS TO BE SOMETHING THAT MAKES SENSE FOR THIS ZONE--HAVE TO PICK THE RIGHT ONE...
THERE--"SHE BLINDED ME WITH SCIENCE." THAT'S IT. HAS TO BE!
NO! THAT'S BY THOMAS DOLBY. HE WAS BRITISH.
Oingo Boingo
Weird Science
0:01
-6:09
menu
THERE. DANNY ELFMAN WAS BORN IN LOS ANGELES.
SHKK

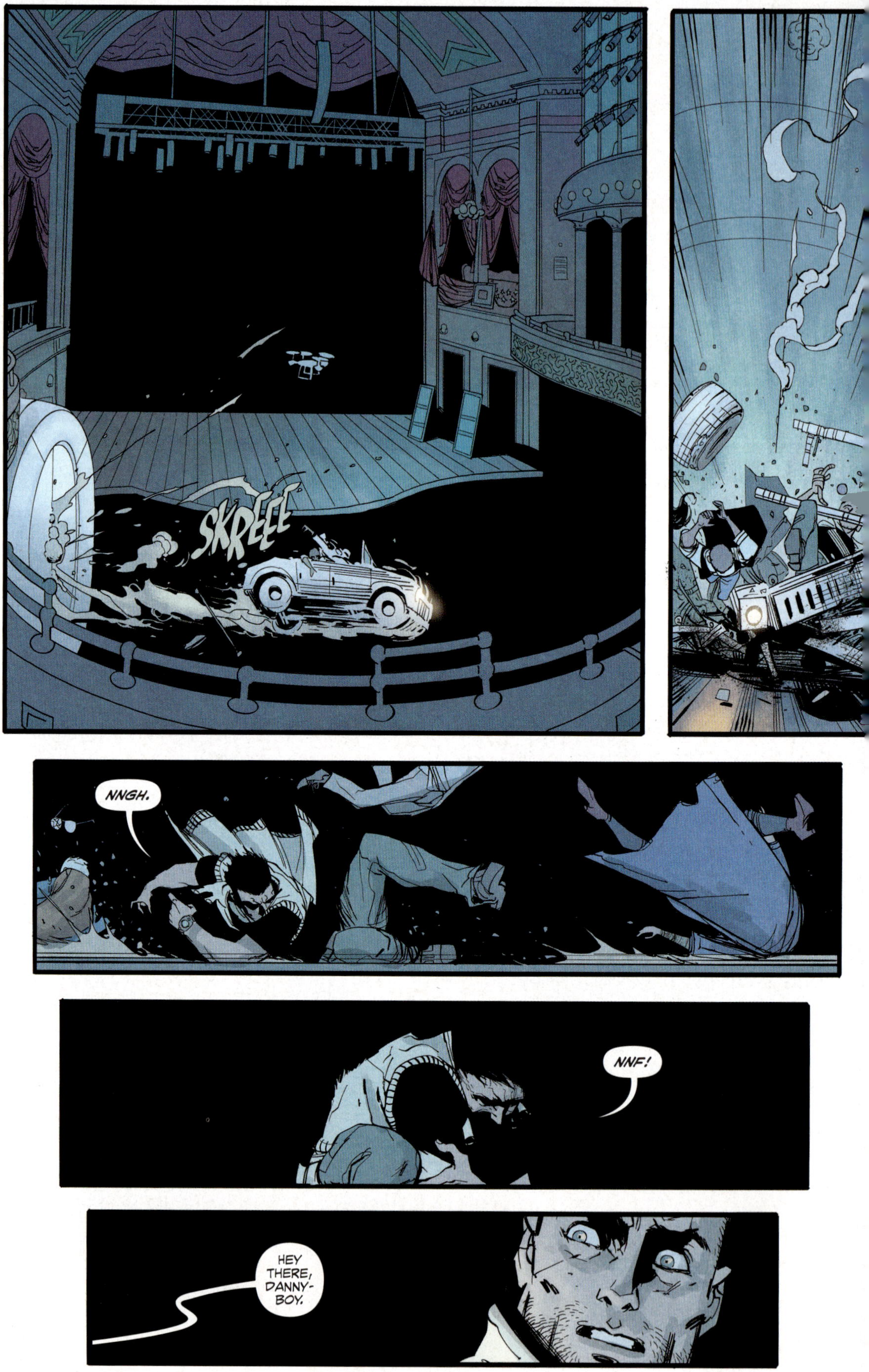
SKREEE
NNGH.
NNF!
HEY THERE, DANNY-BOY.

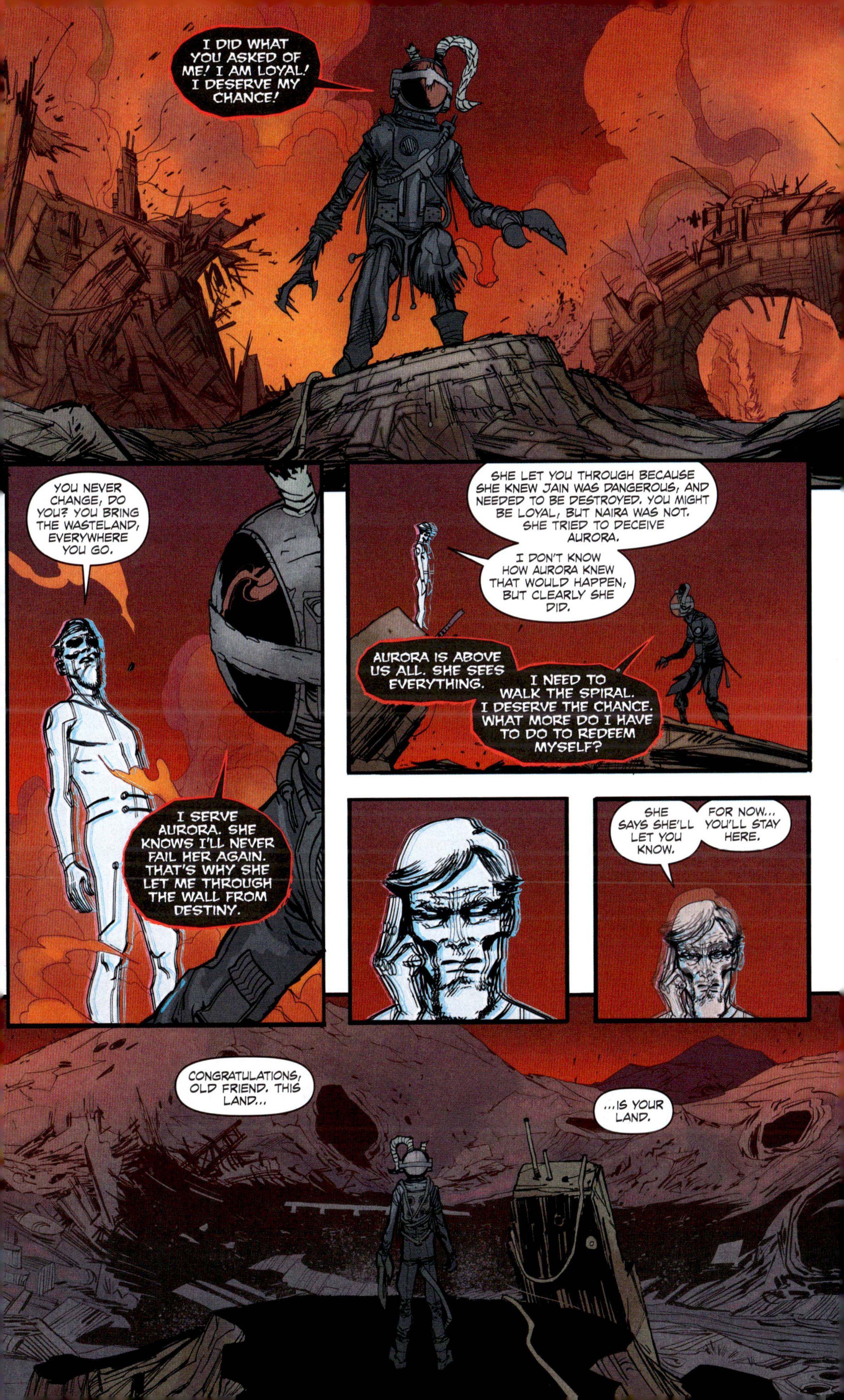
I DID WHAT YOU ASKED OF ME! I AM LOYAL! I DESERVE MY CHANCE!
YOU NEVER CHANGE, DO YOU? YOU BRING THE WASTELAND, EVERYWHERE YOU GO.
I SERVE AURORA. SHE KNOWS I'LL NEVER FAIL HER AGAIN. THAT'S WHY SHE LET ME THROUGH THE WALL FROM DESTINY.
SHE LET YOU THROUGH BECAUSE SHE KNEW JAIN WAS DANGEROUS, AND NEEDED TO BE DESTROYED. YOU MIGHT BE LOYAL, BUT NAIRA WAS NOT. SHE TRIED TO DECEIVE AURORA.
I DON'T KNOW HOW AURORA KNEW THAT WOULD HAPPEN, BUT CLEARLY SHE DID.
AURORA IS ABOVE US ALL. SHE SEES EVERYTHING.
I NEED TO WALK THE SPIRAL. I DESERVE THE CHANCE. WHAT MORE DO I HAVE TO DO TO REDEEM MYSELF?
SHE SAYS SHE'LL LET YOU KNOW.
FOR NOW... YOU'LL STAY HERE.
CONGRATULATIONS, OLD FRIEND. THIS LAND...
...IS YOUR LAND.

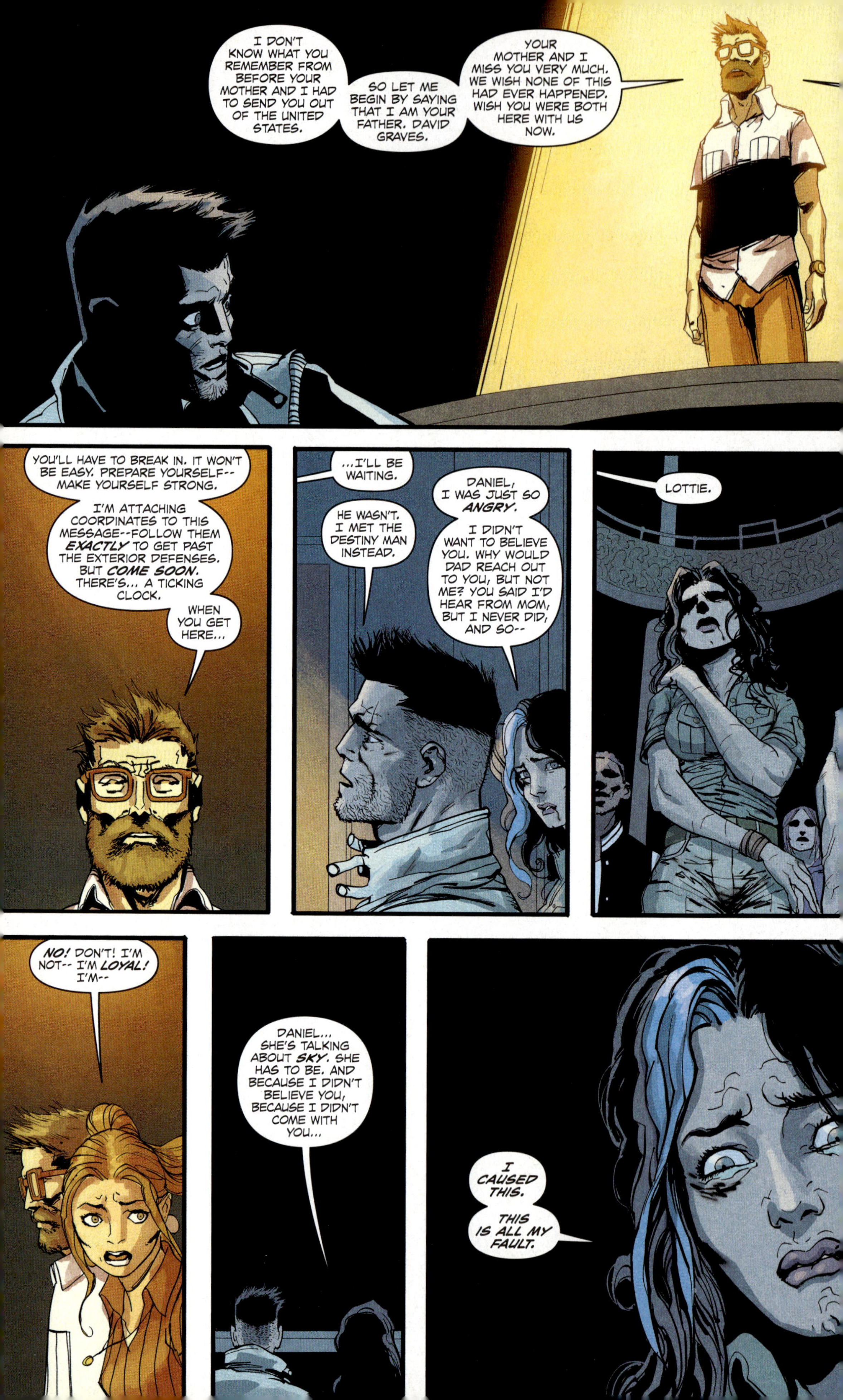

I DON'T KNOW WHAT YOU REMEMBER FROM BEFORE YOUR MOTHER AND I HAD TO SEND YOU OUT OF THE UNITED STATES.
SO LET ME BEGIN BY SAYING THAT I AM YOUR FATHER. DAVID GRAVES.
YOUR MOTHER AND I MISS YOU VERY MUCH. WE WISH NONE OF THIS HAD EVER HAPPENED. WISH YOU WERE BOTH HERE WITH US NOW.
YOU'LL HAVE TO BREAK IN. IT WON'T BE EASY. PREPARE YOURSELF-- MAKE YOURSELF STRONG.
I'M ATTACHING COORDINATES TO THIS MESSAGE--FOLLOW THEM EXACTLY TO GET PAST THE EXTERIOR DEFENSES. BUT COME SOON. THERE'S... A TICKING CLOCK.
WHEN YOU GET HERE...
...I'LL BE WAITING.
HE WASN'T. I MET THE DESTINY MAN INSTEAD.
DANIEL, I WAS JUST SO ANGRY.
I DIDN'T WANT TO BELIEVE YOU. WHY WOULD DAD REACH OUT TO YOU, BUT NOT ME? YOU SAID I'D HEAR FROM MOM, BUT I NEVER DID, AND SO--
LOTTIE.
NO! DON'T! I'M NOT-- I'M LOYAL! I'M--
DANIEL... SHE'S TALKING ABOUT SKY. SHE HAS TO BE. AND BECAUSE I DIDN'T BELIEVE YOU, BECAUSE I DIDN'T COME WITH YOU...
I CAUSED THIS.
THIS IS ALL MY FAULT.

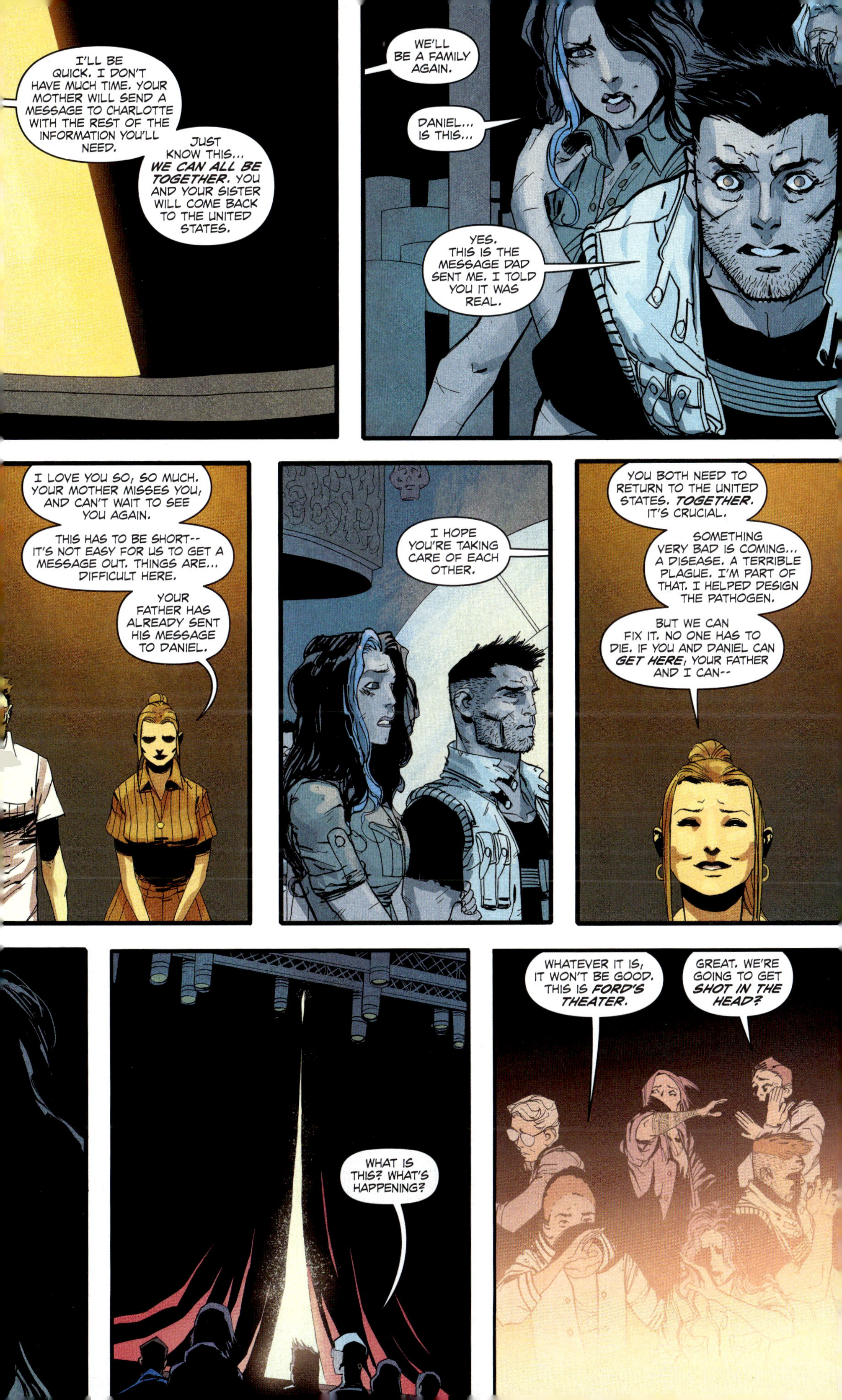
I'LL BE QUICK. I DON'T HAVE MUCH TIME. YOUR MOTHER WILL SEND A MESSAGE TO CHARLOTTE WITH THE REST OF THE INFORMATION YOU'LL NEED.
JUST KNOW THIS... WE CAN ALL BE TOGETHER. YOU AND YOUR SISTER WILL COME BACK TO THE UNITED STATES.
WE'LL BE A FAMILY AGAIN.
DANIEL... IS THIS...
YES. THIS IS THE MESSAGE DAD SENT ME. I TOLD YOU IT WAS REAL.
I LOVE YOU SO, SO MUCH. YOUR MOTHER MISSES YOU, AND CAN'T WAIT TO SEE YOU AGAIN.
THIS HAS TO BE SHORT--IT'S NOT EASY FOR US TO GET A MESSAGE OUT. THINGS ARE... DIFFICULT HERE.
YOUR FATHER HAS ALREADY SENT HIS MESSAGE TO DANIEL.
I HOPE YOU'RE TAKING CARE OF EACH OTHER.
YOU BOTH NEED TO RETURN TO THE UNITED STATES. TOGETHER. IT'S CRUCIAL.
SOMETHING VERY BAD IS COMING... A DISEASE. A TERRIBLE PLAGUE. I'M PART OF THAT. I HELPED DESIGN THE PATHOGEN.
BUT WE CAN FIX IT. NO ONE HAS TO DIE. IF YOU AND DANIEL CAN GET HERE, YOUR FATHER AND I CAN--
WHAT IS THIS? WHAT'S HAPPENING?
WHATEVER IT IS, IT WON'T BE GOOD. THIS IS FORD'S THEATER.
GREAT. WE'RE GOING TO GET SHOT IN THE HEAD?

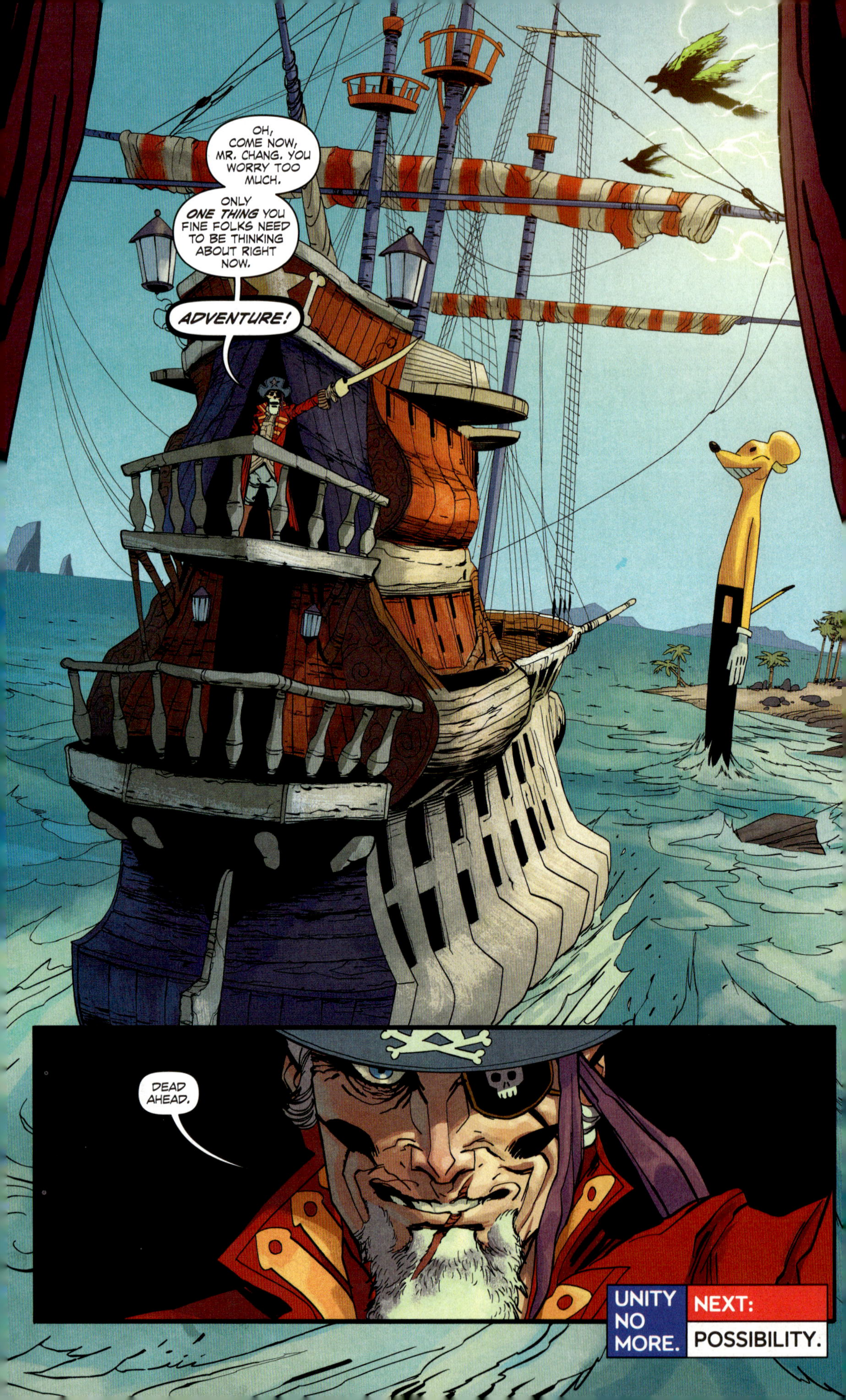
OH, COME NOW, MR. CHANG. YOU WORRY TOO MUCH.
ONLY ONE THING YOU FINE FOLKS NEED TO BE THINKING ABOUT RIGHT NOW.
ADVENTURE!
DEAD AHEAD.
UNITY NO MORE.
NEXT: POSSIBILITY.

DRONET

"Time's up.

You might not be hearing much from your old pal Ace Piñata for a while, friends. I think I've got this all figured out – what's really happening in there, inside the walls, and I'll tell you what...

...it's about time.

I got a little birdie's gonna confirm even my wildest theories, though, so stay tuned. Radio Piñata might be off the air for a while, but I'll be back someday. I promise you that.

   Stay healthy until we speak again. Keep away from that Sky stuff. That's some real bad shit.

   For now, it's time...

   ..to go."

—Posted by Ace Piñata on the 'America Unsealed' Dronet, December 7, 2058

AFTER THE SEALING

The following depicts the best possible reconstruction of events inside the United States of America in the days and years following the Sealing—the complete removal of the US from the world stage. This timeline presents events on a national scale as opposed to a local or individual level, as most of the smaller, personal stories of the Sealing have been lost. But even with the limited picture painted by these few verified events, it is possible to see a country and a people reeling from change, trying desperately to reinvent themselves, seeking any possible way forward as a nation.

THE SEALING
July 20, 2029

Day 0:

The Sealing; July 20, 2029. The United States closes its borders to all travel, trade, and communications. US citizens outside the country are not allowed to re-enter. Likewise, any foreign residents inside the US are not permitted to leave.

Pre-existing border walls are militarized via high-tech drone weaponry and "Airwall" forcefields to prevent flyovers. Electromagnetic shielding drops into place above the entire continental United States and Alaska, preventing satellite surveillance. Hawaii, Puerto Rico, Guam and other US possessions are abandoned, and are no longer considered to be States or Territories, but rather a loose confederation of American Islands.

Days 1–6:

Widespread public unrest in every major city in the country. Attempts are made to escape the United States via plane, boat, etc. All fail.

Day 7:

The President of the United States appeals to the nation for calm, and explains that the Sealing is part of a larger plan, approved in secret by Congress over a decade earlier, to prepare the country for an extended period of self-sufficiency and isolation from the outer world. The plan is called *Fortress America*, and will be further explained once the protests end.

Day 10:

With the nation mostly stable, the President describes the *Fortress America* plan. In one year, the state borders will be redrawn, dividing the continental US into thirteen discrete zones. Each will have its own laws, tax base, industry, etc. Travel between them will be restricted.

(Nothing is said of what will become of Alaska—but its residents are told they can also choose one of the Thirteen Zones.)

Citizens are given that year to choose which America suits them best, and the government will assist with resettlement for anyone who chooses to move.

Days 11–30:

More unrest—but many Americans find the idea of the Thirteen Zones compelling.

J7-2029

Copyright © 2021 Last Mile Productions, LLC. All rights reserved.

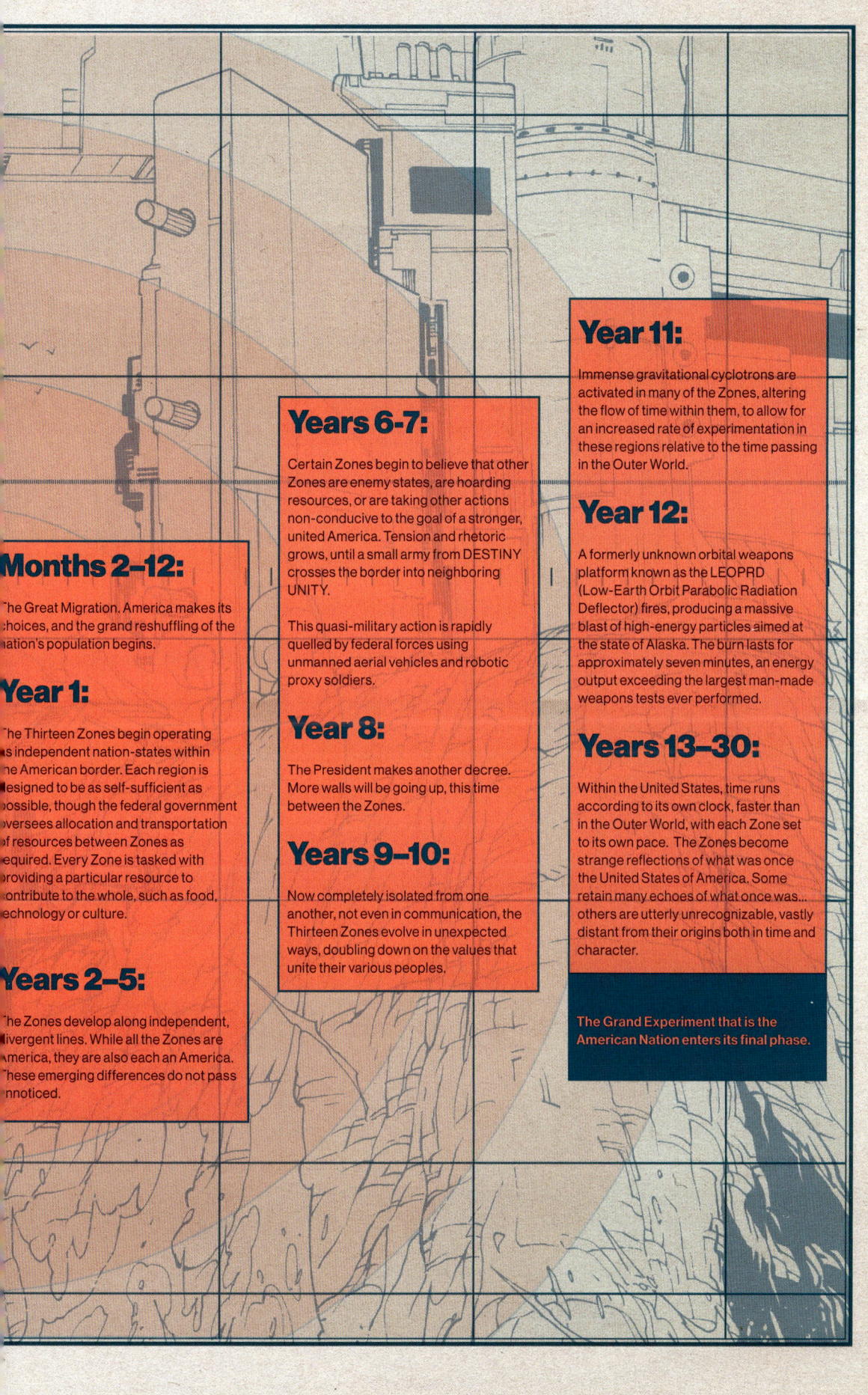

Months 2–12:

The Great Migration. America makes its choices, and the grand reshuffling of the nation's population begins.

Year 1:

The Thirteen Zones begin operating as independent nation-states within the American border. Each region is designed to be as self-sufficient as possible, though the federal government oversees allocation and transportation of resources between Zones as required. Every Zone is tasked with providing a particular resource to contribute to the whole, such as food, technology or culture.

Years 2–5:

The Zones develop along independent, divergent lines. While all the Zones are America, they are also each an America. These emerging differences do not pass unnoticed.

Years 6-7:

Certain Zones begin to believe that other Zones are enemy states, are hoarding resources, or are taking other actions non-conducive to the goal of a stronger, united America. Tension and rhetoric grows, until a small army from DESTINY crosses the border into neighboring UNITY.

This quasi-military action is rapidly quelled by federal forces using unmanned aerial vehicles and robotic proxy soldiers.

Year 8:

The President makes another decree. More walls will be going up, this time between the Zones.

Years 9–10:

Now completely isolated from one another, not even in communication, the Thirteen Zones evolve in unexpected ways, doubling down on the values that unite their various peoples.

Year 11:

Immense gravitational cyclotrons are activated in many of the Zones, altering the flow of time within them, to allow for an increased rate of experimentation in these regions relative to the time passing in the Outer World.

Year 12:

A formerly unknown orbital weapons platform known as the LEOPRD (Low-Earth Orbit Parabolic Radiation Deflector) fires, producing a massive blast of high-energy particles aimed at the state of Alaska. The burn lasts for approximately seven minutes, an energy output exceeding the largest man-made weapons tests ever performed.

Years 13–30:

Within the United States, time runs according to its own clock, faster than in the Outer World, with each Zone set to its own pace. The Zones become strange reflections of what was once the United States of America. Some retain many echoes of what once was... others are utterly unrecognizable, vastly distant from their origins both in time and character.

The Grand Experiment that is the American Nation enters its final phase.

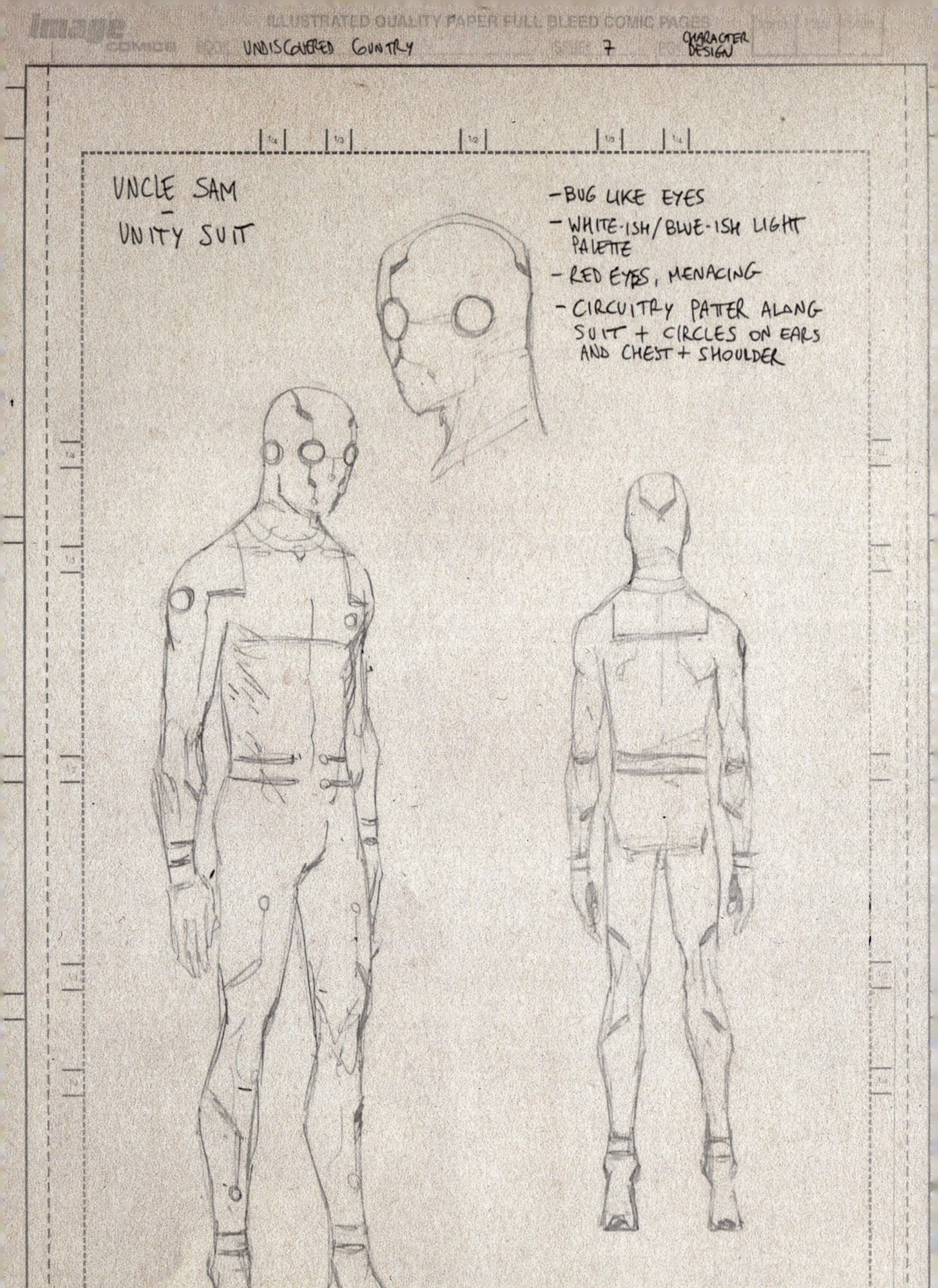
UNDISCOVERED COUNTRY
7
CHARACTER DESIGN
UNCLE SAM
-
UNITY SUIT
-BUG LIKE EYES
-WHITE-ISH/BLUE-ISH LIGHT PALETTE
-RED EYES, MENACING
-CIRCUITRY PATTER ALONG SUIT + CIRCLES ON EARS AND CHEST + SHOULDER

Concept Drawings by **GIUSEPPE CAMUNCOLI**

UNITY

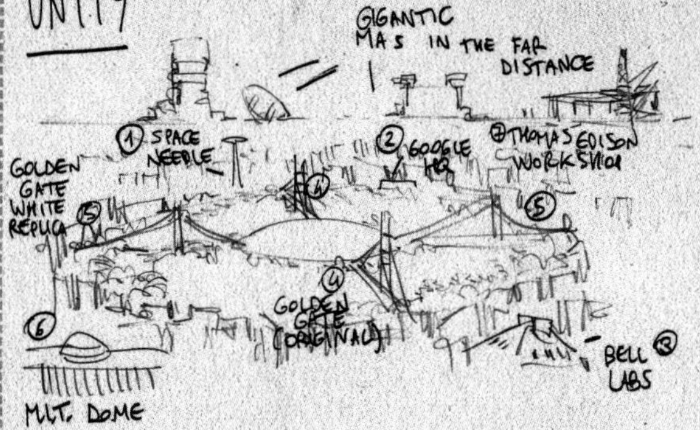
GIGANTIC
MAs IN THE FAR DISTANCE
1 SPACE NEEDLE
2 GOOGLE HQ
7 THOMAS EDISON WORKSHOP
GOLDEN GATE WHITE REPLICA 5
4
5
4 GOLDEN GATE (ORIGINAL)
6
BELL LABS 3
M.I.T. DOME

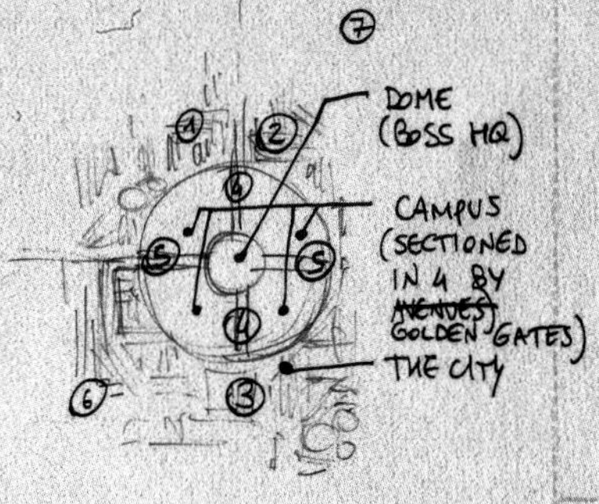
7
DOME (BOSS HQ)
CAMPUS (SECTIONED IN 4 BY GOLDEN GATES)
THE CITY
1 2 4 5 5 4 3 6

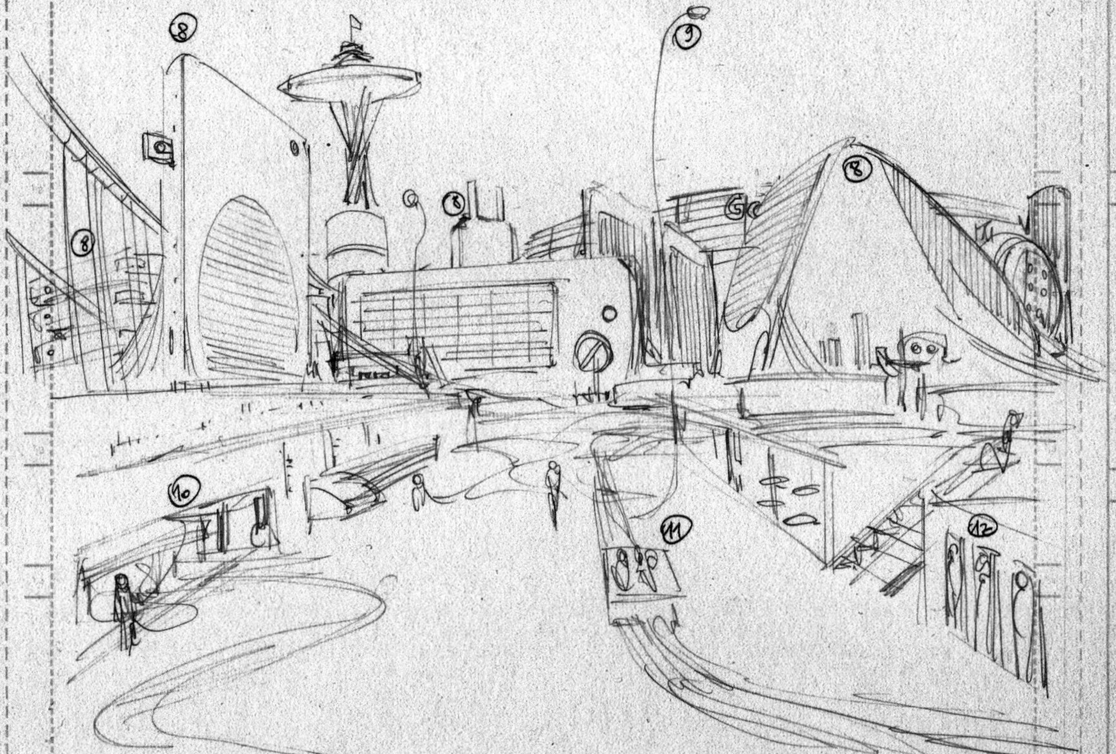
8
9
8
8
8
10
11
12

(8) - BUILDINGS ARE BIG HIVES BUT NOT VERY TALL, AND SHAPED LIKE ICONIC TECH PRODUCTS (iPHONES, iPAD, iMACS, BUT ALSO B&O ETC.). ALL WHITE, WITH CABLES COMING OUT OF THEM (ALSO MADE OF?)

(9) - SOME CABLES CAN LIFT UP LIKE SNAKES, AND ACT LIKE DRONES/SURVEILLANCE SYSTEMS

(10) - STORES/APARTMENTS ARE SHAPED LIKE USB PLUGS OR STUFF LIKE THAT

(11) - CABLES CAN BE ALSO USED AS LINES FOR TRANSPORTATION (WITH WAGONS MOVING ON THEM)

(12) - SOMETIMES CITIZENS CAN GO TO RECHARGE INTO PROPER UNITS/PODS

CITIZENS

- WHITE JUMPSUITS
- SIMPLEST SYMBOL ON RIGHT SIDE OF CHEST, NO LINES
- ALMOST NO SHOULDERS
- (*) - NO NAILS ON FINGERS, BUT TOUCH SENSORS ON FINGERTIPS
- FLUFFY, FLOATED WHEN CLOTHES GO CLOSE TO HANDS AND FEET

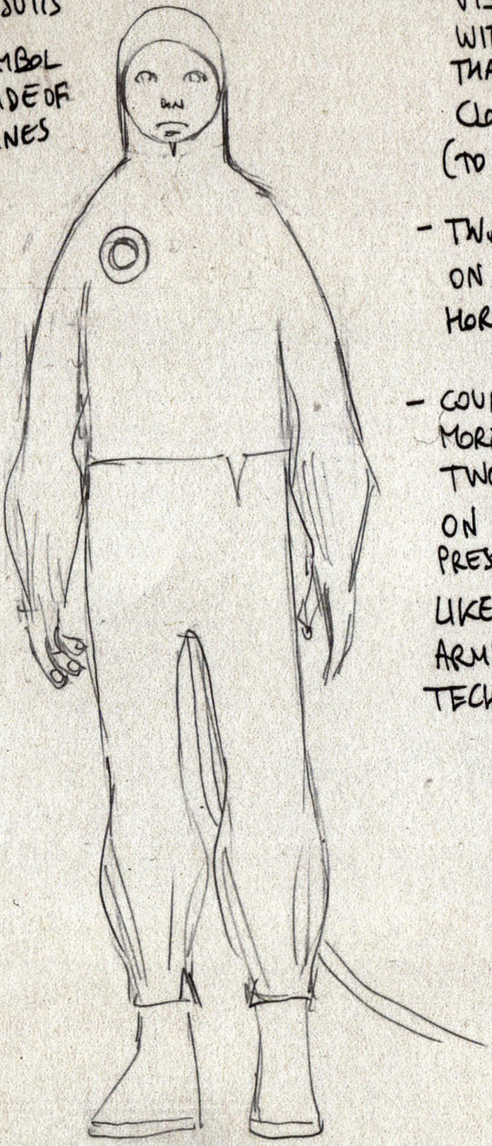

SCIENTISTS

- VISOR IS OVAL, WITH A MOUTHPIECE THAT CAN BE MOVED CLOSE TO MOUTH (TO COMMAND TECH?)
- TWO SYMBOLS ON CHEST, WITH HORIZONTAL LINES
- COULD HAVE MORE THAN TWO, DEPENDING ON LEVEL, PRESTIGE ETC.

LIKE IN THE ARMY BUT HERE TECH RULES

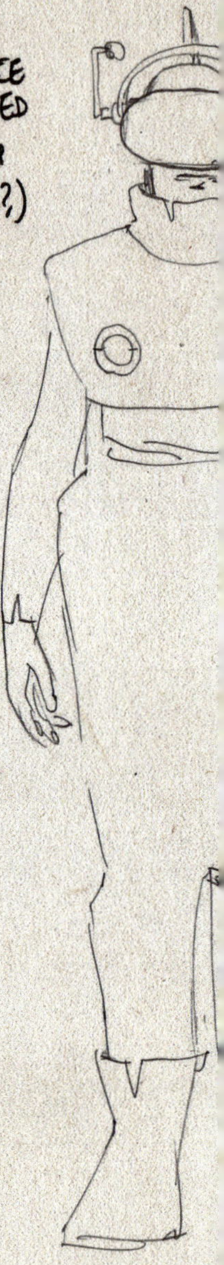

GENERIC NOTES:

(*) THAT GOES FOR EVERYBODY
- EVERYONE HAS GOLDEN EYES, NO EYEBROWS, IS COMPLETELY HAIRLESS
- CAN HAVE DIFFERENT FACIAL FEATURES BUT OVERALL THEY LOOK
- DIFFERENT SKIN COLORS? I THINK IT WOULD MAKE SENSE ...

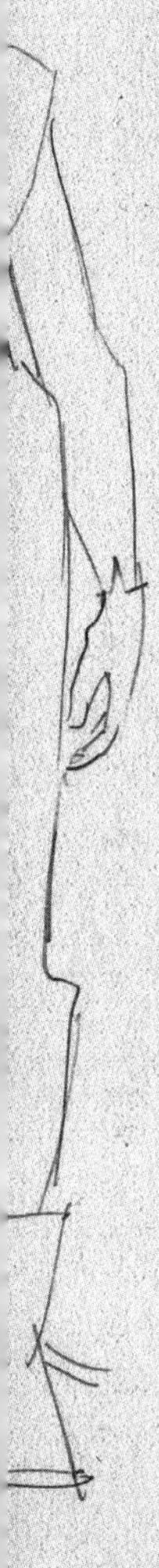

BRUTE FORCE

- ALMOST LIKE AUTOMATONS, CAN BE USED AS POLICE, SLAVES, HARD LABOR PROVIDERS, BODY-GUARDS ETC.
- BIGGER, MORE MUSCULAR BODYTYPE
- ONE BIG SYMBOL ON CHEST, HORIZONTAL LINE

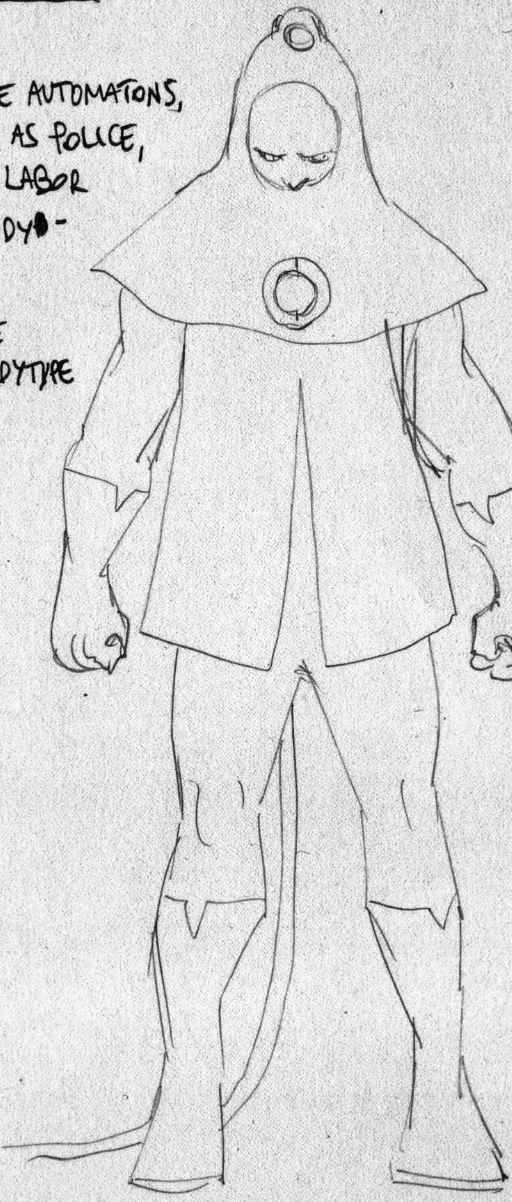

AND WOMEN) AND IS OF THE SAME HEIGHT. WHICH ONE? I'D MAKE THEM TALL
- INDISTINGUISHABLE

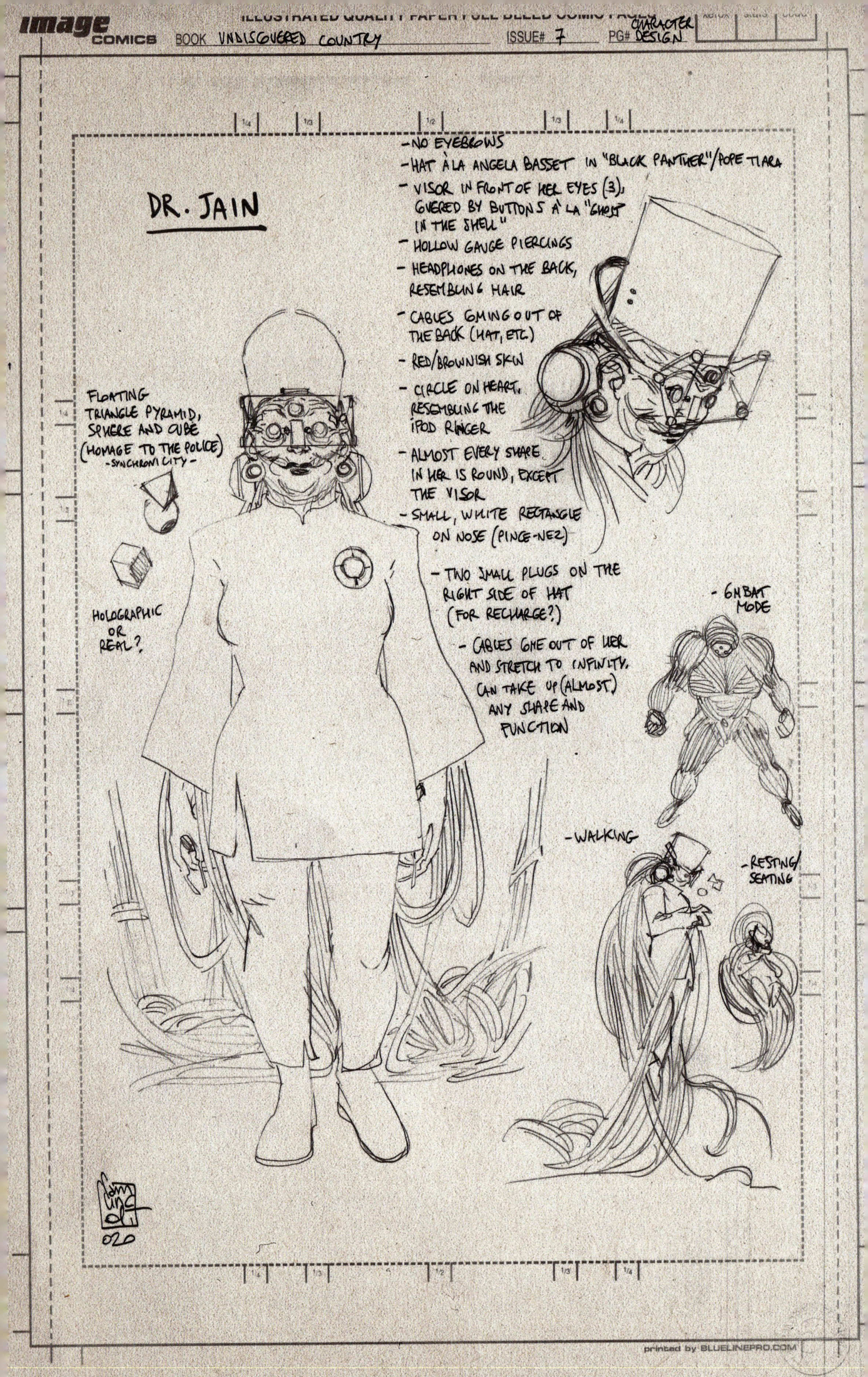
image COMICS
BOOK UNDISCOVERED COUNTRY
ISSUE# 7
PG# CHARACTER DESIGN
DR. JAIN
-NO EYEBROWS
-HAT À LA ANGELA BASSET IN "BLACK PANTHER"/POPE TIARA
-VISOR IN FRONT OF HER EYES (3), COVERED BY BUTTONS À LA "GHOST IN THE SHELL"
-HOLLOW GAUGE PIERCINGS
-HEADPHONES ON THE BACK, RESEMBLING HAIR
-CABLES COMING OUT OF THE BACK (HAT, ETC.)
-RED/BROWNISH SKIN
-CIRCLE ON HEART, RESEMBLING THE IPOD RINGER
-ALMOST EVERY SHAPE IN HER IS ROUND, EXCEPT THE VISOR
-SMALL, WHITE RECTANGLE ON NOSE (PINCE-NEZ)
-TWO SMALL PLUGS ON THE RIGHT SIDE OF HAT (FOR RECHARGE?)
-CABLES COME OUT OF HER AND STRETCH TO INFINITY. CAN TAKE UP (ALMOST) ANY SHAPE AND FUNCTION
FLOATING TRIANGLE PYRAMID, SPHERE AND CUBE (HOMAGE TO THE POLICE) -SYNCHRONICITY-
HOLOGRAPHIC OR REAL?
-COMBAT MODE
-WALKING
-RESTING/SEATING
020
printed by BLUELINEPRO.COM

ILLUSTRATED QUALITY PAPER FULL BLEED COMIC PAGES

Image COMICS BOOK UNDISCOVERED COUNTRY ISSUE# 10 PG# CONCEPT ART

BATTLE ARMOR CHANG

- WHEN CHANG BUILDS HIS TECNO-ARMOR, HE PAYS HOMAGE TO SOME OF HIS FAVOURITE CHARACTERS/HEROES: ~~LANCELOT~~, CONAN, SAMURAIS, MAN-AT-ARMS
- ARMOR IS WHITE, LEAVES PARTS OF HIS CLOTHES UNDERNEATH "OPEN" (BELT, SHOES, ETC.)
- CABLE PENDING ON THE BACK, CONNECTED TO UNITY'S "MATRIX"

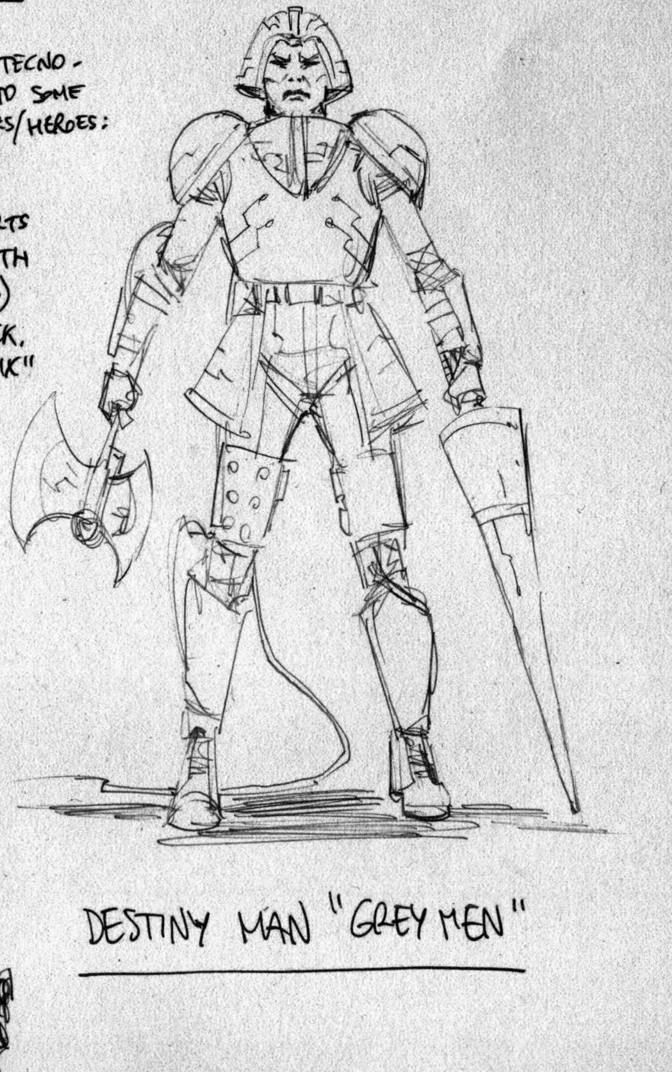

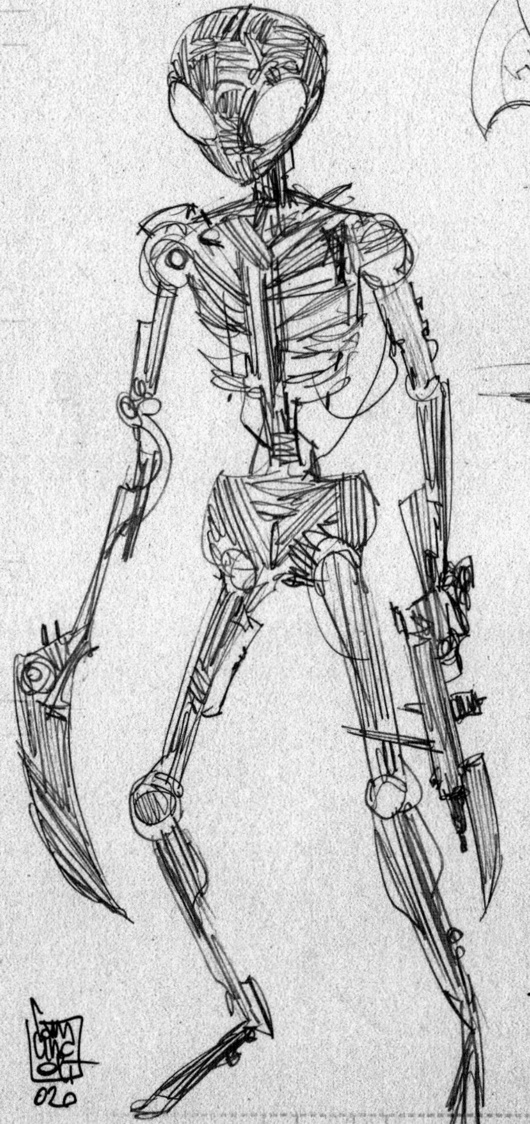

DESTINY MAN "GREY MEN"

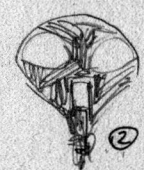

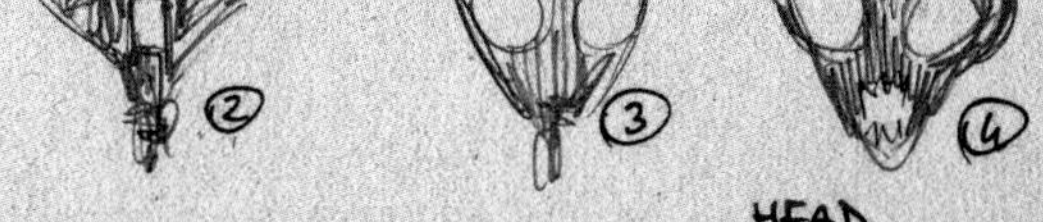
2
3
4

HEAD VARIATIONS

- ALIEN SHAPE
- MIX BETWEEN TERMINATOR AND WARLOCK
- CAN MORPH EVERY PART OF THEIR BODIES, AND TURN IT INTO ANY KIND OF WEAPON (SCYTHE, RIFLE, MACE, AXE ETC.)

020

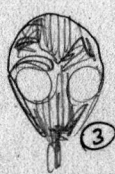

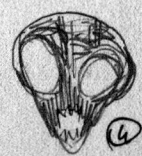

UNITY OCEAN CREATURES

① UNITY SPERM WHALE
(WHITE, TWO EYES ON EACH SIDE + ONE ON THE TAIL)

② DESTINY MAN SHARK ✱
(BLACK, SMALL EYES AROUND MOUTH, TWO ROWS OF TEETH)

③ D.M. HAMMERHEAD ✱
(BLACK, TWO MOUTHS)

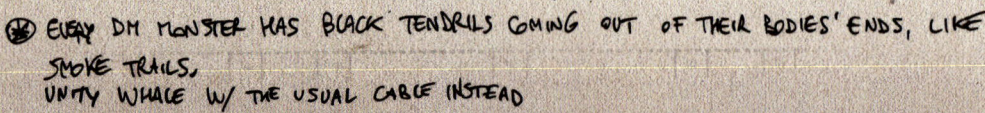

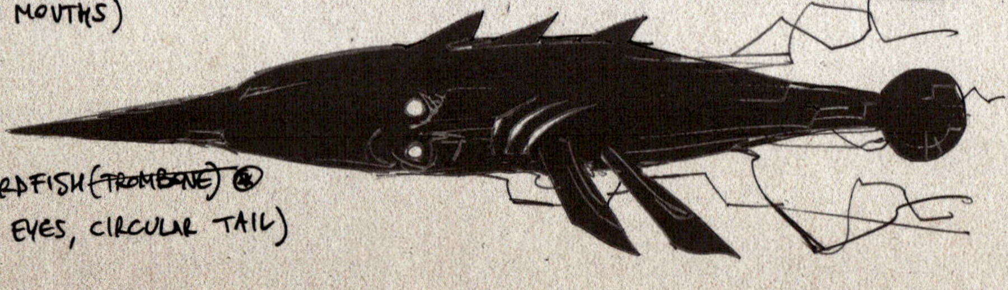

④ D.M. SWORDFISH (TROMBONE) ✱
(BLACK, TWO EYES, CIRCULAR TAIL)

✱ EVERY DM MONSTER HAS BLACK TENDRILS COMING OUT OF THEIR BODIES' ENDS, LIKE SMOKE TRAILS.
UNITY WHALE W/ THE USUAL CABLE INSTEAD

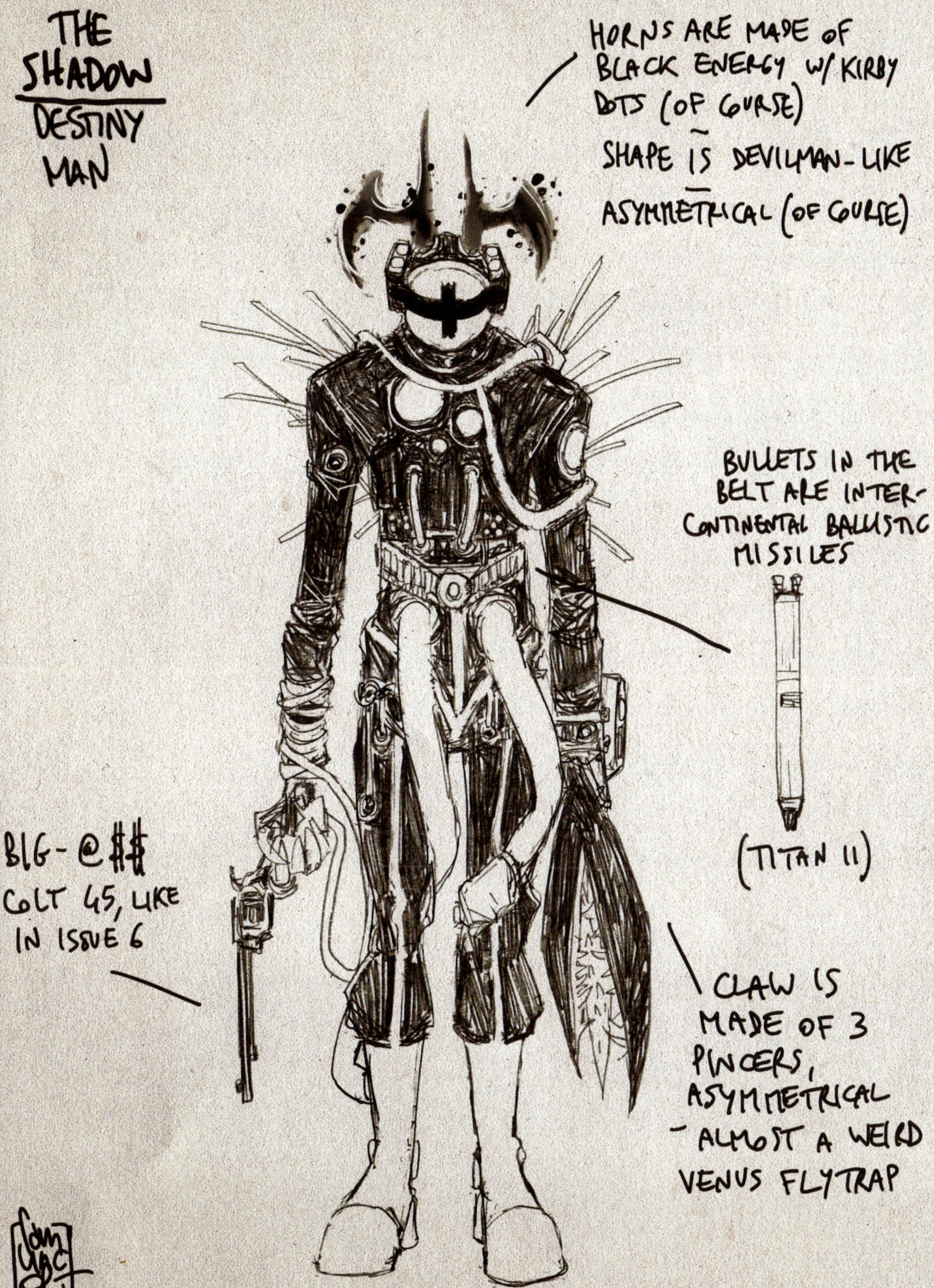
THE SHADOW
DESTINY MAN
HORNS ARE MADE OF BLACK ENERGY W/ KIRBY DOTS (OF COURSE)
SHAPE IS DEVILMAN-LIKE
ASYMMETRICAL (OF COURSE)
BULLETS IN THE BELT ARE INTER-CONTINENTAL BALLISTIC MISSILES
(TITAN II)
BIG-@$$ COLT 45, LIKE IN ISSUE 6
CLAW IS MADE OF 3 PINCERS, ASYMMETRICAL - ALMOST A WEIRD VENUS FLYTRAP
020

MONSTER JAIN

Concepts by Giuseppe Camuncoli

Cover sketches from UNDISCOVERED COUNTRY #9

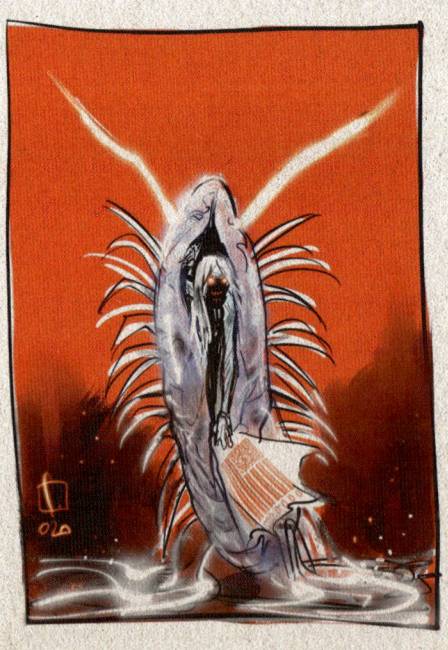

B

C

F

G

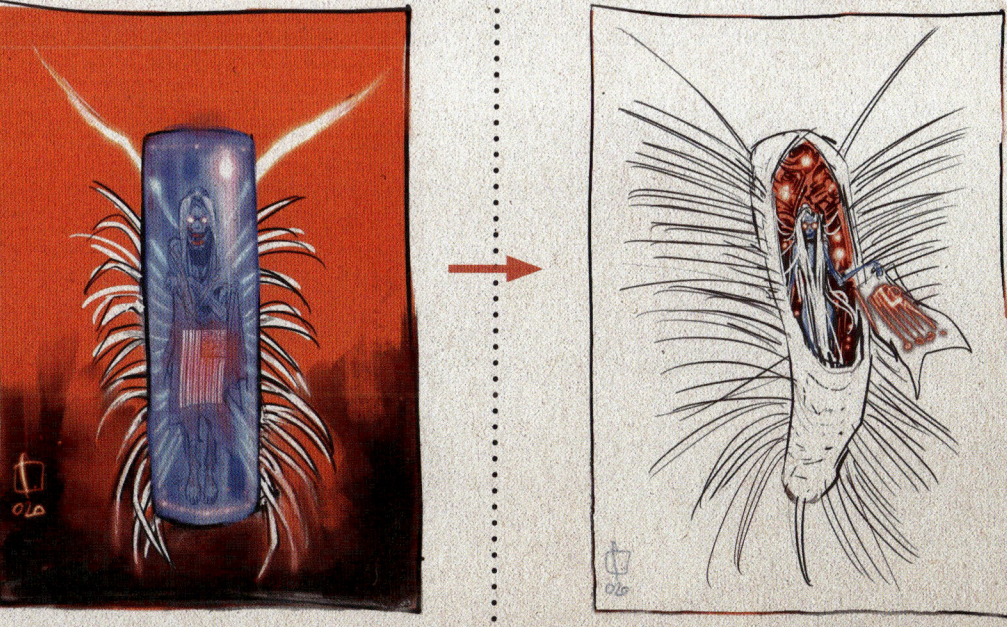

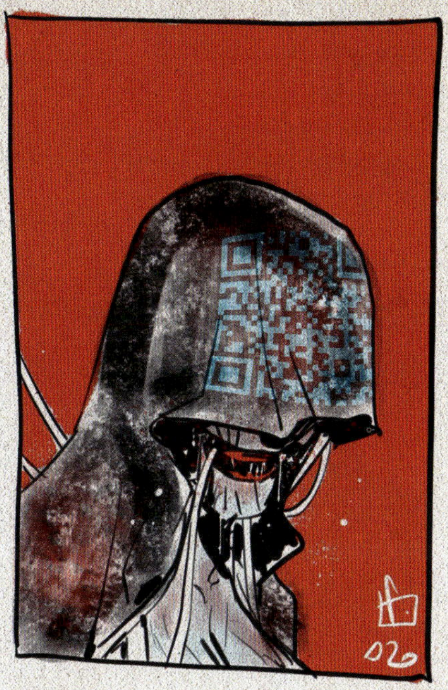

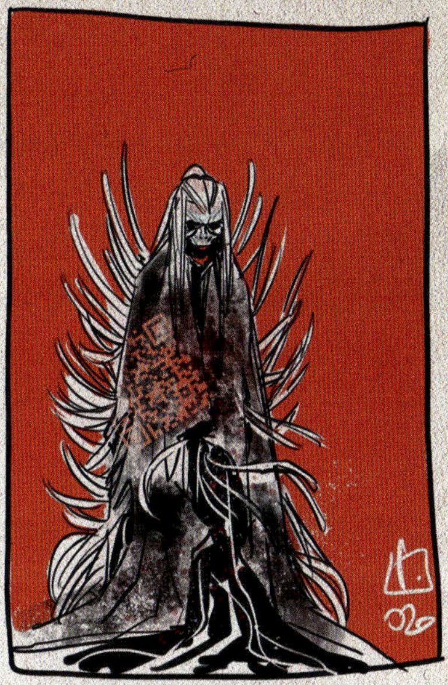

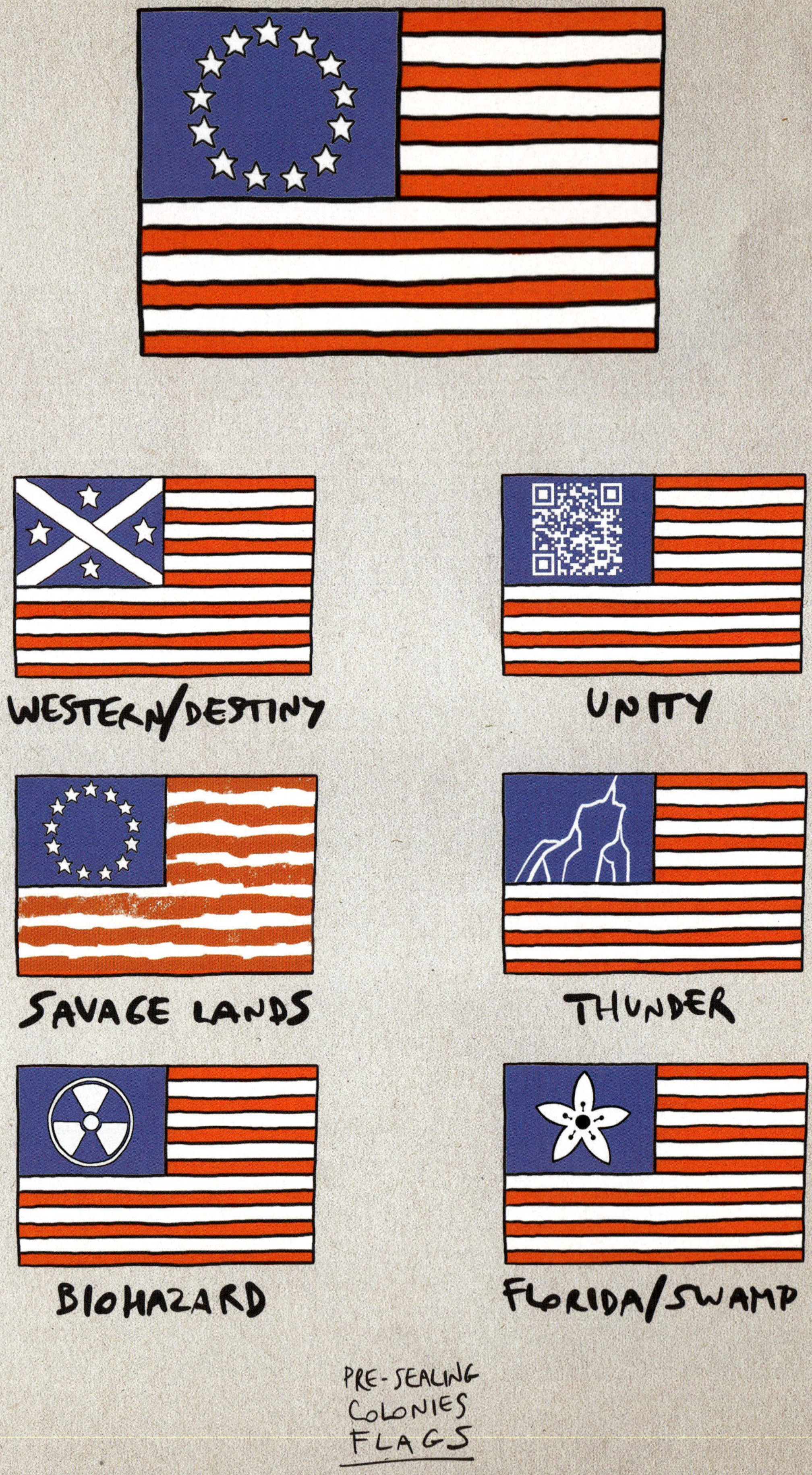
WESTERN/DESTINY
UNITY
SAVAGE LANDS
THUNDER
BIOHAZARD
FLORIDA/SWAMP
PRE-SEALING
COLONIES
FLAGS

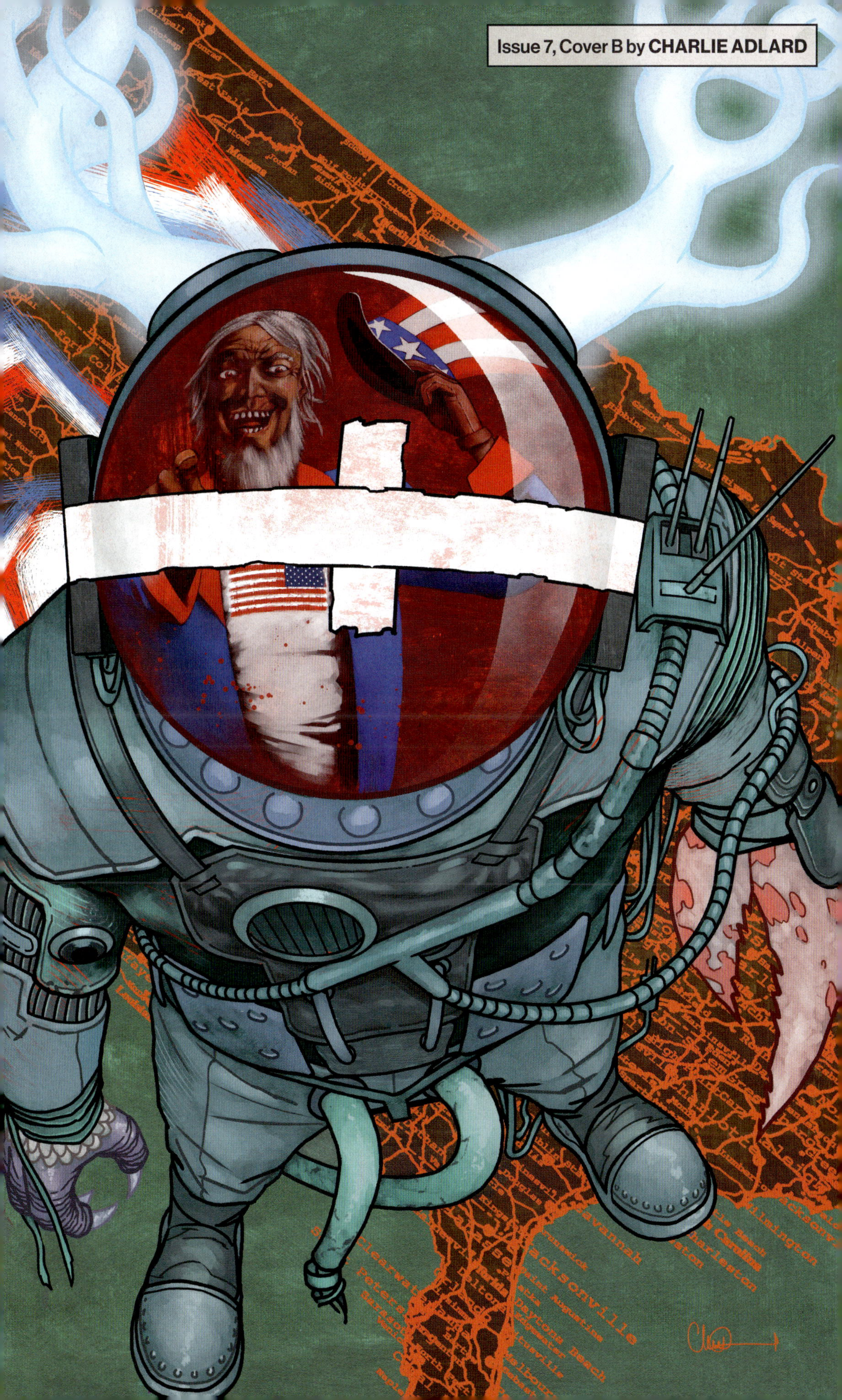
Savannah
Jacksonville
Daytona Beach
Charleston
Wilmington
Issue 7, Cover B by CHARLIE ADLARD

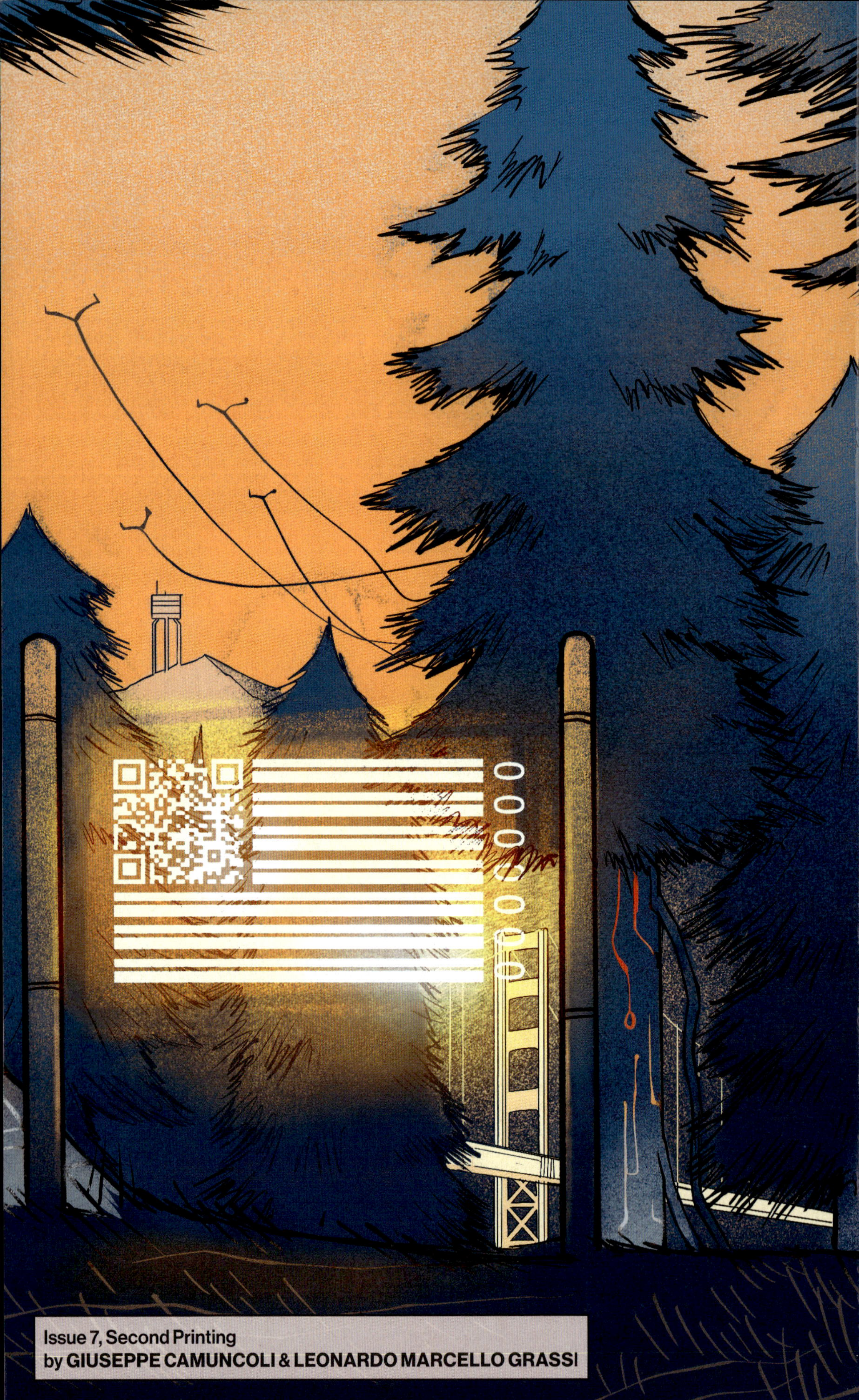
Issue 7, Second Printing
by GIUSEPPE CAMUNCOLI & LEONARDO MARCELLO GRASSI

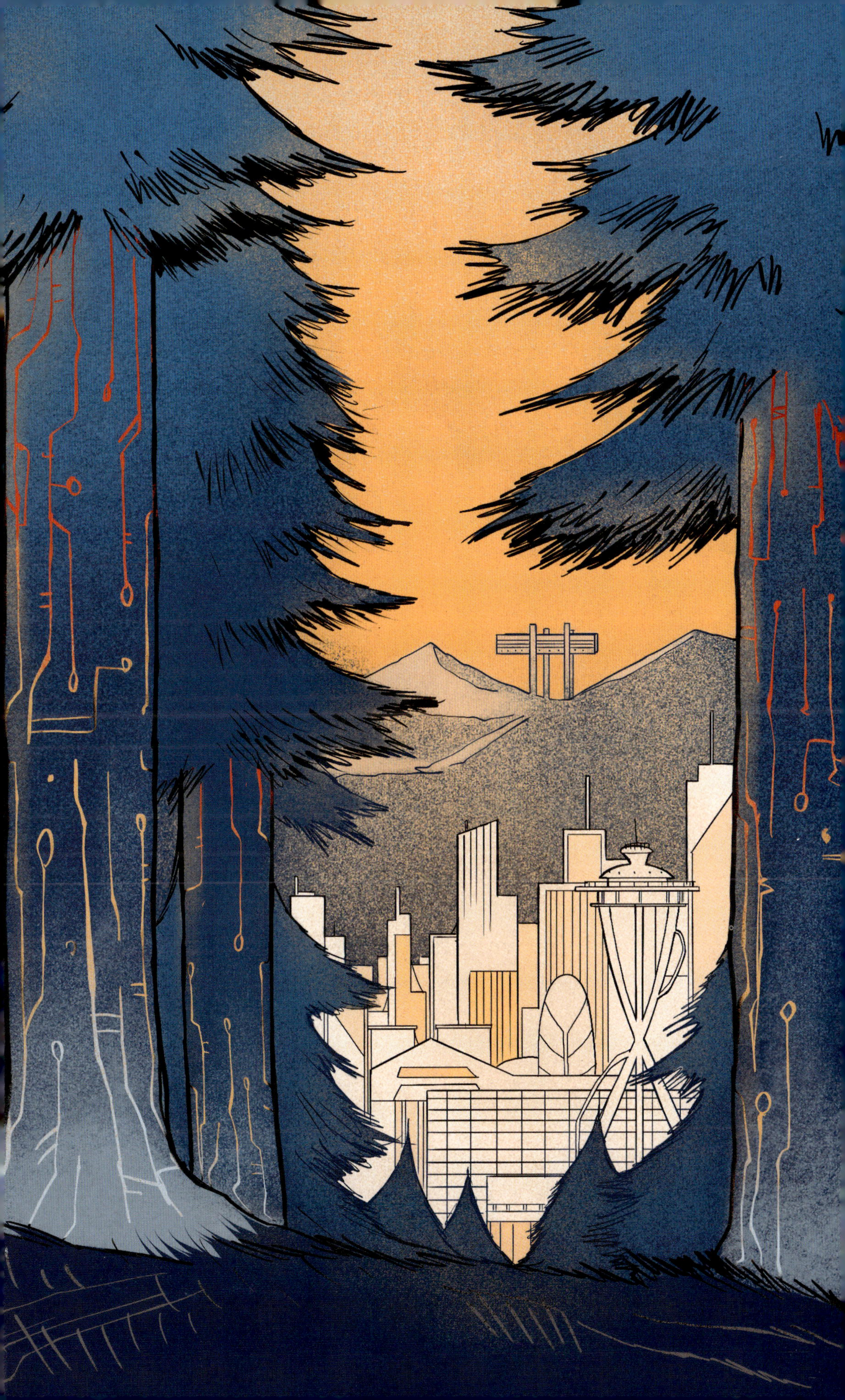

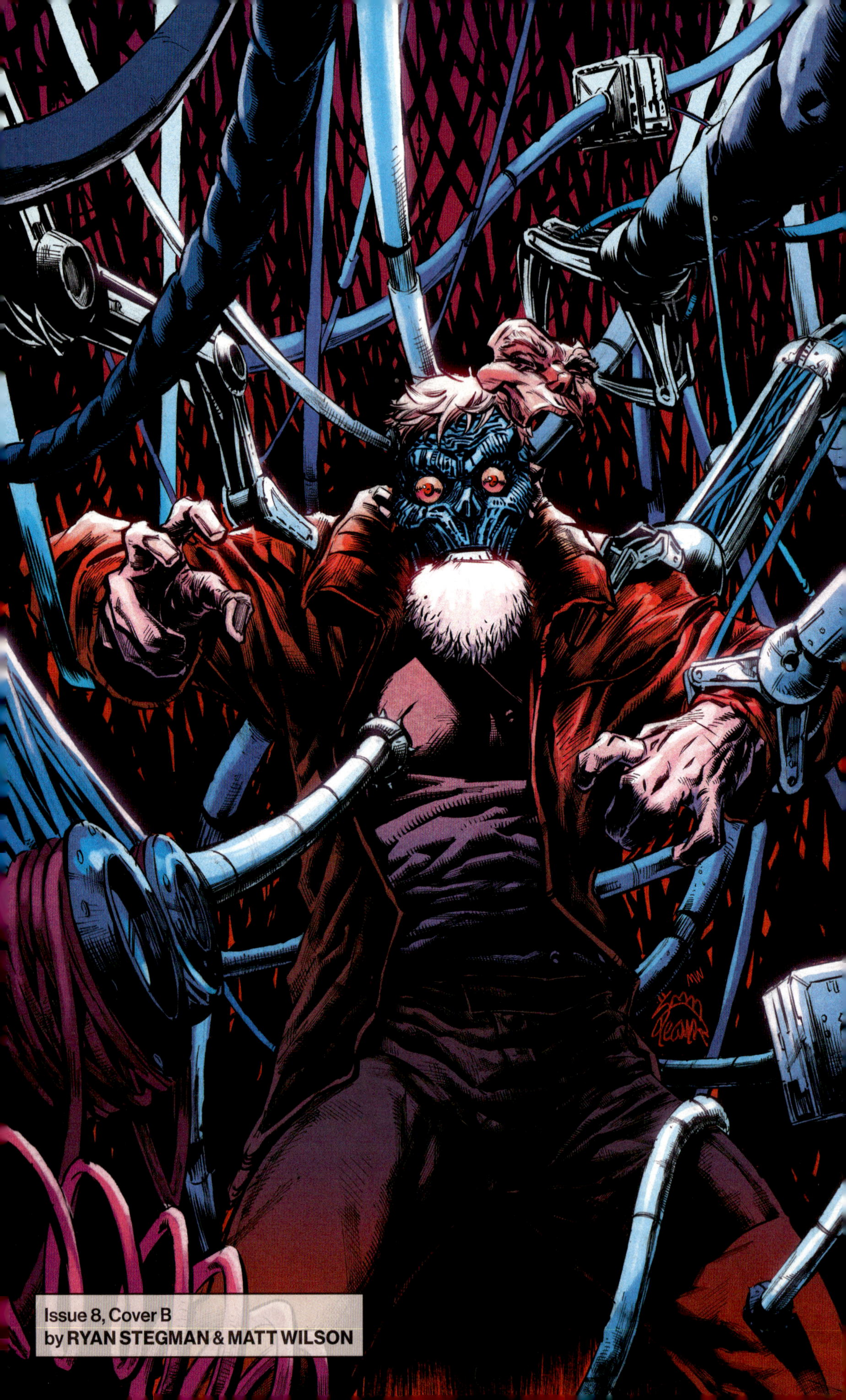

Issue 8, Cover B
by **RYAN STEGMAN & MATT WILSON**

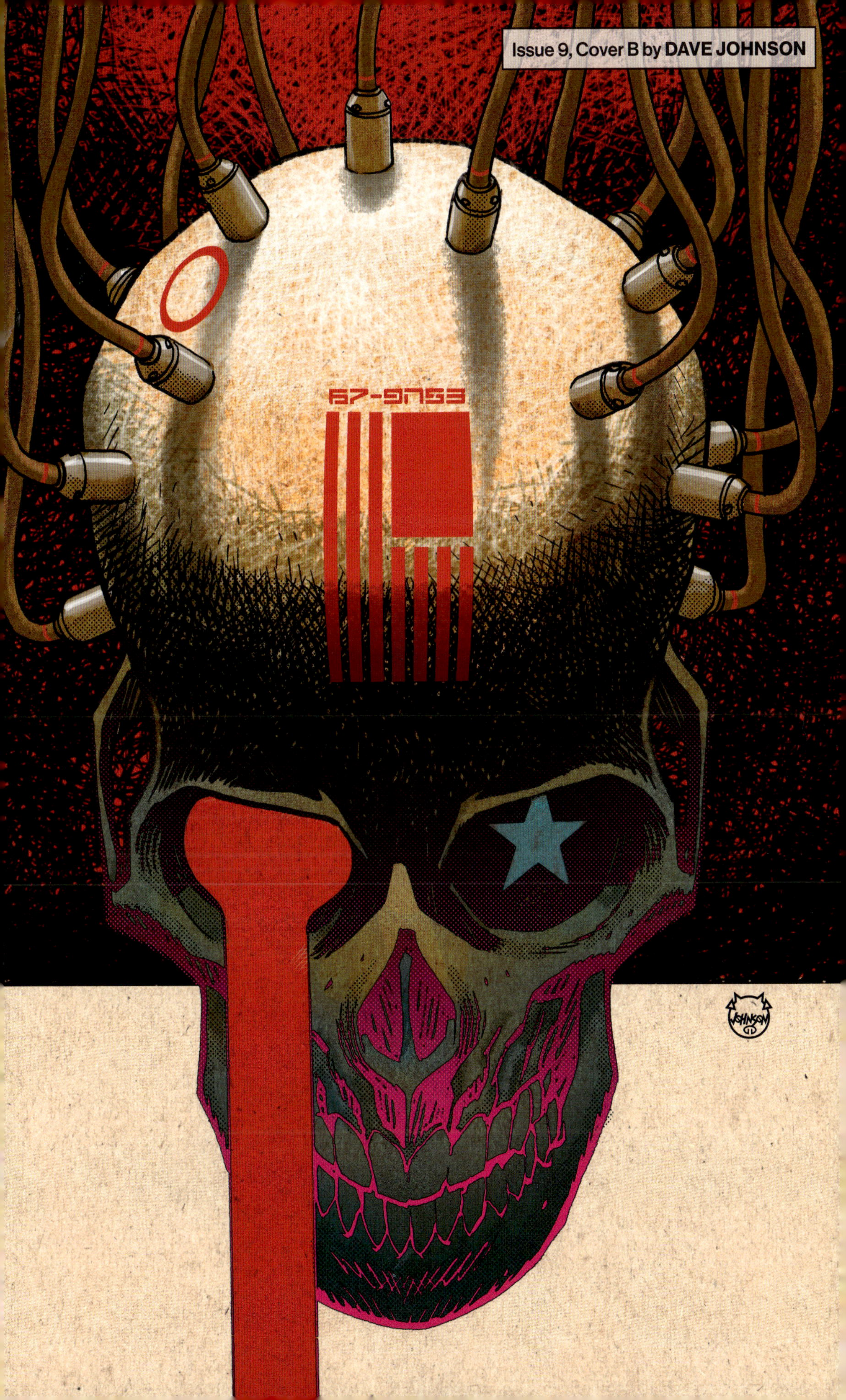
67-9753
JOHNSON

Issue 9, Cover B by **DAVE JOHNSON**

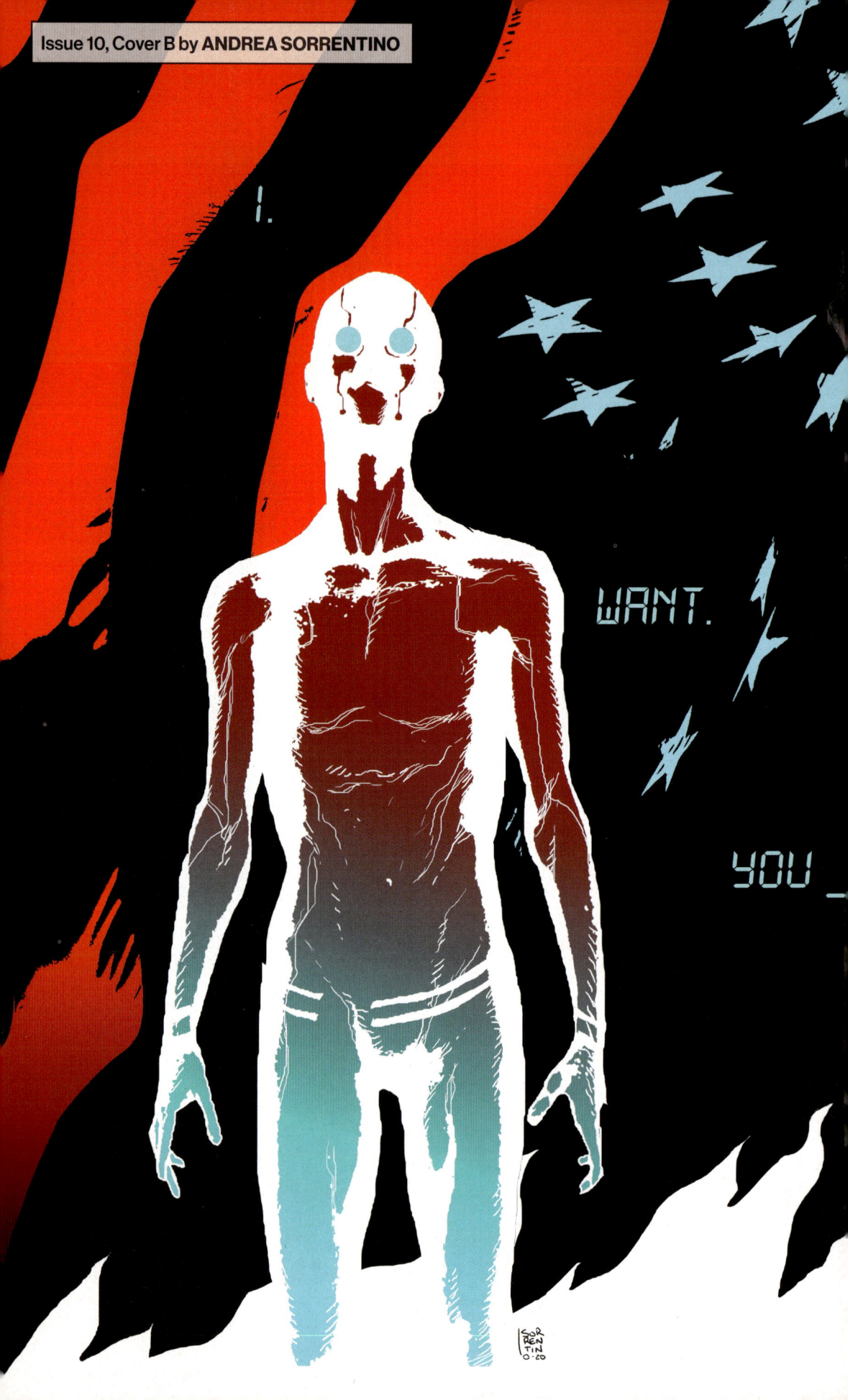

Issue 10, Cover B by ANDREA SORRENTINO

Issue 11, Cover B by **MIRKA ANDOLFO**

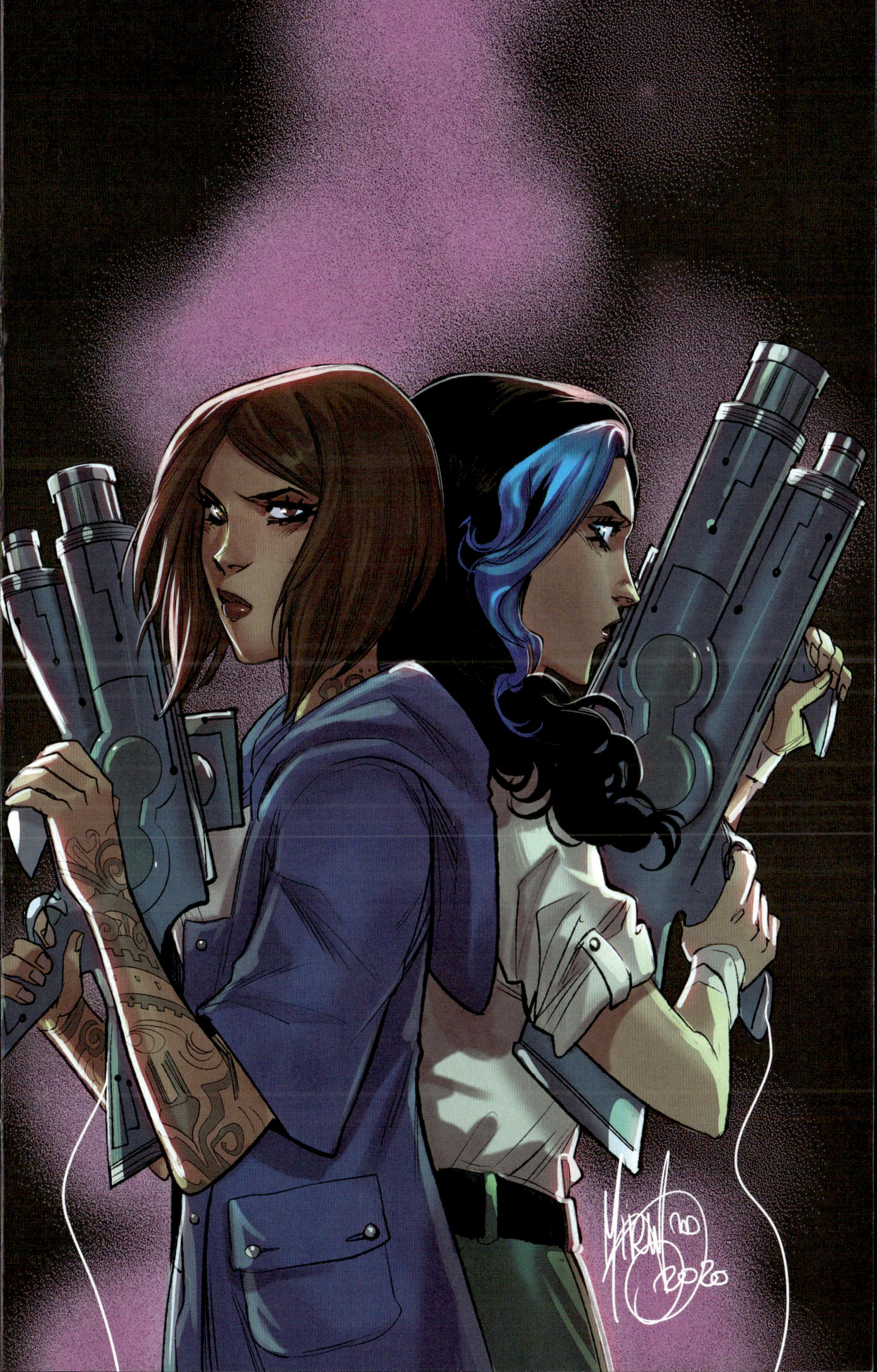

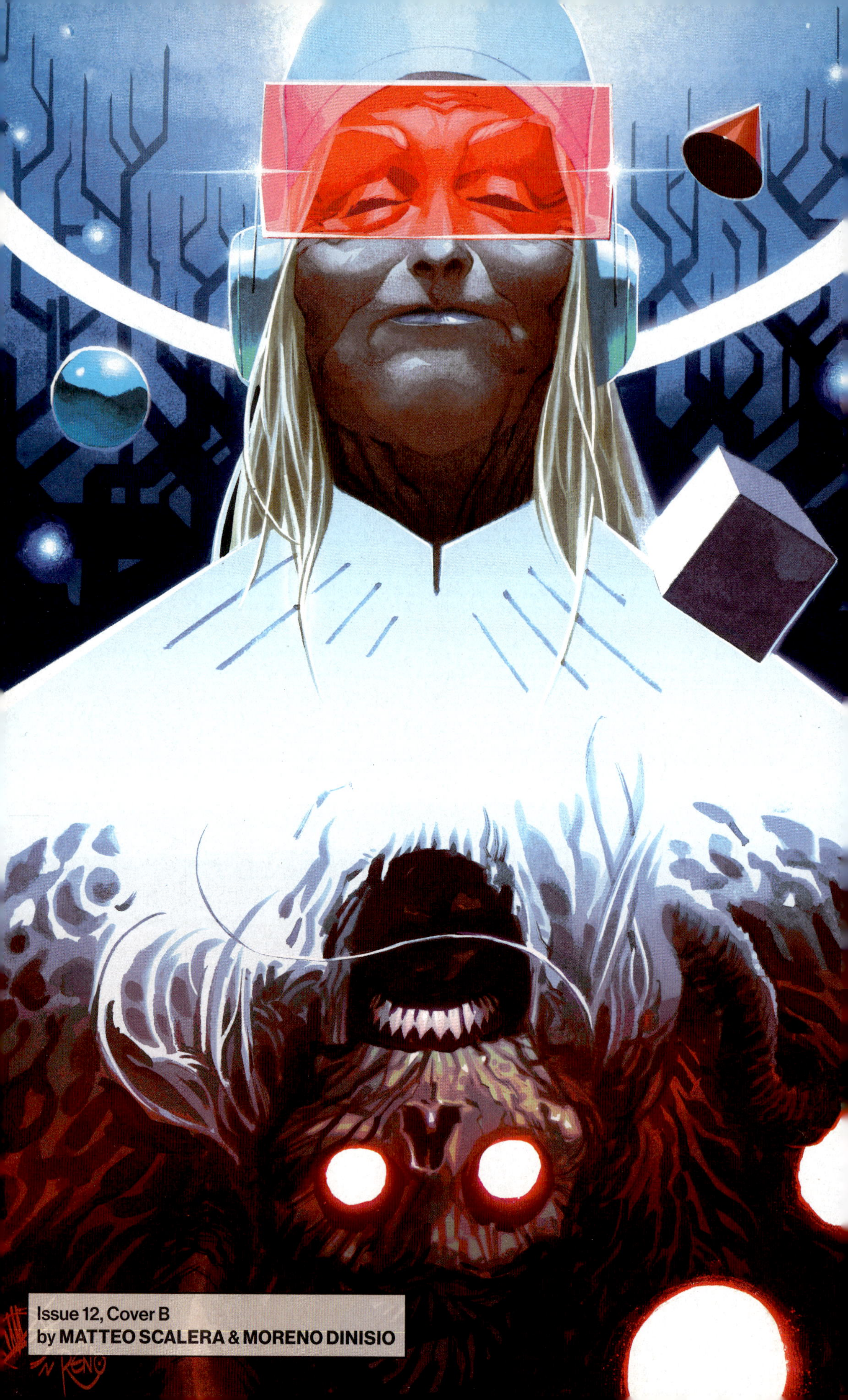

Issue 12, Cover B
by MATTEO SCALERA & MORENO DINISIO